Dawn Melody

Also by the Author

The Beyond the Tales Quartet

The Wanderers

The Storyteller and Her Sisters

The People the Fairies Forget

The Lioness and the Spellspinners

The Guardian of the Opera Series

Prequel: Overture

Book One: Nocturne

Book Two: Accompaniment

Book Three: Dawn Melody

Contributing Author

The Servants and the Beast

After the Sparkles Settled

Dawn Melody

The Guardian of the Opera

Book Three

Cheryl Mahoney

Stonehenge Circle Press

ISBN-13: 978-1-68012-642-6

ISBN-10: 1-68012-642-3

First Edition

Cover images courtesy of Master1305/Shutterstock (ballerina) and pio3/Shutterstock (masked man). Cover design by Cheryl Mahoney.

This book is a work of fiction. Resemblance to any persons living or dead is coincidental, with the exception of Charles Garnier, who is used fictitiously. His Opera is a real place in Paris, but it too has been fictionalized. Box Five is real, but the author can make no guarantees about what's located on the other side of the underground lake.

Dedication

For Mary Bowers

Without whom the Phantom probably wouldn't be
reading Shakespeare,
and I might not be either.

Chapter One

P *lease, God, don't let him be dead.*

    I listened to the silence. It was never silent in the Opera Garnier above me, never silent out on Paris' crowded boulevards. Down here in the Phantom's chambers, deep down belowground, below the lowest cellar of the Opera and across the underground lake, I had sometimes heard silence. In the pauses of a conversation, in the exquisite moment after a musical piece ended.

This silence was deeper, darker, emptier than any silence I had ever heard.

Erik wasn't here.

I walked over to the wall where the door into the rest of his rooms should have been. The wall was as blank as it had been the last time I was here, the door still hidden away by some mechanism I didn't know how to use. If I had known how to find this door I would have searched further, but I knew it didn't make any real difference that I couldn't.

He wasn't here. I needed to see him, I needed to know that the body the police had found in the Seine, the body that everyone in the Opera up above was saying was the Phantom, was not Erik. I needed to know that my friend, the man I'd fallen in love with, the man who had brought me more magic and more mystery than I'd ever known, was still alive. And he wasn't here.

I pressed my palm against the cold stone wall, pressed my forehead to it and felt the roughness against my skin. I closed my burning eyes, breathed in the candle-smoke-and-parchment scent of Erik's rooms. "Please," I whispered, "please, don't be dead."

I had watched him die, but I hadn't believed he was dead. I had watched a mob descend on these rooms, bent on vengeance for the blustering Comte de Chagny who he hadn't even killed. That mob had been made up of practically everyone I knew, the Opera Company that had been my community for seven years, since I was a child of only twelve. I had watched those people, changed in ways that terrified me, drive Erik out of these rooms to the edge of the underground lake. And then the Persian, the one man I had thought might be Erik's friend, had shot him, sending him falling back into the water. And he hadn't come back up again.

But that didn't mean anything. He had promised me he could handle the situation, and pretending to drown was exactly like him. And someone had left a cluster of daffodils on my table in the ballet's changing room the same night he disappeared. Not exactly a signed note, maybe not even from him. But still, it had seemed like a hint, and perhaps he had planned something with the Persian, and I hadn't worried, too much.

Until Commissaire Mifroid announced he had found the Phantom's body.

And now I couldn't find the Phantom.

I curled my hand into a fist, pressed against the stones. How could he leave me like this? I knew he didn't love me the way I loved him. I knew he didn't guess how I loved him. But I was his friend, at least. How could he let himself die—and if he wasn't dead, where was he? It had been three days; surely it was time for a miraculous return.

I pushed away from the wall to look around the room, shadowed with only the light from my lantern to illuminate the empty space. Maybe that was just as well; maybe I didn't want to see more clearly the damage the mob had done while they were here. The tipped over sofas, the scattered, torn sheets of music. The room felt cold and empty, and it was small consolation to know that Erik had moved his paintings and books and violin out of sight himself. So some things hadn't been destroyed.

Though it wouldn't matter much either way, if he was truly gone.

I reached out blindly and grasped the back of Erik's armchair. I could perform a *grand battement* on stage at the Opera, but my legs felt shaky now.

He couldn't be dead. The Phantom of the Opera couldn't be killed like this. Erik was too clever, too careful, too practiced at haunting and teasing and manipulating the crowd. For seven years he'd been doing this, ever since the Opera opened.

But in seven years, they'd never found his home before.

I let go of the chair to touch my gold necklace instead, closed my fingers around it, and unthinkingly started for the door. I couldn't stay here, not for another minute, in this room so oppressively *empty*.

I made my way through the labyrinth of passages below the Opera, dark and silent, through the cellars and up wide stone stairs. I had made this journey many times, in the months since Erik had first invited me into his home. I came out at last through a secret door into the Opera's enormous prop room, closing the wall of masks behind me.

In contrast to the empty blank of the tunnels, the prop room was an untidy display of swords and jewels, stacked chairs and elaborate candelabras. Usually I gave it no thought, but today, in my turmoil of emotions, the chaos of it all felt overwhelming.

I kept my gaze down, made my way out of the prop room to the halls of the Opera, where there was no less to see. Today I had no attention to spare for the gold detailing, or the murals and mirrors that filled every inch of the Opera Garnier. I walked past it all, a little too fast, threading between the dancers and chorus members and scenechangers wandering the halls, grateful this wasn't a busier time of day.

I didn't have anywhere to go, so my feet carried me along the most familiar path, until I arrived in the corps de ballet's changing room. This room was almost never empty but it was sparsely populated now, in the middle of the afternoon. I went to my table, sank down in my seat, and after a few moments realized I was staring at my locked drawer.

The locked drawer where I'd been keeping my directions to Erik's room, the ones that had gone missing and I was far too sure had been stolen and used by the very wrong people.

Even though I had looked for them the day of the mob, I couldn't stop myself from unlocking the drawer and pulling it open. Maybe I had just missed them. Somehow.

It wasn't a large drawer, but I turned over playbills and lifted away hair ribbons and reached way into the back again, just in case.

"Lose something?" I heard a voice ask, and looked up into Jammes' mocking gaze.

Jammes and I had never liked each other. For years we had been in the ballet together, and we had never been friendly. I didn't know exactly why she disliked me, though it had only grown worse when I became friends with Christine Daaé—and since Christine had left, over a year ago. More often than anyone else, Jammes kept bringing up Christine, her disappearance, and all the terrible things the Phantom surely did to her.

I didn't believe any of it was true, but that hardly made it less uncomfortable to hear. Or any easier to continually be asked if I had heard from Christine, when I hadn't.

"No," I said carefully. "I haven't lost anything."

"Oh, I'm *so* glad," Jammes said with a smirk, and turned away again.

I slowly closed the drawer, accepting all over again that I wouldn't find my directions inside.

There was a better than likely chance that Jammes knew exactly what I had lost. And that she was the reason I'd lost it. I'd already suspected that, just by knowing Jammes, and seeing how unaccountably smug she had been the day of the mob.

I wanted to blame Jammes. I wanted to hate her, for stealing my directions and betraying Erik to the police, to the mob. But *she* wasn't his friend. He hadn't trusted *her* with the route to his refuge. That was me. I had left the key information right here. I had thought it was safe enough, but I could have been more careful, chosen a better place.

Maybe Erik had been right not to trust anyone for years. See what happened when he took a chance on trusting me. A mob descended on his home, and now the police thought they had his body.

I wanted to go home and cry. But I'd have to drag myself back for the evening performance, or else explain to my mother, and Madame Thibault the ballet mistress, why I was missing it. Madame Thibault did not accept excuses, and Mother would get a worried pucker in her forehead if she knew I was this upset and—and somehow I didn't feel I *deserved* to escape the Opera Garnier and all the guilt and fear swirling through it.

I went to Box Five, the Phantom's Box. I had come here to think a few days after Christine had left, the evening I spoke with Erik for the first time. Even with the Company believing the Phantom was dead now, I felt sure no one would be in it.

I didn't expect to find Erik there, and he wasn't when I stepped inside.

I sank down into one red velvet seat, stared at the closed curtains of the box and fingered my necklace as I tried to work out how everything had gone so wrong.

I wished I could talk to someone. The Persian would be a good choice, someone with actual answers, but I had no way to find him. And anyone else, someone I could have talked through my confusion of feelings with…Mother would worry, and Erik was missing, and Christine was gone, supposing she even would have understood, and my sister Gabrielle had been dead for seven years, since the time when I was only twelve and had less complicated problems.

"How did I get here, Gabi?" I whispered, my words disappearing amongst the background bustle of voices and footsteps permeating the Opera.

I used to be in control—not of the world around me, never of that. But of myself. Maybe I was only a supporting character, maybe I didn't get to be the lead of the narrative, of the great events happening at the Opera, but I knew how to live within my role.

A supporting character could be left behind, solitary and disregarded when her obviously more heroine-material best friend eloped in the night. It had hurt when Christine left with Raoul de Chagny, when she had barely bothered to write me a farewell note, when she hadn't sent any word in over a year. But sometimes it felt like only what I should have expected.

And at least supporting characters shouldn't have their hearts broken, or do anything important enough to cause anyone's death.

As a supporting character I could become friends with the mysterious man who haunted the Opera, and I should have stopped at that.

I shouldn't have fallen in love with a man who was clearly a title character if there ever was one.

I'd never even told him I loved him. It had seemed sensible, safer, because he didn't see me that way, and why should he, when he was so in love with the glittering, charming, talented Christine? Suddenly the thought of words left unsaid hurt enough to take my breath away. Because if he was dead—if he was really, truly gone—he'd never know. Or did the dead know, somehow?

I shoved that thought away and pushed up from the seat, paced the short aisle of the box. I didn't *know* that he was dead. A body I hadn't even seen wasn't proof, a disappearance wasn't proof, and he had *promised* me he could handle the situation.

Perhaps he had only left, and that thought brought a new pang. Even if Erik was alive, would he come back to the Opera, now that the Phantom was dead?

I stopped at the balcony of the box, looking out over the rows and rows of seats in the auditorium, indistinct in the dim light. How often had Erik stood here?

I wanted to be angry with him for all of this, for dying if he was dead, for disappearing if he wasn't. But how could I blame *him*? Mostly I blamed Commissaire Mifroid and the Opera Company, the mob who had descended on his home. And the Persian, who may have shot him. And Jammes.

And myself.

It didn't feel right, that all of us, including me, especially me, should just go on, unpunished, paying nothing for what we had done to him.

Maybe Jammes would ensure I was punished yet. It was obvious the conclusions she could draw from finding those directions in my drawer. If she told the management, or even the other ballet girls, that I had been spending time with the Phantom, knew the way to his rooms, it would finish me at the Opera Garnier.

Maybe. Maybe not, not if it was her word against mine where those directions had come from. She apparently hadn't told anyone yet, so maybe she didn't feel sure she could convince anyone if I denied it. If I cared enough to do that.

Excerpt from the Private Notebook of Jean Mifroid, Commissaire of Police

25 April, 1882

Coroner's examinations complete, Phantom's body buried this morning in indigent burial grounds. Investigation finished except for paperwork.

Why does it not feel finished? Why can I not put this case away like so many others?

Chapter Two

I began counting the days since the day of the mob, since I had last seen Erik, since he might have died. I counted even though I had no idea when it would be time to give up hope. I had found the daffodils on the second day. The Phantom's body—supposedly—had been found on the third, and I had gone to Erik's rooms that same afternoon.

On the fourth day I was sitting with several other ballet girls on the Opera's front steps, dallying before it was time to go in for the morning rehearsal. They were all abuzz with the management's plans for a new special performance at the end of May; this topic might have taken them comfortably off the subject of the Phantom and his death, except that everyone was sure the managers were only holding it because now they knew the Phantom couldn't interfere. Struggling to make myself pay attention, my gaze drifted out over the busy plaza— and I saw Commissaire Mifroid walking towards the Opera.

A chill went through me as I looked at the policeman, in his dark coat with the shiny buttons down the front. It had been him, all along. He had kept *pushing*, kept trying to find Erik, for months and months. If it hadn't been for him, Jammes never would have gone looking for information, for whatever favor she thought she could curry with the managers, or Carlotta the lead soprano, or Mifroid himself. Without Mifroid, my stupid mistake leaving the directions in reach wouldn't have mattered.

With Mifroid, Erik might be dead.

And Mifroid might be the only one who really knew.

Before I could think better of it, I sprang up to my feet. "Look, there's the police commissaire," I said, making my voice gay and bright. "Let's find out what he knows about the Phantom."

The girls exchanged glances around me. They loved talking about the Phantom, but I wasn't usually the most enthusiastic participant. And no one wanted to talk to the police.

"Come on, Francesca," I urged, picking the girl who *was* the most enthusiastic for gory Phantom stories. It would look less odd, if I didn't approach him alone. "Maybe he'll tell us about finding the Phantom's body."

Her eyes lit up. "Do you think so?"

My stomach turned at her excitement, but I kept my smile firmly planted. It was funny I didn't dislike Francesca the way I did Jammes. But there was no spite in Francesca's love of Opera Ghost stories. She didn't know Erik, and the Ghost was only a myth to her.

"Let's catch him before the managers do," I said, and descended the steps to intercept Mifroid. "Good morning, Commissaire," I called, stepping directly into his path so he'd have to stop and talk to me.

He did stop, looking down at me with his usual cool, remote expression. It was irritating, but less alarming than the fervor he'd shown while leading the mob. "Mademoiselle Giry," he said with the slightest incline of his head. "Christine Daaé's friend." He had spoken to me before, when she disappeared, and I neither liked that he remembered that, nor that he remembered me that way. As though my own identity mattered so much less than hers.

Francesca chirped, "Good morning," too, and he merely nodded to her.

The commissaire began, "I have important business—"

"We want to know more about the Phantom," I interrupted, smile big and voice cheery. As though I was a gossipy ballet girl, just looking for a story. It wouldn't be the first time I had posed that way for the commissaire. "Is it really true you found his *body*?" I let my voice drop low on that last word, as though it was a horribly thrilling idea. Not something that had kept me up last night, something that was twisting me with fear.

"No doubt you have heard the official report already," Mifroid said, and began to step to the side, to work around us.

Desperation made me daring and I reached out to wrap my hands around his forearm, leaning in as though we were old friends. "Oh, but official reports are so dull!" I bubbled. "We want the *details*. How did you *know* it was the Phantom? Aren't there lots of bodies in the Seine?"

Mifroid looked down at my hands as though confused, but didn't immediately yank his arm away. "It is true a certain number of bodies are reclaimed from the Seine regularly. However, we found a body which matched the estimates of the Phantom's height, weight and so on, wearing a cloak of the proper description."

I felt light-headed, and my grip on Mifroid's arm instinctively tightened. Did I really believe he'd tell me something proving he had the wrong body? All I was going to do was horrify myself even more—

"What did he look like?" Francesca chimed in suddenly. "He was wearing that mask, and there's all *sorts* of stories about the Phantom's face!"

"What color were his eyes?" I asked abruptly, because that *would* tell me. That would be proof, even clearer proof than a gunshot wound. Did the body have Erik's green eyes?

Mifroid looked profoundly uncomfortable, shifting where he stood. "It is—difficult to say with certainty…"

"Why?" I demanded. "You had his body. Someone must have looked at the eyes."

"We…did have the body," Mifroid said carefully, carefully eased his arm away from my hold. "But there are…any number of obstacles in the Seine which might be…encountered. And there are, of course…fish, as well."

He didn't know what the face of the body looked like. Because it didn't have one. Blood was pounding in my ears and I didn't want to think about that, I didn't want to imagine that, I didn't want to think of Erik's beautiful green eyes, not even dead or buried but—

"That's so disgusting!" Francesca squealed, with what sounded like genuine revulsion and not the pleased kind that was her usual response to spooky Phantom stories.

"Policemen's work is not a suitable topic for delicate young women," Mifroid said, with paternal sternness in his voice. "I suggest you limit your concerns to dancing in the future."

He said some sort of farewell. Somehow Francesca and I made our way back to the other girls.

They hadn't wanted to come with us, but they clamored for information now. I let Francesca answer, carefully breathing against the nausea roiling my stomach. Or was it guilt?

I'd never told Erik how lovely his eyes were. Had he even known?

The body still might not be him. I tried to hold onto the hope that it wasn't. Mifroid hadn't said anything that proved it one way or the other. In fact, what he'd said suggested that he was guessing, that he had a body that seemed right, but who was there to identify it and say for certain? I could have identified Erik but I hadn't, and there was no one else to do it.

Except the Persian. I should have asked about the Persian too. He still hadn't appeared at the Opera, might be jailed for all I knew. Would they have asked him to identify a body? Would he have been able to? And would he even have told the truth? I still didn't understand him, and his presence in this mystery only added more questions than answers.

But maybe the body wasn't Erik, maybe he was alive. Maybe he was fine.

Maybe I'd go to Notre Dame Cathedral after ballet practice, and light a lot of candles.

It wasn't the first time I went to Notre Dame that week, and it wouldn't be the last.

As the days ticked by, I spent a lot of time lighting candles. I sat in front of my favorite statue in the cathedral, the Madonna and Child, watching candle flames flicker and hoping so hard that Erik could somehow, some way, be all right. When I wasn't at Notre Dame, I was at the Opera. And no matter where I was, I worried. I was exhausted with worrying.

On the fifth day since the mob, I forced myself through ballet practice, through the empty afternoon when I might have gone to see Erik on happier days, and through the evening's performance.

Back in the ballet's changing room after, I only wanted to go home. But that would be giving in, failing to carry on with my life as I was trying so hard to do.

I fastened up the last button on my boot, forced a smile onto my face and turned to Adalisa at the table next to mine. "Do you suppose there will be anyone interesting in the Dance Foyer tonight?" I asked, as cheerfully as I could.

"Ooh, I hope so," Adalisa said with a smile, voice so much brighter than I had managed. "Maybe your Léon will finally bring a friend for me!"

"He's not mine," I said, but mildly, both because I knew Adalisa didn't mean any harm, and because I knew the protest would have no effect at all. Still, Léon de Troyes was just someone I flirted with in the Foyer. He wasn't *mine*.

I moved in a stream of girls in our brightly colored dresses through the halls of the Opera and into the Dance Foyer. It had seemed like a magical place when I first started visiting, with the murals of dancers overhead, the gold decorations, and the mirrored wall multiplying the room and the crowd. It still seemed magical often, but not tonight. Tonight I made myself smile and worried about Erik.

I only spent a few minutes talking with Adalisa about the night's performance before Léon approached us.

"Good evening," he said with a smile that didn't look at all forced—and even in my worries, part of me was pleased to have a charming young man smile like that because of me. As usual he kissed the hand I extended, and said, "Your dancing was wonderful tonight. I was enraptured."

Flirtatious and meaningless, so much easier than the circles my thoughts had been running in. "You wouldn't even know if I danced badly," I said, with a laugh only half-faked.

"I consider myself a great connoisseur of the arts," Léon protested, drawing my arm through his. "Don't I attend performances faithfully?"

"Reliably," I agreed automatically, glancing over to Adalisa.

She had already begun drifting away, and now she smiled at me, mouthed, "No friend," and slipped off into the crowd.

I wished Léon did have a friend for Adalisa. I'd met a few of his friends, over the months we'd been seeing each other in the Foyer, but none stood out. Except for Raoul de Chagny, of course, the original link that connected us, by way of Christine.

"I think my devoted attendance deserves recognition," Léon said with a grin, conducting me along as we began a stroll through the crowded room.

Likely we'd fetch up on a banquette eventually. In the meantime, the conversation was light and harmless, as Léon pretended to know something about dancing and I teased him with a balance of corrections and flattery. The words, mine and his, required little thought but were just distracting enough to make my fears recede. Sometimes I felt a pang as I contrasted a response from Léon with what Erik, a genuine connoisseur, might have said. But mostly I let Léon distract me, and gave in to the half-guilty temptation to stop thinking about all the ways the world was falling to pieces, all the ways it was my own fault, for just a while.

It was harder to keep forgetting, when the evening ended and my mother came to meet me and walk home together. It was harder to pretend with her too.

Not that I didn't try. As I'd been trying for days. I smiled and told her it had been a very nice evening with Léon and managed to keep up a pleasant pretense as we walked out of the Opera Garnier arm in arm.

But I could feel her studying me too thoughtfully, in that way mothers have, and my light-hearted words eventually faded away.

After a few moments of silence, Mother said, not without sympathy in her voice, "You're still worrying about Erik, aren't you?" If her softened tone hadn't already made the question kinder, using his name did too. Usually it was 'the Phantom' from her.

That didn't stop me from saying, with too much force, "Of *course* I am. He's my friend and he—" Might be dead. "—has been driven from his home," I concluded instead.

"I know," Mother said, and patted my hand. "We also know he is very resourceful. No doubt he is perfectly well, wherever he is."

The situation had to be truly bad, if my mother was being this nice about it. I didn't believe for a moment that she really thought he was all right—I was almost sure she believed he was dead, shot and drowned days ago, already buried by the police—but I didn't have the courage to press the point.

"Yes. I'm sure he's fine," I echoed mechanically, because I wanted it to be true, and it seemed too horrible to say anything else.

By the sixth day since the mob, my ability to keep up a normal pretense was fraying. I merely went through the motions at ballet practice, and not very well either.

At the end of practice, Madame Thibault stopped me as we all streamed toward the door, and in her usual imperious voice intoned, "Mademoiselle Giry, I do not know what is disturbing you lately, nor do I wish to know, but kindly tend to it, and renew your focus on your *dancing* as soon as possible."

I felt the eyes of the other girls on me, some curious, some sympathetic; they'd all been in this position before too, many times. All I could do was curtsy and murmur, "Yes, Madame," because nothing else was expected or desired.

In the changing room, I sank into my seat, wondering how long I could carry on like this. How long would it be before I heard from

Erik, if he was alive? How long before I concluded he wasn't, if I didn't?

"Too bad about Madame Thibault," Adalisa said kindly. "You know it's just her way."

"Of course," I said, managing a smile because she was trying to help.

It was less helpful when, with a little frown, she continued, "You *have* seemed distracted lately. Is something wrong?"

Everything. "No, not really," I said, as lightly as I could. It wasn't very lightly and I knew it wasn't enough to address her question. "I haven't been feeling well," I invented, hardly a lie. "Nothing serious, I don't think."

"I thought you might be sad about your Phantom." Not something Adalisa would say, and I wasn't surprised to look up and see Jammes' smirk.

"He isn't—wasn't my Phantom," I said, staring at her mocking eyes. It was true. He had never been mine. Not the way he was Christine's.

But Jammes knew I might have good reason to be sad. That I had broken the rules of the crowd and been friendly to the Phantom.

"Don't be absurd, Jammes," Adalisa said, more sharply than usual. "Meg had nothing to do with the Phantom."

Neither Jammes nor I looked away from each other, but I could feel the weight of stares from other girls around the room. "That's true," I said, and my voice was strangely calm. "I never had anything to do with the Phantom."

I knew I was all but daring her to contradict me, to tell everyone around us what she knew, and yet I felt oddly detached. Maybe it would be better if she did tell them. Maybe that would be preferable to continuing this…masquerade, pretending to be just like all the others, pretending not to care about the most important person in my life.

Jammes broke our gaze first, covered it with a scornful shrug. "Oh well, that's more than can be said of Christine Daaé. And you were supposed to be her good friend."

I was sick of hearing about Christine from her. Sick of Christine's absence in my conversations with Erik taking up far more space than an occasional mention would have. Sick of the whole stupid business. "Why don't you come up with a new story, Jammes?" I snapped. "Christine has been gone for *months*. Surely something else interesting has happened in your life since then."

Her eyes narrowed and I expected a furious response. Instead she merely sniffed and turned away.

I went back to changing out of my ballet costume, making myself respond to Adalisa's light-hearted chatter which, for once, seemed just as forced as my answers.

Jammes left before me, but I encountered her again only a turn of the hallway distant from the changing room, clearly waiting for me.

I didn't bother with a greeting, just stopped walking and waited.

She dove in without preamble. "I'd watch my words, if I was you," she said in a low voice, eyes still furious. "You know I can destroy your whole life, just like that." She snapped her fingers. "Even Adalisa won't be friendly, if she knew you were carrying on with the Phantom. All I have to do is tell them."

This all seemed so...pointless. What was the use of all this pettiness, this gossip and destroying of reputations? Distantly, I knew it should be important to me. But anything the Opera Company could do to me dwindled so much, compared to what they had already, perhaps, done to Erik. I even smiled when I said, "If it's that easy, why didn't you do it?"

She didn't like that response, her frown deepening even further. "I made a promise to keep your little secret. But don't think I won't break it, if you provoke me enough. So you'd better be careful."

She flounced away without another word, before I could attempt any response.

I watched her retreating back, and wondered what that meant.

Someone else knew the secret, if she'd promised someone she would keep it. Probably someone who wanted to be able to use it themselves. Carlotta? That seemed most likely, though a plot that elaborate was subtler than Carlotta usually was. But the lead soprano liked manipulating the Opera Company to suit herself, and Jammes had been paying court to her for years.

I walked slowly on towards the exit, weighing whether this development made the situation any more alarming.

No. Not really. It probably should. But I had no extra worry to spare right now for Carlotta and her machinations.

Chapter Three

On the seventh day since the mob descended, I went to Notre Dame again, leaving the cathedral in the early twilight. I hadn't quite given up hope yet, but my thoughts as I walked were darker than the shadows, and much more absorbing of my attention.

Maybe that was part of why it was such a shock when a man in a black cloak stepped out of a patch of gloom and said, "Good evening."

I no longer jumped when Erik stepped out of walls at the Opera Garnier, but now the atmosphere or the suddenness or my own distraction made me react with a sharp inhale and a stumble backwards and the unthinking protest, "Don't *do* that, it's so much more alarming in twilight than—" And there my brain caught up, made connections, remembered why this perfectly ordinary thing was not ordinary at all. "Oh. *Oh!*"

Erik was standing there with hunched shoulders and a worried expression—at least what I could see of it between the shadow of his hat and the inevitable black mask. Erik, who I had begun to feel sure was drowned and dead and buried, who had haunted my thoughts for too many anxious days while failing to haunt the Opera at all.

"I happened to be in the neighborhood," Erik said, meaningless words I barely processed. "And I just thought…"

He was *there*, alive and apparently fine, and the dark evening was suddenly blazing with light, my cracked and broken world suddenly whole and beautiful again. My breath caught in my throat, my heart gave a jump, and the only natural response was something perfectly unnatural for Erik.

Stepping forward too fast for him to dodge, I hugged him. I wrapped my arms around him, pressing my face to his shoulder, feeling him warm and alive against me. After a few seconds, I felt him hug me back.

Maybe he shouldn't have accosted her in the shadows. He hadn't *planned* to, he'd just gone out to Notre Dame entirely on his own initiative and then when he happened to see her walking out of the cathedral... Some other day his normal self-doubt would have questioned if it was the best moment. But it had been a *week*. Seven days since he had last seen Meg, since the mob had descended on him.

He missed her.

But he probably shouldn't have jumped out of the shadows—well, *stepped*, really, perfectly calmly. And he had managed a calm tone too. She wouldn't suspect from the tiny underlying quiver behind his "good evening" how very, absurdly, ridiculously glad he was to see her.

He had startled her, but she didn't run away. Just the opposite, after an initial step back, she moved towards him again. He scrambled for rational conversation. "I happened to be in the neighborhood and I just thought—oh. Um. Hello."

She hadn't stopped walking when he would have expected, had picked up pace and before he knew quite what to expect she had collided directly into him. No kiss on the cheek this time—though he could still feel the phantom pressure, knew just the spot she had touched, in that moment before the mob arrived. This time she buried her face against his shoulder, arms wrapped tightly around him. Some instinct he had never known he possessed made his arms rise, start to reach around her—then he thought maybe he shouldn't—then decided maybe etiquette said that he *should*, under the circumstances—then decided he didn't care about shoulds because somehow his arms *had* got around her and she wasn't objecting and this was…nice.

"I've been so *worried* about you," Meg said, voice muffled by his shirt.

People didn't worry about him. About the things he might do, yes, but about *him*—no. The thought that she had been concerned about him put a warm glow in his chest even as it made his throat go unaccountably tight.

"Yes, well," he said, inanely, but at least it was evenly. "Ghosts don't die easily."

"Apparently," she said. He felt her weight shift back then and he hurriedly let go. She slipped away, moved a step off and ran a hand over her hair. The hood of her cloak had slipped back and the last of the day's sunlight was tangled in her blond strands. "I'm sorry, I shouldn't have— are you all right? The Persian shot you—*did* he shoot you?"

"No," Erik said quickly. "Clean miss. I mean, he was trying to miss—it looked convincing, then?"

"Yes," she said, her voice growing cool. "It looked convincing."

"Ah. Well. Good." It had been a gamble, a last-minute gambit. He had intended only to jump into the lake, but then he had seen the Daroga at the back of the crowd. There had been no opportunity for more than the barest exchange of glances, but they had had some experience with this before. He had survived to escape Persia, all those years ago, before the Daroga helped him appear dead.

"Did it occur to you at all that you might scare me?"

His brain went into a skitter at this sudden new direction in the conversation. It *had* occurred to him; he had so hoped she wouldn't be scared—this was why she shouldn't have been there with the mob, he had known—and if *Meg* was scared, what did that say about him? "Really?" he said, trying desperately to sound casual. "You didn't think the skull mask was a touch too theatrical?" He had hoped she'd see it that way. See the whole business as an interesting artistic performance, nothing more.

She blinked, forehead wrinkling. "The skull…no, not that part! The going into the water and not coming out part! The *convincingly being shot* part!"

"Oh." He had scared her into worrying about him. He had never thought of that possibility at all. "I told you I'd handle it."

"Yes, but then you disappeared! For a week!" Her voice was rising, and he wasn't entirely sure what emotion was motivating it. She was...angry?

"I left you the daffodils," he offered as some kind of defense.

"You couldn't have written a note? In a *week*, you couldn't write to me at all?"

"I'm supposed to be dead," Erik protested. Were they fighting? Was this a fight? "I was trying to be discreet!"

"I thought you really *were* dead, Erik, do you know what that felt like? Just a few days ago it was all over the Opera that Mifroid had found your body and—" She stopped, resumed in a more reflective tone, "Since you're not dead, whose body did Mifroid bury?"

Did she expect him to have the answer, or was this rhetorical? At least she'd stopped shouting. "I...have no idea. They found a body in the underground lake? There shouldn't be any bodies in the lake, I would know and—" Maybe he shouldn't have said that. "What I mean is..."

"No, I think it was in the Seine."

"Ah, right, see, that makes perfect sense! People die in the Seine all the time, so—well, not *all the time*, I just mean—and not that I have personal experience of this at all, ever, but..."

He recognized the look on her face. It was the look she got when she was trying not to laugh. The corners of her mouth started twitching while her eyes danced. He began to feel better.

He tried to maintain a stern tone anyway. "And there's nothing funny about people dying in the Seine, the crime rate in Paris is a serious concern..."

She gave up holding back the laughter, finally wound up having to sit down on a bench nearby. There were several near the cathedral, unoccupied as evening crept on.

"It's not *that* funny," Erik protested, even though he was smiling himself. How unexpected.

"I know, but..." She shook her head, wiped her eyes with the heel of one hand, and smiled up at him. "I know."

The sun had sunk even lower, the shadows grown even longer, and it suddenly struck him that there was something odd about the scene, about being together like this in the near-darkness. Or maybe it was because he was noticing how her hair still seemed to shine, even in the shadows. He blinked, glanced away. "I suppose your mother will be expecting you home."

"Yes," she said, rising to her feet and pulling her hood back up over her hair. She started across the square and without either of them commenting on it, Erik fell into step beside her. "So was that a proper plan with the Persian?" she asked, voice quiet. "Did you discuss it all with him ahead of time?"

"It was more...improvised. I saw him there, and we've sort of been through this type of thing before, so..." He was sure she was about to ask awkward questions about his past now, and wondered how he was going to get out of answering.

Instead, she asked, "And how did you manage not to drown?"

Erik shrugged, tried for a light tone to offset the heaviness of this topic. "Would you believe me if I said it was magic?"

"That was *not* a parlor trick. And if you couldn't warn me beforehand, you can at least explain afterwards."

"I couldn't warn you because I didn't know I was going to do that," he said, feeling vaguely apologetic and trying to keep it out of his voice. "There were several possibilities—and you weren't supposed to be there anyway."

She turned her head and raised her eyebrows at him. "Because hearing about it would have been better?"

That was a fair question—the Opera Company was no doubt already distorting the story in all kinds of ways, but Meg would have known to dismiss most of it out of hand. So would she have believed more terrifying details than were true, or less? Would he have seemed less frightening in report or more? But apparently she wasn't frightened anyway, so... Right, her original question, that was the point, not this one. "There's an underwater passage in the side of the wall bordering the lake. I just swam through and came up in another chamber, out of sight."

"Of course," Meg said, voice dry. "How simple."

"Exactly," Erik said, consciously ignoring her sarcasm. "I have very good lungs—singing, you know. And the point is that now they think I'm dead, so they won't keep looking for me. Which they would have done, if I'd just not been home when they arrived."

"I suppose," Meg said, running her fingers over the folds of her skirt. "Or you just wanted a dramatic fifth act finale."

"I *can* think outside operatic norms, you know." Although—maybe that had been a factor. He could hardly deny having a flare for the dramatic.

She was looking away from him, off down the shadowed streets, sparsely populated with Paris' residents. "Operas usually end, though. After the finale. And you killed the Phantom of the Opera; that's pretty obviously the end of the story." Her voice grew a shade quieter. "I wondered, even if you were alive, if you were coming back. From wherever you've been."

"The Daroga took me in," Erik said, because it was the easiest unspoken question to answer. It hadn't been an easy or simple thing to achieve—to go knock on the door of the man who had once helped him escape from a death sentence in Persia years ago, who had that same day helped him fool a mob into believing he was dead. Despite that he was never quite certain whether or not to consider him a friend. In darker moments he was certain he was only a duty to the other man.

As for the end of his opera, as for his future plans—this felt less like an ending than it had when *she* left the Opera, choosing the vicomte instead of him, 423 days, 19 hours ago. And his life had continued after that, to his frequent amazement and sometimes frustration.

As for now—had Meg really imagined he wouldn't return to the Opera Garnier? Perhaps it should have been the obvious result of a mob invading his home, and yet—the idea was unfathomable. Where else would he go? Where else could he possibly belong? He didn't want to say that to her though, because how would that make him look?

He tried again to make his voice light, to sound unconcerned. "I'll be coming back to the Opera, of course. I thought I'd block off a passage or two—maybe disengage the magic staircase, make it harder to reach my rooms. Then once I know no one will come wandering in—no one besides you, I mean...well, then it'll be all right, I'll just stay out of sight so Mifroid will think I'm dead and not come hunting again, and...that will be fine. After all, where else would I go?"

He had let himself ramble a little too much, and that last thought had slipped out all unintended. Sometimes he thought it had grown too easy to talk to Meg.

But at least she was finally looking at him and she didn't look disturbed. Just thoughtful. "I don't know. You might find somewhere else."

Somewhere else? There was nowhere else. True, there had been times when he thought wistfully of the larger world, when he talked to Meg about places he had been and places she dreamed of and he thought—but the world he might want to visit, it didn't exist. The world out there wouldn't be for him what he might imagine it to be. It wouldn't be the way it would be for, say, Meg. The world would welcome her. Not him.

So he was staying below the Opera Garnier, dead or not. He thought of the eight weeks he had spent down below the Opera, after Buquet's death, and how excruciatingly boring life had grown. But it wouldn't be like that this time. He could still go up above, merely to observe. With the Phantom dead, he couldn't *do* anything, but...well, he'd manage. He could watch the operas. He could continue selling music to the Opera Company as Erik Rouen the reclusive composer.

And there would be Meg. And that was enough difference to change everything.

"I expect I'll be back to the Opera by early next week," he said, trying very hard to sound casual, to stay casual as he concluded, "So, see you Tuesday afternoon, perhaps?"

Chapter Four

I felt like I could fly as I came in our front door, after Erik walked me home from Notre Dame—or like I could dance the lead in *Giselle* without even practicing.

Mother knew the moment I stepped inside. "You're home late," she said, entering the parlor from the kitchen. And then her eyes narrowed as she saw my face. "You heard from the Phantom."

I practically floated across the room to give her a swift hug. "Erik's fine! I just saw him at Notre Dame. Didn't I tell you he wasn't dead?" I had. I definitely had. And I had been right, and he was perfectly all right, and my world was set in balance again.

Even my second fear, the one I'd barely had time for next to the horrible possibility that he was dead, had turned out to be groundless. He wasn't going to leave the Opera, and in this moment that seemed wonderful too, that Erik would still live in the building where I spent so much of my time.

"I'm sure you must be very relieved," Mother said as she hugged me back. But her tone was guarded.

"You know you're glad too," I said, bouncing away from the hug to set down my bag and take off my cloak. "You *are*."

Mother hesitated, then smiled slightly. "Yes. I would have regretted it if your friend had died in such a way. But you know it does return us to a number of…complications."

"No," I said, shaking my head, unwilling to let anything dampen down my spirits. "Everything was good before, everything is good now. Everything is *wonderful*."

She let it go, but we both knew I was, as Hamlet might say, protesting too much. I found it easy enough to shunt worries aside for the rest of the evening, to talk lightly and happily about pleasant topics.

After I went to bed, I found it harder not to think about...complications.

I lay on my bed, watched the shadows on the ceiling, still happy that Erik was alive—yet in the darkness, the complications lined up for attention.

There were my directions, the ones the mob had used to find Erik. I should have told him about that. But I had been so elated to see him I hadn't thought of it, at first. And then I had hated to spoil the moment.

Because I was a coward.

I'd known even at the time that I should tell him, but I couldn't make myself. I'd have to, though. He should know, and I didn't feel right trying to keep a secret like that. Surely it didn't matter as much now anyway. He wasn't dead. That had to turn a hideous mistake into something forgivable. He had forgiven me for baiting Carlotta, for starting the management down the path that had led eventually to the mob. He'd forgiven me so completely for that, he hadn't even understood why I felt guilty.

So maybe this would be the same.

And there was the fact of his staying. I had *wanted* that, because I didn't know how I'd fit into his life anymore, and he into mine, if he left the Opera. Yet—was it a good thing, if he felt he had no choice but to stay? There was such sadness to that thought, and only more so because he didn't seem to see it. Perhaps I was selfish, wanting him to continue in this partial life hidden away, just so I could see him.

But I *did* want to see him. And that pointed me to the biggest complication. The one Mother had actually meant.

Nothing had to change now. Everything had been good before. Before, when I knew I loved Erik and had resolved not to tell him about it. He wouldn't understand. I had been so sure he wouldn't understand, and that he wouldn't ever feel the same about me. Not when he was so in love with Christine.

I had told myself that not telling him, to continue being his friend and not tell him, was the only option.

But that had never been a comfortable option. Not even before I kissed his cheek when a mob was coming for him, before I watched him (apparently) drown, before I had lived seven days with the possibility that he was dead and I would never again have the chance to tell him anything.

That had been before I saw him step alive out of the shadows, before everything in me had taken wing at the sight of him, before I had impulsively reached out to hold onto him and been embraced in return.

I lay on my back in bed and played with my gold necklace, the little disk with a G on it that had been my sister Gabi's before it was mine.

Sometimes people went away forever, and didn't miraculously return. And knowing how possible that was, could I really continue living with important things left unsaid?

I fell asleep eventually, but questions still danced unanswered in my head the next morning. I dressed and went to the Opera Garnier for the Saturday morning ballet practice, happier than I had been since the day of the mob, but undecided too.

I walked into the high-ceilinged practice room, drifted into the crowd of girls sitting at one end lacing up their slippers.

"Good morning, Meg," Adalisa said as I sat down next to her. "How are you feeling?"

"Fine," I said automatically, before remembering she had actual reason to ask. The supposed illness I'd been blaming my distraction on. I smiled, and it was easier than it had been. "I think I'm feeling better."

She studied me, and smiled too. "You *do* look better. I'm glad."

"How's Madame Thibault today?" I asked, trying to throw the conversation towards less personal subjects.

Every one of us was an expert at gauging the ballet mistress' moods, and it was a safe topic that swiftly had Adalisa thinking of other things, and other girls chiming in with their opinions too.

That left me free to only nod occasionally, begin my stretching, and think my own thoughts.

Was it best to stay silent about love around Erik? Would it be worse to listen to him explain that he didn't love me, or to live with knowing that some day it could be too late to tell him anything? Could we still be friends, if I told him I loved him? If I could only feel the subject out a bit, without plunging headlong in…

Madame Thibault swept into the room and ordered us into our places with sharp claps of her hands. I took up my position next to Adalisa at the barre, and we began the familiar routine of *relevés* and *grande pliés*.

If I could feel the subject out with Erik, what was I hoping to learn? What signal could I see, to tell me to go ahead or not?

He did care about me. I knew that. Was it so impossible that he might, possibly…fall in love with me?

I dipped into another *plié*, the only reason I didn't sigh at the thought. I didn't think so badly of myself that I didn't believe some man some time might fall in love with me. No one had yet, but someone could. But Erik was in love with Christine, beautiful, talented, magnetic Christine, my best friend who'd been gone for more than a year and yet I was sure she was still so present for him. How could I compete with that?

It *had* been more than a year, though. And what if it was worth the risk?

How much was I willing to risk, if there was any chance at all? Any chance that Erik, fascinating, mysterious Erik, the closest friend I'd ever had, not even excepting Christine, might just possibly look at me and—

"Mademoiselle Giry, are you thinking of dancing?" Madame Thibault snapped out, snapped me back into the moment.

"Yes, Madame," I murmured, tried to attend to my posture, to the precision of my movements.

I wanted so badly to know what Erik's incredible green eyes would look like, what his beautiful voice would sound like, if he told me he loved me.

"You are in a good mood this morning," the Daroga commented over breakfast on Saturday.

Erik was thinking what a peculiar thing it was, this eating of a meal in conjunction with another person. What made anyone assume that hunger would hit multiple people at the same time? Not that he and the Daroga had exactly been sitting down and holding formal meals. Usually there'd been pastries in the kitchen in the early morning, and he'd eaten something when he felt moved to do so. Today, it so happened, he'd felt moved while the Daroga was sitting at the table eating as well.

"Am I?" he said, slathering butter onto a croissant. "Seems to be a pleasant day outside." Windows felt like an odd thing too, this viewing of the world outside. He didn't have them in his rooms at the Opera.

"You have been in a good mood since yesterday evening," the Daroga continued, and there was an amused note in his voice. "Since you encountered Mademoiselle Giry."

Erik shrugged. "Why not? Aren't friends usually happy about each other? You can't put a sinister spin on this, even though I'm sure you'd like to." The Daroga, once a police chief in Persia, had a suspicious mind. Perhaps it was one reason they got on.

The Daroga tapped his fingers on the tabletop. "You are fond of Mademoiselle Giry?"

"She's a very pleasant girl," Erik said, and took a large bite of croissant. They had avoided the subject of Meg for the most part, in the days he had spent here. The Daroga had not approved of their interactions when they first began. Had to be more than a year ago, since it had all started just after *she* left, 424 days, 7 hours ago. He swallowed his croissant, remarked, "I promise I'm not going to abduct her or fling chandeliers about or anything else. Besides, her mother would kill me if I did anything untoward. She told me so herself. You know, Daroga, you'd like Meg's mother. The two of you could get together and discuss what a dangerous character I am. Delightful fun for all, I'm sure."

The Daroga actually chuckled. "I do not believe you are as bad as you think I do."

Erik lifted the remaining piece of croissant in a kind of salute. "So I've fooled even you."

"And Mademoiselle Giry," the Daroga resumed, tapping again, "have you fooled her?"

"Meg thinks I'm better than I am," Erik said, "or she knows something the rest of us don't." He had meant the words lightly, even as a joke, but somehow they came out with more meaning than he had intended them to have. He was not in a mood for introspection, which would no doubt turn gloomy soon enough. "I was thinking," he said quickly, before the Daroga could respond again, "I'll get out of your way and back to the Opera tomorrow. It'll be mostly empty on Sunday, good day to rearrange a few things below ground."

The Daroga was quiet long enough for Erik to finish his croissant and reach for another, long enough for Erik to already suspect a turn in the conversation was coming before the other man said, "Regarding that, there is something I have been meaning to discuss with you."

"You want me to pay a higher rent than you said for this past week?" Erik suggested, a delaying tactic, because nothing good ever came after someone said they needed to discuss something, and why couldn't it just be a pleasant, sunny Saturday with no difficult conversations?

"I am leaving Paris," the Daroga said abruptly.

"Oh." This was unexpected. The Daroga had been in Paris almost as long as Erik had—no coincidence, since the Daroga had followed him here. "You don't feel I need you anymore to prevent me from going on a murderous rampage?" These words, too, came out with more weight than he had meant to put on them. Strange, when he was suddenly feeling adrift, bereft of an anchor he'd never failed to resent.

"I told you," the Daroga said quietly, "I do not believe you are as bad as you think I do. And I have received a summons, to return to

Persia. The current chief of police wishes my insights on a very high level matter he is handling. It is a summons difficult to ignore."

"Without jeopardizing your pension."

"I admit that, yes. It seems like a wise time to be absent from Paris as well; Commissaire Mifroid may believe now that I shot you to protect the crowd, but it would be easy enough for him to reconsider murder charges. Besides, sometimes I miss the old life, the old work. And I miss…" The words trailed away. "Well. I do not know how long—"

"You miss what?" Erik prompted, because it was always the things left unsaid that counted the most.

"It is not important—"

"You miss *what?*"

The Daroga sighed, and in a half-guilty tone said, "I miss being in a place where I do not look different from everyone around me."

Erik leaned back in his chair, knowing that it was most certainly not a pleasant Saturday morning anymore. "I see." No place in existence was like that for him.

"I do not know how long I will be gone," the Daroga resumed. "It may be some time. If you are interested—now that the Phantom of the Opera has died—I have already paid the lease on this apartment through the end of the year."

It took a moment for Erik to gather the implication, and he wasn't entirely sure he had it right. "You're offering me your apartment?"

"The landlord is discreet, and quite open-minded—"

"You're wandering off into the world and offering me your *apartment*," Erik said, scorn entering his voice. "I have an entire opera house, remember?"

One of the brief pauses that meant the Daroga would come back with a carefully even tone. "It was merely a—"

"I don't see why you'd want to go back to Persia," Erik said, knowing his own voice was sounding less controlled by the word. But that even tone always meant the Daroga thought he was overreacting, which was always intensely irritating. "Especially to some matter involving the highest levels. You know the court has all the intrigue of an opera, without the same musical quality."

The Daroga passed over this remark entirely, which was just as irritating. "If you prefer to hide away in your opera house, that is your choice. I thought perhaps you were ready for—"

"I am not *hiding*, I have created a personal refuge—"

"—in which to *hide*." It was vaguely gratifying that the Daroga had finally raised his voice too.

As though forcing the other man to react cooled his own temper, Erik found his anger ebbing. His pleasant feelings of earlier did not return in its wake. "The Opera Garnier is what I have," he said finally, quietly. "There's nothing else for me."

"As I said, my apartment—"

"No, Daroga," Erik said with a mirthless smile. Why was everyone suddenly trying to force him out of the one place he belonged? Didn't they understand how impossible an idea it was? That he wasn't like them? "You can go back to Persia. Léon can go travel Italy, *she* and that vicomte can leave the country to escape me, and Meg can dream of distant lands. I remain. *I* have nowhere to go."

The Daroga did not argue, and Erik felt both disappointed and relieved. It was good the Daroga realized how pointless any arguments on the subject would be. Which left little else to say.

He rose to his feet. "If you will excuse me. I should pack, if I'm returning to the Opera tomorrow."

Considering that he had come with little more than the clothes he was wearing, the excuse was patently transparent. But the Daroga did him the courtesy of not pointing this out.

I didn't expect Léon when I came out of the morning's practice. But there he was, standing in the hall grinning at me, clearly pleased with himself.

"Good morning," he said, leaning in to kiss my cheek with an ease suggesting familiarity.

In the back of my mind, I noted that a display like that from a handsome subscriber, where the rest of the ballet girls could see it, was going to both raise my status and spread gossip. "Good morning," I said, putting mercenary thoughts aside and reminding myself that I *liked* seeing Léon. This was just unexpected. Léon was a Sunday afternoon and performance evenings friend, usually, not a Saturday morning friend. "What are you doing here?"

"I wanted to see you, of course," Léon said, drawing my arm through his. "And sweep you away for lunch."

I hesitated. "We have a rehearsal in just a couple of hours, and then the evening performance…"

"Plenty of time for lunch," he said, already walking us down the hall.

"And I was thinking of putting in some extra practice." I had been so distracted this past week, I knew I needed it. And it might deflect some of Madame Thibault's scoldings.

"But you dance all the time already," Léon said, and in cajoling tones went on, "Surely you can spare just an hour or so for me?"

It wasn't that much—and I was hungry—only perhaps it felt strange because these little patches of time between opera business were usually times when Erik appeared. But he wasn't back at the Opera Garnier yet. And after all, if I wouldn't hesitate to go off with Erik, why not go with Léon?

"All right," I said finally, and smiled at him. "Lunch it is."

"Excellent!" He beamed at me. "You won't regret it."

Maybe I should have, maybe it was irresponsible—but I didn't feel any regret.

Chapter Five

Excerpt from the Private Notebook of Jean Mifroid, Commissaire of Police

29 April, 1882

No new information re: Phantom case. Of course. And yet. . .

Still seeking Raoul de Chagny and Christine Daaé. Inquiries remain inconclusive.

Am undecided if it would be advisable to visit the Phantom's hidden rooms again.

Erik returned to the Opera Garnier eight days after the mob had chased him out. Maybe he was being hasty. He knew he had moved with more caution in the past. But after all—no one was looking for him anymore. And he could only impose on the Daroga's hospitality for so long.

And it would be so much easier to see Meg, if he was at the Opera.

So he slipped back into his kingdom, using the secret entrance off the Rue Scribe. He disabled the magic staircase and two secret doors—

he'd have to get new directions to Meg—and set about cleaning up from the Opera Company's destruction. He'd have to buy new rugs too. They'd carried off his Persian ones, though fortunately they'd evidently felt the rest of the furniture was too much trouble to remove. He'd probably be noticing the absence of any number of smaller possessions for days, carried off as souvenirs or Mifroid's evidence. But he had hidden away anything that was truly valuable, and they hadn't inflicted more than a few scratches on his pipe organ. So it could have been worse.

Once his paintings were back on the walls, his Stradivarius placed on its table and the ornamental pistol returned to his mantelpiece, his world felt almost as much set to rights as his rooms.

With his route altered and his next visit from Meg already scheduled, he felt almost as comfortable as he could wish.

There was just one, nagging problem. He didn't know how the mob had learned the way to his home to begin with, learned how to trigger his secret doors and avoid all his traps. Somewhere there was a gap in his defenses, one he needed to find and resolve if he was going to feel truly at ease again.

As much as he ever did, at least.

Early Tuesday morning, two days after returning, he went up to the surface. He dropped a note with new directions on Meg's table in the ballet's changing room, and then went to haunt the managers.

There was a certain risk, of course, but as long as he stayed in the hidden passages and crawl spaces, he shouldn't be detected.

The most immediate risk, far from direct threats, seemed to be from boredom. He was in place to listen behind the wall of the managers' office when Moncharmin and Ricard came in for the day, and for most of the morning they spoke of nothing of any particular interest. He wouldn't have minded if they were talking about production plans, but Moncharmin felt the need to discuss the budget. At length. Even the arrival of Richard, the vocal director's assistant, didn't divert them into a more interesting topic. The man merely delivered some message about plans for the management's next special performance, and then the managers returned to their numbers.

Sitting with his back to the wall in his dark passage, Erik wondered how long he'd have to put up with this. He'd searched their desk before they arrived, without unearthing any clues, so overhearing something was his best chance. But possibly a slow one.

So it seemed like an excellent stroke of luck when Commissaire Mifroid walked into the office. Erik recognized his voice at once, and had never before been pleased to hear it. Although why was the policeman still visiting?

"So, Commissaire," Moncharmin said after the minimum of pleasantries, "I thought our business was resolved? Now that the Phantom is deceased. Unless you're here for tickets to the special performance we're planning. No Phantom to worry about this time!"

"Yes," Mifroid said, but with a considering tone in his voice that Erik did not welcome. "Have you attempted to revisit the Phantom's home across the lake? Say, yesterday or today?"

Erik sat up straighter. Why was Mifroid asking about *that*?

"Of course not," Ricard said, and Erik could picture the shudder that probably accompanied the words. "Nasty place down there."

"I tried," the commissaire said, words even. "The mechanism to trigger the staircase seems to have broken."

Erik felt his stomach sink. Why did the policeman have to be so thorough? So *persistent*? He had the Phantom's body; why couldn't he let go of hunting for the Comte de Chagny's supposed murderer? The Comte had been dead for 427 days, 12 hours, dying the same night *she* left—couldn't Mifroid finally move on to another crime?

"All those people swarming over that staircase, that's not surprising," Moncharmin remarked. "You wouldn't believe the repair bills in a place like this. Always something breaking, and artists never understand the importance of—"

"That's certainly one explanation," Mifroid went on. "But it also seems slightly…suspicious."

Erik tipped his head back against the wall and resisted the impulse to groan. Of course it was suspicious, but why did Mifroid have to be competent enough to notice it?

"But the Phantom's dead," Ricard said plaintively. "We saw him die. He couldn't have…done anything afterwards."

"True enough," Mifroid agreed. "Still. It is a very untimely breakage. Not impossible to overcome with some planning, but it renders our directions far less efficient now."

They might overcome the missing stair, but they'd find the disabled secret doors much harder to get through. Unless Mifroid was planning to break down walls. Erik was still weighing the likelihood of that when there was the sound of a paper rustling.

Mifroid had mentioned directions. Of course they had to have directions, or a map. But where had the information come from to begin with? Erik rose to his feet. There was a small crack at eye-level. The view wasn't much, but if that rustling was Mifroid's directions, if he could see them, that might tell him something. No—his view of whatever Mifroid was holding was blocked by Ricard's black-clad shoulders.

"It's not as though we *need* to go back there," Moncharmin said. "Waste of time and resources. The Phantom's dead."

"Yes," Mifroid said again, and again the tone was too considering. "But I would appreciate having the option to more easily return to the crime scene. An alternate route would be welcome, but our informant had nothing further to offer when I interviewed her this morning."

Informant? Her? Erik was still assimilating those words when Ricard shifted a step, just enough to reveal a glimpse of the paper Mifroid was holding. Only visible for a moment, but it was long enough. The single page contained a neatly written list of bullet-pointed directions, which was not too unexpected. It was entirely unexpected that they were in Erik's own handwriting. His heart started to pound harder.

"If it's so important to you, try offering her more money," Moncharmin said. "That little blond dancer was much more helpful last time after we made it worth her while."

Little blond dancer.

"I considered that," Mifroid said. "I thought it best to let her think about it a while longer before making a new offer. In the meantime, I trust I can rely on your cooperation should any further efforts be necessary..."

The conversation went on, but Erik stopped listening. He sank down to his knees, pressed his forehead against the rough wood of the paneling. His heart beat loudly in his ears, but not loud enough to drown out the words echoing in his mind.

That little blond dancer. That *helpful* little blond dancer, who had given them a route, who had given them directions, who might do it again if they paid her enough, who evidently had been paid enough once already.

Erik's throat ached and his mouth tasted bitter. It couldn't be. It was impossible. Meg wouldn't do that to him.

It would mean that he had been completely, hideously wrong about her.

And so he must have been. He recognized those directions; he had written them and given them to Meg. They had obtained them from a blond dancer. And what was more believable? That an intelligent, far-thinking young woman who had plans for her life had taken a reasonable offer—or that she was unwilling to betray a madman who lived under an opera house?

He clenched his hands into fists, eyes burning. Anyone could be bought. Anyone could turn on someone else for her own gain. He had seen it again and again. Why had he deluded himself into believing that Meg alone was different? Why had he convinced himself that she cared enough about him to make anything different?

Chapter Six

The note from Erik on my table in the ballet's changing room gave me even more of a thrill than usual. I sat down before the table and picked it up at once. There was nothing on it to tell anyone else who it was from, but I recognized the handwriting of the swirling script spelling out my name. I unfolded the note, quickly read the directions and the reminder that he had invited me to visit today. As if I hadn't remembered.

I couldn't contain my smile. I hadn't seen Erik since the night at Notre Dame, four days ago. But now he was back.

My fingers tingled as I refolded the note, slid it into my bag. I hadn't exactly decided whether to tell him how I felt about him. I couldn't stop the idea from revolving in my head, a thrilling and terrifying subject. I was starting to think, if the right moment arrived…after all, how many operas ended tragically, just because two people didn't talk to each other?

"Good morning, Meg," Adalisa called as she passed me on her way to her own table.

"Good morning," I answered automatically. More and more girls were arriving, and the room was filling with its usual noise of voices talking and drawers rattling.

I glanced at my table's locked drawer, and my mood dropped. I'd have to tell Erik what had happened to his last set of directions. Nothing thrilled me about *that* prospect. But I could get that over with, and surely he'd understand, or forgive me at least, and then, maybe, some time in the future…?

I was still toying with ideas when ballet practice ended, and I descended below the Opera. The new directions were simple enough, even if the magic staircase had apparently been something of a shortcut.

As I walked down the last hallway towards Erik's door, I saw that the fallen gargoyle, knocked over by the mob, had been set to rights. It made me smile. I caught the sound of organ music as I drew closer. I'd not heard music in this hall before, though he was often playing when I arrived—so how loud must it be today?

Something about the emotion in the music made me uneasy. I reached out to pat the head of each gargoyle as I walked between them, usually a habit and a kind of totem now. As I stopped at the door, I wondered if he'd hear anything through the music. I tried knocking anyway.

The sound within didn't reduce, but through it I heard Erik's voice say, "Come in."

Once the door was open, I could more fully appreciate the sheer volume and intensity of the music. It was a pounding melody in minor key, a brooding, angry thunderstorm of sound. I looked at Erik, sitting at the keys, and glanced around. The room was cleaned up; that was the only good sign in the situation, and weighed very little compared to the music and to the tension radiating off of Erik.

What was causing that? He had been so cheerful, when I saw him at Notre Dame.

"Good afternoon," I said, trying to sound normal. I sat down in my usual spot on his maroon couch, tried to ignore the worried twist in my stomach.

He only nodded in response, without turning. I watched the relentless movement of his hands over the keys, his shoulders tight beneath his black coat.

"Is something wrong?" I ventured after a moment. It wasn't really a question by this point, but I had to say something.

The music stopped with no concluding chords, the abrupt silence as overwhelming as the noise had been. "Yes," he said, turning around on the organ seat, face dark. He was wearing the metal half-mask today, and it seemed more ominous than his usual white one.

And that simple yes gave me no answers. "Would you like to tell me about it?"

"Would you like to guess?" he asked, voice a growl.

I put my shoulders back and raised my chin. He was obviously angry, but *why*? "Not really, no," I said evenly. "How about you just tell me what's going on?" Had he realized what had happened to my directions? Surely he wasn't this angry about that. Or could it be something to do with Christine?

He stared at me for a long moment, fury in his green eyes. All these months I had been coming down here, I'd never felt afraid. I'd also never seen him look like this. "I found out how the mob knew the way below. They had directions. Written in my handwriting."

"Oh," was all I managed. So it was about this—and I knew he wasn't wrong to be upset. I took a deep breath, ready to apologize. "I was going to talk to you about this."

Before I could continue, he snapped out, "How much did they pay you?"

My brief understanding of the situation fell apart. "*What?*"

Erik's voice was low and dangerous. "How much? I hope you did better than thirty pieces of silver."

My cheeks flamed hot, probably making me look guilty. I felt guilty, but angry too—because I hadn't done what he was suggesting. "No one paid me anything. I didn't sell any information. You *know* I wouldn't do that!"

"Do I?" he said, voice absolutely cold, and something inside of me crumbled.

He was supposed to believe me. He was supposed to trust me. He was my friend and I loved him and did he really think this little of me? I lifted my chin, eyes narrowing, because I'd rather let him see that I was angry than see that I was hurt. "Why would I sell them the way to get here, then warn you they were coming?"

He raised an eyebrow. "No one's ever played both sides of a conflict before? Don't you watch any of the operas you dance in? Intrigue is quite ordinary."

I gritted my teeth. "This is not an opera, and I didn't—"

"At least respect me enough to stop denying it," he snapped. "I *heard* the managers. They were talking very cheerfully to Mifroid about that *little blond dancer* they paid for information!"

At least that explained where all this had come from. But the story made no sense. I took a breath through my tumult of feelings, tried to understand the inexplicable. They had no reason to make up a story; they couldn't have known Erik was listening, couldn't have known that it would mean anything to him anyway—or maybe they did know it would mean something, if Jammes told them the directions were mine—

"Oh," I said, because suddenly it was so obvious.

"Is that all you have to say?" Erik asked, face tight with anger.

"Did you consider for even a moment," I said, hands closing into fists in my lap, "that it might not be *me* they were talking about? That any number of girls—Jammes, for instance—could be described as little blond dancers?"

"Jammes didn't have directions to my rooms."

"No, but she has a habit of sticking her nose where it has no business being." I inhaled a deep breath, forced my hands to uncurl. "I kept the directions in a locked drawer in my table in the ballet's dressing room. I *thought* that was secure enough, and I wanted to be sure I had them whenever I needed them. But I haven't touched them in, I don't know, a couple of months; I've had them memorized for ages. They weren't there a few days ago, and Jammes as good as told me she stole them. I should have told you about it outside Notre Dame, but—anyway, I was going to tell you today. I'm sorry I wasn't more careful. I really am. But it was a *mistake*, that's all."

This time it was Erik who said, "Oh." Slowly the half of his brow that I could see smoothed and his lowered eyebrow rose to a more normal level. His shoulders were still tense, but it looked more like awkwardness than anger now. He looked down at his hands and then up at the ceiling and I waited for him to say something. Finally, gaze on the far wall rather than me, he said, "That does seem…plausible."

Sarcasm coated my words as I said, "I'm so glad the truth seems *plausible.*"

He didn't seem to notice my tone. He half-turned towards the organ behind him, tapped his fingertips on the keys without pressing hard enough for any sound. "Well. I suppose that's all right, then. No real harm done."

I might have felt relieved. He believed me. He didn't seem upset about the part I really was to blame for. But somehow, I didn't feel any better. Not less angry. Not less hurt. "No, it's not *all right*," I said, back stiffening. "You believed that I would hand you over to the Opera Company."

He kept his attention turned towards the organ keys. "Under the circumstances, it was a natural assumption."

The last thing in the world I would ever do seemed like a natural assumption to him? "Was it *really*? You must think so highly of my loyalty!"

"What was I supposed to do?" he demanded, provoked into turning towards me. "Somehow surmise all of that about where the directions were kept and whether Jammes knows anything about lockpicking?"

That was missing the point completely. "You were supposed to *trust* me enough to believe that I wouldn't sell secrets to people trying to kill you! At least enough to ask me about it before you accuse me of doing it."

He was supposed to know me. He was supposed to be my friend who knew me better than anyone else, but if he could believe this of me, then he didn't know me at all. He didn't *see* me any more than all the people at the Opera who still, after all this time, referred to me only as 'Christine Daaé's friend.'

"Ah, yes, of course." His sarcasm was painfully heavy. "Because I've frequently seen the extraordinary depths of loyalty people are capable of."

"I don't care what other people are capable of, this is about *me*—"

"And of course Little Meg Giry is so different from everyone around her."

I hadn't been Little Meg for years, and I *hated* the way it sounded when he said it, as if I was still a child, still twelve years old. "I am not like everyone else," I snapped, fingernails digging into my palms. Fury was making me reckless, making me plunge toward topics best left alone. "And I'm not like *Christine* either."

I had broken our long-standing rule. We never talked about Christine. Not once, in all this time, had I ever heard Erik say Christine's name.

His eyes widened, then narrowed. Dangerously. "Don't say her name."

"Did you trust Christine?" I challenged, a question I had never dared think let alone ask, but that I had always, always wanted to know. "More than you trust me? Because you obviously *don't* trust me. Not enough to tell me your plan when the mob was coming, or to tell me you were still alive, or to believe the best of me when you overheard something that sounded bad. You've never even told me what happened when Christine left, and I trust *you* enough to ignore all the stories saying you killed her!"

"Stop saying her name!"

That was the important part in what I had said? That was the only part he had heard? Anger that had started red hot had turned cold and even harder to control. "I am not Christine," I said, my voice seeming to come from outside of myself, even and steady. "I don't sing like Christine, and I'm not as beautiful as Christine, and I would never betray you *like Christine*."

His voice was barely more than a whisper. "She didn't betray—"

"She *left*," I said, and watched him flinch. And maybe it had been even worse than that, because I still couldn't make sense of why she had gone up to the rooftop with Raoul when she ran away from the

Phantom at the masquerade, why she had stayed to sing at the special performance if she was so afraid. Why she had only written to me once after she was gone. "She left you, and she left me."

"You can't compare the two. You have so much in your life—I had nothing but *her*."

As if my loss didn't matter. And as if nothing else in his life, including me, mattered. "You don't know anything about how I felt— just because I didn't brood around and decide my life had ended—"

"I did not *decide* anything—"

"You decided no woman in the world could compare to Christine! You decided you could never trust anyone or love anyone ever again!"

The words were out before I thought, and they hung in the air in a sudden silence. A long enough silence for me to take a breath, to think what I should have thought before, to wonder if he had, actually, decided all of that—or if I had only assumed that he had. If maybe, after all, I might have been wrong.

He was looking at the floor, and when his gaze finally rose again to me, his eyes were more mocking than angry. "You say it like I had a choice. Which only proves that you understand nothing about pain, or loss, or what it means to be in love. You understand nothing about me."

I understood so much more than he dreamed. Because clearly I had been right all along. I had been right about him, and right that he didn't see me at all. I rose to my feet, head high, and stared down his gaze. "You are not the only person in the world who has lost someone," I said coldly. "You are not the only person who has ever been in love. But obviously, *obviously,* your loss is so much more *meaningful*." I spread my hands as though I was letting it all go, as if it could be that easy. "Fine. Be a martyr. Sacrifice yourself on the altar of Christine Daaé. But she is never going to thank you for it."

It sounded good, strong, even fierce. And I had to leave, now. Because I knew I was going to crumble into tears in another minute, and I wouldn't let him see that. I turned and stalked to the door, back straight.

"Don't walk away from me." If he had said it plaintively I would have stopped—but he didn't. It was hard, a wounded pride, not a wounded heart.

I didn't look back, just snapped, "Try and stop me," and yanked open the door.

I knew he could. I knew he wouldn't. I didn't know if I wanted him to—not to stop me by dragging me back, of course, but to say something, to apologize maybe, to say it was all a mistake and he didn't want me to leave him.

He didn't stop me and I walked out, slamming the door behind me.

Erik was not at all sure what had just happened, and for a while he was too angry and too wounded to care.

He thundered out a few more melodies, until the initial feelings crested, ebbed, and receded. They left an emptiness in their wake that was far more appalling than the anger had been. He rested his elbows on the keys of the organ, head in his hands, and tried to make some kind of sense of the situation.

She hadn't betrayed him—that was good. But she'd been upset that he accused her—and that was bad. He was pretty sure he had followed the thread that far. But then somehow the conversation had ended up being about *her* and by the time Meg walked out, Erik wasn't at all clear anymore what they were fighting about.

He was lucky she'd stormed away angry, instead of fleeing in terror. For a moment the imagined picture came into his head of Meg bursting into tears, looking up at him in fear...

He shoved the image away, skin crawling at the thought. He didn't want that. He didn't ever want that. He couldn't stand the thought of

Meg looking at him with fear in her eyes. If she ever did…then he'd know that he really was a monster.

He drummed one finger against the middle-C key, as though the familiar note could be some kind of anchor.

Did it even matter, that she hadn't been afraid? He had still driven her away, the one person who thought he was worth knowing.

That was as familiar as any note in the musical scale. It was his *leitmotif,* the repeating theme of his life. The melody had some variations this time, but it was still the same recognizable pattern. To care about someone meant to lose them. Often they betrayed him. Sometimes circumstances compelled him to leave. And this time, when someone had proved to be too loyal to turn against him, he had managed to force her away anyway.

Chapter Seven

T he long walk back to the surface was not enough to calm me down. My eyes burned but I blinked hard and held back the tears. I didn't *want* to cry, not over this. Not over him. Why should I make him that important, if I wasn't important to him?

By the time I emerged from the prop room, re-entered the Opera Garnier proper, I was still hurt, still humiliated—but mostly, I was *angry*. It was anger that I had let him see, and it was anger thrumming through me now.

Let him sit below the Opera and mourn over Christine. Let him. It didn't matter to me. If Christine was the only woman he wanted in his life, then she would *be* the only woman in his life.

I couldn't believe I had seriously considered telling him I loved him. It was so painfully, achingly clear that would have been a horrible mistake, leading to nothing but bigger humiliations. I had wondered if I could feel out the subject, and now I knew. He had all but confirmed it, when I said he'd never love anyone but Christine.

If I let it, that was going to hurt so much.

I'd rather stay angry. I stalked through the Opera, thinking furious thoughts, thinking I probably ought to go home where I could throw something—but then I'd have to explain to my mother why I was upset and I didn't want to do that. I didn't have to stay at the Opera, though. With no performance tonight, nothing required me to be here. So where could I go? What could I do with all this fuming energy inside me?

An opera couldn't have timed things better, because at the very moment I asked the question, I encountered Léon. We were in the half-circle hall outside the first level boxes, and saw each other as we approached around the curve. His face lit in a very gratifying smile.

"Meg! Just the girl I was looking for." It was exactly what I wanted to hear, and his smile was exactly what I wanted to see.

This was the second time this week he'd come looking for me in the afternoon, newly attentive behavior. And that was nice. I was about to have a lot more time for Léon. "I'm so glad to see you," I said, and meant it.

He took my hand, as he usually did and Erik never, ever had, and kissed it. "You look beautiful today."

Léon thought I was beautiful. Léon didn't think that I was a child, or care whether or not I could sing. I smiled my most flirtatious smile. "Tell me more."

Still holding my hand, he tucked it through his arm. "Perhaps we could go somewhere."

Why waste time? I was feeling reckless and wild. "There won't be anyone in the auditorium at this time," I said, waving my free hand at the rows of doors leading into the boxes. "We could talk. Or…not talk."

His smile widened. "What an excellent suggestion."

He led me towards the nearest door, and I let him. I spared just a second to glance at the box number—Box Five would have been entirely too strange, but this was Box Seven, so that was all right. That was excellent, perfect.

I didn't need Erik. I didn't need him at all.

By the time Meg had been gone for an hour, Erik was pacing. He felt trapped. His rooms, usually a refuge, felt confining. The weight of the Opera above, normally a protection, felt like it was crushing him. He remembered these feelings, the way the emptiness, the way one person's absence, could be so enormous that no room was left for him.

He needed to get out. He started walking with no particular destination, mind spinning, thoughts tangled. There had to be some way to fix this mess with Meg. Something he could do.

Eventually he looked around and realized that he was backstage. Automatic impulse had drawn him here, to the center of the Opera, the center of his kingdom. It had started here in the auditorium, the first time he spoke to Meg.

He thought of Box Five. He had spent so much time brooding there in the past, maybe the familiar surroundings would help him think today.

He walked out to the stage, moving with his accustomed if likely unnecessary silence in the empty, dim-lit auditorium. No one here to see him at this time of day, the actors departed from the stage. He moved down to the floor, made his way along the rows towards Box Five. As he approached, sounds registered through the noise of his own thoughts.

Breathing. Cloth rustling. A murmur, a kiss.

He pinpointed—Box Seven. A couple was entwined in Box Seven.

He nearly groaned aloud. Of course. The world had plainly turned against him, of course some happy romantic couple had to be in the auditorium, just when all he wanted was peace.

Well. He could get rid of them. A little thunder, a few flashing lights, he could run them off...except that the Phantom was supposed to be dead.

Maybe that didn't matter. Maybe he didn't care. What did he have left to lose?

No. Better not burn all his bridges yet. Maybe he would be able to fix things with Meg still. Maybe.

He started to turn, started to go, cast one idle glance back towards the couple in Box Seven. At that moment, the man moved his head to kiss the girl's neck, and her face became visible in the dim light.

Merde. *Merde.*

What was she—how could she—of course, that was Léon, he could see that now. Meg had her eyes closed and her arms around Léon's shoulders as she leaned back in one of the box's red velvet chairs. Erik couldn't read much of her expression in this light, but it was plain enough that she was not in distress.

Which meant she was willingly, happily, engaging in a—well, in a—in a romantic interlude. With Léon.

He knew they walked about in the Dance Foyer and went out on Sunday afternoons, but this was an entirely different—he hadn't thought Meg was nearly that fond of Léon and—and wasn't she even a little bit upset about what had just happened down under the Opera? No, instead she was up here with *Léon* and—now she was letting Léon kiss her hair and he was whispering in her ear and...

Good God, why was he standing here watching? All she had to do was open her eyes and—the shadows in the auditorium were deep, but not that deep. Silently, silently, praying she would keep her eyes closed, Erik backed away, slipped away until he could slide through a hidden door, close it behind him, lean back against it and concentrate on breathing.

Kissing Léon was not as distracting as I wanted it to be.

This was far more kissing than we'd ever done before, a considerable advancement on the single kiss of Mardi Gras more than a year ago. Then I had been swept up in the exhilaration of the masquerade, and one kiss in the moonlight had been magical.

This was so much more—and so much less.

I didn't dislike kissing him. It wasn't unpleasant. He was good at it, or at least I supposed he was. I hadn't had a vast amount of experience with kissing, but it had happened now and then. He seemed confident he knew what he was doing, and he seemed to be right.

On the other hand, the mere fact that I was thinking dispassionately about whether Léon was good at kissing, while he was kissing me, wasn't a good sign.

It wasn't bad. But it just wasn't anything. No tingles, no thrills, no rising music. It was…boring. I got more thrills when Erik brushed my hand passing me a coffee cup or a musical score…

No, I wasn't going to think about Erik. Certainly not while I was in the middle of being kissed by Léon. I was *angry* with Erik. And at least Léon wanted me.

Chapter Eight

I got home before dark and would have preferred to go straight to my own room. But Mother came out of the kitchen to greet me, and looked at me with narrowed eyes.

Her voice was too carefully not an accusation when she asked, "Where have you been this afternoon?"

"Nowhere," I said, conscious that my cheeks were probably flushed, that my hair, despite my efforts at one of the Opera's many mirrors, was not as neat as it had been when I left home. And that my answer was too short. I waved a hand. "Just…around."

"Ah," she said, too calmly. "And what were you doing while you were around?"

"*Nothing.*" The word came out defensive. At this rate, I was going to sound like I'd been so much worse than I really had been. I gave up. "I was kissing Léon, if you have to know. But that's all I did, nothing else, so you don't need to worry. And you don't need to worry about Erik anymore either."

I shouldn't have mentioned his name. It caught in my throat, made my breath tighten. It wasn't fair, that just saying his name could make me more emotional than kissing Léon did.

Mother's eyebrows rose. "And why shouldn't I worry about your Phantom anymore?"

My riot of feelings erupted. "Because he's not my Phantom and he never will be and I don't care and he's an *idiot*. And he didn't hurt me so don't start looking like that and just—he's just an idiot, all right?"

I slammed off into my room.   It seemed to be my day for slamming doors.

"Supper is ready," Mother said from outside the room, voice still maddeningly restrained.

"I'm not hungry," I announced, flung myself on the bed and wrapped my hand around Gabi's necklace.

I didn't need him and I didn't care and he wasn't worth all this pain.

And I knew perfectly well that every bit of that was a lie.

It took only a single day for Erik to be sure Meg was avoiding him. He went up to the Opera in the morning, watched Meg come in for the day's ballet practice within a stream of other girls.   He wasn't exactly sure he wanted to talk to her, but it was reassuring that she hadn't left the country with Léon.   Not that he had thought she would.   Not that he seemed to have any real understanding of…anything.

He paced behind the mirrors while the ballet girls put on slippers and began warming up, watching Meg's face for some kind of clue to what she was thinking.   This was easier when she came over to the barre, began a series of *pliés* and *relevés*, only a meter and a mirror away from him. She appeared perfectly calm, perfectly serene, in sharp contrast to his own tumult of emotions.

Her gaze turned to the mirror, and he shifted awkwardly, looked away even though he knew she couldn't see him.   She was still looking at the mirror when he snuck a glance back again, her head tipped at a thoughtful angle.

"Good morning," some little ballet girl said, flitting up and landing at the barre next to Meg.

Meg turned a perfectly brilliant smile on her friend. "Good morning, Adalisa. Have I told you what a good time I had with Léon earlier this week? You know, when he met me after practice."

Erik groaned. This was the *last* topic he wanted to hear about—and what possessed her to just launch into it, apropos of nothing?

Adalisa didn't seem to find that strange or off-putting at all. Instead, she sounded simply delighted as she said, "Ooh, no, you haven't, tell me all about it."

"I told him I felt like going to the Café de la Paix—so we went. The inside is almost as grand as the Opera."

A detailed discussion of coffee at the Café followed, and Erik blessed Madame Thibault when she began dance practice proper and ended this absurd conversation. So what if Léon took her to the Café— why was that supposed to be interesting to discuss?

He paced throughout ballet practice, during which Meg gave every indication of thinking only of dancing. He tried to decide what he ought to do afterwards, what he could possibly say to her.

Don't mention Léon, or Box Seven—or the Café de la Paix, in case she didn't like him listening in. But she had to know he listened in, regularly, so—anyway, not important. The important thing was *their* conversation. Eighteen hours ago. Was eighteen hours enough time for her to stop being angry with him?

He should apologize. He wasn't exactly sure what for—not because he doubted he was to blame, but because it had all grown…confusing.

After ballet practice ended, Meg stayed close beside the other girls, moving in a giggling, chattering flock. He paced alongside them in hiding as they wandered through the corridors, settled onto the marble stair at the center of the Opera, eventually picked up again…and then he had to stop following because they walked right out the door. He stood at a window in an empty room, watched Meg's blond hair in the midst of the crowd until they had all disappeared down the street and around the corner.

He consoled himself that she'd have to be back this evening for a performance. And perhaps before the performance, or after, or even on the interval…

By the time the evening was over, and Meg had spent the entire time practically linked arm in arm with the other girls, until she had drifted into the Dance Foyer and let Léon take her arm, Erik was sure—she was avoiding him.

It had never previously occurred to him that was even possible, considering how often he dropped in on her and how rarely she even knew where he was. He had also never thought that she might have been deliberately ending up in empty rooms and corridors, until she stopped. Now, if she was never alone, how could he ever approach her?

The time since their fight had grown to 34 hours, not an extraordinary amount of time to not talk to Meg, but an agonizing stretch of hours under the circumstances. Even if he still had no idea what he would say to her if he could.

I didn't want to see Erik, I didn't want to talk about Erik, and I didn't want to think about Erik. I couldn't do anything about the third point, but at least I could manage the first two. I knew he'd never risk talking to me if he had to face someone else to do it, and Mother couldn't make me discuss the topic if I refused.

I kept to my resolve the first day, the second, and the third. And somehow, I thought it ought to be getting easier.

Only it wasn't.

Chapter Nine

An hour before Saturday's performance, Erik flung himself into a seat in Box Five and stared moodily at the closed curtains, trying to think what on earth he was going to do.

The Phantom, of course, was dead, and the management believed they had sold Box Five for this evening's performance to a M. Laurent, who was entirely fictitious. Erik imagined that if he sat in the back row and opened the curtains halfway, that should be a reasonable balance between hiding and not looking like anyone was hiding. Maybe. He didn't really think he could do this often, but tonight—he needed his box tonight.

It had been four days, five hours since he'd talked to Meg, and he needed the stability of Box Five.

Though he'd probably spend the whole performance distracted anyway.

He was distracted right now, and so it came as a distinct shock when the door to the box opened behind him.

He was on his feet, ready to leap over the front banister of the box if necessary, when Madame Giry said, "Good, you're already here. We need to talk." Her footsteps were brisk as she crossed the box, to sit at the opposite end of his row of seats.

"I—we do?" Erik said, and slowly sat down again. Was this when she killed him for hurting her daughter? He hadn't meant to. He hadn't wanted to. He'd made an absolute mess of things.

Something in the quality of Madame Giry's voice was far more alarming than anything Mifroid had ever done to him, as she announced,

"My daughter has been miserable for four days. What are you going to do about it?"

Erik's shoulders hunched. How could a question sound so much like an accusation? "I...don't think there's anything I *can* do. And she doesn't look miserable to me." She was having so much *fun* with the ballet girls. And with Léon. She wasn't missing him. She was too busy making it abundantly clear that she didn't need him or want him in her life anymore.

Madame Giry made an exasperated sound. "Of course she doesn't *seem* miserable. She's hiding it."

"Then how do you know?" Erik asked in genuine confusion.

"I'm her mother."

People were always saying things like that as though they meant something. If Erik's mother had ever had any special insight about him, she'd hidden that remarkably well.

"All she's willing to say on the subject," Madame Giry continued, "is that you're an idiot. And then she won't talk about you."

"That's encouraging," Erik muttered. True, too. He knew he'd been an idiot. That didn't mean he knew how to fix the situation.

"Do not expect me to sympathize over your wounded feelings. My concern is for my daughter. I suggest you prove that you are *not* an idiot and do something to resolve whatever is upsetting her."

"I can't *do* anything," he protested. "She doesn't want to see me!"

Silence. Weighted, heavy, imposing silence.

He ducked his head. "All right, fine, I'll try."

"Now would be an excellent time," Madame Giry said, quite serenely.

"But she's with the ballet girls and they're about to perform and...and she doesn't *want* to see me."

"Of course she does," Madame Giry countered. "Now go put some of that apparently boundless creativity towards doing something useful for a change."

He was on his feet and stepping through the secret door in the marble pillar before he could manage to think twice.

And he had thought Madame Thibault was fierce.

Everything was perfectly fine and I was perfectly happy and I was perfectly, perfectly content without Erik at all. Or so I kept telling myself.

Likewise, I tried to tell myself that the ongoing chatter of the ballet girls was not irritating, as we sat in the changing rooms, waiting to be called. They were distracting. That was good.

"Tell us more about your dinner with Léon," Adalisa said eagerly, and the three other girls sitting in our little circle chimed agreement. "He really is *so* handsome."

"Yes," I agreed. He was that. And he had grown suddenly attentive. Especially in the last few days. Ever since we had gone into Box Seven and…well anyway, I was enjoying my time with him. And it wasn't as though I was so busy with anyone—anything else anymore.

"Do you suppose that he—" Suzanne began, and then suddenly gave a shriek. She leaped away, pointing behind me, and for one sickening moment I thought perhaps Erik had thrown away the protection of being dead and decided to come looming out of my mirror.

But when I turned, all I saw was a very large spider, standing on top of my dressing table. "Oh, not this again," I groaned, as the girls went through their customary cries over the spider.

I was *positive* that half these girls didn't really mind spiders this much; they just started shrieking because they all set each other off. Usually I was patient about it, but I couldn't muster up the feeling today.

Everyone around me had backed quickly away, and more girls were rising to their feet as they realized what was going on.

"It's just a spider," I said, reaching for an empty glass to trap it with.

And then all the lights in the room went out.

"It's the *Phantom*!" one girl screamed, only to be quickly corrected by a remarkably calm, "No, silly, the Phantom died, remember?"

"Maybe it's his ghost," someone else suggested.

"Or maybe it's just the electricity acting up again."

"Oh. Well, that's *boring*."

"Come on, you can see the door—let's just go, we have to be on stage soon anyway."

Footsteps padded towards the door, visible in outline with light behind it, and as the first girl opened it more light streamed in. Girls around the room headed for the exit and so did I—but I was the only one who hadn't already been retreating when the spider put in its appearance, meaning I was the last one. When I was still this side of the door, it swung sharply shut again.

"Marvelous," I muttered, trying to remember if there had been anything trippable between me and the door, in the now much darker darkness.

Until the lights flared on again, at the same moment that a familiar voice said, "I need to talk to you."

My stomach clenched with anger and nerves—and a little thrill of gladness that I tried hard to shove down. "I don't want to talk to you," I said flatly. "And all of these theatrics?" I waved a hand to indicate the spider, the lights, the door. "Not amusing."

"You didn't give me a choice," he protested. "You've been avoiding me."

I finally turned around then, crossing my arms and glaring at him. "Because I *don't* want to talk to you."

He should have looked imposing. He had his black cloak and black mask on, usually a very unapproachable, uninviting combination. But his head was a little lowered and his shoulders a little hunched, and he looked altogether awkward and uncomfortable. "When do you think you might want to?"

"I don't know!" I snapped, angry with myself for wanting to soften towards him, angry with him for making me want to.

"I'm sorry," he offered.

"That doesn't fix anything!"

His shoulders were growing tighter, his posture shifting more towards frustration. "So tell me what will!"

"I don't *know*!"

"What do you want?" Erik demanded. "I'm *sorry*. *Mea culpa, mea culpa, mea maxima culpa*!"

I took a breath. "Would you like to try the entire Act of Contrition?"

"Would it help?"

"Probably not." I shook my head, turning back to the exit, and reached out to twist the door handle.

"Can't we at least *talk*?"

I stubbornly kept my gaze on the wood panels, turned the handle down in a sharp wrench.

"...I miss you."

If he had said *anything* else. Anything else wouldn't have brought back in sudden sharpness Easter morning at Notre Dame, Erik's voice just behind me, his half-whispered words about missing me. The moment everything in me had woken up to the realization that, somewhere along the way, this man had claimed more of my heart than I ever knew I could give.

I released a breath and slowly let the handle twist back up again. "What do you want, Erik?"

"I want you to stop hating me."

I whirled around at that. How could he be that blind? "I don't hate you, Erik, I—" I cut off a very unwise phrase, replaced it with, "I am *angry* with you. If I hated you, I wouldn't be angry because I wouldn't care what you thought about me!"

"And I don't know what you think I'm thinking that's so awful! I mean, I know you didn't sell me to the Opera Company, that was stupid, and I shouldn't have said you didn't know anything about loss, and I'm sorry and...and I...do trust you." His voice dropped low, and he wasn't meeting my eyes. "More than I trust anyone else."

I knew that couldn't be true. "You trusted Christine."

At that he looked up, looked surprised. "I never trusted..." He hesitated, and I willed him to actually *say* it, to say her name, as though that would prove something. "...her."

Maybe that was true. Maybe not. But he loved her. Enough that he still couldn't say her name after all this time.

"And I know you're not her," he continued. "I never wanted you to be."

"Obviously I'm not," I said flatly. "So that doesn't solve anything." I turned back to the door.

"Please don't do this to me," Erik said, and it was strange to hear a strain in that perfect voice.

I didn't turn back around. "I'm not doing anything to—"

"At least when *she* left me, she was *gone*," he burst out. "I mean, it was over, it was done. But I don't think I can survive it if you leave me while you're still here."

I wasn't with him. I wasn't his and he wasn't mine and, really, wasn't that what this was about? He didn't know it, he couldn't know it, but *that* was what had me so furious with him. And that wasn't fair, was it? And he hadn't exactly said I was as important as Christine, hadn't even managed to say her name out loud, and yet...he had suggested some kind of equivalency between us, hadn't he? He was doing the best he could, wasn't he?

I sighed, a sigh that made my whole body sag. "Don't ever accuse me of betraying you again, all right?"

I couldn't see most of his face when I turned to look at him, so I'm not sure how he suddenly looked more hopeful. It must have been in the eyes. "No. Never. I wouldn't."

"And...it's really none of my business how you feel about..." I hesitated. "Her. I mean, I shouldn't have even brought up—"

"Let's not talk about that," he said hastily. "Can we just—let's just forget the whole thing, all right?"

That was no way to deal with anything. I knew that. But I also knew I desperately didn't want to talk about Christine with Erik. Not like this. "Fine, all right." Then I smiled, and that made him look so relieved that I smiled more, and impulsively added, "I missed you too, you know."

He didn't seem as shocked as he had when I said the same thing Easter morning, though he did say, "You hid it well."

"Then you were watching?" I asked, but said it lightly. Of course he had been. I wouldn't have bothered trying to hide my feelings if I hadn't known that.

"So that I could find a chance to talk to you! Which you did not make easy, you know."

"I know," I agreed, and we just stood there and smiled at each other for a moment.

Finally he said, "I suppose you have the performance to get to…"

The performance. The *performance*. I hadn't given it so much as a thought and— "I'm going to be late," I said, reaching again for the door, "Madame Thibault is going to kill me—do you know a shortcut?"

His eyes slid sideways, thinking. "No. I'm sorry."

I gave an inarticulate groan, pulled the door open.

"Do you have plans?" he said hurriedly. "For after the performance?"

I wanted to say I was available. I wanted to tell him that of course I would spend the rest of the evening with him. "Yes," I said unhappily, "I told Léon…"

"Oh, right, of course," he said. "I understand. Of course."

"Tomorrow, though—I'm not busy tomorrow. I could come by in the afternoon."

"Ah. Good. Grand. I'll be home."

"Good," I said, caught myself standing there smiling at him again, and groaned. "I'm so *late*!"

I ran out the door and didn't actually miss my cue for the ballet number but was definitely not far ahead of it. Not far enough to keep Madame Thibault from giving me a round scolding. But that didn't carry nearly as much weight as it might have any other night.

Chapter Ten

A t first, it was such a relief that Meg had forgiven him (for what, he still wasn't entirely sure, but that wasn't the important point) that Erik felt as though all the world had come right again. As much as it ever was.

It was harder to feel that way after the performance, when Meg went to the Dance Foyer to join Léon.

He didn't blame her, of course, and it didn't have anything to do with him. He was very quick to point that out to himself, as he paced behind the mirror covering one wall of the Foyer, watching Meg laugh at something Léon had said. She had made the plans while they weren't speaking, and he wouldn't want her to break plans indiscriminately. If she broke plans with Léon, she might just as easily break them with him.

But still. It would have been nice to spend the evening with her tonight, instead of wandering about alone inside the wall, watching the world.

It was slightly better here than just going home. He'd only lived with the Daroga for a week, and yet his rooms had seemed unusually empty since he'd returned to the Opera. Nor did it help knowing the Daroga had returned to Persia by now.

So he paced inside the wall, observing, listening—and wondering.

Because now that he wasn't consumed with the problem of Meg being angry with him, he had space to think of other things. And while it was an incredible relief to know that she had not sold him out to Mifroid, that Jammes was to blame, it left too many things still unanswered.

Meg and Léon were deep in the Foyer at the moment, too far away for him to listen in on a conversation—if he had wanted to, that is, though probably he shouldn't—but Jammes was sitting near the mirrors with a couple of subscribers, and her voice was loud.

He wandered that way, even if it was unlikely she was sharing details of her snooping tactics. But how had she known to search Meg's drawer? Maybe she searched a lot of places and that was just the one place that had something useful.

He trailed his fingers along the smooth glass, listened to Jammes chatter and flirt. Nothing mysterious about the pattern of *that*. He'd heard hundreds of such conversations over the years, could probably flirt quite passably himself by now if he wanted to try it.

He grimaced. As if any woman would stay around long enough to be flirted with, after seeing his mask. Not to mention what was under it. And as if he wanted to engage in that kind of meaningless, surface conversation, all so inane and predictable. He was better off discussing music with Meg.

Maybe Jammes *had* guessed that Meg would have useful information on the Phantom. Meg hadn't always been perfectly discreet in her attitudes about the local ghost. He'd heard her try to defend him more than once since they'd become friends.

Had she defended him before they'd been friends too? He suddenly regretted that he'd never noticed. He would have liked noticing that.

Whatever she had guessed before, after finding those directions, Jammes knew that Meg had some connection to the Phantom. Why wasn't she using it or making it public? Probably a matter of wanting future leverage. He might have to do something about her eventually, if she was going to make life difficult for Meg. He'd have to start thinking. It was a challenge, dealing with women. He didn't want to hurt her, because what would that make him? But he'd have to devise some plan.

Meanwhile Jammes' conversation was useless, and his gaze roamed the room again. Meg and Léon had moved this direction, were sitting on a banquette farther down the mirrored wall from Jammes.

He knew he probably shouldn't. But he walked that direction anyway.

Léon was holding Meg's hands, leaning in and whispering something in her ear that made her smile.

Erik frowned. He didn't know nearly enough about this young man, except that apparently Meg liked him much more than she had been letting on. Was there any casual, not awkward way to ask her how she felt about Léon, maybe even hint about the time she'd spent kissing him in Box Seven... Erik only had to contemplate the matter for an instant to wince. No. He was quite sure there was *no* possible way to casually discuss the subject.

He felt uneasy for a new reason when Meg's glance drifted in his direction. In the *mirror's* direction, he reminded himself. She didn't know he was here, and what was transparent to him was opaque to her.

But maybe she suspected something, because just at that moment she leaned away from Léon, pulled her hands free and smoothed her skirt. "Really, Léon, anyone could be watching!" she said with a slight laugh, and Erik wondered just who she meant by 'anyone.'

"What of it?" Léon asked, the brazen tone of a young man who was accountable to no one. He sprawled back into the opposite corner of the banquette, displaying an absurdly turquoise waistcoat.

Erik shook his head. Most people didn't need to wear black to blend into the shadows, but there was no reason to go around looking like a peacock.

On the other side of the mirror, Léon's next words took on a sulky tone. "And if you don't want people staring, why can't we meet somewhere else? Tomorrow afternoon—"

"I told you already," Meg cut in, before Erik could even get bothered, "I have plans tomorrow."

And that made Erik smile. It was good Meg wasn't a breaker of plans. At least, when the plans were with him. He decided to take that victory and retreat. Lingering any longer could only lead to awkwardness. He'd observed the Opera Company very comfortably for years, but just now he felt as though he was being more invasive than usual.

Remarkable how actually interacting with people could change observing them.

It felt so *right* to visit Erik Sunday afternoon, even if it wasn't usually the time I saw him. I knew from Mother's raised eyebrows, when I told her where I was going today, that she had noted that too. Or maybe it was only that I was seeing Erik at all. Mercifully, she had never made me explain why I was angry with him, and she didn't ask me to explain why I wasn't anymore either.

So it felt like maybe life was returning to, well, comparatively normal.

Erik was sorting papers when I arrived, making stacks of his damaged musical scores. The Opera Company had not been kind to his papers when the mob passed through.

"I told you to put all these away ages ago," I said amiably, dropping my cloak onto his armchair. There was something charming in theory about the composer's residence with musical papers scattered on every surface, but it wasn't practical.

"I know, I know," Erik said, trying to smooth out a crumpled sheet. But he was smiling.

That made me smile too. I wandered across the room toward him, picking up stray papers as I passed them. "You know all the music, don't you? If anything's too ruined to read?"

"Yes, of course," Erik said, as though it was obvious.

I wondered if other composers remembered every note of every piece of music they had written. I certainly didn't remember every step of every dance I'd been in.

"Good." I placed one smeared page on top of a pile of similarly unsalvageable sheets, two others on what seemed to be the recoverable pile.

"And how was Léon yesterday?" Erik asked in a perfectly neutral tone of voice, without looking up from the paper in his hand.

My eyes narrowed, but I forced myself to sound casual as I said, "Good." Why did I always feel there was a weight to conversations with Erik about Léon? Or maybe I only wanted there to be. Maybe I wanted him to care that I was spending time with another man—and that was ridiculous. He was never going to care about me the way he did about Christine, that had become very clear, but he *did* care about me and that—should be enough. "Léon's good," I reiterated. "He always is." In fact, he'd been a bit sulky that I wasn't spending today with him, but I didn't imagine I'd stirred any real depths of feeling in him.

"That's nice," Erik said blandly, so blandly that any emotion at all would have seemed more natural.

I almost asked him how *he'd* spent Saturday night. I had wondered, looking at those mirrors in the Foyer. I had taken the many mirrors in the Opera for granted for years, even assumed that the Phantom might be behind them—yet it had given me a strange feeling, when Léon wanted to press flirtations farther than he usually had at the Opera.

"What did you think of Saturday's performance?" I asked instead, diplomatic, sure not to start any new awkwardness.

I thought Erik was relieved by the topic too, from the enthusiasm with which he embraced it. He went on a proper rant about all the things he thought they ought to have done differently, we sorted papers, and life felt comfortable again.

As the days rolled on, it seemed almost as though we had stepped back in time a few weeks, as though the mob and its aftermath had never happened. Except, perhaps, in the details.

Erik was appearing out of walls to talk to me just as he had before—more often than he had before. I was never not glad to see him, with a confused happiness and pain that no one else had ever made me feel. Because it was so good seeing him, and yet so much less than it might have been—if I had told him how I really felt, if he hadn't been all tangled up about Christine...but that hadn't happened, that wasn't how things were.

Erik was full of opinions about the operas and the Opera Company and the plans for the managers' next special performance, just like always—but also more somehow. It took me a few days to realize the difference. Before, he had always seemed to enjoy complaining about them, and then sending a stiff note to the managers, or an insulting one to Carlotta. Now he seemed more frustrated, more truly bothered than before. Maybe because there would be no notes. The Phantom had died, plunging into the underground lake. Erik remained and that was more than enough for me—but by the time I visited him Friday afternoon, I was wondering if that wasn't enough for him.

He greeted me by asking if I'd heard the opera the managers had chosen for their special performance, then proceeded to give me a point by point explanation of why it was a terrible choice. I nodded, took off my cloak, and tried to stay out of the path of his pacing.

I finally broke in when he paused for breath. "If you don't like the songs they chose, send them a new one," I suggested, perching on the arm of one maroon couch. He wasn't entirely without options for influencing the Opera. "Erik Rouen could, I mean. They'd consider it." Only a few months ago he had begun selling his music to the Opera, as the mysterious, reclusive composer Erik Rouen whom no one had ever seen. I was still pleased with myself for convincing him to try the venture.

He shook his head, drumming his fingers along the mantelpiece. "They don't want to hear from me."

"They want to hear from you." His music continued to be very popular, receiving an excellent response every time the Company performed it. The irony of it, when they all professed to despise the Phantom, had not escaped me.

"I just sent them two sonatas last week."

"They still want to hear from you. Moncharmin is convinced the new material is helping ticket sales. He keeps congratulating himself for finding you. Him. The composer." I waved a hand. "You know." Usually I could manage the pronouns for talking to Erik about his various personas, but occasionally it tripped me up.

He didn't comment on my muddle, possibly a kindness, and just said, "Maybe." He stalked over to the couch and collapsed onto it, somehow managing to slouch without rumpling his clothes. "They'll just perform it wrong if I do though."

"You don't know that."

He cast me an expressive look. "Of course I do. I've been watching for years. Do you know how often I've had to steer them off of disaster?" His glance shifted away as he rubbed his palm against his pantleg. "Maybe I could just…send a few helpful notes about properly performing…"

My eyes narrowed. "As the composer or as the Phantom?"

"Well—they don't listen to composers much you know, and—"

"Erik, no!" I protested, my heart suddenly hammering harder. "You're dead! And if you don't *stay* dead, they'll kill you!" If Mifroid knew Erik was alive, he'd go back to searching and it would all begin again. And Erik might not escape so unscathed this time.

He glowered at nothing in particular. "I know, but—"

"Don't you dare get yourself killed just because you're bored!" He had been complaining and pacing and looking restless for days. The conclusion was obvious.

"I'm not bored," he protested, a clear lie. "I just—I don't like what they're doing to the musical standards of…all right, maybe I'm mildly bored but—"

"There has to be other things to do with your time besides give orders to the Opera Company. You could…" And then I stalled slightly, because what *was* there to do for a man who lived under an opera house? Besides write music, and evidently that wasn't enough to entertain him.

His eyebrow rose and I knew he knew exactly what problem I'd run into. "Oh yes, I suppose I'll just go out for a lovely stroll by the Seine and have supper at Café de la Paix."

"Why not?" I said recklessly. "*You* can afford Café de la Paix." So could Léon. Not me, or any other friend I had.

He sighed faintly. "That's hardly the issue."

I hadn't meant it, when I all but suggested he actually go to the Café, and yet… "Why *not*? Why can't you?" It was like a sudden flash of lightning, illuminating an empty room I had always imagined as crowded. I had accepted without question for a long time that Erik couldn't leave the Opera—but just what *were* the reasons keeping him here? "It's only in the Opera that people might suspect a man in a mask is the Phantom, or know that you don't belong here. Out in the rest of Paris…"

"Out in the rest of Paris I will be even more of an oddity," Erik said, in a tone that was plainly meant to warn me off.

"But *why*?" I demanded. "Paris is full of all sorts of different people. Why should you stand out so much? And if people stare, all right, let them!" It had to be less dangerous than his growing bored enough to do something foolish here, at the Opera, where people would certainly do far more than stare. "What terrible thing would happen just because you go outside?"

"Do you really want me to answer that?"

"No, because you'll have some paranoid, impossibly exaggerated answer," I said promptly. "And that's just silly when we could have so much *fun*." The picture was painting itself before my mind's eye, more complete with every heartbeat. The idea wasn't only sensible, it was exciting. "We could go walk by the Seine and see the Tuileries and look in the booksellers' stands for new plays by Monsieur Shakespeare—"

"There are no new plays by Shakespeare. He's been dead for 200 years."

"—and eat pastries and watch street performers and buy you more paper for your musical scores—"

"I don't need more paper."

"That's not the point!" I dropped down onto the couch, cushion sinking beneath me. "And I didn't mean *new*." I crossed my arms and stared at him.

He looked away first. "I don't do things like that."

I leaned forward, hands moving to my knees, unwilling to give the idea up. I knew why *he* thought he couldn't, but I didn't believe it was true. "You can't tell me you never leave the Opera. You came to Notre Dame. Twice. You go out to buy paper and food. You wandered all over the world years ago and you *do* go outside now."

"In the evening. When it's dark."

I threw my hands up. "When everyone expects dark figures to loom out of the shadows, making it the *worst* possible time for you to go out!"

For just a moment he seemed genuinely taken aback as he processed that idea. "I never thought of it that way," he murmured at last.

"Precisely. Then it's settled. Next Sunday afternoon, we go explore Paris." If I was firm enough, maybe this could actually happen. And somehow, suddenly, I wanted it so badly to happen.

His head jerked up. "I never—"

"I'll meet you here, that's simplest." And I didn't trust him to show up at some other meeting place. I might be able to drag him out, as long as I could find him.

"But..." He trailed away. The silence drew out and lengthened until finally he half-smiled and said, "If this all ends with Paris in flames and me fleeing the country, I want it duly noted that I objected to the whole idea."

I had known he'd have a ridiculous expectation about what could happen, even if I suspected him of half-joking now. So I just smiled. "Noted."

He shouldn't have agreed. Obviously he shouldn't have agreed. As soon as Meg left for the afternoon, all the reasons he shouldn't have agreed presented themselves, neatly in a line, demanding attention. It was only—she *had* made it sound pleasant. And he had liked the way she smiled, when she talked about it.

Besides, he was so tired of sitting about underground. Writing music and reading plays and watching operas was all fine, but it was so—so *passive*. He could recall that he had spent entire months in the past doing very little besides that. The Phantom had involved himself with the Opera, yes, but hardly on a daily basis for eight years. During some periods he'd hardly done anything.

He sat at his pipe organ, idly pressing keys without paying any real attention to the notes, and argued with himself that it was perfectly reasonable for him to stay quietly down below the Opera.

Only everything seemed different now. He was used to the quiet, then. Then he hadn't been through a year of emotions of the highest intensity, hadn't pursued and lost *her,* hadn't waged battle with the Commissaire of Police. After all that, sitting about quietly seemed flat. He had hardly been back two weeks, and yet the time had begun to drag already.

And before, there had been no blond girl smelling of lavender and sunlight insisting that yes, of course he could go out, so why not do it?

It was hard to resist her enthusiasm, and the force of her interest had particular appeal, considering something had been distracting her at intervals these past few weeks. Even before the mob, something had been making her look off into the distance or leave rather suddenly sometimes, and he still hadn't worked out what that was all about. So it was nice to see her be so definite about making plans together.

Not to mention, part of him quite liked the idea that Meg wanted to spend Sunday afternoon with *him*, when that was usually time she gave to Léon. Of course, she probably had the idea that going about Paris with him instead would be equally easy and carefree.

He lowered his head into his hands with a groan.

He ought to refuse to go just for the sake of not ruining her illusions.

Yet…what if she wasn't *all* wrong? It had gone all right Easter morning, hadn't it? He'd avoided people, stayed in the shadows of the cathedral and the empty towers, but still. It had gone all right, so…

Maybe he could have just a little bit of what all the rest of the world took for granted.

He used to be out in the world—learning architecture in Rome, helping to build the Opera, traveling through Europe, traveling all the way to Persia. It hadn't ended in pikes and mobs every day. True, the cumulative effect of dealing with people, so many people who didn't understand and couldn't accept his mask or his face, had sent him to build an entire secret world within the confines of an opera house and scarcely ever venture out for a solid eight years.

But *one afternoon*, surely that couldn't end too badly.

So he believed roughly half the time over the intervening hours until the following Sunday afternoon. The other half, he was sure this was an entirely mad idea.

Excerpt from the Private Notebook of Jean Mifroid, Commissaire of Police

13 May, 1882

After repeated attempts, still unable to reach Phantom's rooms. Rope proved effective for bypassing mechanized stair, but cannot successfully trigger hidden door beyond. And cannot go through solid rock.

This cannot be chance.

But I saw him drown. *I buried him.*

Was it not what it seemed?

Chapter Eleven

I was almost surprised when Erik answered my knock Sunday afternoon. I had thought it was even odds that he'd refuse to answer, perhaps make an excuse later about being elsewhere. But he responded as usual and I walked right in, only to find him standing by his piano, wrapped in his black cloak and looking like nothing so much as a very solid shadow. Or possibly a ghoul.

"Oh, Erik, *no*," I said in dismay. "You can't wear that."

His expression, what little I could see of it behind the nearly all-encompassing black mask, was mutinous. "This is what I wear. It's what I always wear."

Based on every conversation we'd had in the past few days, based on everything I knew about him, I knew he was already on the brink of backing out of this whole adventure. If I gave him an inch of space to do it in, he would. I had to take a risk, though—because if he went out in all black, with a black cloak and a mask covering everything but his mouth and chin, *of course* it was going to go badly with anyone he met. I needed him to make changes, without dropping the whole idea.

I put my hands on my hips. "That's fine for your world. Every color looks like black in the dark anyway. But today we're going into my world, so you'd best listen to me. First, leave the cloak at home; it makes you look ten times more ominous."

"That's the point," he muttered.

"If you're haunting an opera house, yes. For a pleasant walk around Paris, no. Especially not on a warm day. Second, where do you keep your masks?"

He broke off fiddling with his cloak clasp. "What?"

"Your masks. I know you have at least five." I had been counting them. "Where do you keep them?"

I think he only gave me an answer because the question was so unexpected. "Upstairs. The door on the left."

I went through the side door of the sitting room, the first time I had ever stepped through that doorway, without giving him time to reconsider the idea. Little to see here, just a stone-lined hallway with one gas lamp casting a flickering light. The kitchen had to be down that way somewhere, but I climbed up the spiral stair I had only glimpsed in the past.

On the second level, I pushed open the door on the left, to be greeted only by dark shadows. I barely had time to think about retreating in search of a candle—but that would lose all the momentum I'd been riding on—when candles on stands around the room flared into life. So he couldn't object *too* much to me venturing in here.

I grinned, stepped inside—and suddenly realized what room I was in. By moving so quickly, I had failed to think of something obvious.

Of course Erik kept his masks in his bedroom. I halted a few steps beyond the doorway, gaze on the wide bed with its carved head and foot of dark wood, and its rich black quilt with shimmering silver embroidery. A setting for the daydreams I shouldn't be having.

Out of the corner of my eye I saw Erik appear in the doorway, and I hastily moved my gaze around the room. Purple-gray paper covered the walls, with scattered bits of music written haphazardly across it; the effect was both more elegant and more homey than I would have expected. A heavy wardrobe loomed from one wall, but my attention lit on the narrow table at the far side of the room. It was a dark wood that matched the bed, and a row of masks lay lined up along its length. I went that way.

There was Red Death's skull mask and the metal half-mask I first saw the night Buquet died. Next to it was the cream-colored one he had worn the day we first spoke in the auditorium, and for Easter at Notre Dame; it matched in style the black mask Erik was wearing now, but the different color made it so much less ominous. A similarly shaped one I didn't recognize lay beside it, pale gray, cut in more gentle curves at its bottom and suggesting a hint of curved eyebrows above the narrower eye holes, a similar hint of cheekbones below. That one actually wasn't too bad, having a serene aspect. Still, I reached instead for the last one, the familiar white half mask he wore most often, covering from forehead to jaw.

"Here." I held it out to him. "It's by far the least forbidding."

He had left the cloak downstairs, which seemed like a good sign. He took the mask almost mechanically, and started to reach for the one he was wearing. Then he stopped, hand slowly lowering.

I should have thought of that too. He had been horrified the first time he realized I had seen the distorted side of his face, when he took his mask off as the chandelier fell. I suppose I didn't really expect he'd just casually remove his mask now to make the change.

That didn't mean I was going to agree with him that his face was some deep, dark secret I might faint on seeing. So I just said, "I'll turn my back if you'd rather, but it's nothing I haven't seen before."

He kept his gaze on the mask in his hand, running one fingertip along its edge.

Evidently this was yet another thing he wasn't willing to trust me with, despite what he might say on the subject.

It was easier to turn around than to argue. And somehow I thought it would hurt less, the less effort I put into failing to convince him to trust me.

I pulled open the thick doors of the wardrobe opposite the table. I was waiting for a protest, about the wardrobe or the mask. None came.

"Meg?" His voice was hesitant. "What do you see when you look at me?"

I risked looking back over my shoulder at him. He hadn't exchanged masks yet, and I wondered if this would be when he backed out of the whole afternoon. "Is that a trick question?"

"No."

I shrugged. Maybe at another moment I would have given this real thought, but just now I wasn't in the mood for games. "I see you. What am I supposed to see?"

His chest rose visibly as he took in a deep breath, mouth set in a hard line. Then he reached up and pulled away the black mask, revealing the familiar lines of the left side of his face—and the less familiar distortion of the right side.

Of course I had thought about his face since I'd seen it, though probably less than he imagined. I recognized the reddish discoloration, the ridge of flesh spreading down from his forehead, around that lovely green eye. His face resembled a wax sculpture set too close to the heat, one side beginning to twist and melt away. And I felt somewhat the way I might have felt looking at a damaged sculpture, at a dancer stumbling in a choreography—a sadness for beauty lost.

But then, who was I to say what Erik's face was supposed to look like?

Evidently, it looked like this.

He looked like this, and it didn't make him any less beautiful.

"And what do you see now?" he asked, words heavy.

The most entrancing, maddening, captivating man I'd ever known. "I see *you*, Erik. I still just see you."

For a moment our gazes held locked together. I was thinking how much I wished I had the courage to kiss him. I had no idea what he was thinking.

He looked away first, gaze dropping down to the two masks in his hand.

I released a breath I hadn't realized I was holding. There didn't seem to be anything else to say, so I turned back to the wardrobe.

After a moment, I even remembered why I'd opened it to begin with.

I scanned the clothes inside, not at all surprised by the rows and rows of black, punctuated by a handful of white shirts. He had far more clothes than I did, although they were almost all identical. No sign of Red Death's costume, and only in the waistcoats was there any color. I turned my focus there, skimming through the row of neatly hung vests. All the clothes were immaculately organized. Why couldn't he try to extend that precision to his papers too?

Even the waistcoats were all dark shades, but I finally found what I was looking for in a forest green one.

"Here, you should wear this one." I pulled it off the rack, and turned to find that he had donned the white mask, and put the black one back in its place on the table. Some of the tension had gone out of the room too. Progress.

He didn't return to the subject of his face, just asked, "What's wrong with the waistcoat I'm wearing?"

It was black. "Nothing, but this one's better." Mostly it was better because it could be paired with a green cravat, and that would be close enough to his face to bring out his eyes.

He frowned but complied, with both the change of waistcoat and the green cravat. I was right about it bringing out his eyes, though that might have been a mistake. Not for him. For me. I didn't need something else to make my breath catch when I looked at Erik, something else to remind me how lost I could get, if I kept looking at his eyes.

It was finally occurring to me, much, much too late, to ask just why I had been so eager to push him into this. Why I was trying to make Erik do, well, what I might have done with Léon or some other handsome subscriber willing to squire me around Paris. Why I was trying to bring the Phantom of the Opera out of his world and into mine.

But it *was* too late, and I didn't voice those concerns, or any other excuse for canceling plans. I just approved the outfit and agreed we could go now.

I had thought we'd need to go back out through the Opera, had wondered whether he'd take me into his secret passages within the walls of the building or want us to separate, but he had a simpler plan than that.

We went out through another secret door off the last hall leading to his front door, into a long, narrow passage.

The passage led to a grated archway. Beyond it, a few more feet of stone tunnel, and then steps up to the Rue Scribe and the daylight above. How many people passed by here every day, never even saw the grating, never guessed where the passage led? How many times had *I* walked by?

Erik ignored the very obvious lock at the center of the gate, pressing instead on one of the bars on the upper right. With a click the door opened an inch. He silently pushed it the rest of the way open and held it for me. I stepped through, walked forward, heard the gate clang shut again. I resisted checking over my shoulder to make sure he hadn't stayed on the far side.

A heartbeat later he fell into step next to me. It was only a few paces to the end of the tunnel, and I went up the steps and out onto the paving. Erik halted, at the top of the steps on the very edge of the shadows, staring into the sunlight.

He was very, very still, except for his hands flexing at his sides.

I bit my lip. Maybe this had been a bad idea. Maybe I was pushing him too far, asking too much. I watched his fingers curl, straighten and curl again. I looked at his face and my throat tightened. All his masks were gone except the physical one, and that one did nothing at all to hide the desperate yearning on his face as he looked out at the sunlight, the street, the wide vast world beyond.

He always said he didn't want that world—but I had found a song in his papers that said otherwise—and I could see a different message in his eyes.

My heart ached with wishing that he'd look at *me* with that expression.

If he didn't want that, I could try to give him this.

I had stopped just beyond the shadows, just a step into the light. I reached back across the border between our two worlds and slipped my hand into his. He didn't glance down or even look at me, but his fingers locked tightly around mine.

I didn't tug or pull. I just waited. After a moment, he stepped out to stand next to me in the light.

"So. There's this lovely bakery just down the street," I said in bright tones, trying to act as if that step hadn't been significant, trying to pretend I wasn't distractingly aware of our fingers twined together. Trying not to pressure him any further by making a big event of either. "We really have to get some of their beignets."

He nodded once in response, which was not easy or enthusiastic, but still an affirmative.

I had chosen this bakery as much for its proprietor as for its beignets. A brisk woman, I had never seen her show interest in anything but baked goods. Today, she blinked at Erik but made no comment on the mask, and the interaction went about as smoothly as I could have hoped. We dropped hands in the course of selecting pastries and paying for them, which was maybe just as well. I didn't know when I would have managed to let go otherwise.

Going towards the bakery had taken us in the direction of the Seine and we continued that way. Erik gradually relaxed, as negotiating pastry and powdered sugar distracted him from negotiating the crowded streets.

The path by the Seine was busy with walkers and lined with stalls, selling books and jewelry and artwork and whatever else they thought might appeal to Parisians out for a Sunday stroll. I kept up a steady, cheerful, slightly meaningless chatter. Erik contributed something, if less than usual, and I tried not to let it be too visible how closely I was watching him and everyone else around us.

It was instructive watching. We passed scores of people, stopped to browse at a dozen stalls, and soon a pattern emerged. Everyone noticed the mask, and I could hardly blame them for that. While a few were immediately scornful or openly suspicious, it seemed to me that most were only curious or surprised or wary at worst. But Erik noticed them noticing, and immediately snapped into what I read as a defense, but everyone else must have seen as antagonism. His shoulders tensed, his face darkened, he seemed to loom a few inches taller and he turned altogether ominous and forbidding.

Then the curious became wary, the wary became hostile, Erik held himself ever more aloof and apart, and the metaphorical distance between himself and everyone else kept growing—until one or the other party created physical distance and ended the interaction.

It all happened in a minute or less, and I had no doubt that if I tried to point it out, Erik would protest that he wasn't doing anything at all.

It was a hideous, devastating cycle. He was sure everyone would be unfriendly, so he reacted accordingly, in a manner that ensured everyone *would* be unfriendly. I wondered what was in his past that had set the pattern in motion to begin with. The only clues were in the topics he wouldn't talk about. Gypsies. Persia. Christine.

I knew I couldn't change the pattern of a lifetime in one afternoon. But if I could just make him see that it wasn't set in stone, that something else *was* possible…then anything would be possible.

No pikes or guillotines yet. That was something. People were hardly friendly though, and every glance at the mask made Erik want to flinch and run. Alone he would have retreated long since but with Meg—well, he could hardly run away in front of Meg, could he?

He followed her from a bakery to stalls beside the Seine to a milliner's shop, because she needed to buy buttons for a dress her mother was mending.

He had doubts about that last place. They stepped inside and he *should* have felt more comfortable. The place was small and dim and the ceiling was low, not too different from his tunnels. It was all full of little drawers and small displays and threads and buttons and drapes of cloth, not too different from the prop room at the Opera.

And yet, he could only see one door, the one they had come through, and no windows, and he was feeling distinctly claustrophobic even before the proprietor started staring at him.

"Hello," Meg said cheerfully, taking half a step to the side and putting herself between Erik and the milliner. Erik was positive that step was deliberate, and didn't know whether to appreciate it or resent it. "I'm looking for small blue buttons, a dozen or so."

The other man's gaze flicked to her for a second or two, then went past her and back to Erik even as he answered, "I have a wide variety. Do you want wooden, enamel, cloth-covered?"

Meg hesitated, biting her lower lip. "Enamel, I think."

"Decorated or plain?" he asked, gaze unwavering.

This could take *forever.* "I'll just wait outside I think," Erik said in a rush and ducked out the door.

He leaned back against the wall beside the door and took a deep breath. For a moment it was such a relief to be out of that unpleasant little man's stare that he felt almost comfortable. Then he remembered where he had taken refuge and his shoulders went up again. He was, after all, standing outside a shop facing on a crowded boulevard along the Seine. Hardly a place that was going to let him avoid stares. And now Meg was inside and he was out here alone.

Only for a few minutes. It would be fine for a few minutes. He tried to gaze into the middle distance and not focus on anyone.

That worked briefly, until some instinct made his spine prickle. He glanced uneasily around the busy boulevard, and stiffened when he spotted the inspector of police across the street. The situation could have been worse; it could have been Commissaire Mifroid. But the man was watching him with a far too intent stare. Erik's hands tightened into fists. It wasn't fair; all he was doing was standing by a shop. That was no reason for anyone to look at him suspiciously. Meg didn't know what she was talking about, with her blithe confidence that everything would be fine. He didn't even have to *do* anything to run into trouble, it came to find him—

"Relax your shoulders and stop glaring," a soft voice said in his ear.

He jumped, looked to his side to see that Meg had rejoined him, and though her expression was impassive, her gaze was on the inspector.

"The glare makes you look much more forbidding," she continued, "and you're alarming the poor police inspector who is, after all, only trying to do his job as a sort of...let's call him a guardian of the city, watching out for helpless girls such as myself."

Erik exhaled in a rush, tried his best to bring his shoulders to a more relaxed tilt.

"Good." She slipped her arm through his. "Now smile and nod at him—and then we keep walking."

He did, and watched as the inspector, who had seemed a breath away from crossing the street, slowly settled back into a relaxed stance. He was still looking this way, but the menace had faded out of his stare.

"A smile and a nod are not going to solve all of my problems," he said in a low voice.

"Maybe not," she allowed, and smiled herself. "But they're a starting place."

He snuck a glance back at the inspector, now half a block behind them. He wasn't even watching anymore. That was...remarkable.

Meg kept her arm through his for another three blocks. For long after that, he could still feel exactly where her hand had pressed. It felt different, somehow, than it had when they had attended the masquerade.

Chapter Twelve

T hings had been going reasonably well, as well as I might have expected, and now the milliner and the police inspector had got Erik's fur all up again—he really did look so much like a cat with its back up when he was uncomfortable—and were liable to ruin everything.

"There's a lovely café just down this street," I ventured, as we walked on beyond the police inspector's gaze.

He offered up at least a ghost of a smile. "You seem to know a lovely café on every street."

"I like cafes," I agreed amiably, relieved to get even a slight smile at the moment. "Come on, let's stop for coffee." I hoped the ritual of it would settle him down. And I knew this shop's owner, and felt reasonably sure he wouldn't be too searching or inquisitive.

There may have been a slightly longer look from the owner than usual, but we were shown to a table and took our seats without any real incident. Erik put his usual six lumps of sugar into his coffee and set about drinking through the cup while I chattered on aimlessly about nothing much in particular. By the time he was on a second cup, he was answering more normally again.

I was just beginning to relax myself, to consider the afternoon back on its desired track, when I heard my name called across the café. Anyone from the Opera Company, who might wonder about this mysterious masked man, would have been awful. This, very possibly, was worse.

"Nice surprise seeing you here," Léon said, loping over to our table.

"Léon," I said faintly. "How…unexpected." I hadn't thought this place was expensive enough for him. I was too surprised to consider whether I should dodge when he bent down to kiss my cheek, or to come up with an objection when he swung a chair around from a nearby table and sat down with us. At least he had never seen the Phantom, had no way to recognize Erik; that was one mercy in the situation.

"Hello, I'm Léon de Troyes," he said, extending a hand to Erik. I saw something in Léon's face change as Erik turned to look at him, and it suddenly dawned on me that he had come at us from Erik's unmasked side. To his credit, his eyes only widened slightly when the mask came into view.

For a very bad few seconds Erik looked down at Léon's hand as though he had no idea what his intention was. Or like he didn't want to shake hands, though I didn't understand what the objection would be. True, he didn't often come into contact with anyone, but it was just a *handshake*.

Which thought indicated how much my mind was spinning, because in calm moments I knew nothing was just anything with Erik.

I got to keep breathing in this moment though, because Erik did, finally, shake hands and say, "I'm Erik…Rouen." I could practically hear him weighing the benefits and hazards of offering the last name, and didn't really know if he'd made the best decision on it. Was there any danger in Léon making the connection to the composer? How could I explain it at the Opera if they heard I'd been having coffee with our reclusive composer?

If Léon recognized the name, he didn't mention it. We talked about performances often, but not on the technical level that would compare composers. It was more opera plots and ballet numbers.

My brain would keep skittering about. Here, in the café, Léon smiled broadly and said, "Meg's never mentioned you."

Erik's face, by contrast, was distinctly impassive. "No, I wouldn't think so."

Which neither explained anything, nor made us seem ordinary and not worthy of suspicion and questions. "Erik is a family friend," I put in hurriedly, because it was sort of true and I had to explain him somehow. But I had to explain his absence from earlier conversations. "He's visiting from out of town. Just for the day. We were sort of touring Paris a bit."

"Charming," Léon said, gaze still on Erik. "You couldn't have better company for it."

Erik glanced at me, very briefly, and said, "I know."

There was *something* about it—Léon was the one who had paid me the more definite compliment and that had gone by with barely an impression, while Erik's simple agreement suddenly made my cheeks warm. It certainly drove whatever pleasant, calming, unsuspicious small talk I might have made right out of my head.

It left too long of a pause, left Léon time to lean back and quite casually ask, "So what's the mask all about?"

Erik's shoulders went very tense.

"It's the new fashion," I said hurriedly. "Haven't you heard? In a month, everyone will be wearing them."

Léon barely flicked me a glance. "Cute. So what's the story really? Some kind of eccentricity?"

"Perhaps." Erik's voice was glacial.

Léon stretched. "There must be simpler ways to stand out, if a person wants to. Why not a red hat? A mask seems extreme."

"So what brings you here anyway?" I asked, desperate for a topic change.

"I was in the neighborhood." He didn't even look away from Erik. "Or you could wear last year's style of coat. A mask is so theatrical, it seems like—"

"He has a facial deformity and he doesn't like showing it, all right?" I snapped.

Erik's head swung towards me, eyes wide. I don't think he could have looked more stunned if I had confessed to murder. My heart pounded in my ears—that had been so *stupid*, I *knew* he didn't talk about this but Léon wouldn't stop asking, and—for a horrible, hideous moment I thought I had really ruined everything, not just the day but *everything*, and that Erik was never going to forgive me for this.

Impossibly enough, I was saved by Léon, who shrugged as though he didn't notice the tension between the two of us. "Oh. Bit of bad luck, that. I suppose the mask makes sense then."

Erik's head swung back to Léon, eyes somehow going even wider.

"Why didn't you just say so to begin with?" Léon asked.

The man was impossibly oblivious—or deliberately so, but I didn't believe he was that tactful. "Why didn't you just drop the subject?" I hissed.

"I was only curious," he said, as though the feeling was perfectly reasonable and he was the injured party here. "If you hadn't made it all mysterious—anyway, never mind all that." He got to his feet and I hoped he was leaving. Instead, he cast a grin at me and said, "Come with me for a minute. I want to talk to you."

I was relieved he hadn't reacted over the facial deformity and I was irritated with him for focusing on the mask to begin with and it was never a difficult choice between spending time with Erik or Léon. "I'm busy."

"Come on, for a minute." He reached out and closed his hand around my wrist. "I just want to—"

"She doesn't want to go with you." Erik's voice was low and dangerous as his fingers locked around Léon's arm. Léon didn't miss this tension, and the two men matched gazes with mutual hostility.

Wonderful. The last thing we needed was a fist fight in the middle of a café. "No, it's all right." I shook off Léon's hand and rose to my feet. "Léon, I only have a minute."

It took them a few more seconds to break the stare, but finally Erik released his arm. Léon straightened up, head high and expression aloof, then led me out a nearby door to the patio beyond.

"What did you want to talk about?" I crossed my arms and tried not to tap one foot.

He was frowning back towards the café. "There's something strange about him."

"If that's all you have to say, I—"

"No." He took a breath. "I'm sorry if I upset you, all right?" He leaned in closer, a trace of his smile coming back. "I have this afternoon free, and I was thinking if you get rid of him, we can spend some time together."

I stared at him, irritation definitely holding sway now. "Léon, what part of 'I'm busy' isn't clear to you?"

He merely shrugged again, didn't back away or stop smiling. "Oh come on, you can't actually want to spend the day dragging all over Paris with your mother's friend."

"He's not my mother's friend, he's *my* friend."

"What, that old man?"

The dismissal was infuriating. "He's not old."

"Well into his thirties if he's a day," Léon said, as though this put Erik into a completely separate class from himself, made any interactions between Erik and myself entirely different from my relationship with Léon.

"Yes, it means he's had time to grow up," I snapped. "Please, call on me again when you've done the same." I turned to go.

"Meg, wait." He caught my arm again.

I glared at him, and in my iciest tones said, "And kindly *stop* holding onto my arm, because if you don't let go I am going to scream, and you are not going to like the consequences."

"Fine, fine." Léon released me, backing away with his hands raised and a half-smirk still on his face. "But you can't intend—"

"Good-bye, Léon," I said, and swept back through the door into the café with as much outraged dignity as I could muster—not as much as Carlotta might have managed, but I didn't do badly.

I dropped back into my seat across the table from Erik, who was carefully, attentively stirring his coffee.

"Léon left," I announced, taking a breath and hoping I didn't look as ruffled as I felt.

"Ah," Erik said without looking up, and we were silent for two more circles of his spoon. "If you would rather spend the afternoon with him, I—"

"I would not," I said crisply. "We have plans, don't we?"

That brought a soft, apparently unconscious smile to his face that made my heart warm and ache to see.

Three more circles of his spoon and then he remarked, "For the record, thirty-four."

And this only confused me. "Thirty-four what?"

He finally looked up, with an apparently more deliberate smile. "Years. I'm thirty-four. If you were wondering."

I hadn't been, actually. I had guessed he was somewhere around there—but somehow he seemed both so much younger and so much older—and that was not the thought occupying the main portion of my mind, or making my cheeks turn suddenly hot. "You heard? That whole conversation, you heard that?"

The smile faded, and now he was the one looking confused. "The door was ajar. And I have good hearing. I didn't *intend* to, I just—I thought you knew! You said, if you screamed—"

"Hearing a scream is not the same as hearing a conversation at normal volume," I said, desperately trying not to let my own volume creep up now. What had I said, had I said anything I wouldn't want him to hear? Not that I could think of…

"I'm sorry," Erik said, if not with any great degree of remorse, and then added almost casually, "You were right, you know. He wouldn't have liked the consequences."

Somehow that comment made me feel both touched and alarmed. I tried to brush past it. "I was being overdramatic anyway. It wasn't necessary."

"Yes," Erik said, gaze unwavering. "It was."

That did not settle me. I tried to plunge on towards a slight change in topic. "Anyway, the whole incident did prove something."

"That Léon is entirely too comfortable grabbing you?"

Not the direction I intended to go. "He did not *grab* me," I said, suddenly on the defensive.

Erik's mouth set in a mutinous line. "So is this business of yanking on your arm a habit or just something he was doing today?"

What did Erik know about it anyway? *He* never touched me at all. "You are overreacting. And that wasn't remotely what I was talking about anyway."

"I am not overreact—"

"My *point* was that he didn't care at all about your face. Proving that if you don't make it important, it doesn't matter to anyone else."

A long moment of silence, long enough for me to wonder if this topic wasn't better than any other. But if he was going to be angry with me for telling Léon about his face, we might as well get it over with. How much could he yell in a crowded café?

He didn't yell at all, even relaxed back in his chair again. "All that proved is that Léon de Troyes is only interested in Léon de Troyes."

I was relieved he was declining to be angry—maybe he didn't want to talk about this any more than I wanted to talk about all the subjects he'd been bringing up—but it felt disloyal to let this remark go by. "That's not true," I protested. "I mean, he was a bit—well, today wasn't his best moment but mostly he's very nice."

Erik's visible eyebrow rose. "I thought you were angry with him."

"I was. I am," I corrected. How had I wound up advocating for him? "Oh never mind, I don't want to talk about Léon."

"I never want to talk about Léon," Erik said with a half-smile. "Though I will point out that his waistcoat really was garish today."

It had been a rather vivid orange, and I was afraid he had a point this time. More importantly the comment made me giggle, and that relaxed the tension somewhat.

"More coffee?" Erik asked.

"Please."

By the time we'd finished that cup, the conversation had moved on and the afternoon had become pleasant again. We left the café and wandered on, through the Tuileries and along the Champs Elysse. Nearing dusk we turned back in the direction of my house. Erik didn't exactly offer to walk me home, but that was clearly what he was doing. I had mentioned the day's plan to my mother, who merely responded with a neutral, "I see," and no further comment. I was not entirely sure how she would react if I turned up at the door with Erik. I suspected, however, that he was going to fade into the shadows the moment I was on my own doorstep.

I appreciated the company, as the most direct route home wasn't through the nicest of streets. It wasn't surprising when I heard a voice saying, "Spare a sous, mademoiselle?"

I glanced to the side, and saw a small boy standing on the street corner. He was maybe ten, clothes patched and face marked with grime. He leaned on a crutch, one foot turned to an unnatural angle. I started to reach for my bag, but before my hand had dipped inside, Erik plucked a coin out of the air and tossed it to the boy.

He caught it, looked down at the coin in his hand, and his eyes grew enormous in his thin face. "A franc, monsieur? Merci!"

"Don't spend it all in one place," Erik advised.

I glanced back as we continued down the avenue. "That's so sad."

"Street children always are, yes," Erik agreed. "But if you mean his foot, he's faking it."

I blinked, as surprised by his matter-of-fact tone as by the words themselves. "You don't know that."

He smiled slightly. "I'm a master of illusion, remember? I know."

"Then why did you give him a franc?"

"Because he really was hungry. Besides, it was a well-done fake. There's a certain artistry in that."

"Do you have any coins, monsieur?"

We halted, three more street children having emerged from a side alley to stand in front of us. Two girls and a boy this time, and the younger of the girls couldn't be more than five. I looked back and saw that the first boy had disappeared from his corner.

"I think word is getting out," I murmured to Erik. A franc was very generous.

"Likely."

Erik pulled two francs out of the air and a third one from the boy's ear, to the giggles of all three children. Then he crouched down to the level of the smallest girl, pressed his palms together in front of her, and drew them apart to reveal a vivid red handkerchief. He spun it about once, and handed it to her.

Erik gave out a dozen more francs, as much as my week's wages, and half as many handkerchiefs before we got out of the neighborhood. He performed a sleight-of-hand trick for every child, and not once did I see him grow tense.

I was smiling as we walked the last few blocks towards home. I had wondered how he could have been so charming to me the first time we met, when I was twelve years old, new to the Opera and lost on my way to ballet practice. How could he be so pleasant then, and so off-putting to everyone else? It made sense now, and I didn't think it was precisely a matter of liking children. Street children, or a girl crying in a corner—they weren't threats, so he didn't have to defend himself.

Erik left Meg on her doorstep; confronting Madame Giry was more than he wanted to face just now, though perhaps earning Meg's forgiveness had put him back in her good graces. All the same, he felt he had confronted enough challenges for one day. He made his way back to the Opera through the lengthening shadows, entering through the passage off the Rue Scribe.

He stepped across the threshold, back into the world of the Opera, with a relief he had expected and a pang he had not.

In many ways it had been a truly extraordinary day. There had been the unpleasant interlude with Léon, but that would be well worth it if the result was that the irritating young man went away. And it hadn't been unpleasant at all, to be the one chosen when Meg was deciding who to spend the day with.

He ran his fingertips along the tunnel wall as he walked, found himself smiling at the memory. That had, perhaps, been the best part of the whole afternoon.

And the rest—strolling by the Seine, drinking coffee in a café, walking through the Tuileries—well, it was the kind of day he had dreamed of, but never actually believed could exist. Nothing extraordinary for anyone else, but impossible for him.

It had hardly been perfect; there had been questioning stares, to be sure. But—no one had run for a pike or the police. No one had even been especially rude, with Léon a possible exception.

Meg was wrong, though, if she thought that it had gone well because of who he was or anything he did. Nodding to a police inspector wasn't enough to make that much difference. No, he knew exactly what had been different about this day.

He had been with her. And when the laughing girl with the dancing eyes, the one who always walked as though she was moving to music, thought the ominous man in black was all right, other people concluded he must be too.

He had noticed the questioning looks thrown to her, the ones from the people trying to determine if she needed rescuing from her companion. Had she even realized how completely in her power he was? All she had to do was look scared just once, maybe make one vaguely alarming comment. The police would be summoned, and then he would be seized and tossed into a cage of a cell, no questions required.

Instead, she had smiled. Every single time.

Thinking of that smile as he turned a corner, he nearly walked straight into a spiderweb anchored in one corner of the passageway. He stopped himself barely in time, lacy strands an inch from his face, and backed up a step. The air disturbed by his near-encounter tore a couple of threads free from their places. Idly, he watched the spider, a big black one, scurry out to fix the damage.

He imagined the spider fussing and scolding, and remarked, "My apologies, Madame." He studied the web, a good two feet wide and an intricate pattern of row after row of gossamer threads. Very impressive artistry, especially since the web hadn't been here earlier in the day when he passed with Meg.

He nodded once to the spider, who was still rushing about on her work, and continued on, making a mental note to walk on the opposite side of the passage for the duration of the spider's residence here. If he was taking this passage again.

He shook his head, amused by his own absurdity. As if one afternoon in the sunlight meant he'd be returning regularly in the future.

His thoughts drifted over the afternoon again—there had been something else too, something he'd had the opportunity to observe. It was familiar, but it had been years since it had been relevant.

Most people only looked at the mask, if he wore a half one. He could always feel it, the way their eyes were constantly fixed just a bit right of center. The mask was on his right side. Even when they tried not to (and many didn't bother trying) their eyes always scanned to that direction.

A few people went the other way, working very hard to only look at the unmasked side. The Daroga did that. But it was always obvious that they were *working* at it, and making such a point of ignoring the mask meant they weren't ignoring it at all.

Meg looked at both sides. She looked him in the eyes and if she was favoring either side, or trying to, he couldn't spot it. She looked at him straight-on as though it was all one, as though, mask and maskless, both sides were just his face.

And that was the secret of it. They were. Somehow she had worked that out, and he didn't know whether to be touched or alarmed.

Chapter Thirteen

I closed our front door behind me, resisted the impulse to peek through the window to watch Erik walk away among the shadows, and drifted into the sitting room where Mother was mending a skirt.

"Good evening," I said, dropping onto our armchair.

"Good evening," Mother said serenely, not looking up from her sewing. "Did you have a pleasant afternoon?"

I couldn't stop myself from smiling. "Yes." It had been a wonderful day. Certainly there had been stares here and there, but nothing bad enough to stop me from feeling that it had been lovely to spend the afternoon with Erik, to take him through my world.

"No one was arrested then?" Mother asked, as calm as before.

I rolled my eyes. "Oh honestly, you sound like Erik. He seemed convinced he'd be arrested just for walking down the street. But of course he wasn't. Everything was fine. He never even came close to getting into trouble."

Well, the police inspector had stared, but that hadn't meant anything serious. And perhaps if he actually had got into a fight with Léon in the café…but they hadn't.

Mother finally looked up, only to raise an eyebrow as though she couldn't imagine why I found her prior remark unreasonable. I was almost sure this was her way of teasing me though. "I can only base my assumptions on the Phantom's apparent attitudes about leaving the Opera."

I waved a hand. "Yes, well. He's paranoid." The day had left me convinced that it *would* be possible for him to leave the Opera, if he'd only do it. If he'd just be willing to take the risk—and having taken it, try to be as relaxed around adults as he was around children.

Had the day convinced him of anything similar?

Perhaps what he really needed was a—friend, to help him. Not to solve the situation for him, he'd have to do most of the work still, but someone who knew at least some of the people he was encountering, to smooth the way a bit.

It was when I began to imagine how I would introduce Erik in Leclair (win over Father Henri at Saint-Antoine-de-Padoue for the best start) that I realized I was in trouble.

I sprang up to my feet, suddenly needing to get away from my mother, who could read entirely too much on my face. "Should I check on supper?" I said, blindly reaching for an excuse, and hurried towards the kitchen.

"There's just soup simmering on the stove," Mother said from the room behind me.

I ignored that, ducking into the kitchen and bracing my hands against our small wooden table.

I was imagining introducing Erik in *Leclair*. The sunlit streets of Paris might be my world now, but Leclair was—it was my roots, it was where my family lived. It was where I had always supposed I might live, someday. When I was married. It was permanent, much more permanent than cafes or even the ballet. And it was as different a world from the Opera as it was possible to find.

I took a breath, crossed over to the pot on the stove and picked up a spoon to give the soup a stir. I needed something to do with my hands as much as I needed to appear normal to my mother.

The most alarming thing was, Erik in Leclair *didn't* seem impossible anymore. Not quite. And that was more painful than thrilling, because I knew I wasn't really picturing him there as a friend.

As delightful as today had been, maybe it had been a mistake to get him out into the sunlight, into the crowds. It was one thing to harbor unrequited feelings for a man I didn't believe I could ever have a life with anyway. It was another to be able to see the life that could be possible...*if!*

It still wasn't possible. Because he didn't love me. And so I should stop imagining anything of the sort. I told myself that, very firmly, very definitely.

I stirred the soup, watched the ripples across the surface, and reached up with my free hand to touch my little gold necklace. Erik was not mine, and this life I shouldn't be imagining was never going to be ours.

I kept calm enough to fool my mother—at least enough that she didn't question me—but I was still awake half the night, trying hard not to imagine anything, not to wish for things I couldn't have.

I was in a somber frame of mind the next morning, a mood that stayed with me as I arrived at the Opera for Monday morning's practice.

I was, probably, in no fit state to be confronted by Léon. He detached himself from leaning up against a pillar as I was ascending the steps to the Opera's doors.

"Meg, I've been waiting for you," he said, smiling at me.

I didn't smile back. "I'm still busy. I have ballet practice." Though truth to tell, most of the fire had gone out of my anger. I had bigger, even more difficult things on my mind.

"Now don't be upset with me," Léon said, holding onto his smile. "Surely you can forgive me for wanting to spend the afternoon with you? I didn't mean to upset you. I was disappointed."

I hesitated. Because, well, *was* I really angry with him for wanting to spend time with me? It seemed silly, put that way. Or was it actually the implied dismissal of Erik that I resented, the way Léon had been so sure that of course I'd want to spend the day with him instead?

Léon took advantage of my silence, and my failure to keep walking, to produce a long thin box from within his coat. "Maybe this will help you decide to forgive me?"

I stared at the box. Jewelry. It was obviously jewelry. He hadn't bought me anything like that before; I hadn't even let him pay for my copy of *Hamlet*, when we were browsing bookstalls a few weeks ago. How could I accept jewelry? "Léon, I can't possibly—"

He lifted the lid on the box, revealing a sparkling blue bracelet within. "Consider it a token of my respect and admiration. And apology."

That sounded sweet, but it didn't make it more all right. I knew the conventions, the rules around this sort of thing. "Léon, I *can't*—"

"I chose sapphires," Léon continued. "To match your eyes."

That did it. It shouldn't have done it. But I wouldn't have guessed that Léon even knew what color my eyes were. I hadn't known he saw me that clearly. "That's...very thoughtful," I said faintly, knowing I was going to accept the bracelet, knowing I was going to forgive him.

Maybe my reason for being angry was ridiculous anyway. I could hardly expect my casual suitor to appreciate the importance of the man I was in love with.

The man who wasn't in love with me. The man I was never going to have a life with.

I told myself that wasn't a factor in deciding to forgive Léon. Separate relationships entirely, nothing at all to do with each other. Nothing serious existed between Léon and me, and nothing at all between Erik and me. So no conflict existed either.

Léon insisted I try the bracelet on, and that we make plans for that afternoon, and by then I had to dash for practice. I meant to take the jewelry off again before I got there, but I was caught up by several girls en route before I could.

"Ooh, that's *beautiful!*" Adalisa said, catching my hand to look at the sapphires draped around my wrist. "Who gave it to you?"

I could have lied or been evasive, but that would have made them assume it was Léon anyway. So I told the truth, to be greeted by a series of delighted squeals.

"You are so *lucky*," Francesca sighed.

"So is Léon, apparently," Jammes' dry voice remarked, and my spine prickled. If I had realized she was walking just behind us, I might have tried to be evasive after all. "Or is he not lucky, and trying to change that?"

Before I could say anything, Francesca said, "Oh, you're just jealous, Jammes."

It was a weak bolt, an easy and automatic remark that likely didn't mean a thing. So I was surprised to see Jammes' cheeks turn suddenly pink. Her voice was smooth enough though, as she purred, "Not at all. I'm simply delighted for dear Meg's sake. So nice that she doesn't have to go delving about below the Opera for a lover anymore."

Suddenly my heart was pounding harder. She knew I had directions to the Phantom's room, and she hadn't spread it around the Opera yet. Was she about to?

She still couldn't prove anything. And beyond knowing about the directions—she didn't know anything else, she was just trying to be nasty.

Our eyes met for a moment, and I held my breath. Lack of proof usually didn't matter, if the gossip was good enough. And I cared very much now about not being fired, now that Erik was back—

But Jammes only smirked, and swept past us towards ballet practice.

I relaxed, hoping my tension hadn't been too obvious to everyone around us. Maybe Jammes did care that she didn't have proof—or maybe she was still keeping that mysterious promise to stay silent. I probably hadn't given that enough thought.

"What was that supposed to mean?" Adalisa asked in blank confusion.

"She must have meant the Phantom," Francesca said; it hadn't been very obscure.

"I suppose it's because Mother was his boxkeeper," I said quickly. "She's just trying to be horrible. You know Jammes."

"Yes..." Francesca said, expression too thoughtful for my taste.

"We're going to be late!" Adalisa said, linking her arm through mine, and we hurried off to practice.

I put the bracelet away before dancing, and left it in my bag afterwards. I didn't exactly mean to cut through an empty corridor after practice, only it had become habit. It was my usual route now— just as Erik appearing through a wall had become a usual thing.

"Hello," I said, heartrate accelerating as usual too.

"Hello," he said in return, with pleasant tones and no doubt none of my inner upheaval of feeling. "The new sets have arrived for the production of *Romeo and Juliet*. They're terrible. Care to come see?"

It was always come see this, come do that, and I usually said yes with no great crisis on the occasions when I said no. Today I felt tentative about it. As if something had shifted the day before. "Actually…I already have plans."

"Oh well, I suppose you'll see them for the next rehearsal," he said calmly enough and I felt a twinge of relief. Until he said, "Plans with the other ballet girls?"

I could have lied. But what was I hiding? No conflict existed between these relationships, and therefore I had no reason to feel guilty. "No. With Léon."

I might have felt better if he had visibly reacted. Instead he just stared at me, expression completely blank. Then something in his green eyes closed off, not going hostile but—distant. I hadn't realized how rarely I'd seen that expression in recent months. "I see," he said, voice flat and expressionless. "He contrived to grow up since yesterday?"

"I was angry when I said that," I protested, and I didn't like having it flung back at me now. It was none of his business, a private conversation he had eavesdropped on. "Léon apologized. He knows he was wrong yesterday."

Erik's gaze did not soften, and I felt a perfectly irrational desire to prove the point to him.

"He *was* sorry, you know. He gave me a very thoughtful gift as an apology."

"Did he." His voice was no softer than his expression.

"*Yes*." I reached into my bag, brought out the bracelet as though it was some kind of evidence.

Erik smiled, but it was a mere turning of his mouth, not reaching his eyes at all. "So he bought you a bracelet, and you decided to like him again."

"It's not the way you're making it sound," I countered. That made it seem so—mercenary! "And it's not the *bracelet*, it's the gesture." I held it up higher. "Sapphires, to match my eyes. That was thoughtful."

He flicked it a glance. "They're the wrong shade. Your eyes are darker. And what good is eye-matching jewelry on your wrist? It's not close to your face. Perhaps I should have given you a gold anklet to match your hair."

Suddenly I made a connection I hadn't before. "Wait, is that what this is about? You're upset that I forgave him too quickly compared to when we were fighting and—"

"I am not upset," he contradicted. "I am very happy for you."

This was an obvious lie, so I ignored it. "It wasn't even the same thing. I was much more upset with you." He blinked and I realized that hadn't come out right. "I mean—it's not as important, with Léon. We have a good time, but—that's all."

And then I stopped. I had to stop. Because I had already, possibly, implied that Erik *was* important to me, and if I didn't stop talking now, when would I? And would it be before I said everything I didn't want to tell him, about how desperately important he was to me, in a way I clearly wasn't to him? In a way that Christine had been, but—not me.

I watched him consider what I had said, wondered what he was already reading between the lines. What he was failing to read between the lines.

At last he tipped his head slightly, smiled in a way that reached his eyes this time, at least a little, and let his shoulders relax. "In that case, have a good afternoon. See you tomorrow?"

I was pleased to see him smile, pleased that we had evaded the awkwardness that could have sprung up, pleased that I had very sensibly not said too much. And I felt strangely, inexplicably disappointed too. But I smiled myself, and said, "Yes. That would be nice."

Then he faded back into the shadows and I went to meet Léon—putting the bracelet back on before I did—and I assured myself that, after all, this was exactly the way I wanted things to be.

Later, after I got home, I stepped in front of my mirror, raised my hand near my face, and studied the sapphires compared to the blue of my eyes. Erik was right. My eyes were darker.

I wished I could believe it meant something, his knowing that.

Excerpt from the Private Notebook of Jean Mifroid, Commissaire of Police

16 May, 1882

Have tracked so-called "Persian." Departure from Paris seemed suspicious directly after Phantom's death. New information indicates he was called to police work in Persia. No connection to Phantom's death.

I should close this case. Why is that difficult?

Chapter Fourteen

I t sounded like Léon wasn't going away after all. Erik didn't analyze too carefully why that was so disappointing, or why he so intensely disliked Léon. He hadn't liked him before, and meeting him hadn't changed his opinion.

But apparently he was going to be around. That meant Erik ought to keep closer attention on him. He didn't analyze that belief too deeply either. He had explored Léon's life before, but never learned anything substantive. If Meg wasn't getting rid of him now, or recognizing the sinister undertones in that exchange at the café, well, then that meant it was his duty to get a better idea of Léon's character and intentions. Surely that was what a friend ought to do. It wasn't as though he was busy anyway, and at least it would distract him from the changes he couldn't make to the managers' planned special performance.

What all this meant in practice was that the Phantom went back to skulking about, mostly following Léon whenever he was at the Opera Garnier. He couldn't learn anything at all when Léon was wandering in the corridors making small talk (although it did seem to him that all that small talk was inevitably with women, usually ballet girls, usually in their rather scanty practice outfits).

He had better hopes for catching some useful information from what Léon might discuss with a friend during a performance. Léon didn't attend Wednesday, but he came Saturday, which seemed like a perfect opportunity. The only problem was that he was boring. Erik eavesdropped on Léon and his friend for over an hour, sitting in a hidden space above their box while they chattered through the performance; he had expected they wouldn't be the rare people who valued art enough to pay attention. They might at least have been interesting though. His right foot fell asleep, and it was all he could do to stay awake himself.

Erik nearly gave up and left when Léon remarked, "Do you suppose this singer is going to keep screeching much longer? They ought to bring out the ballet dancers again. At least they aren't covered in all that drapery."

Signora Carlotta was currently performing a reasonably adequate if not exemplary aria. Although yes, the costume was somewhat curtain-like.

"Of course you have a particular interest in ballet lately," Léon's friend said, and Erik could unquestionably hear the leer. "That's a nice bit you've been keeping time with. Pretty little blond thing, isn't she?"

"Who, Meg? Sure, she's made some of these evenings at the Opera more worthwhile."

"From the length of time you've been seeing her, I could almost think you're planning to propose to that girl."

Erik's stomach clenched. That was not true. That would be a terrible idea.

Léon laughed, a short bark of a laugh. "Do you think I've gone insane?"

Erik exhaled. That was better.

"I just thought…"

"No chance of me marrying some penniless little ballet girl. Let's be realistic here."

And now Erik was uneasy again. He disapproved of Léon proposing to Meg, but now he found that he didn't entirely approve of Léon *not* proposing to Meg. He seemed to be not doing it for all the wrong reasons. But that was beside the point, of course. The point was that there were no marriage plans on the horizon. And if Léon didn't see why he ought to propose to Meg, then that was all the more reason why he shouldn't.

"When I do get married," Léon continued, "I'm going to be smart about it. A rich girl with an indulgent father and a nice title, that's for me."

Good, yes, that was exactly what he should do, and Erik heartily wished him success in finding just such a woman, very soon. With any luck, she'd be a bad-tempered shrew who hated music, and Léon would never come to the Opera ever again. And be miserable into the bargain. That seemed altogether appropriate.

"I suppose a cute ballet girl is a nice diversion in the meantime," Léon's friend commented.

"Exactly. Besides, Meg's obviously not suitable as a wife, but she has great potential as a mistress."

Mistress? *Mistress?*

He was going to kill him. He was going to drop down into the box and personally throttle Léon for his insolent audacity, for his presumption, for his daring to even *think* about Meg like that.

Erik had one hand on the trapdoor mechanism before he stopped. He couldn't kill Léon now, the curtains of the box were open, the entire theater would see and he'd be tossed in jail before Léon was cold. All right then, later. Later, some time when Léon was in some dark alley, he'd step out of the gloom and...

He slammed his fist against the floor, not even caring if anyone below heard him. He couldn't kill Léon like that either. Meg would figure it out. If Léon turned up strangled—even if he mysteriously disappeared—Meg would know he had done it. Or at least she'd suspect, and that would be bad enough. That would be enough to ruin everything.

And even if she didn't suspect...Erik would know, and he'd never be able to look her in the eyes again, without imagining how she would react if she did know.

He pressed his face into his palms. There had to be something he could *do*.

He should have seen this coming. He should have known—he *did* know—that this was the only likely end result of a wealthy subscriber keeping company with a ballet dancer. He had just, somehow, never thought about it that way. Meg wasn't *a* ballet dancer, she was—Meg.

Suddenly he could not stand listening to Léon's voice for another moment. If he wasn't killing him, he had no reason to stay. He climbed through a trapdoor, into the upper reaches above the auditorium, and then continued up ladders all the way to the roof. To where he could pace. And think. And try to work out a solution to this intolerable possibility.

He didn't usually set himself up as a morality police. He knew perfectly well the exact state of relations between any number of the Opera Garnier's women and the wealthy young men who came to call. As long as no one was being mistreated, he regarded it as none of his business what they chose to do.

Chose. He brightened momentarily, pressing his palms against the wall at the edge of the roof, facing the Avenue de l'Opera. He was entirely overreacting, because of course Meg would never agree to something like this. She knew the social consequences, what life that would lead her to. She wouldn't want that. It was unthinkable. He was sure of it.

Mostly sure. He thought of Léon kissing Meg in a dark corner of the theatre and was not as sure as he'd like to be. If Léon sort of coaxed her along...and it wasn't as though Meg didn't occasionally do wild, impulsive things, like talking to the Phantom of the Opera...and if she *loved* Léon...

She had said she didn't, of course. He seized onto that idea. Only, she had said that months and months ago. Anything could have happened since then. Like interludes in Box Seven. She had said just this week that Léon wasn't important—but she was spending time with him and accepting a bracelet and...and was it really true, or was it just what she thought he wanted to hear?

He groaned, turned away from the roof edge and resumed pacing. If she did care for Léon, if she let that sway her choices, he could imagine more clearly than he liked where it would all lead—what eventually happened to girls who went down that path. First they became mistress to a rich young man, probably handsome and charming. But then in a month or a year he would get bored, and move on to someone new. By then the girl would have a Reputation, no marriage prospects, and no choice but to become mistress to someone else, probably someone else who was less palatable than the first had been. After that, it was a spiraling cycle, man after man, and always it was the men who had the power to toss away a girl on a whim, to discard her and leave her to the next one, as she sank lower and lower down. Finally she'd be left desperate and destitute, with no choices but to enter a workhouse or a brothel.

He would not allow it to happen. Not to Meg.

If that wasn't the path of *every* woman in this situation—he was in no mood to take a hopeful view of the situation.

And apart from all that, apart from every justifiable concern—there still remained the fact that the thought of Léon with Meg made his stomach churn, made him want to lock the door the next time she came below the Opera and keep her there safe forever, made him want to…to…

Erik sank down to sit at the base of Apollo's statue and held his head in his hands. He was thinking like an opera again. People locked women up in operas and had it turn out well. That wasn't what civilized people in the real world did.

So what did civilized, rational people in the real world do?

Damned if he knew.

Chapter Fifteen

Excerpt from the Private Notebook of Jean Mifroid, Commissaire of Police

21 May, 1882

Have advertised again in international papers for Raoul de Chagny and Christine Daaé, after inability to trace earlier letter from RdC. Have included information of Phantom's death in notice; may draw them out if hiding from him. Maybe finding them will finally bring resolution?

Léon, perhaps thinking he needed to get a claim in early (not a bad idea for him to have), had arranged for Sunday afternoon plans days before. And so I spent the afternoon wandering through Parisian shops and cafes again—just with a different man. No one stared at Léon, not in the same way at least, and it was a nice afternoon, but…different.

I had never noticed before that I was shifting what I looked at in the shops, turning towards some things and away from others, less for my own preference than because I knew Léon was watching. Today I passed over the booksellers quickly and went on to the jewelry because I knew it was what he'd expect me to find interesting.

I hadn't done that, with Erik. There was no question Erik found me confusing at times too—he certainly was sometimes himself—but it wasn't the same. He tended to be confused and want to know more, while Léon would rather the confusing element simply went away.

Erik had been impressed when I read *Hamlet*, while Léon seemed to find the idea odd and slightly amusing.

"Perhaps we should stop soon for coffee," I suggested, turning away from a collection of Verne novels in a bookseller's window. I didn't really have time to read them anyway.

"Perhaps," Léon agreed, slipping an arm around my waist as we walked on.

I wouldn't have let that stand for long—it was forward for out in the city, even if this was a quiet street. And besides, it was harder to walk that way. But I did let him, for a few paces, and suddenly found myself being pulled sideways into a narrow space between buildings.

Before I even had my feet properly under me again Léon's mouth was on mine. My eyes traitorously slid shut, some instinct I'd hardly known I'd possessed—then snapped open again as my mind caught up with the situation. I pushed against his shoulders, managing a half-smothered, "Léon!" in what was intended as protest.

I don't know how he took it. He may have responded with, "Mmm," but nothing more eloquent than that. He also went right on kissing me.

I pushed harder, palms against his shoulders, and gained an inch of space between our faces, just enough room to say, "Not here!" Strangers were walking past just feet away.

He didn't seem to find this off-putting. He didn't back away, just grinned at me and said in a low, suggestive voice, "Where would you suggest?"

"You're very sure of yourself," I said tartly, a flicker of anger joining my initial rush of embarrassment. What made him think he could just pounce and kiss me any time he liked?

Possibly that interlude in Box Seven. And the bracelet I had accepted. I had known what that would suggest to him—but that still didn't give him any right to assume I was simply here for the taking.

"I'm sure of what I want," he said, bending to kiss my neck.

I twisted away before his lips more than barely brushed my skin, pushed harder against his shoulders and slipped out from between him and the wall. "*I* want coffee," I said, smoothing down my rumpled dress.

He just gave an easy smile to that, and I was more relieved than I liked to think about that he didn't get angry—or force the issue. But even though he strolled next to me to a café, nothing in his eyes suggested he felt he'd been rejected.

He was perfectly polite the rest of the afternoon, left me at my door with an entirely inoffensive kiss on the cheek. But I kept thinking about that brief moment in the shadows, and it wasn't comfortable. I had hoped we could go on indefinitely, friendly—but not too friendly. Instead, of course, it couldn't be so easy.

Why did life always have to grow *complicated*?

The rest of Sunday passed uneasily away, and I went to see Erik Monday afternoon, which would at least be a different kind of complicated. Certainly no chance he was going to press advances. Unfortunately.

I may not have been in the best of moods, and it probably didn't help that Erik seemed inclined to play music in minor key, if less thunderously than when he had been angry. This was more melancholy than passionate. He was unusually quiet too, which took me a while to notice, tangled up in my own thoughts as I was. I sat curled up in his armchair while he played at the piano, and at some point I also noticed that, while not talking, he was looking at me often and I couldn't read his expression.

I straightened up. I'd been growing possibly too relaxed down here, especially on a day like this when I was thinking of other things. I cast about for a conversational topic, hoping to break whatever strange feeling was in the air. "Did you see Saturday's performance?"

Erik's shoulders tightened for absolutely no reason that I could discern, though his hands continued moving smoothly over the piano keys. "No. Not really. I caught a piece or two, but—no."

"Oh." I had not been prepared for that answer. For all that the Phantom had died, Erik was still attending every performance. Or so I'd believed. "Busy with something else?"

His shoulders got tighter. I had *thought* I was good by now at navigating around the topics that made Erik tense, but I had no idea what was bothering him this time. "Something like that. Have a nice Sunday?"

I blinked, tried to roll with the topic change. "…yes." Too bad it wasn't a topic I especially wanted to talk about. "It was—nice." Mostly.

He nodded, and now he was looking at his hands on the keys instead of at me. "Did you spend the afternoon with Léon?"

He knew that, I'd mentioned it before. Maybe he didn't care to remember. "Yes. I had a…good time." Mostly.

Another nod. "And how is Léon?"

"Fine.   He's fine."   This stilted conversation was utterly ridiculous. I never had a lack of things to say to Erik. In a kind of wild search for something else to talk about, my brain went sideways from what I was trying *not* to think about and I said, "I almost bought an entire collection of Jules Verne novels. Any you'd recommend?"

It was a desperate shot, but getting off the personal and on to the artistic was always less charged.   He paused a moment, possibly making a mental shift, then said, "I always found *20,000 Leagues Under the Sea* surprisingly tedious, but I enjoyed *The Mysterious Island*, even though it's something of a sequel."

For the rest of the afternoon, we stayed strictly on impersonal topics. I tried to keep it that way, and perhaps Erik did too. It didn't stop me thinking about Léon at intervals. Or from wondering what Erik was trying to avoid discussing.

Erik kept pacing, and stewing, and hatching wild, improbable plans he knew he wasn't going to carry out. He had to stop pacing when Meg came for a rather awkward visit. The inability to pace drove him to his piano, where nothing but depressing music came to mind.

He *could* have actually asked her about the elephant that had landed in the middle of the opera. He thought about it. He considered saying the words out loud to Meg, "I hear Léon wants you to be his mistress, what do you think about that?"

Right. That was about as likely and as feasible as an actual elephant arriving on stage—and not that fake one they used in *Hannibal.*

After Meg left he went back to pacing, until finally the Monday evening performance came around. He didn't hunt for Léon this time. This time he meddled with the books to make sure Box Five stayed empty for another performance, then waited in the front seat, curtains closed, until Madame Giry walked in to prepare the box for the performance.

She must have been surprised to see him. He'd only been visible here twice in all these years. She only betrayed it with the very slightest pause before saying, "Good evening, Monsieur Phantom. To what do I owe the honor?"

He was too upset to be charming, or even to ease into this gradually. "You have to get rid of Léon."

A long, excruciating pause as Madame Giry took those words in, and finally said only, "Would you like to elaborate on that comment?"

How could she be so *calm?* "He's trouble, he's bad for her, he…" How could he say this to Meg's *mother?* Finally, in desperation: "His intentions aren't honorable!"

Madame Giry sighed. "No, I don't suppose anyone imagined they were. Certain vicomtes aside, members of the aristocracy don't marry girls from the Opera."

He gaped at her. It wasn't that he hadn't known this, but—he had never expected Madame Giry to say it so definitively. "Then why have you been letting him run about with her?"

"I thought we established long ago that I do not choose my daughter's friends," she said, tone implying he ought to have realized this for himself. "You and I would not be having this conversation if that were the case." The slightest pause, and then her voice changed, finally tinged with some faint emotion. Regret? "I did rather hope, however, that this entire business with Léon would fade away before progressing to anything—serious."

"Yes, well, that's not *his* plan."

"I take it you overheard something?"

"Yes," he said shortly, and did not clarify how much effort had gone into the overhearing.

"I see."

That was *it?* "But—but—you can't possibly be all right with the idea!"

"No, of course not," she said sharply. "This is not what I would have chosen for my daughter. But it is not in my power to control what choices Meg makes. I will talk to her about this, but ultimately I can only hope she makes the right ones."

That wasn't enough. Of course he knew this was up to Meg, not to her mother, certainly not to him—and yet! This was no comfort at all, and he reached wildly for what might be more reassuring. "Does she love him?"

The silence drew out for another long moment, much longer than her answer took when she finally just said, "No."

His sudden rush of relief made him almost dizzy. "That's all right then. She won't choose—this."

"I don't think so," Madame Giry said quietly, which was certainly a negative—but it was so much less definite than that simple 'no' to the previous question.

Much of the relief ebbed away. "It's just—he doesn't love her." It was all too intolerable, and he shoved up to his feet and resumed pacing in the small space the box afforded. "No, it's even worse than that. He doesn't *appreciate* her. And if she stays with him, she's going to end up believing that she's no more than what he thinks she is. And she is *so much* more than that."

Caught up by his own words, Erik was not prepared for Madame Giry's suddenly tense question, "What are *your* intentions towards Meg?"

He stared at her, uncomprehending. "My intent—I don't *have* intentions. We're friends."

Madame Giry exhaled, not quite a sigh. "That is as I thought. Negating the easy solution."

None of that made sense, but Erik felt an irrational hope at the possibility of an easy solution anyway. "What's the easy solution?" He'd take any solution. Easy would be a bonus.

"If you don't already know," she said dryly, "I cannot begin to explain it to you."

That was just being deliberately unhelpful. He slumped into his seat again. "Then apparently we have nothing further to discuss."

Again a silent moment, and he wished he knew what she was thinking. With Meg, he might have been able to make a guess, but her mother was far more mysterious to him. At last she said, "Thank you for your concern."

That sounded like a cold formality, but somehow, he thought she meant it. She dropped a program on another seat with a thunk and took a step towards the door.

"Did you threaten Léon?" Erik asked without looking at her. "If he hurts Meg?" He still remembered that conversation vividly, when she had told him with such quiet, unbrooking assurance what would happen if he harmed her daughter.

"No," Madame Giry said, continuing her soft tread towards the exit.

Something inside Erik sank. Of course. Why threaten the handsome aristocrat? "He didn't seem dangerous enough to need a warning?" he asked bitterly.

"On the contrary. He didn't seem perceptive enough for such a warning to have effect," Madame Giry said, stepped out of the door and shut it behind her with a click.

Erik wasn't sure, but he thought possibly he'd just been complimented. Some other time, he might have dwelled on that longer. Right now, he went back to formulating wild, improbable plans.

Chapter Sixteen

I grew no better at focusing my thoughts as Monday wore on, and Madame Thibault gave me a stern lecture after the evening's performance about keeping my mind on my dancing. As a result, I was the last one back to the ballet girls' changing room, the last one still there after the others had gone on to the Foyer.

I was just buttoning the top button of my second boot and about to pick up my bag to leave when the door opened again. I barely glanced up, expecting one of the girls returning for some reason.

It was lucky I was sitting down, as I was definitely not expecting to see Léon stroll confidently in and shut the door behind him.

"I heard you were the last one still here," he said with a grin, as though he had done something clever.

I was too shocked by his arrival to think about where he would have heard that. "You can't *be* here!" I protested. "Subscribers don't come in here!"

"They go into the singers' dressing rooms," he countered, strolling closer.

"That's—different." Maybe it didn't make sense, but the rules were different and that was what mattered. "They'd fire me if they caught you in here."

"I won't let that happen," he said, in a tone meant to sooth that just irritated me more. By now he was next to me, bent down to kiss my cheek—and then leaned further, lips questing for my neck.

I rose to my feet, backed-up a couple steps. "Léon, you *cannot* be here. I'm not discussing the idea, it's a fact. And this is not the time, place or circumstances for—"

"Yes, yes, I know, it's never the right moment," he said, still grinning. "So let's find the right time and the right place."

With a sick twist in my stomach, I knew I was going to have to deal with this, right now. We weren't going to just go on as we had been, innocently friendly. "Léon, I can't—"

"Or is it the circumstances that worry you?" He sat down in my vacated chair, reached out to catch my hands. "I hope you know this isn't some casual thing," he said, looking up into my eyes. "I would never mean that."

This could not possibly end well. "Léon, please don't." I tried to extract my hands, but his grip tightened.

"I want to take care of you. Buy you furs and jewelry and perfume and anything you want."

Probably not Shakespeare or Verne books, a voice at the back of my mind whispered. Probably not trips to Vienna or Rome.

"Do you want an apartment on the Champs-Élysées? Better parts at the Opera? Just name it and I'll get it for you."

'Let me give you the moon and the stars' wasn't a bad line, really. But it was a long way from 'I love you, will you marry me?'

Because that wasn't what we were talking about.

But no one else was making that offer either. Maybe no one ever would. Inevitably, unavoidably, Erik with his music and his green eyes and all his magic rose up in my mind. He had been so distant this afternoon, so impersonal. And he was so in love with Christine.

I could spend my entire life waiting for Erik, and what kind of life was that?

Léon stood up with a suddenness that surprised me, closing the already slim gap between us. He leaned in, breath warm against my ear as he whispered, "Let's go find the right place." Then he was kissing me, mouth hard, fingers tight around mine.

And everything in me said *no*.

It didn't matter how Erik felt, it mattered how *I* felt. And it wasn't even how I felt about Erik that counted—except that those feelings told me, with absolute clarity, that I didn't love Léon. Not the way I loved Erik. Not the way I needed to love any man I was going to be with.

I wrenched my hands free, stumbled back a step, then another and a third. "Léon, I'm not going to be your mistress."

In an opera, I would have sung an entire aria, or at least delivered a gracious, heart-tugging monologue. In life, all I could manage was that blunt sentence.

Léon stared at me with the confusion I had noticed more and more often. "But of course you are. Why do you think I've been waiting around all these months? Where did you think this was all leading?"

My cheeks were hot. "I didn't think it was *leading* anywhere. I thought we were just having a good time." He had been so polite, so gentlemanly—at least, until recently. And he'd made me laugh. Somehow I'd never pictured a wealthy, heartless Don Juan who'd seduce me and leave me to the consequences as someone who'd make me laugh.

He brushed right past my words—and took a step closer, smile returning to his face. I didn't like that. "I don't mind being patient, but it's been long enough. I find a certain amount of maidenly demurring attractive, but you can take it too far."

"I'm not—*demurring*. And I'm not delaying, I'm saying—no." He didn't love me. I *knew* he didn't love me, and I tried to use that fact to make me feel less like I was hurting him. "I'm sorry if we had different ideas about what was happening, but I don't want to be your mistress."

He stopped smiling, and in a cold tone I'd never heard from him before he said, "What did you think I was going to do, ask you to marry me?"

I wasn't that naïve. "No, I didn't think—"

"Because that was obviously never going to happen. I mean, a ballet girl? As if I could ever introduce you to my mother."

I very carefully breathed in, tried to keep the pain and shame off of my face. Of course I knew that was how the subscribers thought of us, but it stung hearing it like this. From him. "I think we're done here," I said, as evenly and firmly as I could manage, and took a step towards the door.

Only one step, because he reached out and grabbed my wrist. "You really think you're going to just walk out of here and leave me with nothing, after all the time I spent? After that bracelet I gave you?"

Damn the bracelet, I knew better than to accept it. "You can have it back," I snapped. "I don't want anything from you."

"I don't want it back," he said in a low voice. "I want what it was meant to buy."

I could not believe that only moments ago I had actually, if briefly, considered accepting him. "That's not for purchasing." I wrenched against his hand on my arm—and couldn't pull free.

"If it's your reputation you're worrying about, don't bother." He smirked, a kind of parody of the grin I was used to. "I'll tell everyone you slept with me either way."

My heart was pounding loudly in my ears and my wrist was beginning to ache. "The people who matter won't believe you." I hoped that was true. I was afraid it wasn't.

"Or maybe," he said in a low voice, yanking my wrist in a sharp movement that forced me a step closer, as he raised my hand up towards his lips, "I'll tell them about your dear friend the Phantom."

I froze, staring at him, barely even feeling it as he kissed my fingers. "What—what are you talking about?"

"Your friend Jammes tells me that you and the Phantom were *very* close," he drawled, lips brushing over my knuckles. "Maybe I shouldn't have described it as *maidenly* demurring."

I couldn't breathe. "That's—ridiculous."

"I asked her to keep it quiet, and she was very happy to oblige me." He kissed one fingertip, looking at me over our hands. "Nice girl, your friend Jammes. Pretty, too."

Was he attempting to make me *jealous*? I could feel an absurd laugh trying to rise in my throat. "She's not my friend."

His fingers tightened on mine, hard. "None of them will be, if I tell what I know. The Opera Company won't be happy about a traitor in their midst. I expect they'll fire you." The tip of his tongue ran along the pad of my finger. "So there you'll be, no job, no reputation, no future. You better hope I'm still willing to take you back by then." His teeth closed on my finger.

I yanked my hand back, and this time fear or anger or desperation pulled me free of his grip. "I don't want you and I don't need you," I said, backing away even as my voice shook. "And I *never* will."

The door was behind me, past the lines of dressing tables and mirrors. I should have moved toward it faster.

Before I could reach the exit, the hall beyond, he had closed the space between us. Suddenly his hands were on my upper arms, shoving me back against a dressing table. His palms pressed against the mirror, arms locking me in on either side, the sharp edge of the table digging into the back of my thighs. "I didn't want it to be this way," he said, breath hot on my face. "I *like* you, Meg. But I don't like not getting what I want."

My heart felt as though it was going to pound out of my chest, my stomach was a twisting mass of fear—I could try to twist away, but I already knew I couldn't break out of his grip if he didn't want me to. I tried to shift my legs, muscled from so many years of dancing, but they were tangled in my long skirts, his legs pinning me against the table.

I couldn't move and I couldn't escape and terror was making my breath tight. There was nothing I could do and no one to help—after so many years surrounded unendingly by other ballet girls or guarded over by my mother, when I really needed it there was no one…

Through the haze of desperation, one possible answer came to me. One single idea. "Don't you think it's rather stupid to try to this at the Opera Garnier?" Distantly, I was surprised by how steady my voice sounded. "What if I screamed right now?"

He grinned, or was it a leer? "Right now? No one would hear."

I knew he was right, but that didn't stop me from saying, "Are you sure? Because maybe I am friends with the Phantom. And maybe *he's* listening."

He wasn't. If he *was*, he'd be in here by now. *Maybe* he'd hear a scream. But he'd expect me to spend the evening after the performance with Léon. Even if he'd attended the performance, he wouldn't be waiting around to meet me now.

But Léon didn't know that.

He thought he knew something else. "Are you insane? The Phantom's dead; everyone says so."

It took all my acting ability from years at the Opera to smile and arch one eyebrow and say, "That's what everyone thinks. The police found a body, but they never knew what he looked like. They're wrong about him, you see—and if I scream—do you remember Joseph Buquet? He was hanged, right on stage, with hundreds of people in the auditorium. And Philippe de Chagny? Drowned under the Opera. It was *weeks* before they finally found his body in the Seine. The Phantom could kill you without hardly trying."

He hesitated, and it gave me the first glimmer of hope. "You're bluffing," he said, but he didn't sound sure.

I managed to keep my smile. "He would do it, you know. Kill you for me. He *will* do it, if you hurt me."

And slowly, so slowly, the pressure of his body against mine lessened—and his hands came away from the mirror—and he moved back just far enough for me to slide off the edge of the table. I wanted to run but that would ruin the effect, make him sure I was lying, and he could still grab me before I got to the door.

I forced myself instead to walk deeper into the room, to pick up my bag—I had a knife inside, could I get it out if I needed to?—then walked to the door. Still smiling. And still watching him. He watched me, and didn't move.

I reached the door, opened it and stepped out into the empty hallway.

His voice followed me out from the changing room. "See if your friend the Phantom can help you after the management fires you. You'll still need me. Wait and see."

Then I ran.

I ran until I was one corner away from the antechamber to the boxes, then made myself walk. The boxkeepers should still be straightening up. Hopefully.

I passed two who weren't Mother, averting my gaze and hurrying by without entering into a conversation. My breath was catching in my chest and my throat hurt and my eyes were hot.

Finally I saw Mother coming out of Box 16, just a moment before she saw me. "Meg? I thought you'd be in the Foyer..." Her voice trailed away, eyes narrowing as she looked at my face.

To the extent I had any plans at all, I had meant to be calm, collected, adult. Make some rational, reasonable excuse for now, so that we could leave. But when I looked at my mother, all I managed to say was the distinctly childish, "I want to go home. Now."

"What's wrong?" she asked. "What happened?

"Not *here*," I said desperately. Why did no one seem to be able to understand about appropriate places for things? "I just want to go home."

Her gaze grew no less searching, but she didn't press me about what was going on. She just went to another motherly concern. "Where's your cloak? Did you leave it in the changing room? We should—"

"Mother, it's *May*, I don't even need the cloak, can we please, please just *go*?" My voice was wavering badly by now.

She drew my arm through hers, pressed my hand with a warm and comforting pressure, and said, "Yes, of course."

I didn't make eye contact with anyone we passed as Mother steered us through the Opera and along the short walk home. It was a relief when the door closed behind us, when I could sink onto the couch and close my eyes against the hot pricking behind them.

I felt the cushion shift as Mother sat next to me, one hand settling lightly over mine. "Meg, can you tell me what's wrong?" she asked, voice gentler than I'd almost ever heard it.

I scarcely knew how to tell her. "Léon...came to talk to me. After the performance."

"In the Dance Foyer?"

"No," I said past my tightening throat. "He came into the changing room. I was the last one there, I was about to leave." Her hand pressed mine harder. I didn't look at her face. "He asked me to become his mistress."

I heard her exhale. "I see. And what did you say?"

My eyes jolted open. "I said no, of course!" Indignation gave me a surge of strength. "You didn't think I'd say yes, did you?" The incidental fact that I had, however briefly, considered it mattered not at all.

"No," Mother said firmly. "No, I did not think that."

My stomach twisted again, nauseous. "Léon did. Léon was sure I'd say yes. And he didn't like it when I said no."

She shifted to look directly into my eyes, voice carefully controlled as she asked, "Did he hurt you?"

I blinked, wanted to look away but then she might think I was lying. "No." Not the way she meant. "I think...that he wanted to. But I slipped away and ran and... Or maybe he was only bluffing, but—" I pressed my free hand against my eyes, pricking even hotter now. "He scared me. And *I* bluffed, and it worked but—I said things I should not have told him, and now...now it's all going to fall apart, everything."

Tears were sliding down my cheeks by now. Mother pulled me into a hug and I sank into it, face against her shoulder. "It's all right now," she said, stroking my hair. "You're home and safe and that's what matters."

Yes. And no. "You don't understand—he knows that I know Erik. I mean, the Phantom. Oh—no, he knows that I know *Erik* too, he saw us that Sunday. And I just told him the Phantom's still alive, and he's going to go to the management and tell them that I'm friends with the Phantom because Jammes told him—and they're going to fire me. Of course they'll fire me for that."

"They may not believe him," Mother said, but the words even sounded unconvincing. "What proof does he have?

I shook my head. "It doesn't matter. He's a subscriber. They might have believed me over Jammes, but Léon—they'll fire me just because he says so." It was true and we both knew it. "But it's so much worse than that, because he'll tell the managers I said the Phantom's still alive and they'll tell Mifroid and...I keep doing this to him! I got Carlotta upset and the managers went after him using my directions and now this and—"

"Commissaire Mifroid believes the Phantom is dead," Mother said. "He will not take it simply on faith that he's still out there."

My thoughts were racing on in a crazed, terrified sort of way. "But Mifroid knows that the Phantom always wears a mask. That's the only way to explain trying to catch him at the masquerade; he knew he couldn't take his mask off for some reason. And Léon saw me with a *masked man*. He doesn't know that's the Phantom but if they talk to each other—Erik even gave him his real name—his composer name, I mean, so they'll figure that out too and..." Everything. *Everything* was falling apart. "They're going to kill Erik. They're going to fire me and kill Erik." If I was fired, I wouldn't be there to help him anymore. They would find him. And this time, they'd kill him.

"You don't know any of that," Mother said, hands firm on my shoulders. "You are speculating—"

"But don't you see, it's like a—a puzzle, and everyone has a few pieces, and if they all get together and put their pieces together, then—I can't let Léon talk to the managers." This seemed the clearest, most blinding of insights. "I can't. That's what will make it all start, if he talks to them. I can't let him."

"You are not going to do anything at all involving Léon de Troyes again," Mother said sharply. "You are not talking to him or going near him or—"

"No, no, of course not." The idea made my stomach hurt. Léon. *Léon* scared me. How had the world turned this far upside down so quickly? "Talking to Léon wouldn't work anyway. But don't you see, the only way—I have to counteract his threat."

"I don't understand."

"I have to quit," I whispered. "I have to quit the Opera. Then there's no reason for Léon to have me fired. He won't talk to the managers, and they won't talk to Mifroid. It's the only thing I can do. To keep them all away from Erik."

Chapter Seventeen

Mother and I talked about options well into the night. She didn't want me to do anything rash, didn't want me to throw everything away. She couldn't see that it was my fault, that it was being friends with me that had put Erik in danger to begin with.

But she did eventually end up by agreeing that, taking Erik out of the question, resigning quietly was still best for my own reputation and any future career I might have.

That was not uppermost in my mind—what did any of it matter, when I knew Mifroid wouldn't come to kill *me*—but if it meant she agreed with my choice, I wouldn't try to persuade her otherwise.

I cried a lot of tears in the night, but by the morning I was calm. If you can call a black void in the pit of my stomach calm. Maybe resolute was more accurate. This was what I *had* to do, so I was going to do it. I never could have stayed at the Opera forever. I could survive giving up my position with the ballet. It was never my dream, not really, not like so many other girls. Not like it might have been for Gabi, if she had lived. I had other dreams, and while I had loved being part of the Opera—I could survive giving that up. I could even imagine I might be all right with it, someday.

The part I couldn't imagine, the part I couldn't bring myself to think about, was—how was I ever going to tell Erik? And then—what happened to the two of us then?

I was working very hard to not think about that.

Mother came with me to the Opera Tuesday morning, and wanted to come with me to talk to Madame Thibault. But I was nineteen, an adult. I could handle this without my mother.

I arrived before ballet practice was due to begin, slipped into the practice room before any of the other girls were present. Madame Thibault was standing by the piano, going over a stack of notes on upcoming performances.

I tried to approach her confidently, but probably failed. "Madame?"

She looked up, fixed me with the piercing stare I'd seen hundreds of times in the past seven years. "Ah. Mademoiselle Giry. Arriving early to rededicate yourself to your craft after that negligent inattention at last night's performance?"

I bit my lip. "Well—no." I glanced over at the mirrors lining the walls. If Erik was behind them, listening…it would be his own fault if he found out like this. "I've come to resign my role with the ballet."

She set down her papers, stare shifting into one I'd seen far less often. Was it surprise? Confusion? Even—concern? "One poor performance is no reason to give up."

I winced inwardly, tried not to do it externally too. "No, that's not it. I have—I have personal reasons for…"

"Has there been a death of an immediate relative?" she snapped out.

"What—no, it's not—"

"Serious illness? Yours or someone else's?"

"No, I—"

"Then I cannot accept that," she said crisply. "I have dances arranged for our upcoming operas, including the managers' special performance next week. You are a part of those dances, and you expect to simply walk away from that responsibility?"

I stared at her, baffled. In all my painful thoughts throughout the night, I had never imagined a resignation being refused. I *could* just walk away over her objection, but that would ruin any future career I might ever care to have in dancing and, more importantly, lead to trouble for Mother and her job. But if I didn't resign—then Léon would talk to the managers—and then... "I'll stay a week," I said quickly. "I'll stay until the special performance. Then I have to go."

She was studying me now, gaze measured, thoughtful, maybe concerned after all. "Why?"

Unexpectedly, humiliatingly, I felt my eyes growing hot again. Hadn't I cried enough already? "I can't," I whispered. "I just—have to leave."

"I see," she said, voice crisp and distant again. "Until next Tuesday's performance then. Now, we have practice."

Practice. I had expected to walk out of here, not to end up going about an even semi-normal day. "I...didn't bring any practice clothes."

"There are extras in the changing room. Quickly now."

The ballet's changing room was empty when I walked into it. I was already sorting through the extra clothes in one cupboard when I suddenly remembered. Léon. So many memories in this room, and now that *one* was overwhelming all the rest.

My gaze slid over to one of the dressing tables, the one he'd had me pinned up against and...

I shivered, snatched up a set of clothes and found another room to actually change in.

As soon as practice was over, I told the ballet girls that I was leaving. I didn't want to have this conversation—but if Léon didn't know that I had resigned, there would be no point to it. And no one spreads stories as fast as the ballet.

A gratifying outcry of distress arose as the girls clustered around me. "But why are you leaving?" Adalisa demanded.

"Personal reasons I would rather not discuss," I said as firmly as I could manage, because I had been in no state of mind to make up a better justification.

That prompted a curious murmur among most of the girls—and from Jammes, the drawled question, "What's wrong, are you expecting a child?"

The murmur rose and I snapped, "*No.* Of course not."

She arched an eyebrow at me. "Oh? I'm sure you'll get there soon enough. Going off with Léon, aren't you?"

"I'm not doing that either," I said, voice steadier than I had expected. I took a breath, managed to smile at her—not a pleasant smile. "I ended things with Léon. So you can finally have him. If you still want him."

It was only a guess that she was interested in Léon—but her cheeks flushed pink and I knew I'd hit the mark. "Oh, *you* ended it?" she said, too sweetly. "Are you sure he didn't get tired of you?"

By comparison to the truth, I wished he had. My smile turned brittle. "Quite sure."

"Oh, stop being horrid, Jammes," Adalisa said impatiently, linking her arm through mine. "Meg, you must come out with us—tell us all about your plans now."

I couldn't. I had no plans. And I had somewhere else I needed to be. As gently as I could, I extricated my arm again. "I wish I could, really. But I have an appointment. I'm so sorry, I have to go."

I managed to get away from the crowd, though I didn't retreat too fast to hear the rising buzz of gossip behind me as I left. Good. That was good. I *wanted* them spreading the word; that was the whole point. I wanted people to hear about this.

Except for one person, who should hear it from me first. If he hadn't overheard it already.

Chapter Eighteen

E rik was not expecting Meg early Tuesday afternoon, but he was quick to straighten his cravat and let her in when she knocked.

Something was clearly wrong from the moment she walked in the door—her pace was too slow, her shoulders set at the wrong angle, her "hello" in response to his own entirely too subdued.

"Ah, how are you?" he asked tentatively, because surely that was more diplomatic than demanding to know what catastrophe had occurred.

She smiled, a mirthless smile quite unlike her usual sunny ones, and said, "I've been better." She sat in her usual spot on his couch, and he hastened to sit on the opposite one.

"Do you want something to drink?" he asked. "I can get coffee—or tea—or something to eat—"

"No, nothing," she said, shaking her head. "Thank you. I just—I need to tell you something."

Almost automatically his gaze darted down to her hands. Her right hand was in her lap, twisting at a fold of her skirt. Not a happy something, not something she wanted to talk about—though that should have been obvious enough already.

Léon. What if it was about Léon? What if she had said yes to Léon? But no, that couldn't be right, she wouldn't do that—and if she had, wouldn't she be happy about it? Would she? *He* would be horrified, her mother would be upset, but if that was what Meg wanted then Meg ought to be happy and she wasn't, so that couldn't be it. Could not.

He cleared his throat, feeling as though words were going to stick. "And—what would that be?"

She looked him right in the eyes, resolve on her face, shoulders squared for a difficult task, and said six words that did not make the slightest bit of sense to him.

"I've just resigned from the ballet."

He stared at her, mind absolutely unable to take this in. He could read Shakespeare without difficulty, the denser parts of Hugo, even Goethe in the original German. But this, *this* made no sense at all. He understood the words, yes, but the meaning of them…

"What?" he finally managed.

Her jaw was tight. "I've just resigned from—"

"No, no, no, I *heard* you, I meant—that is, I don't—you said that you—*what?*" He hastily raised a hand as her mouth opened, lest she was about to say it yet again. "No, I don't mean what, I mean…" There had to be a sentence that would actually be what he was trying to ask—or if not a sentence, because he couldn't seem to get from beginning to end of a sentence right at this moment, then a—a different interrogative… "*Why?*"

She smiled that non-smile again, gaze sliding away. "Personal reasons I would rather not discuss."

"What the *hell* does that mean?"

She sighed. "I have no idea, it's just what I told the ballet girls."

"But…" He was still floundering. "But why? And what does that even mean, you resigned, and…why would you do that?"

"I shouldn't even tell you," she said in a low voice, gaze on her hands in her lap. "You won't like it."

"Of course you should tell me," he protested. "Whatever it is—we'll fix it and—there has to be another—I don't *understand*. You *like* the ballet and everything was fine and…"

Her gaze rose but didn't meet his, staring into the middle distance somewhere over his shoulder. "Léon made me a—proposal last night. If you could call it that."

Léon. It was Léon after all. But it couldn't be Léon, he had decided it couldn't be Léon and—she had said yes and was leaving the Opera because she had said yes and—he was going to *kill* Léon, that was clearly the only solution. "Oh."

"I turned him down."

Erik exhaled. "*Oh.*" Well, that was—that was much better, and the world was not as hideously far awry as he had thought, but this still didn't make any *sense.* "I still don't see…"

"He was going to have me fired. So I quit before he could."

"I'll kill him," Erik said, entirely without thinking about it first. "How dare he—he can't do that, I won't *let* him—"

"Erik, *no!*" Meg's eyes had gone very wide. "You can't…" He watched her swallow, close her eyes for a heartbeat, and say in a steadier tone, "I don't want you to do that."

He had known she wouldn't like the idea and if he was thinking rationally he wouldn't be trying to convince Meg that murder was an appropriate step—but rational thinking had stepped out of the room. "Whatever you feel for him, he doesn't deserve—"

"I don't care about him. I care about you. And I don't want you to kill anyone for me." She sighed. "I appreciate that you want to…defend me. But not like that."

It was a miracle she didn't think he was a monster. An absolute miracle. And this miracle was about to walk out of the Opera Garnier for good, and then… "Maybe you didn't have to resign. Maybe he was just bluffing. Or even if he wasn't—nobody badgers Madame Thibault, she won't want to listen to him anyway. I mean, if he goes to her and says you refused to be his mistress, she's not going to fire you for that." He could hear the desperate, pleading hope in his voice. For all his vocal abilities, he couldn't seem to stop it.

"That's not what he's going to say," Meg said in a low voice. "Listen, it doesn't matter—this whole thing is done already and—"

"What is he going to say?" Erik asked, suddenly alert to what she wasn't saying. "What don't you want him saying?"

She was shaking her head. "No, you don't need to—I shouldn't—"

"If you're going to take yourself out of my Opera," he said sharply, "I would like to know *why.*" Unless he didn't want to know. What if she hadn't said no? What if she had actually said yes? What if she had said yes and then no? Was that what she was trying not to—

"He knows about us," Meg said flatly, and Erik narrowly managed not to say, "What?" again. "He knows," she continued, "that we're friends. Jammes told him. And he knows you're alive, so I can't let him talk to the managers about you, because if they know you're alive—I can't let him, that's all."

It was for him. She was doing this for him, and he didn't know how to take that fact in, or what to do with it. He carefully set the information to the side, to look at later, and tried a different direction. "How does he know I'm alive?"

She looked down at her hands, toying with her skirts again. "I told him," she said faintly. "I—got scared. And I told him that if he hurt me, you'd kill him. He believed me. I'm so sorry, Erik, I shouldn't have—"

"Don't apologize," Erik said desperately, because it was wrong that she should apologize when he had utterly and completely failed her—he should have been there, he should have…what was the *point* of being a ghost if he didn't protect his only friend? "And you don't have to quit for me, you shouldn't quit for me, and are you sure you don't want me to kill him, because—"

"He didn't hurt me and I'm *fine* and no one needs to die and—and I have to quit." She clenched her hands in the folds of her skirt. "I already quit. This whole mess, this never would have happened to you without me and this—this is how I fix it."

"Nothing would have happened to me in the past year without you," Erik said quietly. "Not the good things either." He would have sat down here, endlessly brooding. At the best.

Her eyes crinkled, too bright. "I'm sorry the cost has been so high."

She really didn't understand, did she? "It's been worth it. More than worth it. And you don't owe me anything. You don't have to—"

"You don't get to decide what I do," she said over him. "And this is what I'm doing. It's done. Please—let's just leave it."

He didn't want to leave it. He wanted to talk her out of it—but he also didn't want to fight again, and he could hear her voice rising. With a valiant effort, he tried to refocus. "All right. All right then. So what happens now? What are you going to do?"

"I don't know. Madame Thibault won't let me actually leave for a week—I told her I'd stay through the special performance that she already has choreographed."

Never, ever, had Erik so fervently blessed Madame Thibault.

"And I don't…really have any plans yet. I suppose—find another job. Or something."

Jobs. "Your mother—she's still working for the Opera, yes?"

She tipped her head slightly, an expression he couldn't quite interpret. "Yes."

He nodded. Good, that was good. Meg would still be coming back, if her mother worked here. It wasn't like she was *leaving* leaving, she was just—things were changing but life was change and—it would be fine. It would all be fine. Eventually. Somehow.

"That's assuming I can find a new job," Meg said slowly, fingers twisting in the fabric of her skirt. "If I can't—then we'll probably have to leave."

"The Opera?"

She looked up at him. "Paris."

No, no, no, that was *leaving*!

Her gaze drifted away again. "Mother has a friend—she offered us work in Bordeaux, last year when Mother was fired. Or we could go back to Leclair with our family, I suppose."

Bordeaux? Leclair? Those were far away. There would be no casual dropping by to discuss music, no afternoon coffees, no strolls by the Seine. That last one was fairly unlikely anyway, but— "I don't think you should leave Paris. Too many changes all at once. I think leaving would definitely be a mistake."

"I may not have a choice, Erik," she said, words sharp. "If I can't find a job, we'll have to leave."

"Why do you need a job at all?" he demanded recklessly.

Her lips tightened. "Because not all of us have drawers full of francs."

Of course. Of course, that was the perfect answer, his hidden drawer with all that money the managers had been paying the Phantom; 20,000 francs every month added up, when he spent only a fraction of it. "If that's what it's about—how much do you need? It's just sitting there—"

"No."

"Really, it is, I don't have plans for it, I'd rather—"

"No, I don't want your money, Erik."

But she needed it, why shouldn't she take it? "But it would solve everything, why not—"

"Because there's a name for girls who take money from men they aren't related to!"

Merde. His face went hot and he tried a frantic verbal retreat. "That's not remotely what I—I wasn't suggesting—" This was all Léon's fault, on so many levels.

"I know." She pressed one hand to her forehead. "I didn't think you meant that, I just...I can't, Erik. I just can't."

"I see." He didn't know whether to be hideously embarrassed or deeply disappointed or—it was too many feelings, all at once. He felt a bit like crawling under his own couch and never coming out, but he also felt like maybe it would all be much easier if he could find some way to be angry with her about this. How could she make him care about her, and then *leave?* He carefully steadied his gaze on the opposite wall, steadied his tone to say, "I trust you'll be good enough to let me know, when your plans have been settled. If you care to inform me."

"Don't do that."

"I'm not doing—"

"You just put your Phantom mask on."

Automatically his hand rose up to touch his white half mask, sitting in its customary place since well before she had come in.

"Not *that* mask," Meg said. "The other one, the one where you go all stiff and cold and distant. Don't do that. Not with me."

She really was miraculous. He felt his shoulders sag; he hadn't noticed tensing them. What was he supposed to do, without this woman who actually understood him? He suddenly knew what he was feeling, more strongly than anything else. "If you leave...I'm going to miss you."

She blinked twice, and were her eyes wet? He couldn't be sure; she looked away, rising to her feet. "I should be going—I wanted to tell you about all this, but Mother wouldn't have expected me to be gone this long so she'll be worrying and—I should go."

He rose awkwardly to his feet. "I could walk you out..."

"I know the way, thank you," she said, turning away.

"You will let me know, won't you? About your plans?" Maybe she wouldn't leave Paris after all. The sick feeling in the pit of his stomach didn't believe in that rosy possibility though.

"Of course," she said, and in another moment was out the door and gone.

He stared at that closed door for a long time. He really should be used to this by now. How many times had his world shattered already?

Erik did not take the news well. Much worse than the ballet girls had taken it. In a guilt-tinged way, I was glad. I wouldn't like to think that it wouldn't matter to him, my leaving. Though I had felt awful having to tell him about it.

I suspected I was going to feel awful for most of the next several days, these last days at the Opera.

By the time I was halfway back to the prop room, I wished I had taken the short cut out to the Rue Scribe. I wouldn't miss this long trek through the dark tunnels, up the stone stairs, if I stopped making it.

Except the thought made my stomach turn, because if I wasn't making this journey anymore—that would mean I was losing so much else, too.

I stared at the shadowed passage ahead of me, thought of the corridors and stairs still ahead. I definitely should have taken the shortcut out. This way gave me too much time to think.

Not being at the Opera anymore didn't mean never seeing Erik again. It just meant…things would change. In ways I couldn't define yet. Life didn't even have to change in bad ways.

So I kept telling myself, but I wasn't convinced by the time I put out my lantern and stepped through the secret door into the prop room. I swung the wall of masks closed again, and tried to calculate the fastest route out through the very different labyrinth of the aboveground Opera.

I didn't calculate the best route.

I tried to go by way of the grand marble stair, but had descended only a few steps when I realized who was standing on the broad landing, near one of the posts.

Jammes, leaning back against the post, and Léon, standing a little too close to her. His head was bent towards her, and she was smiling.

Maybe I was a coward, but I turned around and retreated back up the steps, to find another way home.

Chapter Nineteen

A limited quantity of things could be done at three in the morning, but it was the perfect time to break into the Parisian home of the de Troyes family.

Erik had identified the building weeks earlier, just in case he ever needed the information. Tonight it took some further investigation to find the right room, but he had been walking silently through occupied buildings for years. When it was occupied by sleepers, it was even simpler.

And so Léon de Troyes was awakened in the deep dark of the night to the banging of his window, wide open and swinging back and forth in the wind. He awoke cursing, struggled out of bed while making rude comments about the maid, and stumbled over to close the window. Then he fell silent, transfixed by what appeared to be a pair of glowing yellow eyes on the balcony outside.

Erik knew that's what they looked like; he'd gone to a deal of trouble with the illusion.

After a few seconds Léon muttered another curse and yanked the rustling curtains closed.

From the far corner of the room, wrapped in shadows, Erik asked, "Are you the sort who believes monsters go away if you can't see them?"

Léon gave a gratifying yelp, whirling around and backing right up into the curtains with a rustle and a thump. The curtains thrashed as he disentangled himself. "Who—what?"

"It's the monsters you *can't* see," Erik continued, "that are the real danger." He stepped away from the wall, glided silently along the perimeter of the room, was in quite a different place by the time Léon managed to fumble and clatter a candle alight.

"Show yourself," Léon growled, thrusting the candle towards the direction of the voice, revealing the empty corner.

"And then there's the monsters who don't look like monsters." Erik sent his voice into the empty patch of light Léon was gaping at. "The ones who smile and laugh and charm young women—until they don't get what they want."

Léon turned, sending the candlelight skittering around the room as he looked one direction and another. "Who *are* you?"

"Surely you can guess who I am. You're not quite that stupid." Erik moved in front of the banked embers of the fire, knowing his black cloak would lend him the appearance of a living shadow. "Did you think it was only the Opera I could haunt?"

"What is this about? Why are you *here*?"

Erik gritted his teeth. Did the man have so little respect for Meg that he actually had to ask this question? "*Obviously* this is about Mademoiselle Giry."

"I didn't hurt her," Léon protested.

"You had plans for her. And you did not like it when those plans were refused."

"It's over, all right?" Léon said, plainly trying for defiance, plainly missing the mark. "You want her? You can have her. I have girls lined up and waiting, I don't need Meg. There's this pretty little dancer I'm already—"

"Your conquests are irrelevant," Erik said coldly, keeping a tight rein on his fury. How dare this ridiculous, arrogant imbecile talk about Meg as though she didn't even matter? "Your flirtation with Meg is over because *she* said so. And *I* say you will never speak to her or of her ever again. In fact, you will take great pains to ensure you never even see her again."

"You just come in here—and to threaten me—I could yell right now and have a dozen people in here—"

"Through your bolted door?" Erik said. He turned his back on Léon, reached for a fire poker and stirred the crackling embers. "I could kill you before they even reach the door, let alone before they get it open."

The words lingered without response, as Erik listened to the faint noise of Léon trying to walk soundlessly.

"If you believe you can sneak up on me," he said conversationally, "you're stupider than I thought after all."

Léon abandoned stealth and charged. Erik turned at the calculated last moment, catching Léon by the throat. The other man flailed wildly, barely managing a glancing blow, as Erik slammed him down hard into the armchair by the fire. He pinned him with one forearm on his chest and leaned in close.

"Give me one reason," he hissed, "why I shouldn't kill you. Go on. Try."

"I didn't hurt her!" Léon gasped, twisting ineffectually. "I didn't— Meg said, if I did, that you—but I *didn't*."

"Meg is more forgiving than I am. She imagines you have positive qualities, and she also overrates the depth of my mercy. You didn't hurt her—but you wanted to. And you scared her. And that is enough reason for me."

"No, please," Léon protested. "You can't—"

"Of course I can," Erik said, leaning harder on Léon's chest. "Easily. But Meg asked me not to. I want you to fully and entirely appreciate that that is the *only* reason you're going to survive this conversation."

The idea that he was not going to die penetrated into Léon's mind, judging by the way he slumped in the chair, relaxing his struggling.

In one movement Erik released him, turned away, snatched up the poker he had left in the fire and turned back with it raised, tip radiating heat. "I could scar your face. That would interfere with your amorous pursuits. But I prefer a subtler approach."

Léon gave one strangled gasp of horror and tried to scramble sideways out of the chair. Erik caught him with his free hand, shoving him back into place even as he brought the poker down and drew a burning line down the inside of Léon's thigh.

Léon shrieked. Erik threw the poker back into the fire with a clatter, clamped a hand over Léon's mouth and leaned over him as he thrashed and squirmed. Noise was already starting up elsewhere in the house.

"Listen very closely," Erik thundered over Léon's muffled cries. "You tell anyone who asks, police included, that you just had a terrible accident. If you *ever* go near Meg again—if you ever hurt any woman—I will find out, and I will be back. And the next time you have an accident, I'll aim higher."

Erik shoved Léon's head back, using the leverage to turn and leap for the window. Pounding was starting at the door. Wrapped in his cloak, he hit the curtains and the window behind them shoulder first. The unlatched windows crashed open, the curtains billowing out into the cold night air and he went out with them, running by the time his feet hit the balcony.

Chapter Twenty

I arrived Wednesday morning for practice, expecting another day that I could at least pretend was ordinary. The ballet girls were clustered into intense conference in the practice room when I walked in. It did not bode well when Juliette looked up, saw me, and grabbed Francesca's arm. Francesca looked over, made a hasty hushing gesture, and everyone suddenly went silent and wouldn't meet my gaze. Not even Adalisa.

Grand. I gritted my teeth and strolled over to them, because I might as well confront this instead of pretending I hadn't noticed anything. At least I had enough courage for that. "Good morning," I said as pleasantly as I could manage.

There was a moment of silence, an awkward, "Good morning," from somewhere in the group, and then Francesca was demanding, "Is it *true*?"

I wasn't certain, but hadn't she been there yesterday when I said I was leaving? If she knew about that already, what was she talking about? "Do you mean that I quit my position with the ballet?" I asked, even though I doubted it, even though my stomach was twisting nervously.

"No!" she said with an impatient gesture. "That you were consorting with the Phantom!"

Being ill suddenly became a very real possibility. "I don't— where did you hear that?" I asked, heart pounding in my ears. If Léon went to the management after all, if he told them everything, if they talked to Mifroid... "Did Léon say something?"

She waved a hand. "*Everyone's* saying it." All around her, girls murmured agreement.

I might have been disturbed by the idea that this story was already so widespread—but I was too scared to see this as anything but useless information. *Everyone* was always the source for any piece of gossip. "But did Léon start it?" I persisted, digging my fingernails into my palms.

"Never mind where it started," Isabelle said, an ugly frown on her face. "Is it *true?*"

"No," I snapped. "But Léon said he was going to spread that lie when we—ended things." Somehow, I still didn't want to share the details of just how it had all ended. It was too hard to talk about, too humiliating.

What I had said received a moment of considering silence. Then Francesca said slowly, "But your mother *was* the Phantom's boxkeeper before he died."

"Francesca, she *said* it wasn't true," Adalisa snapped, taking a half-step closer to me.

"But she's always been strange about the Phantom," Francesca countered, "you know that."

"She has said," Juliette murmured, "about how maybe he's not so bad."

"And how could she believe that unless something was going on?" Isabelle asked. "Considering she's Christine Daaé's friend."

"I'm right *here,* you know," I said loudly. "And this is all completely ridiculous."

"And she was upset, when they found the Phantom's body," Francesca added.

"I was *with you,* when we all went marching on his home," I countered, trying to find some kind of defense.

"And...you were upset when he drowned," Adalisa said, eyes confused and alarmed.

I was in trouble, if even Adalisa started believing this story. "You know this is silly!" I protested. "Why would I have *consorted* with the Phantom of the Opera?" But how convincing could I be, when everything they were saying was perfectly true? I reached up to touch my gold necklace, some kind of anchor in this new crisis.

"I thought you were upset because of Christine," Adalisa went on, "but if that wasn't it—if it was about him…"

"Girls!" Madame Thibault said sharply. I hadn't even noticed her entering the room, possibly the first time that had ever happened. "That is enough gossip; let us try to make time for dancing."

We all scattered, all hurrying off to our appropriate places. I didn't move as quickly as the rest, trying to get my mind around this new crisis. I had resigned, Léon had no reason to go to the managers— but if he had, what did they know about Erik? What were they going to *do*?

I missed a step, jostled by Jammes as she passed me towards the barre. "So glad you gave us notice before you left," she hissed in my ear. "I'd hate to have lost the opportunity to let them know what you're *really* like." She tossed her head in the air and strutted off, likely quite pleased with herself.

But I was exhaling with relief. Jammes, not Léon. Jammes had spread the word, and whether it was with Léon's permission or not didn't really matter. Just as long as Léon didn't go to the managers, to the police, as long as he didn't match up his stories with theirs. Erik was still safe. And for me—I was already leaving. When the world's already ending, what else can they do to you?

I held onto that happy thought for perhaps two hours. Just for the length of the practice, when we all had to focus on our dancing instead of each other. Madame Thibault was her usual harsh taskmaster, but if she had heard the rumors about me or cared if she did, it didn't show.

It was so normal that I could almost forget, let habits take over again. When practice ended, I turned automatically to the other girls for discussions on plans, perhaps to arrange doing something for the afternoon before the performance.

No one would meet my eye. Not any of them.

I swallowed, not surprised that at least some of them would believe the rumors, would turn their backs on me. But all of them?

Every one of them turned away—Jammes smirking, Francesca already in whispered conference with two friends, many girls looking scornful, Adalisa looking sad. All of them walked away together.

Perhaps I wouldn't spend the afternoon at the Opera. Perhaps I'd take myself out into the boulevards, where surely the opinions of the Opera Company would seem to weigh less. Where at least no one would know the reason why, if I let my bruised feelings show on my face.

Maybe if I had lingered, Erik would have stepped out of a wall and I could have spent the afternoon with him. But I wasn't sure I wanted to see him, to add the usual sting of his blindness about me onto the fresh hurt of the ballet girls' rejection. He should be told that our secret was out—but if he was paying any attention at all, he could hardly have missed this new rumor sweeping the corps de ballet.

Erik spent most of Wednesday pacing his parlor and playing music in minor key. Finally, late in the afternoon, he hit on what he was sure was the perfect solution, the answer to everything. He hurried directly to Box Five. Sooner or later the management was going to notice that there had been a clerical error in selling (or rather, not selling) Box Five—but as long as it wasn't tonight, he could put that out of his mind.

He waited impatiently for Madame Giry to arrive. When she finally did, he listened from inside his hollow pillar as she moved around the box. The usual rhythm seemed unbearably slow today. Finally, a faint scrape of paper against polished wood, and he knew she had picked up the envelope he'd left for her. There was one footstep, and then silence. The envelope looked normal enough, but on feeling it she must have noticed its unusual thickness.

After a moment, the rustle of paper, of an envelope being opened and bills rifled through. 20,000 francs, in thousand franc notes.

There was an even longer silence, and he waited in tense nervousness for her to just take the money out of Box Five, settling the matter.

Instead, she cleared her throat and said, "I can't accept this unless you can explain exactly what you think you're buying, Monsieur Phantom."

Erik dropped his head into his hands. Why was it so impossible to *help* someone? Why did everyone have to assume a dark motive? Surely she didn't class him with the likes of Léon too? "I am not trying to buy anything," he projected out to the box. "I don't want *anything*. I just— want to help, and Meg refused to take money from me."

This silence seemed to stretch for eons. At last, the folding sound of an envelope re-closing, a rustle of paper sliding into a pocket. "Very well. Thank you for your generosity, Monsieur."

He didn't respond, half-afraid he'd somehow make her change her mind. He wasn't being generous. The money was no sacrifice for him. And he'd give much, much more to keep Meg in Paris.

Footsteps, then another pause, without the expected opening of the door. And then Madame Giry asked, "Did you take care of Léon?"

Erik smiled grimly in the darkness. "Yes."

"Good." The door opened, and closed again behind her.

Erik leaned back against the wall. At least he and Madame Giry understood each other about something.

It was not any better that evening, before, during or after the performance. No one tried to run me out of town, perhaps because they didn't have definite proof—but no one would talk to me either. And Erik didn't appear in any shadows.

I didn't go to the Dance Foyer. I didn't want to see Léon, with or without Jammes, and I didn't want to see any of the girls who were now shunning me. The girls I had known for years, who I had always thought liked me.

I had thought they were my friends. Like I had thought Christine was my friend.

Mother was waiting to meet me just outside the ballet's changing room. I had dressed quickly, making sure I wouldn't be the last one there.

"There seems to be a new rumor flying about the Opera," Mother said carefully, studying my face as we fell into step together.

I grimaced. "That I've been involved in illicit activity with the Phantom?" Right from the beginning they'd accused me of 'consorting' with him, but the comments were getting more direct. Not so much *to* me as within my hearing.

"I told everyone the very idea was ridiculous, of course," Mother said, taking my arm.

"Of course," I said dully. It wouldn't matter. They might stop talking about the topic near Mother, but they wouldn't stop talking to each other. So much for protecting my reputation by quitting before Léon could spread any stories. I supposed I ought to care about that. Mostly I just felt…bruised. It was all so ugly. So stupid.

And both true and not true, in infuriating ways. It didn't seem fair, that I could be accused of all kinds of scandalous activities when I'd never had the chance to so much as kiss Erik.

I didn't make that comment to Mother. But I did pour out my other woes on the subject, about Jammes and how terrible the ballet girls were being.

I didn't mention either that I hadn't even seen Erik today. Even though we were talking about the Phantom, somehow we didn't talk about Erik.

Mother was sympathetic, but practical too. "Of course it's an unpleasant way to end your time at the Opera," she said as we arrived home, as I finally began to run out of unhappy details to tell. "But it doesn't make any tangible difference, since you were leaving anyway."

"I suppose not," I sighed. It felt like a difference though.

"Although—if word spreads through the artistic community, it could be harder to obtain a position at another theatre in Paris."

"I hadn't even thought of that," I groaned, flopping onto our couch and rubbing my eyes. I stared up at the ceiling. "I know I brought it all on myself, I made choices that led to this, but…" But it was still hard.

I had been secretly, quietly hoping we might at least stay in Paris. I might at least still see Erik, sometimes. Sneak back in through the Rue Scribe. Maybe I couldn't go back to the Opera Garnier, but I could see the Opera's Phantom.

Only I suppose I had known that wouldn't happen. That wasn't how this story would go.

I'd known all along the risk I was running, but I hadn't known how horrible it could all end up being. I hadn't known a year ago, how much more gut-wrenching the thought of being forced to leave the city would feel this year, compared to last year. "You'll want to go to Bordeaux, won't you?" I had been carefully avoiding the subject since yesterday, but I couldn't dodge it now. And it made sense. Outside of Paris, no one else would care about the Phantom. A scandal with a subscriber would have been universally understood; a scandal involving a ghost would be easily dismissed as nonsense anywhere else.

"Perhaps," Mother said, sitting down next to me. "But I think we might do better than Bordeaux." She folded her hands in her lap, face quite impassive. "I've been looking at our finances. I think we can manage a trip somewhere. Some time spent abroad. Not indefinitely of course, we'd have to return to Paris, or Leclair, or Bordeaux eventually. But perhaps a few months. Wasn't it Vienna you always said you wanted to visit?"

I might not normally have left her talking on for that many sentences, but I was trying to assimilate this new shock. "We…can't afford that," I said finally. "We've never been able to afford something like that." I knew this. I had always, always wanted to do something like that, and it had never been in the realm of possibility.

Mother's expression didn't change, and her hands didn't move. "I assessed our finances, and I believe it would be possible. We have been frugal for many years, and have been saving. This may be the right opportunity. The right moment."

I didn't know all the details of our finances, true. But months abroad in Vienna, neither of us working? We couldn't afford that. So I stopped asking questions about it. As long as she didn't explain, I had plausible deniability. The money could be from—anywhere.

"If we can afford to go to Vienna," I said slowly, twisting my necklace, "we could afford to stay in Paris. Even if I can't find a new job."

Her lips tightened, just a fraction. "You have always spoken of how much you would like to travel."

"Yes…" And I did want to. Part of me. And part of me desperately, desperately wanted nothing but to stay. "But I can't leave…Paris."

Mother looked at me hard and I knew before she spoke that I hadn't fooled her. "You're not really thinking about Paris, are you?"

I looked down at my hands, let my necklace go and twined my fingers together in my lap. "How can I do that to him?"

She sighed. "You are not doing anything *to* him. You are making a choice about *your* life."

"I know, but…"

She reached out and wrapped one hand around mine. "Meg, listen to me. If you are happy right now, *truly*, and if this is what you want for your life, if you can honestly tell me that, then we'll stay in Paris. But I want you to seriously think about whether it would be better to start fresh somewhere else."

Was I happy? Such a simple, complicated question. Not at this moment, but I knew that wasn't what she was asking about. She meant something bigger, and the answer to that was…no. And yes. Because when I was around Erik lately, I was both the happiest and the most miserable I had ever been.

Leaving would break my heart. But staying was already doing that.

I took a breath. "So. Vienna, you were thinking?"

Something in her eyes relaxed, in a very subtle relief. "Yes. I think Vienna would be an excellent choice. So much music and culture."

So at least there would be good musical accompaniment for my heartbreak.

I had been dreaming of traveling, of Vienna specifically, for what felt like my entire life. I tried to remember that feeling, to find that fire of excitement and adventure. It was still there—but all I could feel right now was the faintest flicker, and all I could say was, "Good. That's good." Which didn't fool her at all. We both knew exactly what I was thinking of, and it wasn't Vienna.

Eyes unusually soft, Mother reached out to squeeze my hand. "There will be someone else. Someone who sees how special you are."

Everything in me clamored that I didn't *want* someone else. But maybe I would, someday. Even if I did, I didn't share Mother's confidence that this mythical person would materialize. "Unless I'm not special."

"That's nonsense," she said, a more usual sharpness entering her tone.

"Why?" I dragged the back of my hand across my eyes. "The truth is that I've never been important to anyone. Léon doesn't think I'm good enough to marry. Erik clearly feels I don't compare to Christine. And the closest friend I ever had vanished with only a two-sentence letter to say good-bye. I'm not beautiful and I'm not especially talented at anything and I'm not special to anyone but you— and you're my *mother,* so you're biased."

"No," she countered, "it means that I see you more clearly than anyone else does."

"But I'm *not*—"

"And you were always special to Gabrielle."

My eyes, already pricking, brimmed up with tears. We almost never talked about my sister. "But maybe she wouldn't think so," I whispered. "Not anymore." I could hardly remember who I had been, all those years ago, when my little sister thought I was as magical as…as the Phantom of the Opera.

"Of course she would," Mother said firmly, reaching out to hug me. I rested my head against her shoulder. "Of course she would, my Little Meg."

Chapter Twenty-One

Excerpt from the Private Notebook of Jean Mifroid, Commissaire of Police

24 May, 1882

New rumors at Opera Garnier re: connection between Meg Giry and Opera Ghost. Long suspected same, but no proof or useful information gained in conversations with Giry.

Things always looked better in the morning. Not better enough that I was happy—but better enough that I was calm. Resigned. Feeling like I could at least live with a choice, even if it wasn't a perfect one. It didn't feel quite so unrelentingly hopeless, in the sunshine.

As I walked through the morning light to the Opera for ballet practice, I wondered how Erik ever found the courage to face anything, living in darkness.

And I wondered if I would ever be able to stop thinking things like that.

Mother was right. I needed to go somewhere new, live a different kind of life. This one hurt too much. And Vienna *was* exciting. If I couldn't have one dream, *the* one dream that I wanted most of all, then I ought to be grateful that I could have another one.

It was easy to feel that it was time to leave during ballet practice, a long one as we prepared for the upcoming special performance. The whole thing was a nightmare of averted gazes and scornful comments made in what the speakers knew perfectly well was within my earshot.

It was harder to believe in the benefit of leaving Paris when practice ended, and I had to go tell Erik about it. I had meant to visit his apartment, but didn't have to walk that far. I hardly stepped into the empty prop room before I heard a voice behind me say, "Good morning."

Even *now*, it was that easy for him to make my heart race. It didn't seem fair. Maybe that's why I said, "Not very," as I turned around.

I regretted it, because for just a second I could see an almost hopeful expression on his face, before it faded away and his shoulders sagged. "Nothing's…looking brighter?"

What a strange reversal of roles. How often had I been the one preaching optimism to him? And some things *did* look brighter. Just, not right at this moment, fresh from the ballet girls' rejection, when I was about to tell him… I seized on the memory of the ballet girls instead, trying ridiculously to avoid the inevitable for another few moments. "I suppose you've heard?"

He blinked, looked doubtful. "About…?"

He didn't know. If he had known, he couldn't possibly fail to realize what I meant.

Where had he been for the past day? How did the man who always knew everything about the Opera Garnier possibly miss *this*? Somehow I felt resentful that he wasn't omniscient. That apparently the shunning and the veiled comments and the open remarks had been only mine to deal with.

"Our secret's out," I said bluntly. "The Company knows about us." That seemed suddenly to suggest something more than I meant, more than we were, and I hastened to add, "That we're friends. Not that you're alive, but that we were friends before."

I watched Erik's eyes shift as he processed this, waited for some expression of sympathy. "I *told* you I should have killed Léon."

That was not sympathy. I just shook my head. "No, not Léon. Jammes spread the word." Maybe Léon told her to, but it hardly mattered.

"Oh." Erik frowned for a moment, sighed. "I can't kill her."

"Nice to know you have standards," I said dryly.

"Of course." He sat down on a stray trunk, rubbing the back of his neck. "What is the Company doing about it?"

I slowly sat down on a fringed footstool that was part of some Italian opera. "Just the usual things they do when they get someone between their claws. I mean, they can't *do* anything. They can't fire me. So they're just—being nasty about it."

He winced, and I felt better to see remorse now on his face. "I'm so sorry. This is my fault. They hate *me*, not you, and you shouldn't have to—"

"I knew the risks," I interrupted, swinging around to wanting to reassure him almost as soon as he set in to comfort me. "I started it all. I practically coerced you into becoming friends with me."

"Yes, well." He kicked one heel against the base of the trunk, looking down. "I'm glad you did."

My throat ached and my eyes were getting hot again. Why did he have to be *nice*? Why did he have to show me he cared about me, if he couldn't care about me the way I wanted him to? I swallowed hard, stared harder at the fake galleon looming up behind him, and we were silent for a long few moments.

"So..." Erik said finally, peeking up at me. "Any more plans made?"

Plans. The real reason I had to talk to him. The conversation I'd been scripting in my mind all night, without getting to a satisfactory version. "Yes," I said, and plunged recklessly on to, "Mother and I are going to Vienna."

I could see him struggling not to say "what." He froze, staring at me, and his mouth actually opened and closed once before he finally said, "Vienna?"

"Yes." I nodded, very firmly. "I always wanted to go there, you know, and Mother decided we could afford it."

"Oh, she decided that, did she?" he said with an odd twist to his mouth.

If he told me he gave her the money—I was going to have to refuse it, there was nothing else I could do. I had enough self-respect left for that. But I couldn't make myself ask him—and instead of confessing anything like that he just said again, "Vienna. Well. That's…lovely."

"I think it will be," I agreed. Someday.

"When do you leave?" he asked in a low voice.

"I don't know exactly—we need to make plans, and I'm supposed to be at the Opera through Tuesday. But maybe…a couple of weeks?"

"So, fourteen days," he said with a marked intensity to the words.

"Something like that." Was he planning to count it down? Now that he'd put the idea into my head, I knew I wouldn't be able to stop myself from doing the same. I tried to rally some kind of cheer. "You know, it's not that far away." Only a thousand kilometers, more or less, and most of three countries. "I'll write. And visit."

He smiled, though it wasn't much of a smile. "That would be…very nice."

So this was what he was supposed to hold onto now? The promise of a letter, of a probably mythical visit? How was that supposed to be enough?

He had barely managed a week without her at Easter—no, he hadn't even managed it, he'd gone looking for her halfway through—and those days after the mob, even with everything else to distract him, he had missed her so much then—and now he was supposed to somehow survive *forever?*

This was not what was supposed to happen. This was not what he had intended, and he did not have the patience to wait until the next performance to confront Madame Giry about it. Thursday to Saturday was far too long. She was at the Opera today, cleaning boxes. He knew which were hers, and it was easy to slip into the next one on her route.

Then he waited in the shadows. She barely had the door shut before he stood up to face her. "I did not give you that money so you could take Meg out of the country," he growled.

Madame Giry sounded neither surprised nor alarmed as she said, "You included no conditions and no requests. You were buying nothing and you wanted nothing. Those were your exact words, Monsieur Phantom. I presumed that you wanted done what would be best for Meg. As do I."

"And going to Vienna is best for her?" he demanded. "What's wrong with staying in Paris?"

"Meg has always wanted to travel."

He knew that. He had talked to her about that, so many times. He knew he was being selfish, but...how could he face this? "I know I said I didn't want anything, but I thought—she was going to go to Bordeaux if there wasn't any money, and I thought..."

"Now there is money, and she's going to Vienna."

The common factor was *leaving*, and it wasn't hard for Erik's paranoia to take him to a conclusion. He sank into the nearest seat. "Tell me the truth; are you trying to get her away from me?" A new, horrible thought occurred. "Is *she* trying to get away from me?" No. Why would she? She was his friend—maybe he shouldn't have made that comment about killing Léon, but she had seemed to understand.

"Not everything is about you, Monsieur," Madame Giry said crisply, so reprovingly that he almost, but not quite, missed what was absent from that response.

"That doesn't answer the question," he pointed out. Was it because of the ballet girls gossiping? Maybe Meg had finally been swayed by their opinions of him. But no. That was absurd.

"Do you really want to know the truth?" Madame Giry sighed, but her voice was unsympathetic as she said, "I think it is best if Meg has some distance from you."

Disaster. "You think I'm bad for her." Of course she thought that. She must have always thought it, he had just deluded himself after all these months that perhaps they understood each other somehow.

"Yes. I think you're bad for her." She paused as though expecting him to comment, but he had nothing to say to that. Nothing at all. "I don't think it for the reasons you no doubt believe. But it is doing her no good spending all of her time with a man for whom she will always be *not-Christine*."

This was so unexpected that Erik found himself gaping at Madame Giry. This was not one of the dozen reasons he could think of for her to be worried about him being around Meg. This was—he didn't even know what this meant. "But that's—that's ridiculous. I don't think of her that way!"

"Really?" Madame Giry's voice was glacial. "You were convinced Léon didn't appreciate her. I suggest *you* take a good look in the mirror."

"I don't look in mirrors," he said automatically. He already knew too well what he would see.

And how dare she accuse him of not appreciating Meg?

"The matter is closed, Monsieur Phantom," Madame Giry said, calmly but definitively. "I wish you well, truly. But this decision is what is best for my daughter, and if you care about her, you won't interfere."

That gave him a sick twist of guilt. "There must be another way."

This time she did sound just the slightest bit regretful as she said, "No. There isn't." For a moment, there was only silence. Then she said, "Good day, Monsieur Phantom," and left him alone in the box.

He slumped back in his seat.

This was going to happen and he couldn't change it. There was nothing he could do. Was there?

He could kidnap her. Erik briefly imagined that. Getting Meg below the Opera would be easy enough. Locking the doors, or blocking a tunnel…he could do that too. It wouldn't be hard to get in and out himself by alternate routes for supplies.

It was all perfectly possible. The practical details all seemed quite reasonable.

Where he got stuck was in how he would explain it to Meg. He tried to picture telling her that he was kidnapping her, and groaned.

It was no good. She'd laugh at him. And if he locked the doors and she couldn't get out and actually got upset, then she'd yell at him. Still not the goal.

Which begged the question, what exactly *was* the goal?

Not losing Meg, that was the easy answer. But it was a more complicated question, because he didn't want to lose...the way it felt between them, and kidnapping her would ruin everything even more completely than if she left town.

Also Madame Giry would kill him. There was that.

Maybe he could follow her to Vienna. Would that be disturbing? He was almost sure that would be disturbing. Could he somehow raise the idea hypothetically and see if *she* thought it was disturbing? She was much better than he was at knowing what was normal.

She was much better than he was at a lot of things. Oh, not writing music or magic tricks or speaking six languages. But many skills that mattered much more.

He hadn't told her that enough. And now, he wasn't going to have the time. He had fourteen days, and a lifetime of things to say.

Chapter Twenty-Two

I began packing Friday afternoon. It was not a cheering activity, but Mother was out on errands and I could either flop on my bed, stare at the ceiling and brood, or I could drag out the trunk I took to Leclair every year and start packing whatever I wouldn't need for the rest of our time in Paris. For the next thirteen days, more or less. After I told Erik about going to Vienna, we had agreed to meet in Box Five this evening. That left me a dreary, empty afternoon to fill until then.

I hauled the trunk out from under my bed, then opened the top drawer of my dresser. I was greeted by a muddle of ribbons and old Opera programs and handkerchiefs and empty perfume bottles and endless other nonsense I never even noticed anymore, just pushed aside to get to whatever I needed.

I sighed and started piles on the bed of things to pack and things to throw out.

More of the programs were smoothed out and packed into the trunk than probably should have been. But they were all tangled up with memories, of dances and operas and even eras in my life.

It was harder to let go of those tangible symbols just when everything around me was about to change. When I had to let go of the Opera Garnier, of dancing, of Paris.

Of Erik.

I unbent a corner of a program for *Carmen,* stared at the beautiful singer depicted on the cover, and told myself this was how it should be—how it was supposed to be. The Phantom of the Opera had been the symbol throughout my childhood of the impossible, the magical, the wonderful. Now it was time to grow up. To let go of childish fantasies.

I put the program in the trunk, reached out for the book sitting on top of my nightstand. *Around the World in 80 Days.* Erik's Christmas gift to me. I ran my fingertips over the embossed cover, felt my throat go tight. I opened it up to where I had pressed one of the daffodils he gave me after the mob.

I didn't want the symbol. I didn't want the ghost or the magician. I wanted the *man*, the real person, the one who wrote music and told stories about Rome and lit candles by snapping his fingers, but also the man who needed courage to walk through a crowd, who didn't understand the fear of the dark, who struggled with the ghosts of his own past and who missed me over the long Easter holiday.

I could let go of the Phantom. Letting go of Erik was something else entirely.

Slowly I closed the book, set it down inside the trunk too. For a man who had loomed so large in my life for so long, I had few mementos of Erik. A novel and a flower. A handful of notes and letters I kept in the empty box that had once held chocolates he gave me for my birthday.

I didn't have anything that had ever been his. No necklace I could wear to help me remember.

Maybe that was better. If I was going to…move on.

Wherever I went, whatever happened, I was never going to meet another man like Erik. I tried telling myself *that* was better too. It would be better to meet a different man, one who was less complicated, less haunted, one who smiled easily, who laughed and knew how to have a casual conversation with a stranger on the street.

But that man wouldn't tell stories about faraway places, or do tricks of illusion to make me smile, or write music that haunted my soul. He wouldn't make me fall in love with him by whispering that he had missed me on an Easter morning.

I reached back into the trunk for my book, replaced it on the nightstand. Maybe I wouldn't pack it yet.

A knock at the front door at that moment made me jump, then exhale with something like relief. I could use a distraction. I went to answer the door, trying to shake away cobwebs of thought.

I felt the tiniest thrill as I touched the door handle. It *could* be Erik. But it probably wasn't. It was probably only the postman. I turned the handle and wrenched open the door.

"Hello, *chérie*, it's so lovely to see you!" Christine said, flashing a perfectly brilliant smile.

I stared at her with not the slightest idea what to say. My best friend who had vanished in the night so long ago, suddenly standing on my doorstep.

I had given up hoping for even a letter months ago, had never had much hope that she'd return in person. And as I stood in the doorway and looked at beautiful Christine Daaé, I realized that somewhere along the way I had even begun to actively *not* want her to come back.

I even knew when that had happened. Right around Easter.

"Christine," I managed finally. "How…unexpected."

"Oh, I suppose I should have written to you I was coming, but I couldn't resist a surprise!" she said merrily, sweeping right past me into the room.

I slowly shut the door, just in time to have a free hand when she took off her fur wrap and handed it to me. It was heavy, incredibly soft, and probably expensive. I took a surreptitious glance at her stomach, flat beneath her red silk dress. Not expecting a child, then, and probably hadn't had one already. Considering she had run away with Raoul more than a year ago, it had seemed like a possibility.

She took off her gloves and handed them to me with her left hand, giving me an unavoidable view of the diamond ring on her finger. It also looked heavy and expensive.

We didn't have a coat closet or a receiving room or whatever, so I just laid the coat and gloves on a chair. I had barely set them down before Christine was hugging me tightly. "It's *so* good to see you!" she trilled. "I just can't wait to tell you all the news!"

I made myself smile, pat her back, tried to lower my shoulders that had suddenly gone up nearly to my ears. I extricated myself from the hug quickly. "So you and Raoul got married," I said, not a question at this point, just trying to get to the heart of the matter.

"Yes, of course, the day after we left Paris," Christine said, and sat down pertly on the edge of the couch. The light shone on her brown curls, caught up on her head in a style that was the height of fashion and wouldn't work at all with my straight hair.

I sat down too, unable to stop staring at her. She was *here*, and I had no idea what to say or do or think or feel— "Congratulations," I said. But I didn't want to talk about her marriage, her happy life of the last year, not after she had left with barely a word—that's what I felt, I was *angry* with her. "About when you left Paris—"

"And Raoul has been such a dear," she said, beaming. "I just couldn't be happier. Except for one *little* problem."

I was supposed to ask her what it was. Only, I didn't care. I had problems too, after all, and she hadn't asked about them, not now or in all those months since I'd seen her last. She hadn't bothered to send even *one* letter. "Is that so," I said flatly.

"Yes." She smoothed out her rich red skirts, still smiling at me. "You see, I feel so badly over the Phantom."

Whatever I'd been planning to say about how she left went right out of my head. "You feel badly..." I scrambled to make this not mean what I didn't want it to mean. She had said she was happy with Raoul; she couldn't regret leaving with him, marrying him. Couldn't regret leaving the Phantom behind. What *had* happened the night she left? Erik never talked about it—but Christine had *left him*, she had made a choice that was *not him*, that much was obvious. "I think you did exactly what you had to do," I said. "Nothing else was possible."

"Well, you are a dear to think so well of me," she said, reaching out to squeeze my hand, too tightly. "But still, I think he may have been rather hurt when I left, and I do feel regretful about that."

Regretting hurting Erik, not regretting leaving Erik. I might have actually appreciated that sentiment, if 'rather hurt' wasn't so dramatic an understatement to describe Erik's grief that it took my breath away.

"And now, of course," she went on, "it's too late to do anything at all."

I felt like I kept lagging a moment behind in every new turn of the conversation, constantly trying to puzzle out a missing piece—that had happened sometimes before, hadn't it, when I talked to Christine? Why had I never thought about that? I tried to focus on the moment—it was too late to fix anything because…too much time had passed, too many changes, her marriage to Raoul… And then I realized.

The Phantom was dead. Christine thought he was dead. "You heard about—about the Phantom's death?" There had been news stories. She could have seen one easily.

"It was *so* sad, and must have been *so* difficult for you. After you became such good friends with him."

My jaw went slack. "What?" With a sudden twist I thought of Erik's response, when I told him I was leaving the Opera, and sympathized better. But—how could she know I was friends with Erik? True, rumors were flying at the Opera, but who could she have talked to? The stories had only started two days ago. And who would she have talked to before she came to see me?

Christine smiled sweetly. "Oh, I'm sorry, it was a secret, wasn't it? But you see, Léon told me."

An explanation, but it didn't make me feel better. "Léon," I said numbly. "You've been talking to Léon."

"Well, naturally, Raoul wanted to see him when we came back. Which was just a few days ago!" She squeezed my hand again. "I wouldn't want you to think I didn't rush right over to see you too, just as soon as I could."

Somehow it was embarrassing that she thought I'd worry about that—even more so because she wasn't entirely wrong. But that wasn't what was important here. "But Léon must have told you…" I stopped. Because did I want to tell her, what Léon surely must have told her?

She tipped her head inquisitively. "Told me what, *chérie*?"

"That…it's all over, between us." Because he must have told her that too, even if that wasn't what mattered either. I wondered how much he had said, about how it ended, and what his version of the story had been like.

Immediately Christine's expression welled up with sympathy. "Oh yes, he did mention that. And I'm so *sorry*. I thought you'd be such a nice match. What a pity it didn't work out. But of course, everyone can't be Raoul."

The two utterly absurd ideas of describing what had happened with Léon as *not working out* and that I might *want* someone who was like Raoul collided in my head and left me with very little concept of what to say.

That meant Christine kept talking. "And it must have been such a blow, coming right after the Phantom's death too. I do feel *so* sad about that. I just wish I'd had the opportunity to apologize to him."

I didn't have to tell her. Léon must not have told her. She thought Erik was dead, he didn't know she was back in Paris, she would presumably go back to her new life as the wife of a vicomte (no, comte now, his brother was dead) which had nothing to do with the Opera. She never had to know. *He* never had to know. Two different lives, never meeting. If I could do that to them.

Honestly, I probably *could* do that to her. But I couldn't do that to him.

"Erik's still alive," I said abruptly. Christine's rosebud mouth formed a perfect O, but I kept talking. "He faked it, and the stories aren't true, and he's still alive. He's fine, actually."

"*Oh*," Christine said, and sagged back on the couch, one hand pressed to her chest. "That is *such* a relief—I can't even tell you! I felt so horribly over the whole thing, and the idea that he was dead and I could never try to make things right…and you'll help me now, won't you?" She leaned forward, eyes bright, and reached out to clutch my hand. She kept doing that. "You'll help me find him, won't you, *chérie*?"

It was the inevitable next request. Of course it was exactly what she would ask for. I had *expected* it, there was no reason for it to turn my stomach now. "Yes," I said, lips tight. What else could I do?

Could she make anything better for Erik? Probably not. I remembered how bleak his beautiful green eyes had turned every time her name came up, until I learned not to mention her. How furious he had been, when I had dared to suggest that maybe her departure shouldn't be the end of his life. After all the months I'd watched him grieve, how could I not give her a chance to try to help, however unlikely she was to succeed? "I'm supposed to meet him in a couple of hours. In Box Five."

"Oh, that's so perfect, *chérie*," Christine said with the wide smile I remembered so well. "You are *such* a good friend!" She dived in and hugged me again.

I patted her back and wondered if I was. Not if she broke his heart all over again. Not then. And that seemed as likely as anything else— even with the best of intentions, it would be difficult to avoid—and was I sure she had the best intentions, after all? There had been things that hadn't added up, in those last few days, in the choices Christine had made. But maybe that was just me trying to convince myself, because I didn't want to do this, to let her go see him. To let him see her. But if he ever found out I knew she was back in the city and didn't tell him— that felt like a betrayal.

And this was who I was. The person who wouldn't betray him.

I got myself out of Christine's hold again. "So it's not until later—that gives us time to catch up."

"I want to hear *everything* about the Opera! Is Carlotta still singing?"

We talked about Carlotta, and the chorus, and the latest with the managers, and we didn't actually talk very much about, well, us. Christine didn't volunteer hardly any details about her own past year, and I found myself oddly reluctant to share about my life. I suddenly felt that she wasn't going to understand. Recent events would have meant talking about Léon, and Erik, and I didn't want to talk to Christine about either one.

Before I would have thought it was time to go, Christine rose to her feet. "I had better be leaving, hadn't I? I don't remember the Phantom being a patient man."

I wasn't often late, but he'd never wandered off the rare time when I was. Still, I got up too. "I suppose we can go now."

Christine looked pained. "Oh, *chérie*…I do hope you don't mind, but I really think I'd better have this conversation alone. You understand, don't you?"

No, I did not understand that. I did not like that. That wasn't what I had bargained for when I told her where he would be, and if I didn't go along, perhaps step into the box first to warn him—hadn't I just set him up for an ambush of a sort? "But really I think I—"

"It's all just rather *private*, you know."

That stung. I hadn't been there before. This was part of Erik's life I had never been invited into.

I'd never even heard him say her name.

That fact, not Christine's opinion about it, sent me sinking back onto the couch. What right did *I* have to decide whether she had any right to see him? "Well. Perhaps that's so."

"You see, you're just so understanding!" Christine said delightedly, and swooped in to kiss my cheek. "Raoul is lovely of course, but he simply doesn't understand some things. It's so lucky he's out of town today, and of course I know *you'll* keep a secret. You're so wonderful that way."

Before I could even comment, she had darted over to pick up her coat and gloves, and swept right out the door.

I tried to remember how I had felt a year ago, resentful when Christine went to see the Phantom without me. It had seemed like such a strong, powerful emotion then.

It was nothing compared to now.

I drew my feet up beneath me on the couch, wrapped my fingers around my gold necklace, and stared unseeing out the window.

Chapter Twenty-Three

Thirteen days. He was counting. He wasn't even pretending that he wasn't counting. He knew two weeks had been a vague, semi-schedule that might prove inaccurate, but he was still counting until the day Meg was leaving Paris.

Thirteen days, and the only bright spot at the moment was that she had agreed to meet him this evening. She had also remarked that she should spend the afternoon packing. But the evening, he got the evening. That was valuable. He appreciated that.

He should have told her to meet him in the Grand Foyer. It was hard to pace in Box Five. He was early, she wasn't even supposed to be here yet, but he was pacing anyway.

He heard the door open while his back was to it (he was getting lax, before he would have been more careful about the direction of his pacing) but he couldn't even feel alarm about it. Only glad relief that finally she was here, that he at least had the next hour or two to not be alone. Speaking as he turned, he said, "Oh good, there you—oh."

Erik sank into the nearest red velvet seat and stared at the smiling woman in front of him. "Christine," he said, the name unfamiliar on his tongue.

"Hello," she said, voice warm and soft and exactly the way he remembered it.

She couldn't be here. It was impossible. But she was, looking at him as though she expected him to make conversation with her, even though she was clearly a figment. "I…don't know what to say."

She tilted her head slightly, brown curls catching the light, and suggested, "You could welcome me back to Paris."

"Welcome back to Paris," he said by rote. Probably that meant she had recently returned. Even if he had heard she was in the city, he wouldn't have expected her to come here. He hadn't expected to ever see her again, because surely she would never want to see him. She had left him behind, forever, and this wasn't forever, this had been only—

He realized with a new shock that he didn't know how many days ago she had left.

He had counted every single day, every hour, for more than a year, and somehow, without ever noticing he was stopping, he had just…stopped. When had that happened?

She sat down in the chair next to him, still looking at him as though she expected him to say more. Somewhere along the way, he had worked out all sorts of speeches, for the impossible possibility that she ever did come back. He couldn't remember most of them anymore, and what little he could bring to mind seemed like it must have been influenced by some very bad operas. So what could he say? What should he say?

"Um, how are you?" He glanced at her left hand, saw the large diamond ring. That was as expected, gave him no surprise or any other intense feeling. "And how is Raoul?"

The smile disappeared as fast as a candle blowing out, and with a moan, Christine buried her face in her hands, shoulders shaking.

"I'm sorry!" he said hastily. "I…didn't mean it?" Maybe he should have gone with one of the operatic speeches after all. What had he even said? And had she always been this dramatic? He fumbled about to pull a handkerchief from his pocket, too unsettled to bother with any sleight of hand. She probably wouldn't notice it anyway.

She took the handkerchief, dabbed at her eyes and said, "Raoul doesn't understand me!"

Erik exhaled. "*Oh*. I thought you might say he was dead or—"

"No, no, he wants to stop me from singing! You were so *right*." She reached out and clasped his hands. "You warned me and I didn't listen and now he won't let me sing."

He looked down at their hands and wondered why he suddenly felt so trapped. He flexed one hand and hers tightened, pinching two of his fingers together. "Well," he said, still staring at their entangled fingers, "noblemen's wives usually don't—"

"My voice is a gift that I should be using but he won't listen—and I knew *you* would understand."

That was more than he knew. Why on earth was she here telling him about her marital problems? That was really, wildly none of his business, and he desperately didn't want it to become his business. Although, oddly, not because it was painful to hear but just because it was…awkward. And a lot of trouble he would rather avoid. "I'm sorry, I don't quite—why did you come—"

"I need help, and I didn't know where else to go."

"I was your best option?" he said, unthinking, because of all the people to for help, surely he had to be at the bottom of her list. When she stared at him, he realized that had probably not been a diplomatic thing to say. "That is…I mean, things didn't end well between us."

"No—but we were such good friends, and after all, it was such a long time ago now—"

"That doesn't change what happened," he protested, and yanked his hands free. "I don't understand why you're here, but you are, and there's something I need to say." If *she* was going to ignore what he had done, then that was all the more reason why *he* shouldn't, because someone had to keep this in perspective.

She dropped her gaze, folded her hands on her lap. "Yes?"

Maybe those speeches he'd planned had been fairly ridiculous, but they had held a few ideas—even if they had involved phrases like throwing himself on her mercy and asking her to find it in her heart etc., etc., well, there had been *something* in there that did need saying even if all of that wasn't the right way to say it. "I need to tell you…" How could he say it? How would he say it if he was talking to Meg? "I am so sorry, for so many things. I lied to you, I threatened you, and it was wrong. And I am sorry for all the ways I scared you or hurt you. And considering all that, I cannot imagine why you would ever speak to me again."

"Well, I don't think it was quite that bad," she said with a smile that felt patronizing. "I mean, you didn't hit me or anything like that."

He blinked. That was supposed to make it all right? "No, I just kidnapped you, and tried to coerce you into marrying me by threatening to blow up the Opera. And I could blame it on, I don't know, temporary insanity or having watched too many operas, but those are just excuses. The fact is, it was wrong and I know that and—"

"You were carried away by your feelings for me," she said with an airy wave of one hand. "And I did provoke you, after all, by planning to run away with Raoul."

Maybe he really was insane. Maybe that was the only explanation. Except—he was so *sure* that Meg would not describe an abduction as being carried away by his feelings. "There's no provocation that can justify *kidnapping* you! And that wasn't love, that was selfishness. I might not know much about love, but that wasn't it."

"Perhaps, but—"

"No, there's no *perhaps* about it! I'm trying very hard not to make excuses here, and you're...making them for me."

She looked at him, eyes wide. "I don't understand. What do you *want* me to do?"

He wasn't sure himself. It wasn't exactly that he wanted her to do anything, it was that he could not fathom why she wasn't angry. Why she wasn't horrified and blaming him and—how could she possibly want to have a friendly conversation? "I don't know," he said finally. "But it doesn't matter because...what I want doesn't matter. I tried to make you feel the way I wanted you to before, and that was wrong too, so...you should feel however you want to feel."

"And I want to forgive you," she said, smile blossoming again. "I want to go back to the way it was, when we were such good friends. And I need your help."

She kept saying that, about being good friends. Had they ever been good friends? There had never been a time when he wasn't lying to her, or scaring her. Or, for that matter, when she hadn't been carrying on with Raoul while swearing the nobleman wasn't important to her. Funny, he hadn't thought about that before.

Still, there had been so much he did wrong—if she was coming to him for help, if there was something he could do to start to make up for it... "What can I do?"

She lowered her gaze again, said softly, "I need some time to think, to make decisions about my life, and I need to be away from Raoul while I do it...but I don't have anywhere to stay."

The possibility of a hotel came to mind, but he was surely the worst person to go to for a hotel recommendation—and that was surely not what she was getting at. There was, really, only one thing she could be getting at, absurd and implausible as it seemed. "You want to stay under the Opera?"

There was that smile again—a dispassionate corner of his mind noted the way it seemed to turn on and off like an electric light—and she clasped her hands together. "Oh, that would be so perfect! I think it's so essential that I be somewhere I can really focus on my singing, on what's most important to me. And I just knew *you* would understand."

She kept saying that too. She clearly had no idea how confused he was by this entire situation. He needed to talk to Meg, maybe she could explain this to him—Meg. He was supposed to be meeting Meg. It had to be past the time by now, and she hadn't come. Something must have delayed her.

"Shall we go?" Christine asked brightly.

She really expected to go below the Opera with him, right now. But of course, what else could she expect? And he didn't want to, he wanted to stay here and meet Meg. He only had thirteen days left before Meg was leaving Paris and if he had to spend any amount of time dealing with Christine—that brought him up short. Surely he wasn't thinking of *Christine* as an awkward duty he had to *deal with*?

Selfishness, that's what these thoughts were about. And whatever he was feeling beyond that was too confusing to puzzle out while Christine was sitting here looking at him expectantly. He'd have to take her below the Opera. He owed her too much to refuse. And hopefully Meg would understand, when he explained it to her later. Whenever he saw her next.

"Yes, of course, we can go," he said, because it was the only thing to say, and rose to his feet. "I'll show you the way."

Chapter Twenty-Four

C hristine followed him without a murmur, out of Box Five and through the nearest hidden door. He usually walked through his passages with only what little light filtered through cracks and vents, but he had stocked them all with candles long ago for darker nights. Considering Christine's presence, he laid hold of a candle just inside the entrance, lit it with a snap of his fingers. She followed a step behind him as he held up the light, and it was several minutes before he thought that maybe he should have offered her his free hand—but by then it seemed too late, too unbearably awkward to extend it now.

So they just kept walking in silence, while he tried to figure out how he could make this situation work, and how long she expected to stay, because obviously he couldn't leave her alone down in his home, but missing this meeting with Meg meant he didn't have any specific plans with her, so how long would it be before she came looking for him, meaning how many days was he going to end up wasting—

A sudden draft from a branching passage swirled past, caught the flame of the candle and plunged them into darkness.

Immediately Christine cried out. "What happened? What put out the light?"

"It was just a draft," Erik said, shoulders hunching instinctively at the shrill note in her voice.

"Light it again, quick! It *scares* me being down here in the dark!"

Then maybe she shouldn't have asked for refuge underground. He thought it, felt guilty about it, and forced himself to concentrate on relighting the candle. The flame caught and burned with a steady glow, once again illuminating the passage around them.

Christine exhaled a deep sigh. "That's *so* much better. I just can't stand darkness like that. It's so…creepy, so ominous."

He watched the shadows on the wall dance in the candlelight, thought of all the years when darkness had been his best sanctuary. "I've never understood what people find frightening about darkness. It always seemed to me that—"

"Perhaps you should put some electric lights down here," Christine remarked. "It would make these tunnels so much easier to manage."

For a moment, he could think of absolutely nothing to say to that. Finally he managed to echo, "Electric lights?"

"Yes. You know, like on the Avenue de l'Opera. It's a terribly clever invention, isn't it? It practically turns the night into day. It would be so much pleasanter down here if you put proper lighting in."

"I'll…consider it," he said, and resumed walking at a brisk pace.

He was sure of it now. They had never been good friends.

I did not go to the Opera Friday evening. What would be the point? If Erik wanted to see me, he knew where I lived.

But he was with her instead.

I tried, very hard, to be *so glad* that I was leaving for Vienna. To a life where I would make sure I didn't have to be second place to anyone.

As if I had planned this current situation.

Christine didn't comment on the stacks of musical scores spread all over his parlor, or on the Bouguereau painting of the angels, new since she had last been here. She went immediately to the pipe organ and suggested a singing lesson.

It was pleasant hearing Christine sing again. No one at the Opera could sing the way she did. And yet...her voice didn't seize his emotions the way it once had. He could acknowledge her technical proficiency and appreciate the artistry involved—but when his attention started wandering during an aria, wandering back towards calculating how many days and hours it was until Meg's train was leaving Paris (13 days, 11 hours if he assumed a morning train), then he knew for certain what he had known, unacknowledged and unadmitted, since he first saw Christine again.

He wasn't in love with her anymore.

He had spent *months* mourning this woman, months when he was utterly convinced that he would never stop loving her, and somehow, while still believing that was true, it had all...ended. His life had changed, *he* had changed, and his feelings had too.

Probably even before he had stopped counting the days since she had left. Even that had grown rote somewhere along the way, no longer laden with the despair that had once consumed him.

He stared at Christine, barely hearing the notes as she continued the song, and tried to decipher how he felt about this realization. Numb? No, not numb, just...it was strangely uninteresting. Old news. Because now that he thought about it, he *hadn't* felt much about her for...months probably, two or three at least. Even when he had had that fight with Meg, even when he had vowed to her that he would always love Christine—now that he looked back on it, he had been so much more wrapped up in his anger with Meg than in any feeling about Christine. He'd kept avoiding her name in an almost superstitious habit, but if he had ever said it, maybe he would have noticed the lack of pain involved.

If he felt anything now, it was relief. It wasn't as though loving Christine had ever brought anything good into his life.

Although the relief was tempered by the observation that Fate, with its usual cruel caprice where he was concerned, had orchestrated his recovery from one woman's leaving just in time for another woman to leave him and implode his life all over again.

Not that it was the same thing, of course…was it?

"Do you have any advice?" Christine asked, and from her tone it likely wasn't the first time she'd asked the question.

He blinked. Right. The song. The song he'd stopped listening to. "It was…very nice. Though…you still need some work on the lower end of your range."

They talked about singing for the rest of the evening and he did his best to keep his thoughts on point.

He slept badly, uncomfortable with the knowledge that Christine was in the next room. And not uncomfortable the way he would have been a year ago. Now he had an instinctive itch to lock his door because—well, it wasn't that Christine was frightening exactly, it was just that he didn't trust her. He never had.

He was awake again at five, pacing the parlor. He wanted badly to talk to Meg. But how could he do it, when he couldn't leave Christine alone here? She would be upset if he did that and besides—he didn't trust her. It felt strange to think of her in his home alone. He couldn't bring her with him. He'd have to look for Meg upstairs, and that meant a lot of narrow passages and crawl spaces and—no, bringing Christine would be completely absurd.

After more passes up and down the parlor than it really should have taken, he thought of a letter. He couldn't go find Meg, but she could come to him. Because unlike Christine, Meg knew how to get to his home, with a reasonable probability that she'd want to.

He sat down at once to draft a letter, snatching up the first paper that came to hand. Black-edged, but that was all right, Meg wouldn't mind that. He should have thought of this sooner—maybe he would have, if he hadn't got stuck in a mental loop fixating on the idea that he just wanted to see her, talk to her, not waste any more very limited time. 13 days, three hours left now, and a letter wasn't as satisfying, especially with that count running in his head. But if it produced the desired end…

He dipped his quill in the ink pot and quickly scrawled, *My dear Meg, my apologies for missing our Friday meeting. There's been the most…*bizarre, unsettling, unexpected, baffling, inconvenient? *…extraordinary turn of events.*

Christine has returned to Paris, returned to the Opera, and requested sanctuary below while she makes some decisions about her possible singing career. He had the distinct feeling that this sentence made no sense at all, though it was perfectly factually accurate. *I thought you would want to know, and also this leaves me rather...* trapped, overwhelmed, confused—that wasn't even close to what he had meant to say. *...occupied and unable to find you above. Clearly I will be home, though, if you find an opportunity to visit today.* Please, please come visit. Please, I need to talk to you so you can help me make sense of all of this. Not so much the part about not loving Christine anymore, but what to do about her now that she's here. And also, I miss you.

He almost wrote that last thought down, hesitated, wrote *Hoping to see you* instead and signed an *E* at the bottom.

It was a terrible letter. It was oddly formal and remarkably short, when he looked at what he'd actually written down. Maybe she'd read between the lines. Though if she managed to gather everything that was behind the written words, that would probably just convince her that he was completely mad, so maybe it would be better if she didn't.

He groaned, gave up, folded the letter into an envelope and went upstairs to leave it at her table in the corps de ballet's changing room. It was barely six, so even the earliest-rising ballet girl wouldn't be there yet.

Chapter Twenty-Five

W hen I went to the Opera the day after Christine's unexpected
return, I told myself it was because I was, after all, still a
member of the corps de ballet for a few more days, and I had a
responsibility and it was really the...responsible thing to do.

And I also knew perfectly well that I was going because maybe
I'd see Erik. Or even Christine, because I'd talk to Christine if that was
the only way to get news about Erik. Not Friday night, I wouldn't have
expected to see him Friday night. But surely by Saturday morning...?

In the changing rooms, the ballet girls ignored me so I ignored
them. I sat down at my table, and immediately saw the black-edged
envelope tucked into one barely-open drawer.

I stared at it in a rush of relief and irritation. He had sent me a
message; he hadn't completely forgotten I existed. But he *had*
apparently forgotten that this room was crowded, and everyone in it
thought I had consorted with the Phantom—and knew that the Phantom
sent black-edged envelopes.

I carefully slid the drawer open, pushing the envelope down out of
sight. I rifled through the papers inside the drawer, until the envelope
was tucked into the middle of a stack of programs, then brought the
whole pile out and slid them into my bag. I would have had to clean
this drawer out soon anyway.

Then I changed for practice in a positive fever of impatience. As
soon as I possibly could I picked up my bag and left, as though on my

way to practice—and took a side turn almost at once, ducking into the first empty room.

I drew the letter out of my bag, held it in my hands with a conflicting rush of eagerness and dread. It was a letter, that was good…unless it said something bad. And I could already tell it was thin.

So help me, if he was leaving the country and said good-bye with a two-sentence note, I would—I took a deep breath. That was ridiculous. Erik wouldn't do that. Leave the country *or* leave me with just a note to say good-bye. Like Christine had done, when she left. All Christine had gone to do now was talk to him. That wouldn't have changed anything.

I tore the letter open, read it quickly.

It wasn't a good-bye. But it wasn't much better. She was *staying* below the Opera? Only in my wildest, most paranoid thoughts had *that* seemed like a possibility. Why on earth was she doing that? She had told me she was happy with Raoul, that she only wanted to apologize to Erik—I clearly understood even less about Christine than I had thought, and I hadn't imagined I had a full picture anyway.

Did I understand less about Erik too?

I read the letter through again, more slowly, and felt a new anger uncurl itself in the pit of my stomach by the time I reached the end a second time. One time had been enough to be angry with Christine. A second time had me angry with Erik too.

There had been an "extraordinary" event and he was "occupied" and he didn't have time for me but I could drop by if I wanted to.

Yes, I'd just *love* to do that, to spend ballet practice under fire as the Phantom's friend, then go traipsing about below the Opera to walk in on what exactly when I got there? I had a brief image of Christine sitting on one of his maroon couches in a state of *déshabillée*—or perhaps I'd arrive right in the midst of—I shoved those thoughts away, I was not going to think about that.

And besides, it just so happened that others of us could also be *occupied*. Perhaps that hadn't occurred to him, but I was going to be *very busy* today.

Excerpt from the Private Notebook of Jean Mifroid, Commissaire of Police

27 May, 1882

Raoul de Chagny and Christine de Chagny, née Daaé, returned and taken up residence in Paris. Sent letter informing me of same, received today. Should have come in-person immediately. Attempted to find at home – RdC gone to country estate. CdC's whereabouts unknown to housekeeper, seemed unalarmed. Where would she go? Must have interview at earliest opportunity.

Meg did not come to visit. The world did not grow any less unsettling.

Christine was not interested in anything but advice on her singing, or occasionally reminiscing about her beloved father. Erik threw out haphazard alternative topics at random intervals, but never got anywhere with any of them. Christine would just look blank—or laugh. It wasn't a mocking laugh, but it still made something inside of him curl up tighter and hide deeper away. For every topic he raised, there were at least half a dozen he didn't even bother trying.

All of Saturday slipped away from him. He missed the evening performance, a minor matter compared to Meg's complete silence. Had she received his note? Was there some reason she couldn't come to visit? Was the corps de ballet being horrible to her?

He didn't *know* and he hated it.

It was incredible to think that he had actually contemplated in the past having Christine stay under the Opera for an extended period of time, perhaps forever. He had imagined it guiltily, worried about how limiting it would be for her. How had he never considered how limiting it would be for *him*?

Sunday morning dawned, somewhere far, far above him, with no material change in circumstances. It was unlikely Meg would visit today. Sunday had rarely been their day—except for Easter morning, and for the one time she had brought him out into her sunlight.

His rooms seemed particularly dark today. Christine appeared happy to go on with more singing lessons, while he fidgeted and lit extra candles.

She finished an a cappella aria from Bellini's *La Sonnambula*, standing beside his piano while he sat in his armchair, and promptly said in the most cheerful of voices, "And what shall I sing next?"

He didn't know and he didn't care. "Perhaps you should rest your voice," he suggested. Perhaps they could actually do something else, talk about something else—or not talk. Perhaps she could amuse herself and let him compose, or even just think. Meg had always been happy enough to listen while he played music.

"Oh no," Christine protested, "it's so *delightful* to sing again! I'm really so out of practice and I missed it so much—especially singing for someone who really *understands*."

She kept on saying that and it kept becoming less true. Maybe he understood singing, but he did not understand why she was here. "How long do you suppose you'll be wanting to stay?" he asked, not because it was entirely apropos to the topic but because they hadn't discussed it, at all, and he wanted to know. He'd waited long enough for the subject to come up more naturally, and it hadn't.

"Oh—I really can't say," Christine said, and already her voice had grown cool, no longer tinged with the bright delight of when she spoke about singing. "It's all so—so complicated. And I just feel so conflicted, you know. And it's really all so—"

"Won't Raoul be worrying about you?" If *he* had a wife he'd certainly notice if she was gone for several days. Or hours. Never mind a wife, if he cared about someone at all—he had a decent working picture of Meg's schedule and—

"Raoul doesn't understand me," Christine said. "I don't know how long it would be before he even cared that I was away."

That seemed very much at odds with the annoyingly ardent young man Erik remembered. Though perhaps after a year things had changed. It would be like a smug nobleman to take his wife for granted.

"And besides, he's away at the country estate. So much left unattended while we were gone, you know," Christine continued. "But of course—if I'm becoming a burden to you—if you'd rather I left…"

He would, very much so. But her voice was wavering and she was sounding hurt and distressed and it made him feel guilty and after everything he had done before… "Of course not," he said grimly. "You must stay as long as you wish."

"Oh, you're *so* kind," she said, perfectly happy again. "Now what shall I sing?"

He gave up. "Why don't you pick something?"

"Oh, I know—a duet! We haven't sung anything together since I came back."

It was like a rush of cold air across his soul. "I don't sing anymore." He had stopped singing when she left.

He had told himself then that he had no music left. That hadn't turned out to be true, he was composing again, so perhaps, after all, he might sing again some day too. But not today. The idea of singing a duet with Christine—it was so personal, so intimate. The very thought made him feel exposed and vulnerable.

"Oh, but you mustn't say that!' Christine protested, and he could hear the pout in her voice. "You had such a wonderful voice and—"

"I *don't* sing anymore," he repeated. Certainly not for her. "If you'd rather not sing something else yourself, there's no need of it." Maybe he'd get some quiet after all.

"Well, I didn't say that," Christine said with a little laugh, dashing his hopes. "Now let me see, the best thing to sing…"

A sudden idea, a delaying tactic— "I have a book," he said hurriedly, rising to his feet to go to his bookcase. "Opera scores. You could look through it, find just the right one." Give him at least a few minutes of quiet.

The tactic worked. She settled onto the couch in a rustle of skirts, the book on her lap, and Erik dropped back into the armchair, to brood in the new silence.

It was Sunday morning. That made it 11 days, 21 hours until Meg was leaving Paris. There had to be some way he could arrange to see her. What was she doing this morning, right now? He knew more of her schedule during the week, but she was probably at mass. Probably at the little church in her neighborhood. Though today was Pentecost, the end of the Easter season. She went to Notre Dame Cathedral for Easter. Would she go there for Pentecost too? She'd never said so, or else he would have been sorely tempted to try to ambush her again. It had worked at Easter. Was that really a mere seven weeks ago? It felt like longer.

"Is it painful for you, to hear me sing?" Christine said suddenly, and Erik started.

Was he that transparent? He had tried to be polite.

"Considering," Christine continued, "that's what led you to fall in love with me."

It was the first time either of them had said anything on this subject since she came below the Opera, and now that it had been raised it was so—so absurd. She thought her singing would stir *too much* emotion in him, when the truth was exactly the opposite. "It's—not too painful, no," he managed, because he didn't want to talk about his feelings, there was no way that would be a comfortable conversation.

"I'm *so* glad," Christine said cheerfully, and quiet fell again.

Erik let out a breath. It was ridiculous, absurd—and on an even larger level than the present moment. Because was it even true? Had he fallen in love with Christine because of her voice? He tried to remember that first moment when she was singing in the auditorium, when he had looked out through the curtains of Box Five and seen her standing alone on stage. So vulnerable, so harmless, so in need of help. That had mattered just as much, if not more, than her voice.

No, wait, he was still getting this wrong—Christine hadn't been alone on stage in that moment. *Meg* had been there too. He had never told her about the significance of that afternoon, but had she guessed? She seemed to think it was Christine's voice he cared most about too. The only time they'd really talked about Christine, when Meg got so angry a few weeks ago, she had said something about not being able to sing like Christine as if it was important to him, as if he was somehow judging her based on that.

He should have told her that he didn't care about that, that it had never been as important as she seemed to think, even with Christine. True, he couldn't imagine himself forming any meaningful connection with a woman who couldn't appreciate music or singing or operas, but appreciating was a long way from being able to sing Marguerite in *Faust*. And the ability to sing Marguerite didn't mean a woman would have any interest in discussing composers with him, or listening to his music, or digging through his piles of papers to find the right concerto for the Opera—or encourage him to send music to the Opera to begin with.

Really, a good singing voice was much less important than being interested in him and the things he cared about, far less important than being able to look at him and see some value in the man behind the mask. He cared much more that he could trust her about…everything, from not betraying him to the Opera Company to not flinching when he took the mask off to genuinely listening and not laughing when he risked confessing something private.

A singing voice dwindled to utter insignificance compared to the way he heard concertos every time she smiled at him, and days never meant as much when she wasn't in them, and he could still feel the touch of her lips the one time she had kissed his cheek. And she made him want to do…not dramatic things, but just things like walking in the sunlight and visiting Notre Dame and actually engaging with life, made him want to write symphonies and paint pictures and go out to the Café de la Paix for pastry on Sunday morning even when he said he couldn't, made him want to be good enough, made him want to be a man she…could love.

Oh.

Oh no.

He had been staring into space, unseeing, unaware of his surroundings, and it was a jolt to remember suddenly that he was not alone. No mask in the world was concealing enough to hide the secret that could be written on his face, and if Christine looked up from the book right now—he surged to his feet. "I'll go get more coffee, shall I?" he said in a rush and all but ran out of his side door.

In the corridor beyond, with the door closed behind him, he sank down onto the bottom step of his spiral staircase and dropped his head into his hands.

How could he—Meg was his *friend*, how could he think of wanting more than that? And how could he not have realized for so long how very, very much more he wanted? But she wouldn't—she couldn't ever— how could he possibly even imagine...

Why hadn't he realized this was happening and stopped it? He tried to search backwards, to work out when the turning point must have been, to maybe then be able to engineer forward what he ought to do now, but it was no good, every memory he looked back on felt like it had already been too late—*now* he could see that, he hadn't seen it then. That Sunday they walked around Paris—why hadn't he realized what it meant, how good it had felt when she took his hand as he stepped into the sunshine? Or that hideous, wrenching heartbreak when he'd thought Meg had betrayed him to the mob? Before that, the day the mob came—oh yes, it had been too late by then too, why hadn't he seen it in how he felt when she came in to warn him, when she kissed his cheek? Back further, Easter, that empty dull week with the shining morning at Notre Dame in the middle. Already too far, even then.

Plainly he didn't recognize love when it was making him happy.

Chapter Twenty-Six

I went to Notre Dame Cathedral Sunday morning. It was Pentecost, the end of the Easter season, and though I didn't usually go to Notre Dame for Pentecost, there might be only one more Sunday before we left Paris. I wanted to visit Notre Dame while I could.

Mother, looking too thoughtful, decided to come with me. I wasn't sure how I felt about that. I knew she was trying to be supportive. And I didn't have any special plans for the day anyway. Not really. Just a trip to mass.

It was nice to have her sitting next to me in the pew during the service. It was steadying. My mother was even more a constant in my life than Notre Dame, for all its centuries-old history, its great solid stone architecture. Between my mother, the cathedral, and the familiar Latin of the mass, I was feeling more grounded than I had in days.

After mass I lit a candle by my favorite statue, the Madonna and Child, but without the anguish I might have had in another moment. I felt hopeful, even.

The mood lasted until Mother and I had walked out into the sunshine again, turned a corner and were walking beside the cathedral. Until I glanced to the side, glanced into the niche Erik had occupied on Easter morning.

It was empty. Of course it was empty. And yet the sight gave me such a stab of loneliness that I could almost have hated him for not being there.

"Do you have plans for this afternoon?" Mother asked as we walked on.

I didn't turn to look at her, in case my feelings were on my face. I took a breath, felt the loneliness ebb a fraction.

I didn't have plans. And yet, I hesitated. I *could* go to the Opera. Erik had told me I was welcome to come by, I could…go interrupt him and Christine mid-duet? If she was still there.

I could go to the de Chagny residence. Christine and Raoul were likely living there now, I might find out if she was home and…

Did I really want to spend my day chasing after Christine, trying to find out Erik's business?

No. No, I did not.

I slipped my arm through my mother's, forced a smile on my face. "I don't have any plans. Let's think of something nice to do."

Monday morning. Ten days, 20 hours left, and Erik was starting to think he was going to lose his mind if he had to sit under the opera house any longer. He couldn't face another day like the last two. When Christine still made no indications she intended to leave any time in the foreseeable future, he was driven to the point of saying, in as bright a tone as he could muster, "Do you know what would be nice today?"

"Practicing the Queen of the Night aria?" Christine suggested.

"No," Erik said, trying not to clench his hands as he sat on the organ bench, back to the keys. "I was thinking of some fresh air. Let's go out."

Her laugh came again. It had grown too familiar. All merriness, no mockery, and yet it still brought his shoulders up. "But you don't go out."

"Even a ghost has to eat." Meg would have laughed at *that*.

No laugh now from Christine, just a pause as though he wasn't quite making sense, and then the comment, "Well, perhaps this evening."

At dusk, no doubt, when everywhere was dim and shadowy. Worst possible time for a cloaked figure to loom out of the darkness. He almost said it out loud, but what would be the point? "No, I think now is the ideal time," he said firmly, rising to his feet. Now was when the practices up above would be finishing, when it just might be possible to not very accidentally bump into Meg when she was done with ballet practice but hadn't left the Opera yet. "We can go up to the roof."

He wanted to see Meg. Probably. He knew he couldn't stand sitting down here anymore, and he knew he wanted to see Meg, but he also knew it might be a terrible idea to see Meg right now—and he was no longer as sure about anything he might do as he had been two days ago.

Life was more complicated than it had been two days ago.

"Well," Christine said slowly, fitting an enormous amount of reluctance into a single syllable, "if you really think…"

"Excellent!" Erik said, just as though he couldn't hear her tone at all.

He led her up through the cellars, through hidden tunnels and secret stairwells up through the levels of the opera house, realizing but ignoring her obvious distaste for the whole enterprise.

He had few thoughts to spare for Christine, because if he *did* manage to bump into Meg…then what? Would she be able to see it on his face, all that he had realized he felt for her?

Christine hadn't noticed anything. As long as he praised her singing and kept his mask on, Christine would be completely oblivious to whatever he was feeling.

But if he saw Meg—she would notice something was different, because she paid attention, she was interested, she actually cared. The thought gave him a warm, pleased feeling in his chest—but that didn't help anything. He didn't *want* her to notice this.

But he wanted to see her. He took a deep breath as they ascended another staircase, gave his vest a tug even though it didn't need straightening. If they bumped into Meg, he would simply be calm, and in control, and…and *calm*. It was just another mask, that was all, and if anyone knew about masks, it was him. He would be aloof. But not too aloof, he'd be friendly…but not too friendly.

Because if she somehow guessed…he had no idea what would happen. None at all. And he was not in any way prepared to deal with that. After an entire day of not being able to think of anything else, he still didn't know how *he* felt about this. He couldn't possibly handle however *she* was going to feel about it.

Although if she didn't hate the idea…

No, he was trying particularly hard not to think about *that*. He'd have to think this all through first, carefully, calmly. It might be easier if he could just get some space from Christine's constant presence, enough space to really think. And then later—but there wasn't any *time* later, Meg was leaving Paris in ten days and 19 hours, and how was he ever going to—but that didn't mean he should think about this right this minute. Right now he'd just see if he could bump into Meg, and maybe that would make something seem clearer, and mostly right now he just needed to be…calm.

He did not feel calm when they reached the hidden passage behind the mirrors in the ballet's practice room, to be greeted by a silent, empty room beyond.

Ballet practice was already over. Meg could be anywhere in the Opera Garnier. Anywhere in Paris.

For just a moment he flirted with the idea of going to the ballet's changing rooms. She might still be there. But of all places, he couldn't go *there*. Certainly not with Christine.

And then Christine chose that moment to rebel. "I think this is enough light and air for me," she announced, looking through the mirrors at the sunlit practice room. "And I've had quite enough staircases too."

He could feel the bars of the cage locking around him. This wasn't good enough, this wasn't any better than if he'd simply stayed underground. He still felt just as trapped, just as confused. Could he leave Christine here, go search for Meg? But how could he abandon Christine—and how could he stay here, do nothing— "That's fine," he said with reckless desperation, "you stay here and I'll just climb on up to the roof." It was only two more flights. It wouldn't be as good as finding Meg but at least it would give him some space. "I'll be back in a few minutes."

She didn't agree to the idea, might even object if he gave her time. Before she could say anything, he hit the nearby wall paneling with his palm, stepped through the next secret door before it had even slid all the way open, and quickly shut it behind him.

In the darkness, he leaned back against the closed wall and took a deep breath. Better. A little space, a little solitude.

If someone had told him a year ago that he'd someday be grateful to get some space from Christine, he'd have said they were mad.

But even still, he rather wished someone *had* told him.

He wasn't sure what he would have thought, if someone had told him he'd someday fall in love with Meg.

I finished my second-to-last ballet practice, full of whispers and sarcastic remarks and no one talking *to* me while they all talked *about* me. Except for Madame Thibault, first when she scolded, and then when she handed me a note from the managers, saying they wished to meet with my mother and me later in the day. No topic was specified, but it had to be about the new gossip, about the Phantom and me.

After that practice, and with that new prospect, I decided this was a day for going up to the roof. I needed some space, some sky. Even the arching ceilings of the Opera Garnier felt oppressive. There was sky outside the Opera too, freely available in any of Paris' boulevards, but it was different from the roof. And I wouldn't have many more opportunities to visit this particular sanctuary.

I was still all twisted round about Erik and Christine and leaving the Opera and everything else, but I could breathe easier on the roof, started to feel calmer…until I walked around a corner and nearly tripped over a ghost sitting in the shadows.

I stumbled backwards a step, and Erik half-rose to his feet, every line gone tense. His gaze focused on my face and he visibly relaxed. "Oh. It's *you*." He smiled at me, making my heart jump. For a moment we held gazes as I searched for something to say in this unexpected meeting. He looked away first, abruptly, and resumed his position sitting on the tiled roof, back to the low wall. He added in an undertone, "Thank God."

This gave me a glimmer of something to say. "You're lucky it wasn't someone else from the Opera Company." It wasn't a clever observation, but my stomach was churning with absurd nerves and I had to say something.

"That too," Erik said, or I thought he said. It didn't make much sense, so maybe I misheard. Maybe what he really said was "that's true," except Erik never slurred anything.

I was still standing above him, hesitating. A week ago I would have settled in sitting next to him without a thought. Now I finally, slowly, sat down anyway, studiously tucking my red-flowered skirts around my ankles.

"Did you get my letter?"

I kept my eyes on my skirts. "Yes. I did."

"You didn't come visit."

I wasn't looking at his face, but the tone was wistful. I made a snatch at my resentment. "I've been busy."

"Oh. Yes. Of course." The wistfulness had grown into a hollow sadness—and yet it was more the resigned acceptance beneath the sadness that made me want to revise my answer.

"And I thought you'd be…busy too," I said, not quite willing to say it more directly, to actually say out loud that I hadn't thought he'd have time for me.

He responded just as though I had said that anyway. "I *did* want you to visit," he said, and then, more softly, "I missed you."

I'd be in a great deal of trouble if Erik ever figured out how easily he could soften my mood by employing that simple phrase. I tried to resist, told myself that he couldn't really have missed me very much, when he'd been so *occupied*. With her.

So I didn't say anything in response, just drew my knees up and folded my arms over them, staring out over the rooftop towards the great dome of the Opera, and wished I could be less acutely aware of

Erik sitting next to me. It didn't seem fair, when I was trying to be angry with him.

We sat without speaking for a long moment, and I could feel the silence building up between us, as thick and heavy and oppressive as a thunderstorm, as real and substantial as a third person—and I knew exactly who that third person was.

"How's Christine?" I asked.

Erik sighed, ran a hand over his hair. "Honestly?"

"Of course," I said, though I didn't want to know, wished I hadn't asked the question, didn't want *any detail at all* about Erik's feelings for Christine.

"She's driving me mad."

I laced my fingers together around my knees, tried to work out what that meant. "Well. They do say love is madness and all that."

"What?" He blinked and turned towards me. "I didn't say anything about love, we weren't talking about—oh, you mean—no, not like that. I mean, *mad*. All Christine wants to talk about is singing. All the time!"

He was ill at ease and I wondered why. Wondered what he wasn't saying, because there had to be something, if I was any judge of his slightly incoherent rambles. As to what he *had* said, that made no sense. "You like singing."

He liked Christine's singing. He had always liked—suddenly a shiver ran down my spine. He had said *Christine's name*. For the first time ever in my hearing, he had said Christine's name. But—well—of course he did, she was here, we were talking about her. Of course he said her name, that didn't mean anything. Did it? And what did it mean, if it meant something?

"I know, I know," he groaned, and I had to stop to think what he was responding to, what I had actually said out loud. Oh, right, liking her singing. He tipped his head back against the stone wall behind us. "*Mea culpa*. My fault. I brought this on myself. I had the whole insane idea about Christine living under the Opera and the singing lessons and all the rest. *Why* did I think that was a good idea?"

The name again. And furthermore, this was not remotely what I had expected him to say about Christine. He seemed to be relaxing slightly as he warmed to the topic, but I hadn't the slightest idea what to say in response. Fortunately, he didn't seem to expect me to have answers.

"Now she's here, she wants to stay, she wants to practice singing, and it's *boring*. I mean, singing lessons are fine, but to the exclusion of all other topics? No, wait, she does talk about her sainted father now and then but that's a whole different...never mind that, the point is...what was my point?"

"She's driving you mad?" It was half an answer, half testing the idea out.

"*Yes*. There are so many other things to talk about besides singing. I keep thinking of other ideas, only that doesn't work, because some of them I'm sure she won't understand, and some ideas I try to mention and she *doesn't* understand, and then some of it I know I don't even want to say to *her*..."

He had turned his face towards me again, and I found myself staring into those green eyes.

"I guess it's not Christine's fault," he said softly, "if she's not who I want to talk to."

Staring into Erik's eyes felt like looking down from the edge of the rooftop, terrifying but exhilarating, making me dizzy in a way pirouettes never had. We were only inches apart; I found my head tipping just slightly to the side, and was he leaning a little farther forward...?

Quick, light footsteps sounded on the tiles of the roof.

I jerked my head back and Erik all but sprang to his feet and we both looked to see Christine come walking up with a smile on her face. Her cheeks were flushed from the climb up the stairs, her eyes were bright, of course she looked beautiful, and suddenly the idea that Erik didn't want to talk to her did not seem as clear-cut as it had a moment before. It didn't, for instance, definitively indicate that he didn't want other things from her.

Chapter Twenty-Seven

E rik was not at all sure what had just happened.

A lifetime of self-control was apparently not enough to keep himself in line around Meg right now. He had found himself staring at her immediately and forced himself to look away, even though he wanted to keep looking. It had been easier to talk about Christine, still a pressing problem if no longer the most significant one. He had relaxed into Meg's presence, his whole world feeling brighter, safer because she was here. But then he had relaxed too much. It had felt so comfortable, had been such a relief to be talking to Meg, and the next thing he knew he was an inch away from confessing too much, an inch away from—from— what would have happened if Christine hadn't walked up just then?

But she had, she was here, he had to deal with now, not whatever might have almost happened.

"Christine. Hello." He scrambled for his charming façade; that was the mask he needed right now.

There was movement beside him as Meg started to rise to her feet, and he hastily, automatically, offered her a hand. Charming, yes. She took his hand without looking at him, and he fought not to hold on too tightly, not to run his thumb along the back of her hand. She let go as soon as she was standing, and seemed intent on brushing off her skirts.

"I certainly didn't expect to find both of you here," Christine remarked.

It suddenly occurred to him that this situation required explanation. "Well. You see. Over the last year, Meg and I—"

"Yes, I know," Christine interrupted, "Meg told me you had been speaking with each other."

She had? When had they talked? He looked at Meg, but she was looking down, apparently flicking dust off of her red-patterned skirt. He looked back at Christine. "You never mentioned that." It would have been too different a topic from singing lessons, perhaps.

Christine laughed lightly, the laugh he was truly coming to dislike. "It didn't seem quite right for me to bring the subject up first. It would have looked as though I was prying into your business! And I couldn't bring it up *second* because you never talked about Meg at all."

His friendship with Meg had seemed…private, separate from anything to do with Christine, part of a different life, even. And he certainly wasn't going to bring up Meg after he realized that friendship was only the half of it. She was one of the subjects he had doubted Christine would understand, and now when she started talking about it, it seemed clear that she didn't.

He was ready to dismiss this as just another thing that Christine didn't grasp, only Meg had stopped looking at her skirts now and was staring at him with a very strange expression. That was worrying. What had he done wrong this time?

"Since you never mentioned it," Christine went on cheerfully, "naturally I assumed it couldn't be very important."

It. "It" meaning…his conversations with Meg? Their friendship? And by implication, Meg herself?

Oh. Now he saw what he had done wrong.

He almost said something noncommittal and restrained, about that not being quite right…but what good had restraint been doing him lately? Maybe a less restrained letter would have convinced Meg to come visit him.

"Actually I'm far less likely to talk about important things," he said with studied firmness. "Unimportant things can be talked about to anyone."

All unintentionally, his gaze flicked to Meg. She looked away—but she was smiling, so that was all right. And if Meg understood, then it didn't matter whether Christine did or not.

Christine laughed again, though he couldn't see anything funny, and said sweetly, "I do quite envy you. Meg was always *such* a good friend before I left. And now it's been so long."

What was he supposed to say to that? Yes, it had been…he still hadn't recalculated the days since Christine left. Four hundred and some. Maybe he wouldn't mention that thought, so he just said, "Mm-hmm," not at all eloquently.

"It has been a long time, especially without any letters," Meg said suddenly, gaze resting thoughtfully on the statue of Apollo.

Another momentary pause, then Christine picked up the conversation again with a lot of cheerful, meaningless remarks. Erik only half-listened, if that.

It would have been hard enough to pay attention to Christine, after the last few days of so much endless chatter. But trying not to stare at Meg was also occupying a good deal of his attention. He couldn't help darting looks in her direction, enough to realize that, as far she was concerned, he likely could get away with staring.

She wasn't looking at him. And something else was wrong. He gave up trying not to look as he tried to work it out. It was subtle, in the way she was standing, in the angle of her shoulders.

Without moving at all, she was somehow in full-flung retreat. They were standing more or less in a triangle, but from Meg's angle, it was a triangle that paired Erik and Christine, and left her on the outside.

He didn't *want* that. Could he slide a step over, change the angles, change the bigger picture? But the way she had her arms crossed, the way her chin was raised, was altogether forbidding towards coming any closer. Was this still about him not mentioning her to Christine? Or maybe it was simpler than that. Maybe she was assuming things were the way they had been. How many times, back before, had both women been present and he'd only noticed Christine?

He didn't know. That was the point. He hadn't noticed her.

How could he *not* have noticed her? How might it all have turned out differently, if that day in the auditorium, that day he'd heard Christine sing for the first time, he had looked a little to the side instead, noticed Meg instead… But he hadn't. And he couldn't change that. The question was *now*, what he was going to do now, and he still had no idea.

The conversation meandered and lurched along about inanities— they were going to be onto the weather in a minute—and all the while Erik felt as though he could see Meg moving farther and farther away.

Finally Christine remarked, "We ought to be going back down below. It isn't really safe for you to be up here, Erik."

He supposed that a year ago he would have been thrilled by the expression of concern. Now it didn't seem like any of her business, and furthermore they couldn't end the conversation here, before he could figure out what to do about…everything. Anything.

But Meg was agreeing with Christine, and the women were saying perfunctory good-byes, and in a moment it would be too late if he didn't—"You should come with us," he said abruptly.

Meg stared at him, blue eyes wide. "I don't think that's a good idea."

"Of course it is," he said. "It's a brilliant idea." They only had ten days and 19 hours left, and he felt that if he let her out of his sight now, he was never going to find her again.

Her smile was wan. "You don't really want me to—"

"Yes, I *do*, that's why I suggested it." She had never been so reluctant to agree to his suggestions, to agree to a visit. Now, when it mattered even more…

"Don't push her if she doesn't want to come," Christine interjected. "And we can't blame her, it's such a dreadful dark walk down there, with those hideous gargoyles at the end."

Meg's chin rose and her eyes narrowed. "I would be *delighted* to come. And I'm very fond of gargoyles. They're deeply misunderstood creatures."

Erik felt his lips twitch, and he suddenly had the strangest pressure in his throat. He coughed. "Right then. If that's settled… Shall we go?"

I could think of few more uncomfortable ways to spend the afternoon than sitting around Erik's parlor with Christine. But that didn't mean I was going to let her run me off. Erik wanted me to come. He wanted to talk to me.

And if he didn't want to do anything else with me, well, it was still something and I wasn't going to let Christine and her delicate shudders about gargoyles interfere.

So I did what I usually did when Erik beckoned. I followed. Even if having Christine along too made it all very, very awkward.

We descended down through the levels of the Opera mostly in silence, apart from an occasional "turn left here" from Erik. I didn't need any of the directions, and tried to be pleased by that. To believe that it mattered somehow.

When we finally reached the last tunnel, Erik stepped up to the heavy wooden door to push it open. I automatically reached out to pat the head of the nearest gargoyle as I passed. I didn't know when I had started doing that. It was habit by now, and my fingers were brushing stone before I thought to be self-conscious about it. It hardly mattered though; no one was looking at me.

Across the threshold, Erik snapped his fingers and all the candles flared into light, illuminating the familiar room. Nothing looked different, but after all, what had I expected? Christine's petticoat tossed across one couch?

I swallowed hard and ordered myself to *stop* imagining things like that. He had said she was irritating him with endless discussions about singing, but would he have said, if they were…doing other things?

Christine herself tripped lightly across the room with an air of belonging and possession that I was probably imagining but deeply resented anyway, and dropped onto one maroon couch. It was the logical place to sit, if there were going to be three of us in the room.

So I followed her, and sat down in what was my usual spot anyway, on the opposite couch from Christine, the one that faced the pipe organ. I smoothed my skirts over my lap, tried to think of some conversational gambit before the silence, grown heavier now that we were sitting, stretched even longer.

Erik had lagged a few paces behind us, tossing his cloak over the armchair by the piano. Now he approached while I was still trying to think of something to say—and then I forgot about thinking of a topic because he sat down on my couch. Mine, not Christine's. At the opposite end, but still. What did that mean? Did that mean anything?

"So tell me about where you've been traveling," I blurted out, as much to silence the voices in my head as to break the external silence.

"Oh, here and there," Christine said with an airy wave of one hand. "We went to Rome for a bit."

"Rome?" I seized on that. "I'd love to see Rome."

She laughed lightly. "But you'd love to see everywhere."

I was less annoyed by that than I might have been, because I was engaged in trying to convey to Erik by facial expression that he should talk about Rome. I *knew* he had a virtually endless trove of stories about Rome, but he merely stared at me like he had no idea what I wanted. "I hear the view from the Janiculum is the finest in the city," I said desperately. *He* had told me that, and spent a good thirty minutes discussing every significant building on view, aided by the painting hanging near his bookcase. "The...architecture, and everything." If that didn't start him, nothing would.

But Erik still didn't say anything, and Christine just shrugged. "I suppose, if you like old buildings."

"Right," I said faintly. "So. Seen any operas?"

That topic lurched the conversation along for a few minutes more, during which Erik so entirely failed to hold up any end of the discussion that soon I was itching to kick him. Maybe that's why I finally said, "But Christine, tell me about your *singing*."

On the edge of my gaze I saw Erik's eyes widen—a palpable hit, as Hamlet would say—but I kept my attention firmly on Christine. She straightened up on the couch, eyes widening in an entirely different way and smile lighting her face. "Of course I've been a bit out of practice recently, but Erik has been *so* kind helping me and I really think I'm seeing the difference already. Perhaps I should sing something for—"

"No," Erik interrupted, and when we both turned to look at him he added, "You should rest your voice." His gaze met mine for just a second, then looked away again, and I knew he was lying.

He didn't want to hear her sing. As confusing as that was, I still felt my spirits lift.

Christine's lips tightened ever so slightly. "I suppose. If you say so." She took a breath, smiled again. "If you think I shouldn't sing, then why don't *you* sing instea—"

"*No*," he said, more sharply.

My spirits plummeted again. Had he been singing for her? After refusing to sing all this time she'd been gone? Somehow, Erik and Christine in a duet seemed…almost as bad as anything else I might imagine them doing together.

Christine pouted prettily. "I don't see why not. I think this is very silly."

"I *told* you," Erik said, voice tight, "I don't sing anymore."

So at least that was one question answered. I drew in a long breath, ridiculously, selfishly glad that he wouldn't sing for *her* either. And ridiculously, contradictorily disappointed too. I had never forgotten the one time I had heard him sing, when I had eavesdropped on his singing lesson with Christine. I would have loved to hear that beautiful voice again.

Still, his unwillingness to sing for Christine made me want to forgive his unwillingness to talk. "Maybe some coffee would be nice?" I suggested.

Erik blinked once, then caught onto the idea like it was a life raft. "Yes. Yes, that would be nice." He surged up to his feet. "I'll go…get that."

He was out of the room in a few paces, and I set myself to tackling Christine and the conversation again. It was somewhat easier, without him sitting a distracting two feet from me. "I suppose you and Raoul are living in his house in Paris now?"

The details of Christine's front parlor were not exactly scintillating, but it kept the conversation moving until Erik got back, balancing his silver coffee tray.

"Does it seem warm in here?" he asked as he set the tray on the ivory table. He didn't wait for an answer—mine would have been no—and said, "I thought it seemed dark before, but maybe there are too many candles lit. I'll just...put a few out..."

I expected him to extinguish them with a snap of his fingers, but instead he went to do it the normal way. Probably an excuse to continue avoiding conversation. For a moment I was aware of him moving around the room somewhere behind me, but then Christine caught my attention again, as she leaned forward toward the coffee pot. I reached out, caught the handle first.

"I'll pour," I said, and made myself smile. I was not going to have her pour my coffee like I was the guest here. "Weren't you telling me about your lace doilies?"

She sank back onto the couch, and after a moment resumed her former thread. I wasn't more than half-listening, until she interrupted herself to say, "Isn't that rather a lot of sugar, Meg?"

I glanced down at the cup in my hand, though it couldn't tell me anything since the lumps had dissolved with stirring already. I had counted, though, and it had been the usual six. "No," I said, and set the cup down near Erik's former seat. How many days had she spent down here, and she didn't know how he took his coffee?

And why, above all else, *why* did he want this woman who didn't notice how he took his coffee and didn't care about architecture and didn't like gargoyles and didn't—

What might have been a very interesting train of thought cut off abruptly at a pounding against the door.

My gaze flew to Erik, whose gaze was on the closed wooden door—for a moment, until it came around to meet mine.

"The Persian?" I suggested into the sudden silence, because it was the only good option I could think of. Even though Erik had mentioned the Persian leaving town, he could be back. Maybe.

Erik shook his head, one tight movement. "Not his knock." He set down the lit candle he'd been holding, reached inside his jacket.

A renewed pounding and now a voice demanding, "Open the door, I want to see Christine!"

I was still watching Erik, and I saw his shoulders relax. He drew his hand out again, still empty. "Oh. Him."

This told me nothing at all. I didn't want to, but I looked at Christine, as though an answer might be there. She was sitting straighter again, hands clasped in her lap and cheeks pink. Something in her face told me she knew too. I carefully looked back at Erik before I asked, "Who is it?"

"Raoul," he answered with a dismissive shrug. He looked past me to Christine and said, "So why don't you talk to him, and Meg and I will just go into the kitchen. So you two can talk."

That was a good plan. I liked that plan. I was surprised by that plan, but I wasn't going to complain.

Not so Christine. "You can't leave me alone with him!" she protested.

Erik blinked. "...why not?"

"He'll want me to leave with him!"

"Do you want to leave with him?" Erik asked, and despite my closest attention I couldn't tell how he felt about the idea. She was driving him mad...but she was *Christine*.

"No!" Christine said, inexplicably. She had told me she was *happy* with Raoul.

"All right, so don't go with him," Erik said with another shrug. "But there's still no reason you can't talk to him while we—"

"I *think* you should *stay*," Christine said, an edge in her voice that I didn't recognize.

Erik sighed. "All right. But you talk. And don't blame me if this all turns into a farce."

He crossed the room towards the door, where Raoul continued to pound ineffectually, and I realized Christine was looking at me.

"Perhaps it would be better if you left," she said delicately.

My fingers tightened on my coffee cup. "I'm not going." Leaving with Erik was very different from leaving without him. I didn't like this new plan, and I liked walking away even less. Raoul could not possibly be here with friendly intentions, and I didn't trust Christine to have Erik's back—so I had to.

I didn't know what I could possibly do, but that wasn't the point.

Christine's lips tightened and I thought she was going to argue the question—but

the door swung open and the Vicomte de Chagny charged in. The *Comte* de Chagny, I corrected myself. Except that was always going to be Philippe for me. Even if he'd inherited the new title, Raoul was always going to be the vicomte in my mind.

"Do come in. Make yourself at home," Erik said dryly, Raoul's forward momentum having already carried him a half-dozen steps into the room.

Raoul halted well beyond the piano, ignored Erik, didn't even glance at me, attention locking straight on Christine. "Are you all right?" he demanded, voice hoarse.

I felt the most absurd pang. I didn't even like Raoul, I mostly thought he was silly and rather dull—but I found something to envy in that single-minded focus. I'd like to be...someone's priority like that.

Christine was twisting her hands in her lap. "I'm fine. You shouldn't have come."

"Agreed," Erik said. "How did you even get here anyway?"

Raoul leveled a glare at him. "I've been here before, and the Persian's route by the Rue Scribe isn't that complicated. Or didn't you think I'd remember?"

"I didn't know you went that way, or I would have blocked it," Erik said dryly. "Though I am surprised you remembered enough."

"If all you can say is insults, I don't want to hear them!"

"That's fine," Erik said, raising his hands in a gesture of innocence. "I don't want to talk to you anyway. Talk to her," he said with a nod to Christine.

And yet Christine, who had seemed perfectly content to talk away about nothing interesting, now was silent. She merely darted anxious looks at both Raoul and Erik—and I couldn't tell which one was making her alarmed. Which made no sense, since I couldn't see why she had any reason to be alarmed by either one.

I cleared my throat. "So...I hear you've been abroad," I said, looking at Raoul. As though we could somehow have a polite, conventional conversation. And then maybe he'd leave and maybe he'd take Christine with him, and we could try to pretend none of this had ever happened.

"Yes," Raoul said with a ferocious glare. "And we should have *stayed* abroad." He swung around to turn the glare on Erik again. "You were supposed to be dead! We never would have come back if we knew you were alive!"

"So sorry to disappoint," Erik said, sketching a slight bow. He was wearing his Phantom mask again, the cool, elegant, unemotional mask.

"Oh, Raoul, please don't be angry," Christine said, voice going plaintive. "I know I've been weak."

"I don't blame you," Raoul snapped. "I blame *him*." He stalked closer to Erik, getting at least a step within Erik's usually-imposed invisible walls.

I half expected him to back up a step but he didn't. Maybe it was a point of pride. He crossed his arms, looked down at Raoul and said, "Have you been drinking?"

"I haven't, though I don't see how it's any business of yours!"

"Very well," Erik said with a shrug. "I just thought you seemed braver than usual."

Raoul sneered. "Sure, take cheap shots."

"Or it could be a compliment," Erik suggested. "If you wanted to see it that way."

Raoul glared at him, turned his back, and swaggered—yes, actually swaggered—over to the phonograph machine near the fireplace. He reached out to grasp the edge of the horn.

"That's fragile," Erik said pointedly, and as Raoul moved onto the next item on the table, his voice rose in volume. "And don't touch my violin!"

Raoul whirled to face him again. "Why not, you've been touching my wife!"

Erik sighed, a very weary sigh. "No, I really haven't been, so this is all completely unnecessary."

My fingers tightened on my coffee cup in spite of myself. He *really* hadn't been, or was he just saying that? If he was lying, I couldn't tell.

Raoul walked past the fireplace now, running his hand along the mantle.

"Could you just stop touching things?" Erik said through gritted teeth.

"Which things?" Raoul said. "Maybe things like *this*?" He swung around to face Erik again, and his hand wasn't empty anymore.

I hadn't given any thought in a long time to the gold-decorated pistol sitting on Erik's mantle. It was part of the décor, like the paintings and the gargoyles and the shelves of books. But now it was in Raoul's hand, his arm extended, gun aiming directly at Erik.

My heart beat loud in my ears, without drowning out the memory of a long ago conversation. I had asked my mother if it seemed at all possible that Raoul could kill the Phantom of the Opera. With his bare hands? No. With a gun? Yes.

The air in the room had gone brittle. I carefully set down my coffee before my suddenly shaking hands could slosh steaming liquid onto my lap.

Erik didn't look as disturbed as I felt. His hands rose, but his stance remained relaxed. "This is completely unnecessary." His voice, too, sounded calm. "I haven't done anything to Christine and I'm not trying to stop her from leaving with you if she wants to go."

"If?" Raoul snarled. "How can she possibly make a rational decision with you manipulating her, twisting her mind around?"

"I'm not manipulating anyone. Christine, would you please tell him you're here of your own free will and I'm not hypnotizing you or whatever ridiculous idea he has in mind?"

All attention went to Christine, who stared back at us with wide, scared eyes and said, "This is all so—I just don't—I really can't…"

I *knew* she'd be useless if there was a confrontation.

If she wasn't going to say anything worthwhile, I had to say something. Whether I had anything worth saying or not. "You don't want to do this, Raoul," I said, the first thing that came to mind. I didn't have any reason to think he didn't want to do this; I just knew that *I* didn't want him to do it. I grasped for an argument. "If you really wanted to kill anyone, you would have come prepared. You would have brought a gun."

"Good point," Erik said, even though I wasn't sure it was. Maybe we were both only trying to distract him. "So rather than doing something impulsive, put the gun down and we'll talk about this."

Raoul nodded deeply. "I suppose that makes sense, I can't *really* want to kill you if I just impulsively picked up a gun, right?"

"It makes sense to me," I said quickly, even as a voice in the back of my head warned that he was agreeing too easily. But after all, it was only Raoul, and if he'd just put the dangerous weapon down…

And he did. Dropped it, in fact, and gave it a kick that sent it spinning off across the room, to glance off the base of the coffee table and disappear under my couch. I was lucky it hadn't hit my foot—but I didn't care *how* he put it down, just so it wasn't pointing at Erik anymore.

"That was expensive too," Erik muttered, and I shot him an exasperated look. Who cared if he broke the gun, as long as he didn't *fire* it? Erik spared a second to shrug at me, then said to Raoul, "If you're done thinking about killing me, then Meg and I are leaving so you can talk to Christine. Which we should have done to begin with."

Back to that plan. Such a better plan. I was on my feet, coming around the back of the couch towards the side door before I glanced at Christine again. Her gaze was darting between Erik and Raoul and I didn't know what to make of her expression. She started to say something that might have begun, "I don't think—" when Raoul spoke over her.

"You're not going anywhere, Phantom. There's just one problem with the theory that I don't want to kill you, that I'm only acting on impulse." His hand was already reaching into his coat, out of the corner of my eye I saw Erik tense and start forward, but he only made a step before Raoul was leveling a second pistol at him. "I did bring a gun." And then he smiled, with the most frightening smile I had ever seen on the Vicomte de Chagny's face.

Chapter Twenty-Eight

W hat a completely stupid way to die. Killed by Raoul de Chagny. Erik had imagined his own death any number of ways, had always rather expected it to be violent, but had also expected to at least have a competent adversary.

"Christine, will you please tell him this is ridiculous?" Erik said, keeping his gaze on Raoul's gun, trying to keep his voice even because yelling at Christine was unlikely to help right now. Raoul wouldn't listen to Meg, and Erik didn't imagine any argument he could make himself would carry weight.

"I just—it's all so…" With a sob Christine crumpled down, couch creaking as she buried her face among the pillows.

Of course. What else should he have expected?

"Stop upsetting Christine!" Raoul snapped.

Clearly he might as well have yelled at her. "I did not—"

"And come over here," Raoul continued, with a sharp gesture of the pistol. "I don't want any furniture getting in the way."

"Fine," Erik said, more cooperatively than he might have otherwise—but moving as Raoul suggested put him farther away from Meg. He didn't know how bad the nobleman's aim might be, so he didn't want to be in remotely the same direction as Meg right now. Besides, this also put him closer to Raoul…

"All right, stop there," Raoul said, when Erik was still a half-dozen paces away.

Too far to easily jump him. Not too far for a difficult jump, but Raoul had both hands gripping the gun now, meaning Erik wouldn't be able to disarm him quickly. Assuming Raoul didn't get a shot off before he even reached him—big assumption—there would still be a struggle for the gun with almost certainly a wild shot then.

Erik was willing to risk being shot. But there was a chance of a stray bullet hitting Meg—or for that matter, Christine—and even if it wasn't a high chance, any chance of that was too much.

So much for that potential plan. He had a lasso tucked into the inside pocket of his jacket, but with his hands above his shoulders he couldn't get it out before Raoul would have time to shoot. He could light a fire snapping his fingers but that would do no good unless he was close enough to burn Raoul, which he wasn't.

Parlor tricks. Nothing but parlor tricks, and not enough to defeat even the Vicomte de Chagny. Comte, technically, but that was never going to sound right. Though it didn't look like he'd have much time to think about it.

Talking might be his best hope after all. An unpleasant thought. But how serious could the *vicomte* be, really?

"I know this is hypocritical of me, but are you sure you want to kill someone in front of the woman you love?" Erik asked, pitching his voice conciliatory, trying for time. "That seems like a good idea to you?"

"How can you say that after everything you did the last time we met?" Raoul demanded.

He shrugged. "I *said* it was hypocritical. But I learned something, all right? It was a bad idea."

"Wonderful, you think trying to murder me was a bad idea. I feel much better now!"

Professional pride compelled him to say, "I did not try to murder you. If I had *tried*, you would be dead. I just..." He snuck a glance at Meg. Maybe he shouldn't be saying this. "...threatened you, a little."

Meg looked pale, her lips tight and her hands gripping the back of the couch. But she didn't look hysterical, which was good. He couldn't tell how she was reacting to this discussion, which was less good. He had a sudden uneasy realization that he didn't want Raoul talking to Meg about him. There was...a disturbing amount Raoul could say that would put him in a very bad light.

He had barely thought it before Raoul said it. "So you were just *contemplating* the idea while you had me in your torture chamber?"

"No, now, wait—he's making it sound worse than it was," he appealed to Meg. "I mean, torture chamber conjures up knives and racks and—it wasn't like that."

Raoul's voice turned hideously smug as he addressed Meg with, "Did he never mention this room he has? Where he likes to bake people?"

Worse and worse. "Oh come on, that makes it sound like I had you in an oven! It's just a…sort of…fake equatorial forest. And you were really pathetic about it, by the way."

"Enough!" Raoul raised his gun to sight between Erik's eyes. "I'm ending this! It should have ended a year ago and today I'm fixing that mistake."

"Please don't do this." A whisper, a thread, the first words Meg had said in a long time.

"You don't understand," Raoul said, words cold. "He is a dangerous madman. When a dog goes mad, we shoot him. This is the same. I'm removing a menace to society, and there is no one who will be sorry. No one will even care."

Erik's world was narrowing rapidly. A new note had entered Raoul's voice, a disturbingly serious one. He had been talking wildly all this time, but maybe it hadn't been at random. Maybe it had been working himself up, to finally, truly do something.

Erik had looked death in the face before, and he knew when it was looking back.

If there was one other thing he knew, it was that he did not want to die looking at the Vicomte de Chagny. His gaze shifted away from Raoul, to rest on Meg. She was still holding the back of the couch, her knuckles white and her expression stricken. She was looking at him.

It didn't matter that she was four meters away. As he met her eyes, as their gazes locked together, the two of them might have been on the rooftop again, her face so close to his, the blue of her eyes as deep as the sky.

Raoul was wrong. Someone would care if Erik died. Meg would care very much, and while he didn't want her to be sad, it was *good* to feel that she would care. That someone would remember him and mourn him and miss him. Maybe that was the best life had to offer him, to be remembered fondly by the woman he loved. That wouldn't have been the situation at any earlier time, so in the end, maybe this was all as it should be.

She was so beautiful. Gold hair that shone even in candlelight, blue eyes that were plainly meant to be bright and laughing, yet could convey so much concern and compassion too—and that had somehow seen through so many of his masks.

How had he not seen it before? How had he wasted so much time, not seeing her? But what could he have done, if he had realized sooner? He couldn't have asked her—he couldn't have expected—no, this moment, this one moment was all there was, all there could be.

Raoul was doing him a favor. Meg had been leaving him, slipping beyond his reach, about to disappear even as he realized how desperately he wanted her. Needed her. Loved her. Now he wouldn't be forced to live through long empty years. It could all end, right here, holding Meg's face in his gaze, and trust that he would be held in turn in her memory.

He should tell her. If all he asked of life was to be remembered, then she should remember all of it. If he was dead, he couldn't frighten her, couldn't upset or impose. This was the only way he could tell her he loved her and have it be perfectly safe.

Raoul was still ranting and Christine was still sobbing, but he had stopped listening to them and didn't wait for a pause now. "I have to tell you something."

"I don't want to hear it," Raoul interrupted his own rant to say.

"I wasn't talking to you, I was talking to Meg." His focus didn't waver from her face. "There's something I have to say before I die."

At that last word, she bit her lower lip and looked down, finally breaking their long-held gaze. And then her eyes widened, she released the back of the couch, and ducked down behind it. Erik barely had time to be surprised before she was rising up again—and in her hand was his gun that had slid away under the couch.

Meg's face had assumed an expression he had never seen there before, a steel determination that suddenly reminded him that she was

Madame Giry's daughter after all. She leveled the gun at the vicomte and in a cold voice said, "Put down your weapon, Raoul."

Raoul just blinked at her, his own gun unmoving. "You can't be serious."

Could he not see the determination in her eyes?

"If you hurt Erik," Meg said, voice low and dangerous, "I will kill you."

Memory stirred as his breath caught in his chest. Primal instinct, nature's highest imperative…Madame Giry had used the same tone, warning him not to harm her daughter.

No one had ever unleashed that kind of power on his behalf before. He had never belonged to someone like that before.

The prospect of death wouldn't wring tears from him, but to be defended like that, to matter to someone like that—suddenly he had to swallow, tip his head back and widen his eyes in a desperate effort not to lose all control. How ridiculous it would be, to cry in front of Raoul, in front of Christine, in front of… Meg, perhaps, would understand.

"Meg, what are you *doing*?" Christine demanded, and Erik was surprised to hear from her at last, though he welcomed the distraction before emotions got the better of him.

"I'm stopping your husband from committing murder," Meg said, coming around the end of the couch, gun still aimed at Raoul. "You might have been outraged a little sooner, Christine."

"But you can't be taking *his* side!" Raoul protested. "You're Christine's friend!"

Meg's eyes narrowed and her chin trembled, though her hand stayed steady. "That's what you never understood. That's what no one ever understands. I am *so much more*."

Raoul was staring at her now almost as intently as Erik had been doing—and that was his chance. Erik edged one step closer, than another. Raoul had shifted his grip by now, he only had one hand holding the gun and it was drooping down to point at the floor besides. Watching the vicomte's eyes, Erik chose his moment and jumped. He caught Raoul's wrist, pressing hard on the muscles that forced his hand open, the gun falling to the floor. One kick sent it spinning away out of anyone's reach. With his free hand, Erik grabbed Raoul's collar and shook him once, just to prove he could, then shoved him towards the couch with Christine. He stumbled back and collapsed on the seat.

Meg exhaled, her whole body relaxing, and sank onto the opposite couch. She set the pistol down on the cushion next to her, and kept her hand over it.

He knew he shouldn't hug her, even though he wanted so much to take her into his arms and... He clasped his hands behind his back, tightly, and forced himself to remain standing by the fireplace. "Are you all right?"

It was a second before Meg's head lifted towards him, and then her glance slid away again almost at once anyway. "Of course. No one held a gun on me. Are *you* all right?"

"I'm fine," Erik said, somewhat gratified she had asked but wishing she would look at him. How odd. Had he ever in his life wanted to be looked at before?

Never mind, he couldn't think those things, not yet. He resolutely turned his attention towards the vicomte. "For the record, I did not abduct Christine, I have not been threatening her and she isn't a captive."

"I knew that," Raoul muttered, "but you still lured her here."

"I did not lure—" Erik blinked. "What do you mean you knew that?"

The vicomte's sulky tone did not change. "I got back from my trip to my estate this morning, and found Christine's note."

"Christine's note?" Erik said, hearing the words echoed from Meg's direction.

"She told me I obviously didn't understand how important singing was to her, so she had to go back to her Angel of Music."

Erik stared at Christine. "You *told him* you were coming here?" He barely stopped himself from voicing his next thought: I didn't think you were that stupid.

Christine sniffed, voice tremulous. "I thought it would be cruel to not even leave a message."

For a fleeting instant he remembered that departing without a word had been her plan for leaving him, a long time ago, and that might have hurt—except that he was distracted by something very different. Whether it was the intensity of what had just happened or only that he'd been surprised into really looking at her, he seemed to be seeing Christine clearly for the first time in days. And he was noticing something that didn't make sense. She was rubbing at her cheeks, which were red—and she had spent five minutes sobbing into his couch cushion—and yet her face was dry.

She had been crying for several minutes, and there were no tears on her face.

Memory pictures flipped through his mind. When Carlotta was so horrible about Christine's promotion, and Christine so clearly needed rescuing—when she pulled his mask off—when he took her down below the second time, the disastrous time—and just now... Had he ever seen actual *tears*, any of those times she'd dissolved into sobs? She had always hidden behind her hands, shoulders shaking and breath gasping.

That was an old stage trick. It was easier to gasp and shake than to produce tears, when the moment called for looking distraught.

How had he never thought of that? He was supposed to be so good at spotting illusions and deceptions.

But no, this had to be a ridiculous line of thought. The woman he knew, the woman he had fallen in love with, she was innocent, artless, not in any way capable of deliberately putting on distress during trying moments. Why would she even *want* to do that?

That answer came to him all too swiftly. Because in each of those times, hadn't he always done what she wanted whenever she cried? The ghost of his own voice came back to him, telling Christine not to cry, because he couldn't be angry when she cried.

He had never trusted Christine. Maybe he had been right not to.

Maybe he had never really known her at all.

He had mentally stepped out of the conversation for a moment, and now as he stepped back in it was to hear Raoul making extravagant vows to Christine that he really did understand the importance of music to her, and that he'd never try to stop her from singing again.

And that was it. The vicomte, for once, had exquisite timing, because that was the piece Erik needed to complete a puzzle he hadn't realized was showing only half a picture.

"It wasn't stupid leaving that note for him at all," he said. "You knew this would happen." He stared hard at Christine, not sure what he hoped or feared to see. "You told me he didn't want you to sing—he was interfering with your career, and you knew if you scared him badly enough by coming here, he'd let you do whatever you wanted."

Christine's eyes widened ever so slightly—then narrowed, and for a fleeting instant, so brief he might have imagined it, her face took on an expression he had never seen there before. Frustration, annoyance, anger? He wasn't even sure he'd seen it, let alone identified it, before her eyes went big in an expression that was entirely familiar, wounded and confused. "I don't know what you're talking about!" she protested. "That doesn't make any sense!"

He didn't bother arguing with her. He looked at Meg instead—and knew her expression easily enough. Head tilted, eyes with that distant look she got when she was thinking hard, trying to work something out. It wasn't her perplexed or confused look. It was her *thoughtful* one. So something he was saying did make sense, whatever Christine said.

"It fits together, doesn't it?" Erik said slowly, half working it out as he spoke. If he assumed that Christine was much cleverer and much less transparent than he had thought... "You knew I felt badly about what happened last year—you knew I'd help you if you asked—and you knew how Raoul would react. Even *I* could have guessed how Raoul would react, and you've been living with him for a year."

Raoul chose that moment to put his voice in again. "Christine would never go to you for help unless you lured her somehow! We only came back to Paris because the newspapers said you were *dead*. You should have been dead!"

The last sentence was only worth ignoring, the first could be dismissed since he knew perfectly well he hadn't lured Christine into anything. But the second raised a question he should have asked days ago. "How *did* you know I was alive, Christine?" Maybe it hadn't been as planned as he'd thought—but she'd clearly expected him to be in Box Five, she had left the note for Raoul...

"I told her," Meg said, raising one hand—as though she had to do that to catch his attention, which she didn't. "I'm sorry, I thought you'd want me to. I didn't expect all of—" Suddenly she frowned, and now it was her puzzled frown. "No, wait, that's not right. If Christine learned it from *me*, she couldn't have left the note for Raoul *before* she saw me—"

"I don't know what either of you are talking about!" Christine said plaintively. "You're saying I had some plan and I was just trying to decide—"

"Léon," Meg said in tones of sudden clarity, with a satisfaction Erik didn't altogether like infused in that particular name. "That's it, isn't it, Christine? You talked to Léon and *he* told you Erik was alive. But you needed me to tell you how to *find* him. You could have just said so."

Christine hesitated, biting her lower lip in a way that Erik was pretty sure he would have found very distracting a year ago. Now he just wished she'd get on with confessing any answers. "I...*did* hear a rumor from Léon," she said finally. "But I didn't think it was quite right to tell you—I wasn't certain how much you knew, and if Erik hadn't told you he was alive, that would have been rather painful to find out..."

"I think that was very considerate," the vicomte said immediately.

Christine sniffed. "Thank you, Raoul. I'm glad someone understands."

"But Léon learned it from me," Meg said, voice dry.

"He didn't *say* that!" Christine said, so swiftly that she must have been prepared for the point.

Erik never would have thought that about her words, even ten minutes earlier. But more and more pieces were coming together, things he'd half-questioned, things he'd never even thought to question but should have, all lining up in light of this new understanding of Christine. "I've felt so badly about everything that happened to you last year, but it actually worked out for you, didn't it? I've never helped another singer like I helped you, and noblemen very rarely marry chorus girls. It...couldn't have gone better for you if it had been planned." And maybe it had been.

Christine went back to sniffling, and he wondered in a detached sort of way if she was going to try crying again. "Everything that happened was so—so *frightening*! If you think I wanted all that—you're mad!"

Maybe he was. Maybe he was, at least, overreaching the limits of this rather unexpected theory. But maybe he wasn't. "Am I?" Erik asked, and he looked not at Christine, but at Meg. The one he trusted. The one who would understand.

Her gaze had gone back into the distance, thinking again, but now returned to him. She hesitated, fingers twisting at a fold of her skirt. "Something strange is happening now, but—I don't know if you really want my opinion on...before."

They'd never talked about it, had they? He'd never wanted to talk about what had happened before, and now suddenly he wondered how much that silence might have bothered Meg. He should have thought of that. "I do want to know what you think. Please."

"Well..." Her lips tightened. "No. You're not mad. Because I've always suspected that Christine knew you would follow her to the rooftop the night of the masquerade."

"Meg!" Christine protested. "How can you say that?"

Meg crossed her arms, expression troubled but posture firm. "I'm sorry, Christine, but it's the truth. I tried to ask you about it then, remember? I couldn't figure out any other reason you'd choose to run away from the Phantom by *not* leaving the Opera. And by running upstairs."

"That would explain a few things," Erik said, thinking back to that night, more dispassionately than he ever had before. "Like that terrible job you did of sneaking out of the masquerade. I mean, I would have had to *try* to miss it."

Raoul, by contrast, was anything but dispassionate, and only growing more irate. "Our moment on the rooftop was very private! Christine would never *want* you there!"

"Unless she thought it would make me go away," Erik said. "That was it, wasn't it, Christine? I had been very helpful up until then, gave you singing lessons, got you better roles at the Opera—but you knew my secret then, and a man with a face like mine is not going to do well in the drawing rooms of Paris as you advance your career." He pointed to Raoul. "Enter the handsome nobleman at the crucial moment, and all you had to do was use the threat of me to get him to propose, and the engagement with him to get rid of me—which you'd expect, because I *did* go away for days, when you first showed an interest in him." The puzzle was fascinating, a kind of artistic achievement, and in the end he felt a grudging admiration. "If I'd reacted on plan, that would have worked beautifully for you. Really, Christine, you're much smarter than I ever thought."

Her eyes were wide, much the same wide distress he'd seen often, but her face was white in a way he hadn't seen before. "You're mad."

If repeating that was the only defense she could give, then he had to be making sense. Erik grinned in spite of himself, because there was something *satisfying* about finally understanding. And he didn't care a bit if she wanted to call him mad. "I am but mad north-north-west. When the wind is southerly, I know a hawk from a handsaw."

A giggle escaped from Meg, hastily swallowed. Erik turned to catch her eye, watched her lips twitching towards a smile.

"Mad," Raoul snapped. "Utterly insane."

Meg's smile escaped her control. "It may be madness...but there's method in it."

Even in the moment, he knew it wasn't that funny. Except—she had *understood*. She had understood and tossed the conversational ball back. The realization that Christine had betrayed him far more deeply and intentionally than he had ever imagined mattered vastly less than that Meg had recognized his quote from Hamlet's mad scene, and been able and willing to throw a quote back to him.

The pressure in his throat and the clenching in his stomach got away from him, erupting into—a laugh.

Meg's eyes opened wider in surprise, and her smile grew. That made him laugh again, and by the time she began to laugh too, he didn't even know what he was laughing *at* anymore—it was just an uncontrollable, irrepressible bubbling-up of laughter.

He laughed until his legs wobbled and he couldn't breathe and he had to sit down against the post of his fireplace, still laughing. Meg had one hand over her mouth, shoulders shaking with mirth, and every time he thought he might get control he looked at her and lost it again.

It had been more than a year since he had laughed at all, and he had never in his entire life laughed this hard.

Raoul and Christine had been silent and ignored as all this went on, but finally Christine said, "They're *both* mad. Raoul, let's *go*. Now."

She rose to her feet and Raoul was only just a beat behind her as she swept towards the door.

Erik felt vaguely that he ought to say something—but he didn't have any breath available for talking. And besides, he didn't have anything left to say to Christine.

Between laughs, Meg managed, "Christine, wait…"

"We have nothing to say," Christine said coldly. "I can see where your loyalties lie."

That seemed like simple truth. And Meg nodded agreement—and that was more important than anything Christine had to say.

Nothing more was said. Christine marched out the door with Raoul trailing a step behind her. Erik suspected that was going to be their pattern for the rest of their lives.

The closing of the door put a punctuation on the moment. The laughter began to die away, and he was confronted with the absolute realization that he was going to live after all.

And that meant he had to decide what to do next.

Chapter Twenty-Nine

T he room grew much quieter after Christine and Raoul left, after the laughter finally ran its course. Laughing, Erik and I had understood each other, had shared some confused tangle made up of *Hamlet* quotes and endless conversations and standing on the same side when Raoul waved a gun around and even when Christine set about breaking hearts and betraying friends and we were just...*together* in all of it.

But when I swallowed my last giggle, awkwardness entered the room. At least, I felt that. I didn't know what he felt. That was the problem.

I looked down at my hands, started fingering the gold design on the pistol sitting on the couch next to me. Then I realized what I was doing and hurriedly put the gun on the table by the coffee, out of absentminded reach.

I finally let my glance go to Erik, and found he was watching me. "So. Are you sure you're all right?" I asked, because I had to say something.

He smiled. To my eyes, a genuine smile. "Alive, not shot and not mad. So, yes."

I would have liked to laugh again, but my heart wasn't in it. I knew he was physically all right; that wasn't what I had been asking. But I didn't quite have the nerve to ask him about Christine. Anything about Christine. I reached up to play with my necklace.

He was saying her name again, and he was laughing. He wasn't singing, though. And had I even got it right, when I thought those three things were the indicators that he was not—would never be—done with mourning Christine? And how did all these fresh revelations, about her true intentions all along, change things? Was it freeing, or did it only tie him more closely to her, by deepening the pain she had caused?

I didn't even have an answer for myself in that regard, let alone figuring out how he felt.

While I wondered and hesitated, he got to his feet and came to join me on the couch. He dropped into the opposite corner, leaned back and closed his eyes for one long breath. When he opened them again, he said, "Thank you. For…everything."

I tried to put analysis aside and smiled, just a little. "You're welcome."

"I mean, no one has ever—it was really…" He ran a hand over his hair. "*Thank you* is so inadequate, but I don't know how to say…"

"It's all right." Erik only lost control of sentences when something was important to him. My smile grew slightly. "Anyway, you were the one who actually disarmed Raoul."

Erik shook his head. "I could only do it because you distracted him. And he would have dropped the gun in another minute anyway if I hadn't stepped in. Which is fortunate, since it would have all fallen apart if he'd tried calling the bluff instead."

My smile vanished. "I wasn't bluffing." I had never been so sure of anything, as I had been in that moment when I could see only one way to stop Raoul from doing something unthinkable.

"Oh—no, I know, that was obvious." He hunched one shoulder, obviously fumbling for clarification. "I mean—well, you didn't know, so—"

"Know what?"

"That gun," he said, gesturing to it. "I, ah, requisitioned it from the prop room. It's loaded with blanks."

I blinked once, then again.

"The detailing on the handle is really excellent craftsmanship," he elaborated. "It was being wasted on stage where no one could see it properly. It's from that Russian opera, you know the one—"

"I don't care *what* opera—you have multiple secret exits from your apartments, you carry a lasso around in your cloak, but you never put real bullets in your gun?" I was irrationally, ridiculously outraged by this. It made no difference. It was a reasonable safety precaution. And yet...

"It's meant to be a decorative piece! Besides, guns were never my style, they're too...imprecise." Erik frowned, shook his head again. "Never mind, the gun doesn't matter. You still rescued me from the mad vicomte, and I was trying to say thank you, but that feels so inadequate, I just..." He groaned, rubbed his palms against his pantlegs. "I'm more articulate with music notes than I am with words."

My brief outrage had already faded, and now I only shrugged. "You could write me a song then."

His gaze met mine, those green eyes that still made my breath catch. "I'll do that," he said, and though I had suggested it almost at random, there was a new intensity in his tone.

It occurred to me, suddenly, how very easy it would be to slide over a little, to lean sideways. He had one arm stretched along the back of the couch, and it created a space that I just knew I would fit into perfectly, I could rest my head on his shoulder...and he was still looking at me and my fingers tightened in my lap and...

And his gaze dropped, breaking the connection, and my body suddenly remembered I hadn't breathed in several seconds and exhaled.

He was sitting almost sideways in the corner of the couch, and he didn't have to turn his head far to look over his shoulder, over the back of the couch towards the door. "You know, when she left, she didn't even look back."

My stomach twisted and my hands, steady a moment before, now wanted badly to shake.

Of course. What did I expect? After all this, after *everything*, he was still thinking about Christine.

I pushed off the couch, rose to my feet. "I should go."

Erik blinked up at me in baffled surprise. "Right now? Right away, after..."

I smoothed my skirts, tried not to look at him, tried to ignore the ache starting in my throat. "I have a meeting with the managers. About leaving, you know. So I'd better...get to that." I didn't care at all about the meeting but it made an excuse. Though I didn't think it was about leaving—more likely it was about the rumors of my involvement with the Phantom, but I couldn't see a way to say that that wouldn't be trying to make him feel guilty.

He got to his feet more slowly, and I furtively watched the gracefulness of the motion. "I should walk you back."

The pressure in my throat said no, because I wasn't going to make it all the way back to the surface without losing control entirely. "No, that's all right. I'm fine. Really."

Did he know what I was feeling? He was staring at me with a focus I didn't recognize. It didn't suggest suspicion, but what it was I couldn't read, only it made me feel guilty and conflicted about going.

"And stop *looking* at me like that," I snapped. He flinched and glanced away. "It's not as though I won't be back," I said, though neither of us had previously raised that topic. "It's at least a week before we're leaving for Vienna."

Part of me clamored that that was still too soon, that I shouldn't leave at all, that I should stay, right here, with him. Another part kicked that first part and said that if I felt like that, I couldn't get away fast enough.

With the voices in my head, I only barely heard Erik say, "Can you come back tomorrow?"

The second voice was still strongest. "I don't know...it's my last day at the Opera, there's the special performance in the evening, it'll be very busy..."

"Please?"

Just that, just the one word, but he was looking at me again and I could almost believe that nothing mattered to him more than my answer to this question.

How could he look at me like that, if he still loved Christine?

She didn't even look back. I reminded myself of the words, tried to bolster up my resolve. And I still couldn't say no. "There's a morning rehearsal. I could come by after that. So about eleven?"

"Eleven," he repeated, as though he was carefully memorizing it. "Good."

"Right." I nodded. "All right then." I turned to go, but made only four steps towards the door before it occurred to me there was something else to say—or at least to ask. I knew I should keep walking, but against my better judgment, I stopped and turned back. "You were going to tell me something."

He didn't meet my gaze now, smoothed his pantlegs. "When?"

"When Raoul was pointing that gun at you." I already regretted stopping. If I thought about *that* moment right now, my hands were going to shake in earnest and I was going to lose whatever vestige of calm I still had. "You said you had to tell me something," I pushed past my tightening throat.

"Oh. Right." His gaze drifted around the room, slid right past me, landed on the mantle. "It was just—if I died, the secret drawer with the money—"

"I remember." I should have known. That was all he'd wanted to tell me before the mob came too, how to find his money if he died. "See you tomorrow," I said, and this time I got out without stopping.

I didn't pause to pat the gargoyles, just hurried down the passage and took the secret door to go out by the Rue Scribe, one hand holding my gold necklace. I hurried around the first turn and then the second, got as far as being able to see the grating that led out to the street before the sob finally rose up from my throat and the tears started, spilling from burning eyes to slip down my cheeks. The grating brought back the afternoon we'd spent in Paris, reminded me of everything that might be but wouldn't ever be, because the most observant man I'd ever known *still couldn't see me.*

I sank down to sit on the stone floor, pressed my wet face against my palms, and hoped the sound of sobs wasn't going to carry back to the Phantom's rooms.

I couldn't keep doing this. I couldn't keep breaking my heart. I couldn't keep waiting and hoping, but in this moment the idea of losing that hope seemed to take every bit of light out of my life, leaving me in a darkness that was not the magical shadowland that Erik knew, but just a black, blank void.

I thought I might stay in that corridor until I ran out of tears.

But instead, a small, defiant, angry part of me uncurled itself and said *no*. And I made the tiny but crucial shift from couldn't to *wouldn't*.

I would not keep doing this.

No Opera Ghost was coming to help me find my way out of this dead-end, to point me along a smooth and easy path to a happy future. I'd have to make my own path.

I pulled my handkerchief from one pocket to wipe my cheeks, pushed hair back from my face, and took a long, slow, deep breath that didn't splinter into a sob.

What was I so afraid of losing anyway? All the pain and heartbreak and...and *absurdity* of pining after a man who didn't love me and never would. I had had *enough,* enough of wondering and wishing and hoping and trying to parse what the angle of a gaze or a choice of couches meant. Every time I had thought of telling him my feelings, he'd managed to do something to show it would be a terrible mistake. So if I was wrong, if any of the other signs meant he did care for me, then he was going to have to *tell* me that using actual words— and since he hadn't told me anything except where to find his money if he died, there was clearly no point in waiting around any longer.

Mother was right. A new life, a new start, that was what I needed. I didn't need to waste any more time crying in dark tunnels.

And if I could face down a mad vicomte with a gun, I certainly ought to be able to face anything else waiting for me too.

Chapter Thirty

L iving was more complicated than dying. Though really, it was just one question that ran relentlessly through his mind as he paced the length of his parlor. Was he going to tell her—or not?

It had been clear enough when he thought he was going to die—one declaration and then a dramatic exit worthy of any magician. But now when he'd have to stay on the stage, and actually face the consequences…it became complicated.

He had promised to write her a song, and in the moment that had felt so right, an adequate response to what she had done for him. But now he had to decide what that song would *say*.

He sat down sideways on his piano bench, rested one arm on the frame and pressed some idle keys. He could always take the easy way. Write a nice melody with no lyrics, which wouldn't technically be a song but she likely wouldn't object. And that would be that. Or he could write something to celebrate friendship, and that would be safe enough too.

And then she would leave for Vienna, and they'd exchange letters, and eventually, likely in the not-distant future, one of those letters would mention meeting someone special. Knowing Meg, she'd probably send him a wedding invitation, and then his choice would be to accept, or to go up to the rooftop and consider voids after all.

Or he could *really* write her a song.

What was the worst that could happen?

He winced, pressed his forehead against his clenched fist. She could be disgusted by the whole idea, terrified by the possible ramifications, run away and he would never see her again.

He dropped his hand again, played a few more notes. Surely that, at least, was paranoia and exaggeration. It wasn't even being fair to Meg. More likely, more realistically, she was going to be very *kind*, and very *sorry*, and just not able to return his affections and it would all be unbearably uncomfortable for both of them.

And then either she'd never want to see him again because it would be too awkward, or she'd be willing to continue as friends, whatever that meant when she was leaving Paris in ten days, 17 hours, but then it *would* be awkward, awkward enough to ruin everything anyway.

He had to be out of his mind to consider this course.

He pushed up from the piano, went back to pacing.

But what if maybe, just maybe, there was the sliver of a chance…

All his life, he had always looked at the worst possible outcomes. But what about the *best*?

What if she didn't hate the idea. What if she thought it was at least a possibility… He stopped, staring at his Degas painting of ballet dancers, seeing a different dancer in his mind's eye.

She cared about him; he knew that. Nobody could look the way she had, staring down that idiot Raoul, if she didn't care about him. But the leap from friendship to love…

If only he had more *time*.

If only he could keep her down here somehow. He toyed with that kidnapping plan briefly, but it was no more reasonable now than it had been before. Less, even. Now he knew all the more clearly that he could never do that to her. Hoping for Christine to stay down here had been just barely a possibility—probably that had been mad too, but at least she had seemed like she might be able to live on music alone, to belong in the shadowy beauty of darkness.

Meg, who dreamed of traveling, who loved daffodils, who ate tangerines on sunny afternoons on the rooftop of the Opera, could never live in the darkness. She might be more willing than Christine to visit his kingdom, but he couldn't force her to stay.

He could never justify that. He might as well lure her into the cellars with a cask of Amontillado, and then wall her up in the darkness.

He flung himself into his armchair, stared broodingly at the gargoyle in the corner. When had the Quasimodos of the world ever succeeded in winning the girl's heart? Cyrano de Bergerac had had no happy ending, and as for Dr. Frankenstein's poor misshapen creature, his best hope had involved digging up a corpse; that hadn't ended well either.

Although…in spite of himself, he smiled a little…he and Meg had already turned gothic tradition on its head. The beautiful blond girl had rescued the shadowy cloaked man from the handsome nobleman. So there was that. But this next idea, this flew in the face of every expectation, not just of gothic literature but of his own world view. Of his own beliefs about what was ever possible for his life.

Most likely the choice was between not telling her and losing her, and telling her and still losing her. So maybe he shouldn't even be thinking about outcomes. Maybe it was simpler after all.

He reached up, ran one fingertip down the cheek of his mask.

Maybe the real question was whether he had had enough of hiding.

I wiped my face and left Erik's kingdom to come out on the Rue Scribe; I had probably been too emotional to find my way through the labyrinth today. It would have been easy now to just go home, to keep my back to the Opera Garnier looming behind me and simply walk away. But there was the meeting with the managers. Even though all I really wanted to do was go into my room and hide under a blanket and not *deal* with anything more today.

Sort of. But I also wanted to prove to myself that I could be that defiant girl who had stood up from crying and promised herself she could face anything. Surely I could face Moncharmin and Ricard, for heaven's sake.

Besides, Mother was at the Opera, and was supposed to be meeting them with me, and she wouldn't be happy if I didn't show up.

She also might leap to terrible suspicions and summon the police to confront Léon. That couldn't end well.

So I made myself walk to the front of the Opera, stepped through the doors and glanced in the first mirror I passed. At least my nose wasn't red, and I didn't look as though I'd been crying. Sort of a relief, though it might have made a reasonable excuse to myself that I ought to leave.

I wondered if there was the slightest chance at all that I was going to bump into Erik again today. Did I want to? I wanted to see him as often as I possibly could—and I wanted to never, ever see him again.

He was probably still down below, brooding.

I tried to shake all thoughts of Erik away—utterly useless exercise—and ascended the marble stairs towards the upper levels and the managers' office.

I took a breath before I entered the office, put on a confident expression and went in with my head high.

Mother was already inside, already with a pinch of worry in her forehead. "Meg, you're late. I was beginning to wonder…"

"I'm sorry, I got a bit distracted at my earlier appointment." That was one way to describe it.

Moncharmin and Ricard were standing behind their desk, both trying to look stern. Moncharmin was better at it than Ricard. Ricard had his arms folded and was making an attempt at a glower, while Moncharmin stood with his hands on the edge of the desk, trying to loom except he wasn't quite tall enough for it.

I had never been able to take them as seriously as I probably should have, considering the power they wielded, and now the idea that they might think themselves threatening was almost laughable. They only held power in this one small corner of the world.

And they were so much less dangerous than so many other people I knew.

Like a jealousy-crazed vicomte with a gun; a wealthy young man who thought too much of his own rights; a smiling, false-faced friend; a man who could break my heart without ever intending to. This was nothing by comparison.

I dropped into a chair in front of the managers' desk without waiting for either manager to invite me to sit down, crossed my ankles and folded my hands over my knee. "I suppose you brought me here to tell me you disapprove of me for getting involved with the Phantom?"

Ricard and Moncharmin exchanged confused expressions. Probably they had expected me to come in repentant and afraid.

They didn't understand. My world was already ending—at least, this one was. That meant there was nothing anyone here could do to me anymore.

Ricard cleared his throat. "We, ah, heard some very disturbing rumors about you which we felt we must address…"

"That I was having liaisons with the Phantom, yes, I know," I agreed. "Would you believe me if I denied it?"

"*Meg*," Mother said in a shocked undertone.

"Well, we like to give everyone the benefit of the doubt, naturally," Ricard blustered. "And of course if you can clear up these little stories…"

"These little stories that are based on—what evidence, exactly? I suppose Jammes started it, she never liked me." It would carry more weight if Léon had talked to them—but he had no reason to do that, now that I'd resigned. Besides, if they had got the word direct from Léon, they probably would have risked Madame Thibault's wrath and taken more drastic action by now. Bar me from the building, or something. Setting Léon aside, that brought it down to Jammes' word against mine. "It seems to me, you have enough support for the stories to ruin me in the Opera no matter what I say. But—not enough to bring in Commissaire Mifroid and try to pursue anything legally." I smiled sweetly. "All you can really do is fire me. And I'm already leaving tomorrow anyway."

"I do not like this insolent tone," Moncharmin said, puffing up with indignation. "We ought to throw you out this moment!"

In barely more than a week, it wouldn't matter. And until we left Paris, I knew how to use the grating on the Rue Scribe to get to the only part of the Opera that really mattered to me anymore. "If you like," I said, maintaining my smile. "You can explain to Madame Thibault about who will be taking my place in tomorrow evening's special performance."

"Ah. Well..." Moncharmin tugged on his collar. "I suppose—as long as you are leaving shortly regardless—though I do hope you have a full appreciation of the consequences of your deplorable actions—"

"The consequences of *my* actions?" My eyes narrowed, and an anger that I'd been keeping back for too long finally saw an opportunity to come out. "I also appreciate the consequences of *your* actions. No one has mentioned the mob in the articles about the Phantom's death. Did you ask Mifroid to keep that detail out? Did you not want the audience to imagine artists hounding a man to his death? How well do you suppose *that* story would go over with your ticket buyers?"

"Now see here," Ricard protested, "there is no reason for all this hostility—"

"I watched someone *die*," I said, glaring at him with all the fury of many reasons, even if the one I said was a lie. "Pardon me if I feel *hostile*."

"You may feel you are outside our reach," Moncharmin said swiftly, "but your mother is still in our employ—"

"Actually, I am resigning as well," Mother put in, voice quite calm, as though this was merely a simple business conversation. "We have plans to travel abroad."

Moncharmin, previously leaning forward, sank back into his seat. "Well. That is...very convenient."

"I thought so," I agreed, and rose to my feet. "I think we're done here."

They didn't object, and Mother and I both turned to go.

"I would have expected better," Ricard said in heavy tones, "of Christine Daaé's friend."

I stopped, but I didn't look back. "Maybe so. But that was *never* who I am."

Erik finally pushed away from his piano in the early evening. He had been there for hours, and he had done all that he could do. So he told himself, and resisted a twitching urge to change one more note, adjust one more word of a lyric. It was *done*. He had made a decision and soon it would all be done, one way or another. She was leaving in ten days, 12 hours. What happened would happen, and a kind of fatalistic freedom dwelled in that.

He could do nothing more until tomorrow. And tomorrow…if it went badly…no, he was trying not to think about that. That was an undoubtedly futile effort and he would spend the rest of the night thinking about all the ways this could go badly—but he could at least *try* to imagine the possibility of it going well.

That was harder to picture. But he wanted that, so much…

He realized with a sudden start that he had been staring at his painting of angels for five minutes. Perhaps…maybe he was wrong, maybe there was one more thing he might try…if he dared. He snatched up a cloak and set off at a near-run.

Notre Dame Cathedral was still open, though mostly deserted this late in the day. No one paid any attention to him among the welcoming shadows. At least, not until he had lit most of the candles in front of the bronze crucifix to the right of the door. Then a priest in a black cassock came gliding up to inquire if Monsieur needed assistance.

"Yes." Erik paused, taper still in hand. "You can tell me how many candles there are."

The priest looked at the rows of candles in front of them. "You mean here?"

"No, no, in the entire cathedral. I want to light all of them."

"Are you aware there is a recommended donation per each—"

"Yes, I know, that's why I'm asking." Erik shook his head, and brought a paper note into his hand with a snap of his fingers. "Never mind, this should be enough."

He handed it over, and the priest nearly dropped the paper as he looked at it. "A thousand franc note—!"

Erik resumed lighting candles. "It's a very large prayer."

"Do you need any assistance?" This in much warmer tones. "Anything at all?"

"No." He stared meditatively at the flickering flames. "Except that I prefer not to be disturbed."

"Of course, Monsieur!"

And he wasn't. And when he had made his way all around the cathedral, and banks of fire glowed before every statue, he came to a final halt in front of a statue of the Madonna and Child. There were more than one, but the first Madonna he'd seen looked vaguely bad-tempered, and this one had a kinder expression. She had clearly been a better mother than his ever was—and a child Jesus was less off-putting than the sad-eyed man on the various crosses around the cathedral. After all, it was a hopeful prayer.

He looked up at the stone faces for a long, long time before he found any words, and then he had to clear his throat twice before he could manage even a whisper. Somehow it seemed to count more, out loud, and there was no one nearby to hear. "I know there's no real reason you should listen to me...although I expect Meg thinks you would, so maybe..." He hung his head, candles flickering at the corners of his vision. "I'm not asking you to make her love me. I don't suppose you do that kind of thing, and anyway it doesn't seem right exactly, but...please, just this once, please, don't let me ruin everything. Just...as long as she isn't afraid, all right? I can live with anything else, just not that." He pressed one palm against the cool stone of the statue's base. "Please help me get this right."

Chapter Thirty-One

W hatever new confidence I'd found to confront the managers, it didn't seem to apply the next morning. My last ballet rehearsal, a final rehearsal for the special performance, went about as well as could be expected, considering. There was a notable lack of proper farewell or expression of appreciation for all my years at the Opera. Even Madame Thibault ignored the fact that it *was* my final rehearsal. I had just enough confidence to keep my head up and ignore their ignoring of the situation.

But then I was going to see Erik. I had left so precipitously the day before. Why should I imagine that today was going to be any easier, any less fraught with emotion?

Maybe we could pretend that yesterday had never happened, that it was still a week ago when we were—well, mostly comfortable with each other.

Or maybe he was going to talk about Christine. Maybe he was going to realize that he really was devastated she had left *again*, and then I was—going to be sympathetic? Tell him that he and his grief could both go jump in the underground lake because I couldn't stand this anymore? Probably not that, but maybe. Maybe that would be the smart response, better than getting all twisted up about it again.

He didn't waylay me en route, and I walked all the way to the last corridor and the gargoyles. I paused to pat each one, with an odd thrill of defiance. On some level, this was still my place and I belonged here. Today. Maybe not ever again. But today.

Then I knocked at the door.

It swung open almost instantly, Erik just beyond the doorstep, unlike his usual trick of unlocking it from across the room. "Hello," he said, even that single word coming out noticeably fast. "You came."

I tilted my head slightly, raised an eyebrow. "Of course I did. I said I would."

"Yes, well..." He stared at me for a few seconds, blinked, and appeared to suddenly notice he was blocking the doorway. He backed up into the room and I stepped past him inside.

So he was in some kind of mood, though it was hard to tell exactly what, or what was causing it. I tried to read something in his eyes, but he wasn't meeting my gaze now. His white half-mask showed more of his face than most, but I still couldn't interpret his expression.

"What's wrong?" I asked. Had something happened with Christine? With Mifroid?

"Nothing," he said, still too quickly. "I mean—well—it's sort of a...difficult week. I mean, you're leaving for Vienna."

"And Raoul tried to kill you," I prompted. "And Christine probably betrayed everyone much more seriously than we thought. And then left. Again." Why was I bringing her up? I didn't want to talk about her—but it was impossible not to think of her.

"Right, all that too," he agreed. "But that's not important, I didn't want to talk about that today."

Neither did I—and yet I couldn't stop myself from saying, "It's not important that Christine left?"

"No, it isn't. Not very. But can we—"

"It was important to you *yesterday*."

His visible eyebrow rose. "No," he repeated. "It wasn't."

I was stubbornly stuck on the idea. "You *said* that she didn't even look back."

His eyes grew distant, as though he was genuinely trying to remember a comment that had echoed in my head all night.

"Oh…right, I was thinking I didn't know why I wasted so much time on a woman who didn't care enough to look back when she left."

"Oh," I said faintly. Could a sentence mean the exact opposite of what I had thought it meant? "That's interesting."

"No," he groaned, "it's really not, and I don't know why we're wasting time now talking about it. Even Christine isn't that interesting; up until the end it was the most boring—never mind, it's not important and I have to tell you something."

My head was still spinning, but this sentence sparked recognition. "I remember where the money is."

He winced. "No, not that. This is different, this is…that is, I…" He took a deep breath, let it out. "You should sit down."

I looked at the armchair across from the piano, looked at Erik again. He was clearly agitated and through my haze I started to worry. "Do you have bad news?"

"No!" He frowned. "Maybe. I don't know. Could you just…?" He gestured at the chair.

As I passed him and the piano, he muttered, "I should have lit more candles."

I stopped in front of the chair, looked at him again in puzzlement. "There are just as many candles lit in here as usual."

He stared at me, seeming more confused by my remark than I had been by his. "Yes," he said finally. "Of course there are. Right."

That explained nothing, and I gave up trying to understand. I sat down, sweeping my yellow skirt out to the sides. I had worn my best dress for my last day at the Opera, though I wondered why I had bothered. "All right, sitting. What is it?"

Another long inhale and exhale, and then finally he said, "I wrote you a song."

This was so entirely unexpected that it may have been good after all that I was sitting down. "You did? I was mostly kidding, I didn't expect—and since yesterday?"

His shoulders hunched. "I write quickly. And that doesn't mean I didn't think about it, because I did. More revising than usual, in fact."

"No, of course, I didn't mean..." I shook my head. Apparently we were both going to be awkward today. I took a breath and ordered myself to be *normal*. "So do I get to hear this song?

"Yes." He walked slowly over to the piano, stared at the keys for a moment, fingers tapping against the top board, then looked at me again. "If you don't like it, we don't ever have to talk about this again. Just so you know."

"Why wouldn't I like it?" I smiled in a way I hoped was reassuring. "You know I love your music."

"Yes." A breath. "Keep that in mind." With a strange air of finality, he sat down behind the piano, placed his fingers on the keys, and launched into the music.

I should have realized that if Erik said "song," he meant *song*. He was the last person in the world likely to use musical terms vaguely or incorrectly. And yet I was so accustomed to Erik *not* singing that I automatically assumed he meant "melody," something instrumental with no words, or that if he did write an actual song, he'd still only play the music and hand me written lyrics. So I was taken completely by surprise when, after a bar or two, he began to sing.

This was completely mad. He *knew* he was going to regret it. But he was committed to this course, he was going to see it through, whatever disaster it might lead to. She was leaving in nine days, 19 hours, and this was his only chance.

At least he had got her to sit down, in case, as in one of his imagined scenarios, she wound up fainting. Not that she seemed the fainting type, but...

His fingers danced across the keys, his melody spilling out of the piano, and he kept his gaze on his hands even though he didn't need to look to play. Another bar and he was up to the first line of lyrics. He took a deep breath, bracing himself, and released it into the song.

"I never dared to dream of daffodils, or sunny afternoons.
Of dancing through a Mardi Gras—not in a hundred moons."

He wished there was another Mardi Gras, another crowd he could hide within, another excuse to hold her in a dance. He'd appreciate it so much more, now. And it was strange, how the terrifying idea of a Mardi Gras seemed so comparatively *safe*, so much less vulnerable than this moment, right now.

"I never dreamed my life could change, or that a dream just might come true,
Not until that day, the day that I met you."

He wondered how she was reacting, if any hint was written on her face. He wanted so much to look, but—no, he didn't have that kind of courage.

"I didn't know it then, I was too blind to see,
That everything would start to change, because you spoke to me.
I never had a friend like this, I didn't know what to do,
Not at all that day, the day that I met you."

He could still deny everything, if he stopped now. He could hide behind that word, *friend*, deny that the melody was already telling a different story, already expressing a different emotion. She had listened to so much of his music, listened to him write his soul in notes so many times—how well could she read him?

"Then days passed days, with stories, notes and tangerines,
You shone through all my shadows, a soft and graceful gleam.
Sometimes you laughed, sometimes you yelled, but you always understood,
Until that day I met you, I thought no one ever could."

He shouldn't have put in the line about yelling, he was nearly sure of that as soon as it was sung. But he *did* love that about her, that if he yelled, she yelled back. No one else trusted him that way. No one else felt that safe around him.

Never mind, on to another verse. The bridge was catching flame behind him, line by line.

"I never thought to tell you—I didn't realize,
The worlds that opened up, when I looked into your eyes.
Though this be madness, there's method in it too,

On this path we've walked, since the day that I met you."
The music was swelling into a greater intensity as he approached the final verse, and his heart seemed to pound harder with every note. It was terrifying enough singing—what was he going to do when the song ended?

"You've seen past all my masks, you've seen my very soul,
Yet I doubt you know how much you have me in your hold.
I didn't have the courage, to say what I know is true,
Not until this day—to say that I love you."

Rubicon crossed. Bridge burned.

A few more notes, and then, silence. He stared at his hands, at his fingers against the ivory of the keys. All through the song, he hadn't dared to look at her. He should, he had to—but she wasn't saying anything, and Meg was not quiet, they had always talked so easily, at least after the first few times...it had only been a matter of seconds, any moment she was going to say something, and—

"The third verse," he said desperately, trying to sound casual, holding himself tightly together because if he relaxed a muscle he knew he'd fall to pieces, "um, the last line of the third verse, it doesn't match the rest. And I'm not sure about, ah, the progression—of the melody, I mean—or the ideas, really. I thought—but I'm not sure—"

"Erik," she interrupted, and his name in her voice sent an ache through him. Footsteps followed, and he looked up instinctively before he could stop himself. She had risen from the chair—no fainting, that was something—crossed the steps between them to stand just on the other side of the piano. "Erik, you just said—"

"I know," he said, and the words felt harder to force out than the entire song. "I just—I wanted you to know." He was seeing her face at last and she was so beautiful it hurt, her eyes wide and bright and not afraid, thank God for that, but he didn't know—he couldn't read what she was thinking and—if he had taken a step too far, if she left him behind, how was he ever going to live without the light from her eyes? His gaze darted back to his hands; it was too hard to look at her. "I'm not expecting anything," he said quickly, a hopeless effort to stave off the worst of what could be coming. "And—I don't want you to feel you have to—and if you'd rather not—"

"What if I'd rather?" she whispered, and he could just see her hands on the top board of the piano, reaching towards him, stopping short.

What if she'd...*what if she'd*...what did that *mean*? He forced his gaze up again, fingers instinctively curling up at the sight of tears glimmering in her eyes. No, no, that couldn't be good. "Please don't cry."

She wiped the tears with the back of one hand, without looking away from his face. "They're not bad tears, Erik, I just—I've loved you for so long," she said, her voice catching on the words, "and I thought you'd never see me."

With one sentence, she had upended his entire world.

"I...didn't see that," he said slowly, repeating her words again and again in his head, trying to make sure they said what he thought they did. Not that it was a complicated sentence—but never, in his most hopeful fantasies, had he imagined *this* response. This had to be impossible, and he couldn't stop himself asking, "Are you sure?"

She laughed, a laugh that was half a sob and the loveliest sound he had ever heard. Then she slipped around the piano, sat on the bench next to him, facing the opposite direction, facing him. He could feel her leg against his, feel her warmth just a breath away. "Yes," she said, "yes, I am so sure."

He reached a hand up, cautiously touched her cheek with one fingertip. Her skin was even softer than he had imagined it might be. "I never dared to dream of that."

He didn't know what to do about it now, he hadn't written a libretto for this so unlikely possibility. But she was smiling and he could feel himself falling into her eyes and she was leaning towards him and he was almost sure he was about to figure out what came next—

"Oh, wait," she said suddenly, straightening up the fraction she'd moved in.

"What is it?" he asked, letting his hand drop. She didn't look upset, but he felt himself tense again anyway, unsure about this new direction.

She reached for his hand, the one still resting on the piano, laced her fingers through his. The warmth of her touch was a comfort, a counterbalance to the small wrinkle in her forehead, the hesitation in her voice as she said, "Would you do something for me?"

"Anything," he said, because he would—but what was it? What did she want?

She lifted her free hand, the hesitation in her eyes now, and touched the mask on the right side of his face. "Please...stop hiding from me?"

Oh. It was this.

It would have been nice, if this dream had lasted for more than a moment.

He knew he could say no, refuse to take off the mask, cling to whatever protection it could still offer him.

But this was Meg. Meg asking him to trust her. Meg who had already seen his face, who hadn't run away yet.

He had shown her his heart and she hadn't run away. Was it any riskier to show her his face now?

Of course it was. She was asking to see the reason this could never work, the reason this dream was so impossible, because how could she look at his face and still claim she loved him?

His lips tightened and his eyes slid closed. Maybe it was better this way, to end this before he had really believed in its existence. "Go ahead," he said, barely more than a breath.

He felt her fingertips curl around the edge of his mask, felt the air touch his face as she slowly pulled his last disguise away.

"Are you still sure?" he asked heavily, unmoving. He didn't open his eyes. He didn't want to see the change that had to be on her face.

A faint thunk as she set the mask down on top of the piano. Then she was touching his twisted cheek, his misshapen brow, disentangling the fingers of her other hand from his, to press her palm against the opposite side of his face. "Yes. Very sure."

He didn't dare open his eyes for another reason now, because he could feel they had grown suddenly wet. Because she still wasn't running away.

Her lips pressed against his skin, kissing just above his eye, where an eyebrow should have been, and he sighed, something that had been tight and hard inside of him all for as long as he could remember suddenly relaxing into her touch. "Did you know," she said, lips moving against his skin, "that you have the loveliest green eyes?" She kissed his temple, his cheek, the corner of his jaw, and he was frozen, afraid to do anything to break this moment, and yet also feeling safer than he had ever felt in his life.

Her breath moved across his skin, and he could feel the warmth on his own lips now, kindling an ache of longing inside of him. "Look at me," she whispered, and he opened his eyes, looking into her face so close to his. "I see you too," she said softly.

No one saw him. No one saw him and accepted him—except her. His breath was tight in his throat. He barely murmured, "Meg…" and then her lips were on his.

He didn't know how to do this. He didn't have enough experience for this—but after one instant of panic it didn't seem to matter because her mouth was moving against his, lips just barely parted, and he drank in the taste of her, drowning in her kiss. Her arms slipped around his shoulders, one hand tangling in his hair, and he reached out to hold her— tentatively at first, but she pressed against him, and he held her tighter, closer, held her as though he would never have to let her go.

Chapter Thirty-Two

Butterflies did pirouettes in my stomach, the whole world spun into a dizzying crescendo and I never wanted it to stop. Kissing Erik was better than I had ever imagined it might be—but I hadn't let myself imagine it often, too sure that it was too impossible. I had never imagined Erik singing me a love song, never imagined what his eyes would look like when every mask was gone.

We kissed and we kissed and we might have sat there for a long, long time if Erik's arm hadn't bumped into the piano keys and set off a discordant clash of notes. His wince was so marked that I couldn't help giggling, as much from the larger moment as from the immediate cause.

After a second, he laughed too, not the intense, extended laughter of yesterday, not the villain laugh I'd occasionally heard from the Phantom over the years, but a low, pleased chuckle that made something inside me melt—and made me set an immediate goal of hearing that laugh again and again.

That didn't stop me from interrupting this one with another kiss. But after a moment he pulled me up from the piano bench, murmuring something like, "Maybe not near the…" And then I wasn't sure if he pulled me or I pushed him but we ended up tumbling into his armchair. I hadn't thought two people would fit there, but he pulled me onto his lap and we went back to kissing.

Finally, at length, I came up for air, giddy with kissing, with music, with knowing that *Erik* loved *me*—and I drew back just far enough to be able to look into his face again.

I traced one fingertip along his brow, down his cheek. It was thrilling that I was suddenly, incredibly allowed to do this. I studied the right side of his face, the side I had seen so rarely. I felt sure, if I looked at his face for any length of time—and I wanted to, I wanted so many days and weeks and years of Erik—I was going to get used to it. The very beautiful or the very ugly, both seem less extreme with familiarity. And he—was just Erik.

I could feel him looking at me looking at him, and I didn't want to talk about the facial deformity, not on this wonderful, delightful day, so instead I said, "Really, has no one told you how lovely your eyes are?"

That made him smile, a broader, happier smile than I'd ever seen on his face, even if he blinked self-consciously too. "No, no one has ever told me that."

I sighed in mock dismay. "I should have said something months ago. Though you might have wondered."

"About your taste?" he said blandly, eyes laughing.

"*No*," I protested, "about my feelings. About you."

This produced a pause, Erik's gaze shifting away, making me suspect it was the kind of pause that meant he was processing something. This was confirmed when he said, in tones of sudden realization, "You weren't going to tell me, were you?"

I knew he didn't mean about his eyes, and now I felt vaguely self-conscious. "No," I admitted. "I wasn't."

He laughed again, delightful laugh, and said, "I thought you hated operas where people never said anything to each other, and—"

"I almost told you," I said, half-laughing myself, just because. "After the mob, after I thought you were dead—but then you were so tangled up about Christine when we had that fight—"

He groaned. "Don't tell me I was being even more of an idiot than I already thought."

I grinned, the memory so much less painful than it had been before, now that it had this sequel. "Why do you think I was so angry with you?"

Another groan. "Why did you put up with me all this time?"

"I like your music," I said comfortably. "And the stories about Rome. And..." I hesitated, tracing my fingers along his shoulder. "...I guess, it made me feel special, to be your friend."

He caught up my hand, kissed my fingertips. "You are special. And not because of anything to do with me."

I still didn't altogether believe that. But it put a warm glow in me to think that he did, warmed something so deep inside me that it was much easier to deflect into levity again than to admit it, to just lightly say, "My mother always said so."

From the sudden alarm in his eyes, it wasn't as light a remark as I'd intended. "We're...going to have to explain all this to her, aren't we?"

"It's going to be fine," I said hastily. "She likes you."

"Yes. Of course she does," he said, but in the kind of deadpan voice that meant just the opposite. "Every mother wants a ghost to court their daughter."

Courting. Was that what we were doing? It sounded so conventional—in a good way. If someone had told me that someday the Phantom of the Opera would court me... "Mother *does* like you. After all, she's been your boxkeeper all these years, so she has a— unique perspective." And she had let this, us, go on for so many months, not exactly happily, but she could have raised far more objections than she had.

"Mmm," Erik agreed, pulling me tighter again and kissing the top of my head. "I did always give good tips."

"Better than any other subscriber. And you were politer than most too."

"I'm lucky she told you so. You might never have wanted to talk to me to begin with, if you thought I was only the terrifying Phantom all the ballet girls shrieked about."

First I giggled again. Then I turned thoughtful. "That's…not exactly the only reason I wasn't afraid of you." It seemed to be a day for confessions, and this one was probably long overdue.

"I find it hard to believe that Christine gave me a good character."

For a moment I savored how easily he said her name. Then I pulled my attention back to the point. "I didn't mean that, I meant, well…" I shifted down so I could put my head on his shoulder—I had been right yesterday, I did fit there, perfectly—and looked out at the room. I fixed my gaze on Degas' airy dancers, and took a deep breath. Even if all my reasons for not telling this story were past the point of mattering, secrecy was a hard habit to break.

"When I first came to the Opera," I began finally, "when I was just twelve, I got lost one day early on. Very lost. I somehow got a level or two below ground, and wound up in an empty, dead-end hallway. Getting to ballet practice looked hopeless and I was terrified of Madame Thibault, so I gave up and sat down and cried. And then I heard a voice say—"

"It can't be as bad as all that."

I shivered suddenly, not scared, just struck. Hearing those words again, in his voice, was more ghost-like than any flaming skeleton had ever been. I lifted my head to look at his face. He was gazing into the distance, and I wondered what he saw. "Yes, exactly."

He blinked, and his attention snapped back to me, to now. "That was *you*?"

I smiled. Those three words gave me a wealth of answers. "I wondered if you knew. Or if you had forgotten the whole thing."

He made a sound of general disbelief. "Yes, because I help little lost ballet girls all the time."

"Well…" I looked down, nervous again. "I wondered that too."

"No, just you." He said it entirely inconsequentially, but a renewed glow spread through me. "Too much of that would have ruined my reputation. It's lucky you didn't get lost six months later. I was more careless at the very beginning."

"Why didn't you ever talk to me again?" the ghost of my younger self asked. My today-self pointed out that Erik had just written me a love song, I was curled up with his arms around me, my lips still tingled from kisses, and surely this didn't matter anymore. But the question had been asked.

"I don't know exactly," he said slowly. "I never found out who you were. I never wanted to." Maybe something showed in my eyes in response to that apparent dismissal, because he quickly said, "It was just that, I assumed you'd be like the others, telling stories about the terrifying Phantom. You'd been nice, and—I didn't want to see everything change." He shrugged. "Obviously I was wrong."

"I forgive you," I said, leaned in and kissed his cheek. And after all, if he *had* talked to me again all those years ago—I'd only been a child. What kind of friends could we have been then, and how would I ever have convinced him I wasn't a child anymore? "So will you tell me *now* how you lit a candle by breathing on it?"

"Of course." A pause. A grin. "*Magic.*"

He had not thought often about that little ballet girl he'd helped so long ago. Her face had gone blurry with time, and even now, he couldn't really say that he remembered Meg, Meg as he knew her now, in that years-old memory. But he knew narrative arcs from watching so many operas, and he liked the fitness of this one.

She had always been the person in the Opera Company he had the warmest connection to, who was the most sympathetic towards him, even when he hadn't known it. And he liked thinking he'd done something good, once upon a time, to start to earn the incredible gift that had been handed him today—even if helping one lost girl weighed only the tiniest amount in comparison to what Meg was offering him now. But it meant that he'd already, long ago, taken one step towards being deserving of her love, and if he spent the rest of his life trying to make up the remaining balance—that was very possibly the best way he could imagine spending a life.

Not that anyone was talking about lifetimes right now. Today was enough. They'd have to work out tomorrow, and then the next day, and—

A sudden, cold breeze blew across his emotions as he remembered the obvious, the glaring detail he had conveniently been ignoring in this new blaze of delight. Meg had settled down with her head on his shoulder again and he was glad she couldn't see his face as he remembered. He fought not to clutch her tighter, to smooth out his expression before she looked at him again.

Because she was leaving. In nine days, 18 hours. How could he have forgotten that? It was the *reason* he had told her he loved her—but implicit in the decision was the assumption that she would decline any romantic involvement, that he was telling her only so that she could take the knowledge away with her.

But now—would she still leave? Could he ask her not to?

And if she did stay—was that even the right decision?

Operas. People in operas never talked to each other and that never worked out, and operas were terrible places to get advice about life anyway, just witness how badly it had all gone with Christine, but—he was not going to go down those paths this time, he was going to get this right, and he didn't know exactly what *was* right, but—talking. Meg thought people should talk to each other, so therefore... "What happens now?" he asked, because he didn't know any better way to put it.

"Mmm?" She didn't lift her head from his shoulder. "Why should anything happen now?"

She meant *now*, and he meant...well, a slightly larger now. He shifted his weight, dared to ask more directly. Somewhat more directly. "I mean—aren't you leaving Paris next week?" In nine days and—he'd sound obsessive if he told her he was counting. Maybe she wouldn't mind. Or maybe she'd think it was strange.

"Oh. Oh..." She straightened up, a slight frown on her face. Was that a bad sign? Or was it just that she'd forgotten for a little while too? "I can't go to Vienna now..."

That was what he wanted to hear.

He thought it was. So why didn't it feel good? Was it because she didn't sound sure? She sounded troubled and what if—what if it wasn't right?

After all the energy he'd spent thinking about ways to keep Meg in Paris, even before he realized the utter devastation he'd feel if she went, it was absurd to think she shouldn't stay. But. She had always wanted to travel. Madame Giry had pointed that out. What right did he have to try to stop her?

And what did he think would happen if she stayed? He hadn't imagined this result of his love song at all, hadn't tried to work out any plan. But the Phantom of the Opera was dead. Meg had lost her job. What was his best possibility here: he continued to lurk around in the undercellars of the Opera to no purpose, living only for whatever hours she could spare to visit him? And the rest of the time she stayed in a city where she had no purpose, only to be able to visit him?

It was all pointing to one path. He just didn't know if it was a path he could walk. Or one she'd want him to.

That, at least, was the first thing to find out. "Maybe," he said slowly, "you could still go."

Her gaze had drifted into the distance, occupied with her own thoughts for the few seconds he had run through his, and now her attention snapped back to him, something like betrayal in her eyes. "You *want* me to go to Vienna?"

Instinctively his arms tightened around her. He had an idea and he had to ask her if it was all right, but it was asking for so much more, and what if it ruined everything, what if he scared her after all—he should just *say* it, he knew that, but his courage failed and he fumbled for prevarication and excuses instead. "I'm just thinking—Vienna, I mean, it's very important. Musically. You know, Mozart, Beethoven, all sorts of developments in musical style. So I was thinking—I mean, it's just a, well, a thought, but really, every composer ought to spend some time in Vienna, just as a sort of, that is, just because, so I was thinking…I've been to Vienna, but that's not really the point, the point was more…"

"You want to come to Vienna," she said in tones of sudden clarity—and it felt like a miracle that she'd made sense out of his ramble.

It was as clear as a mathematical equation. Meg couldn't stay at the Opera. He couldn't face losing her. Therefore he had to go with her. Even if leaving the Opera had always seemed impossible, it had just run up against two more impossible things and something had to give way.

He was more afraid of losing her than he was of leaving the Opera. How extraordinary.

But that revelation wouldn't matter, if she didn't agree with this so inevitable conclusion. "Only if you think it's a good idea," he said hastily. "It was just a thought, you know, just an idea, and if you'd rather I didn't, I—"

She kissed him. She was warm and soft and lovely and the only trouble was that he didn't know if this was a happy kiss or a consolation kiss.

That didn't entirely stop him from enjoying it, but as soon as his lips were free again he had to ask, "Does this mean it's a good idea?"

"It's a *wonderful* idea," she said, eyes alight and smile filling her face. As though she was the one benefiting in this scenario.

"Are you sure?" he asked, because it seemed so unlikely. "It's not, I don't know…" He hesitated. "Too much? It's not going to make you uncomfortable?"

"No. Maybe if you had just showed up in Vienna without saying something first." Her face turned thoughtful, as though she was picturing that. He pictured it too. It probably would have happened, if he hadn't said something today. How long could he have resisted, lived through the loneliness before he had given up and followed her? "Actually," she said in musing tones, "I think I would have been happy to see you anyway."

He wasn't certain he believed that. But it felt like its own small miracle that she did.

Chapter Thirty-Three

I could almost—not quite, but almost—imagine just staying down here forever, curled up with Erik in his armchair. Except that Mother would very possibly show up with the police if I wasn't home eventually. And more immediately she'd worry. Plus I was supposed to be at the special performance tonight, my final performance at the Opera Garnier.

"It's getting late, isn't it?" I said at length.

"I guess. Maybe."

I squinted up at him. "You always know what time it is."

A pause. "Maybe I don't. Maybe if I pretend I don't, you'll believe me."

"All this just means it's time for me to leave, doesn't it?"

"…maybe."

I groaned, wriggled about trying to untangle and extricate myself without losing any dignity. I found my way to my feet, then turned around, reached back to clasp his hands again. "Come on, you can walk me to the surface."

His eyebrow rose, a glint of humor in his eyes. "Oh? You didn't let me yesterday."

"Yesterday…" I smiled. "Yesterday was an entirely different lifetime."

He rose, fingers still entwined with mine, and pulled me into another kiss. We kissed until I laughed and pushed him back. "We're never going to leave at this rate."

He didn't say anything, just smiled an easy half-smile—but he stepped away, let my hands go.

I suddenly remembered trying to push Léon off—not just at the end, but nearly every time we had kissed before that. It had always been harder than this.

It wasn't the only reason it was nicer kissing Erik.

I reached for his hand again, wound my fingers through his, and we walked together towards the door.

He picked up his mask as we passed the piano, and returned it to its place on the right side of his face.

"You don't have to do that," I said quietly.

He paused, hand lingering on the mask for a moment before letting it drop. "Maybe not. But let me pace my breaking of lifelong habits."

I smiled and didn't argue the point as we left his apartment. Even just talking about his mask like this seemed like as much of an advancement as anything else.

Well, almost.

It was slower than usual, walking through his passages and tunnels today. Holding hands had been such a pragmatic thing, the first time he'd led me through this journey—and even more so, the very first time we had met. Now his thumb stroked over my knuckles and frequently our shoulders bumped, not quite accidentally.

Eventually we got to the last chamber before the secret door into the prop room, and he pulled me into a real embrace again, for a proper good-bye kiss. Even when we stopped kissing, we stayed locked together for a long time.

"I should go," I whispered, but didn't move. I didn't want to go, didn't want to break this perfect moment, with Erik's forehead against mine, his breath warm on my lips and his hands resting on my hips.

"Mmm," he murmured, an acknowledgment, not quite an agreement.

Reluctantly, I eased back a little, not far enough to break our embrace. "Really. I should go."

He opened his eyes, blinked a couple of times. "Right. Of course." He lifted one hand, tucked a strand of hair behind my ear. "See you after tonight's performance?"

I nodded. "I can meet you in Box Five."

He nodded too. I could feel his fingers moving as he played with my hair. "So, you won't...disappear or anything, of course. Between now and then."

I nearly responded lightly, because the idea was obviously ridiculous. Just in time I noticed the way he wasn't quite looking me in the eyes, noticed the tension that had entered his shoulders. "Hey." I raised one hand to tap his cheek, the unmasked one. "Look at me." Slowly, his gaze shifted to meet mine, and I willed him to see in my eyes all that I felt. "I am not going to change my mind or run away or suddenly decide that Léon is really wonderful after all." I tightened my fingers on his shoulder. "I love you—and you're going to find me very difficult to get rid of."

The corner of his mouth curved up. "Good," he said, and leaned in to find my lips again.

I did leave...eventually.

Erik watched through a spyhole until Meg had disappeared between the aisles in the prop room. Then he turned to lean back against the wall, let his knees fold and slid down to sit on the ground.

What an utterly extraordinary day.

He felt...he felt...it was a little like when the entire orchestra arrived on time, in place and in tune, when everyone was good at what they were doing and they were playing something he liked and he could sit back and let the music wash over him for two hours and enjoy every note.

No, it was even better than that—more like the much rarer performances, when everyone was better than good, when all the musicians and the performers worked together with a special charge to the air and everyone played better than they ever had and everyone knew that the symphony was never going to sound quite like this ever again because there was something magical in the air this one night, and he didn't even notice each note as it went by, he was just swept off into the music and never thought of anything.

Joy. He was pretty sure this was joy.

For a few moments, he closed his eyes and reveled in the feeling.

But because he was Erik, it didn't take longer than that before complications began making themselves known.

Just like living rather than dying, success was much more complicated than failure. But he could handle that, he could handle anything. *Meg loved him.* That was a miracle so enormous that anything, anything at all, was suddenly, beautifully possible.

He rose to his feet, not because he knew where he was going but just because he was too full of excited energy to sit for long. Better to wander through this kingdom he knew so well. And would soon be leaving.

He hadn't planned leaving, he hadn't thought that far ahead, but it was obvious. Like a melody that could only end with a particular chord, loving Meg, confessing the same and finding it requited could lead only to the conclusion that he had to leave the Opera. A week ago he would have said he couldn't leave—but that in itself should have warned him that he had already stayed too long.

The Opera Garnier was meant to be his refuge. It was the place he had chosen as sanctuary. But a refuge was a place you *chose.* A place you *could not* leave? That was a cage. A beautiful cage, a large cage, one with excellent art and music, but still a cage.

It was time to go. And with her...he could go, with her.

He was going to have to pack. How extraordinary. He didn't have much time, but most of the transitions in his life had involved fleeing in the night. For a rarity, he had enough time to actually fill a trunk.

He was going to have to buy a trunk.

He cut through one of the public corridors, intending a quick shortcut to another hidden passage. Several steps down the hall, he stopped. Like so many other rooms and corridors in the Opera Garnier, this one was lined with mirrors.

There was something else he could do, something else that had always seemed impossible, but perhaps on today of all days...

He cast a furtive glance to his right, where his reflection loomed. He took a deep breath, and turned to face himself. With the half-mask on, not so bad. But he already knew that, and also knew that wasn't what he needed to confront.

Another breath, and then he slipped off the mask. Bad. Very bad. Deformed, misshapen—he grimaced at the sight, which of course only made matters worse.

He closed his eyes, took two breaths, with a conscious effort smoothed the expression of his face. The eyes. Just look at the eyes.

He met his reflection's gaze, leaned in to look closer. Very green, no denying that. Lovely? Well...perhaps if you liked that sort of thing. Which apparently Meg did.

An unthinking smile spread across his face. Maybe they really were lovely. Or maybe it just didn't matter that much, as long as she thought they were.

By the time I got to the surface, where there were things like clocks to indicate time, it was even later than I had thought. Mother would likely be irate—but even that thought couldn't put too much of a damper on my happiness just now.

I threaded through the corridors towards the exit, though really I'd barely have time to go home before I'd have to come back again for the evening's performance.

I was taking a shortcut through the Emperor's Entrance when I heard my name called from the top of the stairs behind me. Surprising.

No one had been speaking to me for days. I stopped and looked back, to see Adalisa descending the stairs towards me.

"Your mother's been looking for you," she explained, stopping a few steps above me. "I just saw her—back by the practice rooms."

"Oh. Thank you." I took one step up, but she was in my way.

I looked up at her to find she had a troubled expression, nibbling on her lower lip. "I heard…that you're leaving Paris."

"Yes." Was this a friendly overture, or was she just leading into more hostility? "We're going to Vienna."

"Oh, that's so nice!" she said, with a smile that only looked slightly forced. "Since you always wanted to travel, I mean."

"Yes," I agreed, rather at a loss of what to do with this conversation.

She could have just stepped out of my way and I would have gone on and that would have been the end—but she went on standing there, looking profoundly uncomfortable. Finally, she said, "Was he—not really so bad? The Phantom?"

I couldn't stop the smile from spreading across my face. The question conjured up the ghost of his lips on mine, his arms around me, his voice, singing me a love song. "He was actually quite wonderful."

She frowned, forehead creasing, but it was a puzzled frown. "I guess—you would know, but everyone always said…"

Everyone said a lot of things. "They're *stories*," I said impatiently. "Did you, you personally, ever see the Phantom do anything really horrifying? Not what Francesca or Jammes or anybody else *said* they saw, but anything *you* ever saw?"

"Well…" Her eyes darted about as she thought. "I mean, he wrote all those letters, and I've seen spiders in the practice room—"

"There are spiders everywhere in this building."

"—and the chandelier fell."

"Did you see him drop it?" I asked swiftly.

"No…"

"All I'm saying is—have an open mind, all right?" I said. "Now I've got to go find Mother before she has my head."

I slipped around her on the stairs, took them two at a time going up.

"Meg!" she called after me. "Maybe you could—write me from Vienna? I can find someone to read it to me."

I looked back and smiled at her. "I'll do that."

It would be nice, to think I still had one friend at the Opera Garnier after I left it.

I found Mother outside the practice room, looking like a thundercloud and only calming down slightly when she saw me. "Do you *know* what time it is?" she demanded. "What happened?"

"Good things," I said, darting in to give her a quick hug. "I have so much to tell you—but maybe not here." I glanced around. Definitely too many people about.

She gave me one of her intent looks, peering into my face. "Everything's all right?"

"Everything's *wonderful*."

She pursed her lips. "Hmm. Perhaps. It won't be if you don't go talk to Madame Thibault. She's reworking a bit of the Act One dance and wants to see you."

Of course, *now* everyone wanted to talk to me. But it didn't matter, nothing mattered, except that I was meeting Erik again after tonight's performance. And then?

The world was full of infinite, magical possibilities.

Excerpt from the Private Notebook of Jean Mifroid, Commissaire of Police

30 May, 1882

All suspicions proved correct. <u>Phantom alive</u>.

RDC and Daaé came in to report kidnapping today. Both witnesses to seeing Phantom. Possible involvement of Meg Giry. Reason to believe Phantom will attend special performance at Opera tonight.

Chapter Thirty-Four

Erik didn't go to Box Five at the beginning of the evening's performance. It had been his practice for years—but tonight he would much rather, instead, watch the ballet dancers sitting in the wings before their first dance. It was easy enough; there were so many people, so many hanging curtains and stacks of boxes, so many shadows filling up the backstage, that it hardly even took his talents for hiding to stay out of anyone's notice.

Except, easy as it was to move about, he didn't see the one ballet dancer who really mattered amongst the crowd. She wouldn't have...no, of course she hadn't left. She wouldn't leave. She had said she wouldn't leave.

All the same, it was probably best for his peace of mind that it only took a little prowling around backstage before he found Meg, in a shadow between two hanging curtains, not so far from the other ballet girls but still standing separate and alone.

He hid in the deeper shadows, watching her as she stood with her gaze on the lighted stage. It seemed impossible that he could have been seeing her for so long, without appreciating what he was seeing. Now he was greedy for every detail, gaze lingering to memorize each one. The angle of her neck, the arch of her back, the slender lines of her legs. The way she stood with one knee bent, toe tapping in an andante tempo against the wooden floor. The fine wisps of hair at the back of her neck, dancing free from the clasp that held the golden mass of the rest. And especially the half smile playing about her lips, the smile that he hoped had something to do with him.

Memories supplemented vision, and he remembered the silken softness of her hair, the touch of her hand against his face. He remembered the taste of her kiss, remembered holding her in his arms, her body warm against his, remembered how his world had narrowed to encompass nothing but her.

He wanted to reach out, even as he wanted to go on watching, to not break this moment as it was. Briefly he savored the fact that he *could* step out, that he had come to a point where this was even an option.

She was in a secluded corner, nearly as deep in the shadows as he was himself. There was little risk of anyone else seeing, and so he could discard that reason for holding back. It was the thought that perhaps she had deliberately chosen a secluded corner that finally prompted him to move forward, to slip silently up behind her and softly say, "Hello," just before she would have become aware of his presence.

She didn't even jump. She turned her head slightly and he could see her smile grow. "Hello, Erik."

He carefully curled his fingers around her shoulders, bare in the sleeveless dance outfit—carefully, even cautiously, because despite the memories of the afternoon, it was still hard to break the habits of a lifetime, to step over walls he had always thought insurmountable. More carefully yet, he lowered his head and kissed the back of her neck, lips lingering on the delicate knob of her spine.

His fingertips explored the angles and curves of her shoulders, then slid slowly down her arms to settle on her hips, already a familiar place, new from this direction. Her hands rose to twine her fingers through his, and then drew his hands together and past each other across her stomach, so that his arms wrapped around her and her arms wrapped over his, fingers still entangled. She leaned back against his chest, so that the top of her head just brushed below his jaw, fitting as naturally there as a violin. He sighed, pressing his cheek against her hair.

"I thought we agreed to meet *after* the performance," she murmured, but her tone was too teasing for even Erik to feel rejected by the words.

So he just whispered, "I missed you."

A tremble went through her, and there was a catch in her voice when she answered, "I missed you too."

And he knew—and knew that she knew—that when they said "missed" they really meant "love." And he knew, too, that it had always meant that, even when neither of them had realized it.

Excerpt from the Private Notebook of Jean Mifroid, Commissaire of Police

30 May, 1882, *Continued*

Secured reluctant cooperation of Opera management and all in place. I will end this. No tricks this time.

I had to return to the ballet girls when the curtain opened on the special performance. It wouldn't do for Madame Thibault to go looking for me, and find me entangled with Erik. I found an empty spot and did my warm-up exercises automatically while I waited impatiently for the special performance to be over so I could get back to far more important things.

Our cue came and I stepped out with the others onto the stage for our Act One dance.

Automatically, unthinkingly, I glanced towards Box Five. I knew that Erik wasn't there; he'd been kissing the back of my neck mere minutes before. But habits are funny things, and I still looked towards Box Five.

It was a miracle I didn't crash straight into the girl in line next to me and thoroughly ruin my final performance.

Erik wasn't in Box Five, even he couldn't move *that* fast, and it wasn't shocking for someone else to be there, now that the management believed the Phantom was dead. But I was not expecting Christine. And Raoul. And Commissaire Mifroid.

Between them in the audience and Erik backstage I passed the dance in a blur. Finally it was over and I could retreat into the shadows again in the wings. I'd find Erik—and not for selfish reasons but because he needed to know about Mifroid—we were so *close*, we weren't even staying in the country, why was she *here*? And why was she here with *him*?

I barely had a chance to glance around for Erik—no sign of him— before suddenly Adalisa was next to me, slipping her arm through mine and saying more loudly than necessary, "Come on, Meg, you can come sit with me." An act of defiant loyalty I would have appreciated at any other time.

How could I politely get away without rejecting someone who was trying so hard to help me? Other girls were glowering at us, and while I certainly couldn't leave Erik to the wolves of the police, I didn't want to leave Adalisa to the ballet wolves either. "I really think, actually, if you'd give me just a moment…"

"We dance again in Act Three," Madame Thibault said crisply, with that trick of voice to be heard perfectly backstage but not beyond the curtain. "Everyone keep together in the meantime; no wandering off, if you please."

Did she *know* things, or was I just unlucky? Either way, I was trapped. I sat down next to Adalisa, made myself smile at her, and tried to decide if the situation was critical enough to warrant defying Madame Thibault.

I knew where Erik had been. Where was he *now*? Maybe he'd see Mifroid for himself. He was clever, he was perceptive, he was…most likely distracted by me right now. Which gave me a warm glow even while it made me worry.

Although, if it was a paying attention kind of distracted... "Did you see Box Five?" I asked, a little louder than I would normally talk backstage, in theory addressing Adalisa. "I'm *sure* I saw Commissaire Mifroid there. And *Christine* too."

"Christine Daaé?" Francesca cut in. "But the Phantom killed her!"

I looked at her coolly. So if my gossip was good enough, she'd talk to me? "I've said all along she was alive. And if she isn't, then her ghost is sitting in Box Five with the police commissaire."

"You must be seeing things," Francesca said huffily, and turned away.

"But I didn't say *anything* about apparitions coming out of a mirror," I said innocently, and watched the backs of her ears turn pink.

There was a certain freedom in knowing I was leaving the Opera. But no tangible freedom for the next two acts, not until the interval.

By the time Act Three was closing, I was jittery with the need to do *something*. If I found Erik, I could warn him—but maybe I already had, and I didn't know how to find him right now. Though I did know how to find Christine.

If I tried to wander off into a dark corner in the hopes of bumping into Erik (again), that was liable to attract attention and questions and maybe even lead someone to him. But no one would think it strange if I went to talk to Christine.

I wrapped my cloak around my dance costume and the moment the interval officially began and Madame Thibault stopped staring at all of us, I rose to my feet. "I'm going to go see Christine," I told Adalisa.

She frowned a little. "Are you *sure* you saw...?"

"I'm certain. And if she asks, tell Madame Thibault I'll be back for Act Four."

I slipped away from backstage, made my way towards the boxes. The whole place seemed to be aswarm with people tonight. I wasn't seeking out an empty corner—but I was keeping my eyes open too, and not seeing any. In fact...were there more tall, unfamiliar men hanging about with no apparent job to do?

Maybe I was becoming paranoid. And maybe not.

I shook my head and hurried on toward the boxes. I knocked when I got to Box Five, though it was somewhat meaningless. I knew they'd assume I was the boxkeeper, and sure enough I heard a voice tell me to enter at once. Male, so either Raoul or Mifroid.

I stepped into Box Five, so much brighter than I was used to it being, with all the curtains wide open. There were Christine and Raoul. No sign of Mifroid, which was both a relief and an alarm. It would be easier to talk without him, but where was he and what was he doing?

Deal with the problem at hand. I fixed my gaze on Christine, only half-hearing Raoul as he bumbled some sort of greeting. "Well, Meg, how—unexpected. It's, well, how, um…" I don't think he knew whether to treat me as the inconsequential ballet girl I'd always been, or as the woman who had held a gun on him and been willing to use it.

I cut through his stammers without looking away from Christine; she, at least, was showing no trace of discomfiture. "Christine and I need to talk."

"Ah, well." Raoul paused, and I think it took a moment before he realized I meant he should leave. He blustered up with, "Anything you can say to Christine you can say in front of me."

I arched an eyebrow, still looking at her. "Can I?" The weight of what I knew about her lay between us like a tangible presence.

"Raoul, go get me a drink," Christine said briskly.

Raoul looked between us, shifting his weight from foot to foot. "Well, I, um…"

"If you would, please, dear," she added, voice softening, accompanying the words with a little smile.

He mumbled some but went.

Once the door was closed behind him, I demanded, "Just what do you think you're doing here?"

Her eyebrows rose, expression perfectly innocent. "Why, I'm here to see the opera, of course. I remember my days here so fondly, and it's such a nostalgic—"

"Oh, be real, just for once," I snapped. "You're here with the police commissaire. Why?"

She stared at me for a moment. Then her eyes narrowed, and a kind of softness disappeared from her face. It was so much part of her usual expression that it was never so noticeable as when it was suddenly gone. "Mifroid and Raoul want to catch Philippe's murderer, and I'm helping them."

My heart pounded in my chest. "Erik didn't kill Philippe. We both know that."

"No doubt he's done other things," Christine said, waving one hand in an airy dismissal. As though Erik's life weighed nothing at all. "I have plans, now that I'm back in Paris, and I don't need a madman playing at haunting getting in my way. After the debacle of yesterday, I had to take more drastic action today."

I had asked her to be real, but it was disturbing to see behind her soft smiles and doe-eyed innocence. So much more unsettling than when Erik took his mask off. What was under Christine's mask was so much uglier. "You *wanted* Raoul to kill Erik yesterday. That was the plan—that was why you told him where you were."

She only smiled. "As I said—I can't have a madman getting in my way."

I supposed I didn't have to feel guilty for not wanting her to come back—for resenting her all those months when she didn't write to me, when Erik spent all that time thinking about her. "You can't do this," I protested. "Erik's not going to interfere with you!" But I stopped short of telling her that we had made plans to leave Paris, to go to Vienna. Because—did I want her to know that? What could this new, calculating Christine do with the information?

"I should just depend on that? Assume that he's going to forget all about me?" She smirked—an actual smirk, very unlike all her sweet smiles of before. "He would be the first man to do that."

"He has," I said through gritted teeth. I had spent all those months believing he'd never forget her too. But I had been wrong—and she was wrong. "He thought you were boring, these last few days."

What I had intended as a biting reproof didn't even impact her confidence. She just laughed. "Of course, *chérie*, if that's what he's telling you."

This was a waste of time. "What did you tell Mifroid? What is he planning to do?"

"Because you think you can rush off and stop him somehow? Go do whatever you like; it's too late to change anything. All the commissaire's men are already in place. And I felt sure the Phantom wouldn't miss this performance. Last time you're dancing here, isn't it? Quite the end of an era."

I had never told her anything about leaving, but why should it surprise me that she had learned more than she'd ever bothered saying?

Mifroid was here and his men were around and they expected Erik to be here too.

All right, all right, that was fine, that didn't matter. Yes, Erik was here—but he surely knew about Mifroid by now, would be able to handle this. He might have noticed on his own, and if he was distracted by me, well, I'd just come all the way to Box Five. He must have noticed and was working out why. So it was fine, it was all fine.

But I wasn't going to be able to do any good here. "I have to go."

"To warn him?"

"I'm sure he already knows." I was sure. Nearly.

"Perhaps. He is clever, I'll give him that." She waved one hand, a shooing gesture. "But by all means, you just rush off to protect your Phantom."

"He's not—" And then I stopped, halfway to turning away. Because in spite of myself, in spite of everything, quite against my intention, a smile was growing on my face. At the thought of *my* Phantom. I turned my head far enough for Christine to see the smile over my shoulder, and did I see a flicker of doubt in her eyes? "Yes, I'll do that," I said, and walked out of Box Five.

It was a good exit. The only problem was that I didn't know what I should do next—what I *could* do. I started to return to my place backstage. It was as good a vantage point as any, and it was where he'd be looking for me. I took a circuitous route, though, trying for less frequented areas. I thought of the changing room, but at the interval half the girls could be in there.

It had been so easy to find a dark corner backstage earlier; why was it so difficult now?

Finally, as I was passing the auxiliary prop room, a small one backstage, I spotted the door ajar, with darkness within. It was worth trying.

I slipped inside, closed the door behind me, blinked against the blackness. There had to be a light in here somewhere, a switch for the gaslamp…

Before I found it, a soft voice said, "Hello."

The rush of conflicting feelings—surprise, relief, happiness, worry, fear—made me dizzy. "We need to talk."

"Should that worry me?" he asked, snapping his fingers and lighting a candle in a heavy silver candlestick sitting on a prop table in the center of the room.

The slight illumination of the candle seemed to mostly cast shadows, but it put a glow around him. Somehow, wearing all black, he still glowed.

This was *not* what I needed to be thinking about right now. Later, I could think about it later. "Mifroid is here. With his men. And he still thinks you killed Philippe."

"Of course he does," Erik said, moving the candle out of the way and sitting just on the edge of the table. He extended his hands towards me. "Victor Hugo would love that man."

Inevitably I took the steps between us and let him take my hands, whether it was going to distract from the main point or not. "I don't have any idea what that means."

"In *Les Mis*—"

"And right at this particular moment, I don't care," I interrupted, squeezing his hands. There were limits to how distracted we could safely get. "Mifroid. Out there. You don't seem surprised."

"No, I saw him during Act One." He smiled at me. "It was nice that you wanted to warn me though."

I couldn't help smiling back. "See, I thought you'd notice him yourself."

"There was nothing worth seeing backstage just then," he said, with his green eyes all soft and it would have been so easy to lean into him and kiss him and...

"So what are you going to *do*?" I asked, trying to rally my focus.

"A few possibilities. Did you learn anything worthwhile from Christine?"

"You noticed that too?" A little voice at the back of my mind asked if he had noticed because he was watching me or Christine. But he was holding *my* hands...

"That you went to Box Five? Of course I noticed *that*."

Good answer, and he had such distracting, distracting eyes... I blinked. "Um, did I learn anything...no, not really. Christine's helping Mifroid, but that was obvious anyway."

"Mm-hmm. So much for all the efforts to pretend to be dead. I'm sorry, especially after you resigned over it."

That hadn't even occurred to me. All my efforts to keep Léon away from the management—pointless, because Christine had cut a much more direct track to the police anyway. Or maybe, not pointless at all, maybe incredibly important because it had bought us these few extra days...long enough for everything to change.

"I don't care about that," I said, shaking my head. "But you shouldn't be here, not if Mifroid's trying to close a net around the auditorium. You know so many ways out, you should just..." He was looking at me, but not in a listening kind of a way. I tugged on his hands. "You're not paying attention!"

"I'm paying very close attention," he protested, pulling me closer.

"But out there, you should..." I wasn't sure where that sentence was going, and it was unconvincing protest as I was letting him draw me in. He released my hands and they somehow drifted up to his shoulders...his heavily cloth-covered shoulders. "Were you wearing this cloak before?" I knew he wasn't; I had gotten close to all of his clothing.

He spread his hands, holding the edges of the cloak out to either side. "Think it'll impress Mifroid?"

He wasn't going to run, and my heart started beating faster. "No! Because he shouldn't ever get the chance to see it!"

"I'm going to handle this," he said in soothing tones.

"That's what you said *last* time!" And I had watched him die, spent days afraid that he was dead. I could not live through another week like that.

"And I handled it," he agreed, as though it had all worked out fine before. "The interval's almost over, you know, they'll be needing you back out there." He slid sideways, off the edge of the table, and stepped over to a shelf I could barely see in the gloom.

"They won't be thinking about *me*!"

"Madame Thibault will be, you have another dance." He held up two masks, both skulls. "Which of these do you like better?"

I had no patience for this right now. "I hate them both."

He looked at them critically. "I suppose they are about equally theatrical, but either will do." He tossed one aside, tucked the other into his cloak. "We had both better go."

"Erik, what are you going to *do*?" I demanded.

He grinned, cocky and unconcerned. "A parlor trick, I expect."

Instead of being reassured by his lack of worry, it filled me with the conviction that he was not giving this due weight. "You don't have a plan, do you? Mifroid is out there with men and guns and—"

He seized me by the shoulders, pulled me against him and kissed me hard. I clung to him, fingers clutching the folds of his cloak.

If there was a message in that kiss, we hadn't been kissing each other long enough for it to come through. For all I understood, it might have been anything from "don't worry" to "good-bye."

His cheek brushed mine, his breath danced past my ear, a whisper: "Watch me fly."

He released me so suddenly I stumbled back a pace. Before my head stopped spinning, he had disappeared.

I looked around the empty room. "Erik?" I whispered, to no response.

It probably served me right for falling in love with a ghost.

"I am going to be so angry with you later for whatever stunt you're about to pull," I said, expecting no answer this time and receiving none.

I picked up the candlestick to guide me to the door, the silver cold in my hand. I blew the flame out when my free hand was on the door handle, and stepped out of the prop room into the shadows and curtains of backstage, letting my hand drop with the candlestick still in my grasp, trying to think out my next steps. I'd go back to the ballet girls, because at least I could see what went on from there and—

"Hello, Meg," an all too familiar voice said, and not the one I wanted.

My back straightened and my head lifted and if I was scared, I was not going to let him see it. "Hello, Léon," I said evenly. "Don't you have anywhere else in the world you could be tonight?"

He spread his hands, grin as cocky as Erik's and so much less appealing. "And miss all the excitement?" He walked towards me, and his walk seemed less relaxed than his tone. He was favoring one leg, but his next words drove that from my attention. "Christine told me so much interesting news about your precious Phantom, and Commissaire Mifroid's plans for him. You must know I wouldn't want to miss it."

"I don't have time for this," I said, moving to step around him. I couldn't imagine Léon having anything useful to say, and I wouldn't tell him anything. "I'm needed in a dance."

His hand closed around my right arm, fingers tight. In a low voice he said, "I don't like it when you run away from me."

My stomach clenched with mingled fear and anger, and I gritted my teeth. "Let. Me. Go."

He laughed, a cold laugh. "Or what?"

I looked him in the eyes, and their blue did nothing at all for me now. "Or I will scream. And he will kill you."

Léon's grin broadened. "Oh, by all means. Scream and scream. How many policemen do you think are in earshot too?" He leaned in even closer, his breath hot against my face. "Mifroid thinks he'll find your Phantom by searching the shadows, but I think we ought to lure him out."

Merde. The easy way out of this was too dangerous—and my arm was aching and if this went on too long Erik was going to notice anyway, from wherever he'd disappeared to, and—and somehow, this time, the anger was emerging stronger than the fear.

I was so *tired* of wealthy men who thought I didn't matter.

I made myself smile, and said, "It's really too bad things have turned out like this," slightly because I meant it, but mostly because I wanted to distract him. He was looking at my face as I lifted one knee and struck him hard between the legs, my own legs so much freer in my dance costume than they'd been in my long skirts before.

His howl was even more dramatic than I'd expected. Maybe I had hit whatever injury he'd been favoring when he walked. Besides the obvious.

He bent over, face red, but his hand still clutched my arm, fingers digging in tighter. "You little—"

I lifted the heavy candlestick from the prop room, the one that had been out of sight amongst my skirts and hit him in the side of the head. That finally sent him sprawling to the ground.

Three policemen arrived with impressive speed. Apparently that's how many were in earshot.

"Monsieur de Troyes has had an unfortunate accident," I informed them. Léon himself only whimpered. "And I am needed onstage." I sketched the very slightest of curtsies to the confused policemen, and retreated.

This was the kind of thing they'd fire me for, of course—but that hardly mattered anymore. And Léon could only press charges by admitting he'd been beaten by a little ballet girl.

I was still worried about Erik, but at least I wasn't worried by Léon anymore.

Chapter Thirty-Five

E rik knew Meg was worrying and that concerned him more than he
let on—but he wasn't concerned about Mifroid. This was the kind
of fight he knew how to handle, the kind of challenge he'd been
facing all his life.

A beautiful girl who only pretended to cry—*that* was confusing.
Leaving the Opera Garnier, starting a new life—exhilarating, but
terrifying. Even Meg herself, this new adventure they were embarking on,
loving and being loved—that was better than his wildest dreams and yet
still so deeply new, and strange, and yes, terrifying too, in a way.

But men coming to kill him with guns? *That* was refreshingly
straightforward. That he knew how to handle.

He left the prop room and ascended up into the catwalks over the
stage. Most policemen didn't like the catwalks. And for a man
comfortable with ropes, they presented far more exits than might be
imagined.

He settled into a central location with a view of the stage and partial
view of the auditorium at what he thought was just a few minutes before
Act Four would begin. Instead, when the curtains opened again it was
with Moncharmin and Ricard onstage.

"Ladies and gentlemen," Ricard began, "we trust you will indulge us
with your patience for just a few moments. The Paris police has
requested that we allow them to do a special test of the arrangements of
the theatre in case of an emergency. Please remain in your seats."

Ah, so this was Mifroid's plan for investigating while there was a full
house. Less likely to create a panic than announcing there was a murderer

in their midst, Erik had to give him that. He wondered if Moncharmin and Ricard knew the truth, or if they really believed this to be a "special test." From what he could see, Moncharmin's tight shoulders, slightly lowered head and the fact that he wasn't the one talking suggested he wasn't pleased. But that could mean he knew the truth, or simply that he didn't like anything disrupting the opera and possibly causing demands for refunds.

Out in the audience, there was a rising murmur, half-amused but with an edge of dismay as well. That prompted the inevitable, "Now, no cause for alarm, nothing to be concerned about," from Ricard. "This is of course merely a test."

Meanwhile uniformed men were fanning out among the audience, clearly working in some kind of pattern, ostensibly checking the rows of seats but to Erik's view they seemed to be paying particular attention to the edges of the room. To the shadows and the crannies and the corners.

What did Mifroid think, that one of his men was going to turn up the Phantom standing in a corner? Please.

Erik was watching among the catwalks too. Mifroid had found him here before; he was sure to check here again. His first warning wasn't visible or even auditory—he felt the railing vibrate beneath his hands, shifting slightly but definitely. Someone new, probably several someones to get that reaction, moving on the catwalk. He scanned left, right—there, ascending the nearest spiral stair to his right, three men in dark clothes that light would no doubt show as police uniforms.

The one in the lead looked up and saw him at the same moment that Erik saw him too.

And the game was on. Erik grinned, raised one hand in salute, and leapt off the front of the catwalk.

I found my place in the wings again, and no one among the girls asked me any questions. They couldn't hear how hard my heart was pounding, and perhaps they didn't notice my flushed cheeks.

I watched as the managers made their announcement, watched the police officers fan out among the audience and explore here too, backstage. Surely Erik would disappear into a wall somewhere. You couldn't catch a man by blocking all the doors, not when he knew twice as many exits as everyone else. That was *true*, it was *logical*, and it did nothing whatsoever to stop my heart from hammering in my ears and my breath from catching in my throat as more and more policemen spread through the auditorium.

And it didn't stop me from screaming when a black-cloaked figure came leaping from one of the front catwalks. All the other ballet girls screamed too; it didn't mark me out. My gaze locked on Erik as he came plummeting down from above, thinking crazily that even he could not possibly land on his feet from fifteen yards up, it was impossible—and then the plummet became a swing and I finally realized he had a rope, near invisible in the shadows but still a rope he was holding onto, sliding down, using to swing out towards the front of the stage and land neatly in the full brilliance of the stage lights just a few feet behind Moncharmin and Ricard.

"Tell me," he said lightly, "am I the emergency you were trying to prepare for?"

He had donned the skull mask, and from the reactions around me you'd think he really was a ghost. Perhaps that's what everyone thought.

Ricard had gone white as a ghost himself. "But—we saw you killed!"

Moncharmin, by contrast, was red-faced and indignant. "Mifroid said he could handle this without disturbance!"

Disagreement within the ranks of the management. Maybe that's why Erik smirked. The mask didn't quite cover his mouth, though maybe I wouldn't have recognized the expression if I hadn't grown so familiar with his face.

"What's an opera without a fifth act twist?" he drawled.

The audience was abuzz more with interest than fear. Perhaps they thought this was all part of the show. More importantly, more frighteningly, by now Mifroid's men were circling in from their places around the auditorium.

Mifroid himself appeared between two curtains backstage, just beyond the ballet girls. He was heading towards the stage, but paused to look over our ranks—and stopped with his gaze on me.

"Come with me," he ordered, and without waiting for comment caught my arm and pulled me along.

"What are you doing?" I protested, letting him pull me because that was better than being dragged. *Why* did men keep thinking they could grab my arm? Mifroid had caught me in the same place Léon had. "I don't—"

"I understand you are friendly with our ghost. You are going to tell him to surrender."

"I am not!"

And then we were out on stage and I was blinking in the lights and the sudden stares of a very large audience. I was used to the audience—when I was dancing.

"I want your immediate surrender, Phantom," Mifroid announced, loud enough for the entire room to hear. "For the crime of murdering Philippe de Chagny."

Distantly I was aware of the crowd murmuring, still an excited murmur. But mostly I was looking at Erik, who was looking at me. And then he very definitely moved his gaze to look at Mifroid instead.

"Yes, of course that's what *you* want," Erik said, sounding bored. "That's no reason for me to do it."

Mifroid shook me by the arm. "Tell him."

"He's not going to listen to me!" I protested—but would he? I didn't know. Probably not. He obviously hadn't run when I told him to, and that was a far more sensible, more reasonable course of action than surrendering ever would be.

"Why on Earth do you imagine I would listen to a member of the corps de ballet?" Erik asked, in clear and blatant tones of dismissal. "They're charming, but that's asking a lot of charm."

Oh—so we were playing it that way. All right. I could do that. "I *told* you, there's no reason for him to listen to me!" I tried to tug out of Mifroid's grasp, but he was standing firm. "He barely even knows me." I couldn't claim to be complete strangers, not with Christine and Raoul to contradict it.

Christine and Raoul. I looked towards Box Five, and of course there she was. He was too, but he was behind her and she was the one that counted. Christine was standing at the front of the box, hands on the balustrade. The light caught her brown curls and she was watching Erik with an intent expression.

I had to look at Mifroid again, when he said, more in defiance than defense, "All the stories say you're *friends*."

Erik laughed. Not that nice chuckle I liked so much, but a proper, villainous ghost laugh. "Mifroid, we're in an opera house. Haven't you learned by now that very little here is as it seems?" In a perfectly audible stage whisper he added, "Most of the gold in the Grand Foyer isn't even real."

I was near enough to see Mifroid's lip curl. "So I suppose you're not actually a murderous, rampaging madman?"

"Oh no," Erik said easily, "that part's true." He didn't reach into his cloak—I would have seen, and he didn't, yet somehow, suddenly, there was a pistol in his right hand, his arm extended. He turned in place, that pistol swinging around the room. "What do you suppose a madman would do if he's starting to feel crowded?"

The onlookers weren't amused anymore. They were rising to their feet, both the audience and the orchestra, alarmed and objecting and starting to push towards the exits. I looked at Box Five again—Raoul was ducking down, trying to tug Christine down with him. She was waving him off, still standing at the balustrade.

"Sit down," Erik thundered. "Everyone back into your seats. I'm a theatrical sort, I want an *audience*!" Few people obeyed the order.

He had a plan. There had to be a plan.

I was going to *kill* him if there was no plan.

Mifroid released my arm at last and paced a few steps forward, empty hands raised. "There is no need for this. You'll only make things worse for yourself."

Erik sighed loudly. "Mifroid, you can't *reason* with me. I'm a madman, remember? Did anyone reason with Shakespeare's Hamlet? Bellini's Elvira? Handel's Orlando?"

Did this really seem like the moment to discuss madness in operas? I should have known, this was his Act Five finale. The mob had merely been Act Four, and now—

Mifroid must have given a signal I didn't see, because a half-dozen policemen all rushed at once, all from different points of the stage, all converging on Erik in their center. My scream caught in my throat as Erik disappeared in the center of the struggling mass.

There was scuffling and shouting and more screams from the audience and I couldn't see Erik clearly or make out what was happening—but out of the crush of bodies, Erik's gun came spinning across the wooden stage. Kicked, I supposed. In my direction.

Automatically I darted forward the two steps and knelt down to pick up the gun. My fingers had just closed on the carved handle when a black-cloaked figure broke out of the knot of men and plunged towards the edge of the stage.

"Do not force me to shoot you!" Mifroid shouted, drawing his own gun.

What few musicians remained were scrambling from the orchestra pit to get out of the way, and the audience was still doing the same, shoving through the aisles now towards the exits—or at least, to a place that wasn't behind the fugitive poised on the edge of the stage.

And I had a gun in my hand. Erik's gun. The same gun from yesterday, the one that had been loaded with blanks.

Mifroid aimed his weapon straight up and fired. There was a click, nothing more. Misfire. Chance? Or had Erik done something in that past hour when Mifroid was sitting in Box Five?

Was Erik's gun still loaded with blanks? Had he put bullets in it, after I got so indignant on the subject? What was his *plan*? I didn't think it was chance his gun had been kicked my direction, but what did he expect me to *do*? Shoot Mifroid?

No, he wouldn't expect that. I was tempted to do that, yes, but it wouldn't be the plan and it wouldn't be right—and it wouldn't work if the gun still had blanks anyway. Bluff? Was I supposed to bluff somehow?

Or perhaps he had a different plan. Perhaps the gun hadn't been sent towards *me* after all.

All this thought passed in a blink, in the time it took for Mifroid to curse and throw his weapon aside and look around for another.

"Here," I said, feeling oddly hollow, feeling as though I was watching myself more than I was acting. And I reached out to hand Erik's gun to Mifroid.

He took it, pausing just an instant to look into my face with a tiny wrinkle of surprise between his eyebrows. I don't know what he saw. I felt—strangely calm. Frozen.

Erik saw. I could *see* him seeing. His head lifted just a fraction, his shoulders tightened beneath the dark cloak, and I knew he had seen. In a fleeting thought I remembered the first time we had talked in this auditorium, how hard I had found it to read his emotions. Likely no one else in the room now, not even Christine, had seen him have any reaction at all. It hurt to be reminded how well I knew him, how desperately I treasured every nuance, now on the edge of losing it all.

A new voice spoke out over the chaos, projecting easily. "Haven't you tormented us all long enough, Phantom?" Christine said, voice pitched to a tragic air. Apparently she thought it expedient to be the victim again. "Can't this finally be over?"

As unimportant as it should have been at this moment, it was a relief to *not* see Erik react more strongly to those words. To her. He merely lifted his head higher, turning her direction, and the words that followed felt more theatrical than genuine. At least to me. "But I finally understand, Christine. I finally see the role you wanted me to play. It wasn't a monster at all. It was a *martyr*. A sacrifice on the altar of Christine Daaé the glorious opera singer." He spread his arms wide, cloak billowing around him. "And haven't I always strived to be what you want? All right, Commissaire, you heard her. Are you going to ensure this is finally over?"

"You are under arrest, Phantom," Mifroid said, voice steady, hand steady as he aimed the pistol towards Erik's chest. "For the murders of Philippe de Chagny and Joseph Buquet, and additional crimes too numerous to list. Do nothing stupid, and no one needs to die today."

"So that you can arrest me and behead me later? And throw me in a cage in the meantime?" Erik's lip curled. "No cages. Not for me. I'd prefer death—even if I have to take you all with me." He reached into his jacket with his left hand, drawing it out closed into a fist.

Christine screamed, the sound mingling with the sharp retort as Mifroid fired.

Erik jerked once, right hand rising to clutch his left shoulder. Red blood oozed between his fingers. His closed left hand opened.

Empty.

His laughter rang loud through the auditorium as he fell backwards—not leaped, not jumped, *fell*—into the darkness of the orchestra pit.

Chapter Thirty-Six

M ifroid ran forward, shouting to his men, and they all converged
on the orchestra pit. I remained where I was, unable to banish
the image of that cloaked figure falling. Of the blood on his hand. I
kept my gaze fastened on the shadows of the orchestra pit, my fingers
wrapped around my gold necklace. Out of the corner of my eye I could
see Christine sobbing on Raoul's shoulder; what did *she* have to cry
about?

Mifroid was the first into the pit, and I watched him turn, looking
around—and then cursing. "There's no way out of here that isn't in
plain sight, how can he be *gone*?"

I exhaled. My legs went suddenly wobbly and I sank down to sit
on the stage.

He was fine. He had got away. He was *fine*.

He had obviously faked the entire thing, because the alternative
was too hideous to contemplate.

Which I then proceeded to contemplate. In detail.

"He has to have gone somewhere," Mifroid called to his men as
they crowded into the orchestra pit. "Tear up the floorboards if you
have to, I want him found!"

"This is going to be expensive," Moncharmin moaned. I had
forgotten the managers were even on stage, and we went on ignoring
each other now.

I got to my feet again before I was stepped on, but I didn't try to leave. If Mifroid even allowed it, he would want to know where I was going and that would be hard to explain. I wanted to leave, I wanted to find out—but he was fine. Of course.

Raoul led a weeping Christine away, and Mifroid didn't try to stop them. He trusted *them*. I watched them go, and hoped I would never have to see either one ever again.

I wanted this to be finished. Just not the way Christine had suggested it might be.

"Meg!"

My name gave me just enough warning to turn before I was engulfed in a hug by Francesca. It did not give me any time to work out why this was happening.

"You were so *brave*!" Francesca squealed, as more ballet girls crowded around me, coming onstage from the wings. "And I'm *so* sorry for believing all those awful stories about you!"

"Um—thank you?" I said, noticing that most of the girls had surrounded me but a few, like Jammes, still stood apart.

Francesca finally let me go, but looked at me with shining eyes. "When you handed that gun to Commissaire Mifroid, it was obvious where your loyalties really lie!"

The other girls chimed in agreements while my stomach lurched. They were happy—they trusted me again—because they thought I'd helped Mifroid kill the Phantom.

"Yes, well," I said, because I had to say something. "It seemed like the right thing to do." It had, in the moment. For a few seconds I had been so sure, but then Erik had bled and fallen and—it was a trick, it had to be a trick—and all the ballet girls were *smiling* at me now—

I looked through the crowd to find Jammes, and it was obscurely comforting to see her still glowering at me. She met my gaze for a moment, then turned and flounced away with all her usual disdain. She still didn't like me, and she probably still believed I was loyal to the Phantom. Somehow, that felt better than all the other girls' approval.

"It must have been rather awful," I heard Adalisa say, and my gaze flew to her face. Adalisa, who I had just told earlier in the day that the Phantom was wonderful.

Adalisa's expression was thoughtful, a wrinkle on her forehead as though she didn't quite understand something. But when our gazes met, she smiled at me. As though she still trusted me to have done the right thing, however confusing it seemed.

I wished I trusted myself that much. I wished I knew it had been right. I wished I knew—

"Was it just terrifying when the commissaire dragged you out like that?" another girl demanded, and a third added, "And you were so close to the Phantom too!" while a fourth chimed in, "I almost *fainted* when the Phantom threatened to blow everyone up!" And then all the voices overlapped each other in a babble of happy excitement.

The death of the Phantom was already turning into the latest gossip. Into the latest story to be bandied about and embroidered and shrieked over. And they were all around me and they were all talking and I felt sick to my stomach because what if I had been wrong, and I couldn't stand all the voices and the crowd and—

"Meg, there you are!" My mother pushed through the group of girls, pulled me into a hug that was more comforting than Francesca's had been. The girls fell back slightly at Mother's arrival, giving me enough space to at least breathe.

"We are going home," Mother announced, inevitably. "This has been quite enough for one day."

She didn't know the half of it—but I *couldn't* leave, not yet, Mifroid was still trying to find Erik and I didn't know what had happened and I didn't know what would happen and— "Mifroid won't want me to leave," I said, clinging to the only excuse that might be acceptable to everyone listening. "He'll want to talk to me. I have to stay."

Mother frowned and the ballet girls said it wasn't fair, but when Mother marched over to Mifroid and told him we needed to go, he found that "inadvisable."

So we stayed. Most of the ballet girls scattered, while Mother and I took seats in the auditorium and watched the police literally tear the orchestra pit apart. They uncovered a very low, very narrow tunnel leading away under the stage. They did not find Erik. They did find blood. Lots of it.

I clenched my hands into fists and tried not to think about what that could mean. The gun had been loaded with blanks. It had to be a parlor trick.

The police spent an hour crawling around in the passages leading off of the orchestra pit. They followed the trail of blood to a passage high enough to walk in, and there the blood ceased. Only when it became apparent that tracking was not going to be easy did Mifroid come to me.

"Are you certain you don't know where he might have gone?" he asked, a seat over in the row, notebook open in his hand.

"For the third time, *I don't know*. I barely knew him. He asked me about Christine a few times, after she left. He always just appeared and disappeared. I never knew where he was." I had had an hour to think about my story, to think about what I could tell the police that would shift the blame as far as possible off of myself. He'd never believe I didn't know the Phantom at all, not with Christine and Léon telling him otherwise. Mother sat tense and silent beside me, and I knew she wouldn't contradict whatever I said.

"And you never felt it advisable to report these conversations to me?" Mifroid said, voice cold.

"I *told* you, he just appeared sometimes." I shrugged, trying to reach for the silly ballet girl persona I often put on around Mifroid. I was afraid I was too upset to do it convincingly today. "What was I supposed to tell you? That he was haunting the Opera? You knew that, and every ballet girl will tell you they saw the Phantom sometimes."

He nodded slightly, which seemed like some kind of victory. "Have you ever visited his rooms across the lake?"

I saw the trap in that, and resisted a full denial. "Twice. Once with the mob, once yesterday with Christine. And don't ask me how to get there; it's such a labyrinth."

He made a mark in his blasted notebook. "And you know nothing about where that passage from the orchestra pit leads?"

I exhaled, blowing my bangs upwards. "That's just another way of asking where he's gone and I told you, I don't *know*. I imagine he crawled off to wherever was most convenient. *You're* the one who shot him. Where do you expect a dying man would go?"

"We have no assurance that he is in fact dying—"

"No, just a quart or two of blood!" I heard the hysterical note entering my voice, and didn't try to suppress it. "It's obvious he crawled away to die, and you had better accept that you'll never find him. There are as many hidden spaces in this Opera as there are rooms. Probably more."

Mifroid looked thoughtful. "We may be able to find him in a few days by the smell. The weather's warm enough."

I flinched, clapping a hand over my mouth. "That's a *disgusting* thing to say."

Mifroid at least had the grace to look uncomfortable. "I apologize if I upset you."

Mother cleared her throat. "If you have no further useful questions to ask, I would request that you stop harassing my daughter and allow us to go home. If you have doubts about her loyalty, I think her actions handing you the gun that shot the Phantom should clarify the matter sufficiently."

Part of me was glad she had said that—it was a useful point, and I never would have managed to get the words out. Part of me felt sick all over again, hearing it laid out so neatly in my mother's voice.

"I do appreciate your…assistance," Mifroid said, but his eyes were still searching my face as though he remained unconvinced. So it was doubly a relief when he closed his notebook and said, "I believe we are done for now. I may want to speak to you again tomorrow."

"Fine," I said crisply, and rose to my feet. I could deal with that tomorrow.

Mother and I walked out the front of the Opera Garnier, had just crossed the plaza when Mother said, "What really happened on that stage?"

I wanted to say that Erik had had a plan, that we had discussed it at length and I knew exactly what had happened. But it wasn't true and I was too tense to lie and my mother always knew when I was lying at the best of times. "I don't know. I'm not sure. I think..." I looked over my shoulder, looking for any men who could be following me, in case Mifroid thought we might be going somewhere useful to him. No one on the street looked out of place. I lowered my voice anyway. "I think Erik had a plan. I think he faked everything. But I need to find out, I have to—"

"We are going *home*," Mother said, her hand firm on my arm. "You are not getting any more entangled with—"

"Mother, I *have* to find out what happened," I hissed, trying not to raise my voice in case the wrong person overheard. "I have to go find him, he might need help or—don't you understand, I have to *see* him."

Nothing else mattered more than that.

"He knows where you live. He can find you if he—"

"*You* go home," I said, disengaging my arm. If I waited for him to come to me—it had been a *week* last time, and maybe he wouldn't wait that long this time, maybe he'd miss me and—I remembered his arms around me backstage, his voice in my ear, and ached with the memory. "I won't be long—I'll be home soon."

I didn't have the least idea if that was true, but it was the only thing to say, and I was already turning, already separating from Mother.

"Meg, wait, you—"

I didn't stop walking and she didn't chase after me. I wondered what had been in my voice, that had convinced her.

I didn't wonder it long. I was too occupied trying to think how quickly I could get back to the Opera, while taking a circuitous enough route to be sure I wasn't being followed. And with trying not to think about what I might find—or not find—when I arrived.

I circled a few blocks, still didn't see any sign of anyone trailing behind me, and made for the tunnel entrance on the Rue Scribe.

I reached the steps down to the grating, and paused, just on the edge of the shadows. I had a long walk through a dark tunnel in front of me, and all the horrible things that could have happened were waiting to fill my thoughts in the darkness.

I took a deep breath, heartbeat loud in my ears, and hurried down the steps. The grating was ajar; fortunate, since I'd forgotten entirely about the lock. I pushed the grating open with a scrape, and entered the dim tunnel. I would *not* think about crying here yesterday, about being here on a Sunday afternoon, about—

Erik appeared from the deeper shadows before I had advanced more than a few steps. "I *knew* you'd come this way."

Thank God.

He was alive and grinning and my knees wobbled and I let him cross the distance between us in a few of his long strides. He caught me up around the waist and spun me around.

I reached out automatically to steady myself against his shoulders, finding them reassuringly solid and not ghost-like at all. "I'd have been here sooner, but it would have made Mifroid suspicious." It suddenly occurred to me where my hands were, and I lifted the one on his left shoulder, turned it over to look at the palm. Clean. "Stage blood?"

"Of course," Erik said, smiling down at me. "And blanks in the gun. Did it look convincing?"

"Very." The image of Erik falling into the pit flashed across my mind again and I flinched, eyes closing as though that would block out the sight.

"What's wrong?" His hands momentarily tightened on my waist, then lifted until his palms were just barely, cautiously, grazing my hips.

"Nothing," I said, fingers on his shoulders clenching in the folds of his cloak. I looked up into his worried green eyes. "Nothing," I repeated, and it was true, nothing was wrong, everything was all right, he was here, that picture of him falling shouldn't matter anymore. Only, my voice and my legs both trembled. All the control that had kept me outwardly calm in the auditorium, talking to Mifroid, walking here, it was all crumbling away at Erik's touch, at the sound of his voice.

I stepped forward the arm's-length between us, slid my hands down to wrap my arms around him. I could feel his heart beating beneath my cheek. I blinked hard, swallowed past the lump in my throat. "You really have to stop dying in front of me," I said into his shirt. "It's extremely disturbing."

He pressed a kiss into my hair. "I'll work on that." His tone was light enough. The tightness of his embrace told a different story. "You were brilliant, though. I thought Mifroid was going to ruin the whole thing by not picking up the right gun."

I groaned against his chest. "Next time, you have to actually *tell* me the plan before it all unfolds."

"It was sort of a...free-form plan, actually—"

"No, I take that back," I said, "because no *next time*, all right?"

"No next time," he said obediently, then continued with a new hesitancy in his voice, "*This* time, you know, I didn't die for Christine."

"Obviously. You're here."

"Yes, but I meant the whole stunt. I could have got out of that six other ways, and I didn't do it *that* way to launch her singing career. But if I had just disappeared in the shadows...Mifroid would keep looking for me. He might be more satisfied about my death this time, shooting me himself—and at the least he'll waste a lot of time hunting for my body. So that will make it harder for him to trace me to Vienna."

I hadn't really had time to worry that he might have still been influenced by Christine—but the reassurance was nice. "I'm sure being chased by Mifroid would interfere with your study of Beethoven."

"Exactly what was uppermost in my mind." He cupped his hands around my face and kissed me—then pulled back just a fraction, far enough to whisper, "I'm trying to tell you that I died for *you*."

"I know," I said, and kissed him back.

Chapter Thirty-Seven

T empting though it was, we couldn't stay in that tunnel forever. Erik might have. At least, I was the one who finally pulled back and said, "Mother is probably very worried right now." It occurred to me that I seemed to say this a lot lately; but it was true, especially right now.

"Oh. Yes."

"So I should go home, but..." I looked up at him, smiled, not sure how he was going to take this idea. "...you could come. I mean, we have to tell her about..." I ran my fingertips along his shoulder. "...you know. This."

"Oh," he said again. "You haven't mentioned that yet?"

"Not much time or opportunity."

His shoulders hunched a little. "Are you sure that isn't a private sort of conversation?"

I really considered. "I think it would look good if you were there." I grinned. "Besides, it can't be as alarming as facing Mifroid, right?"

"Easy for you to say," he muttered. But he walked home with me.

He had already changed masks to the half-face one again, and now he left the cloak behind too. No one gave us any more than slightly odd looks as we passed.

I pushed open the front door, stepped into the sitting room. "Mother?"

"Meg?" Her voice came from the bedroom. "I know you were upset earlier, but that is no excuse for—" She stopped in the doorway, breaking off abruptly as she saw me. And Erik next to me. If she was surprised, it didn't show on her face, or in her voice. "Monsieur Phantom. I see you are less dead than believed." Her gaze scanned down to our hands joined together. As though that was the more unexpected part. Maybe it was.

I felt Erik's hand flex, as though trying to let go. I locked my fingers around his, was gratified to feel his fingers curl tighter again. "It's been a...complicated day," I said.

"So I see," she said, voice dry. But the corner of her mouth twitched just a bit towards a smile, which I took as a good sign on several fronts. "Perhaps I should make some coffee, and we can all sit down so you can tell me about it?"

We did. I did most of the talking, although Erik relaxed slightly when Mother showed signs of taking the entire story calmly. At least, his shoulders relaxed; his grip on my hand did not. I didn't mind that at all. And I could always appreciate a new way to discern Erik's moods.

Madame Giry took things remarkably well. Maybe she'd been expecting this. That would explain a few of her comments, now that he looked back on them. He almost began to relax, emphasis on almost.

"I suppose you've already thought about how this affects our traveling plans?" Madame Giry said halfway through a second cup of coffee.

So much for relaxing.

But Meg just cheerfully said, "We thought Erik could come to Vienna too. He speaks German, you know."

One of Madame Giry's eyebrows rose. "Yes, that's clearly why he's coming."

"I know Vienna very well too," he said doggedly. "I was there ten years ago or so."

What was going to happen if she said no? He might have to kidnap Meg after all. It wasn't really kidnapping if she was a willing participant...

But Madame Giry nodded and said, "I'm sure that will be very useful."

And the tension went down a degree. Then back up when Madame Giry remarked, "Meg, we're rather low on sugar. Would you please go to the kitchen for more?"

The bowl of sugar was low, but it was still an obvious ploy. For a few seconds Meg didn't move, gaze darting from her mother's face to Erik and back again. Then her lips tightened slightly. She squeezed Erik's hand once then let go, though it cost him an effort not to clutch on tighter. "Fine," she said, rising to her feet. "Be nice, all right?"

"I beg your pardon?" Madame Giry said, in what even Erik could tell was mock confusion.

Meg shook her head and walked out into the kitchen.

The frost in the room grew noticeably the moment she was out of it. Madame Giry leaned back in her seat, giving him a cool look. "Well, Monsieur Phantom."

He inclined his head, keeping his face impassive while his heartbeat drummed in his ears. "Madame Giry."

She studied him for a long moment, during which he narrowly succeeded at not fidgeting. Finally, the corner of her mouth turned up. It was the tiniest of smiles, but he'd take it. "You know she's far too good for you," she said conversationally.

"I know," he said with complete sincerity.

She nodded once. "Good. Keep it in mind."

He rubbed his palms against his pantlegs. "Madame Giry, I know you don't trust me, but—"

She held up a hand. "I trust my daughter, and my daughter trusts you. I am...willing to give you a chance to prove Meg correct."

"That's very generous of you," he said, and meant it. It was a wonder she hadn't put a stop to all this, long ago. "I hope you know..." He hesitated, forced himself to meet her direct gaze. "...Meg is the most important person in the world to me."

"As she should be," Madame Giry said, but she was still smiling slightly. "And if you break her heart—"

"—you'll kill me?" Erik suggested.

"No," she said, smile growing a little more. "I'll make you wish I had killed you."

He'd deserve it, and so he merely nodded. "Understood."

Chapter Thirty-Eight

I didn't go back to the Opera Garnier; at least, not above ground. It had been the fifth act finale, and that part of the story was done. I was ready for the next opera.

I was ready to be done with Christine Daaé too. But while I certainly wasn't seeking her out, and she didn't appear on my doorstep again, she still wouldn't quite disappear. Just a few days after the Phantom died (again), I arrived at the Phantom's rooms with a newspaper and a great deal of resentment.

I threw the folded paper down on Erik's carved table. "Look at this."

He leaned forward from his seat on the couch, glanced at the page and raised an eyebrow. "The society page?"

I jabbed my finger at an item near the middle. "There, read that one." I had already memorized what it said, and watched Erik's face as he read the brief lines: *The Comtesse de Chagny is inviting select friends for an exclusive Salon in her home. The reader may remember the Comtesse as the soprano who so enchanted the audience at the Opera Garnier last spring.*

Erik's expression told me very little, with no trace of irritation or even surprise. Finally he leaned back and remarked, "Sounds like a lovely event. Pity my invitation was clearly lost in the mail."

"You know what she's going to do, don't you?" I dropped down to sit on the couch next to him, arms tightly folded. "She's going to start singing at these exclusive Salons for the wealthiest, most influential people in Paris. It's all going to be very proper and very refined and she'll influence and manipulate and connive, and pretty soon she'll have the heads of society telling *her* she ought to sing publicly again. She's going to end up with the wealth and the title and the high place in society *and* the singing career."

There was a long pause before Erik finally said, "Well, that…seems plausible." He frowned slightly. "Why are we talking about it?"

"Doesn't it *bother* you?" I demanded. "She manipulated you, me, everyone we know, and she got away with everything. She's getting everything she wanted. Doesn't that make you angry?"

The Phantom's legendary temper was simply not in evidence. All he did was shrug. "Maybe it would, if I spent enough time thinking about it. But I already wasted too much time thinking about Christine, and I don't plan to waste more time on her in order to hate her. I'd really rather just never think about her again."

A good plan, mostly, good enough to put a warm spark in my chest and blunt the edge of my anger. But not all of it. I swung one foot, not entirely satisfied, wanting some kind of admission still. "Doesn't it seem…like there should be consequences? She shouldn't be able to destroy everyone around her, and then reap all the rewards."

"Are you suggesting I drop a chandelier at her Salon?" he asked, and might have worried me if he wasn't smiling.

"No," I said, smiling back. He really did have such a nice smile when he used it. My own smile faded after a moment. "But it doesn't seem *right*."

He sighed and reached out for my hand. "I'm afraid I'm far too cynical to believe in an overarching justice in the world." His fingers wrapped around mine and I unfolded my arms to let him take my hand. "But I don't really think she got away without consequences. She has to live with herself."

Now my eyebrows rose. "Sorry, but *I'm* too cynical to believe she feels guilty about it all."

"No, I'm sure she doesn't. I didn't mean that." He laced and unlaced his fingers through mine, looking down at our hands as he spoke. "Maybe I meant she has to live *as* herself. She chose to go down a path that means there is no one in the world who sees who she really is. Everyone around her only sees the mask she puts on. That is a very lonely way to live."

"I'm not sure she cares," I said softly.

"And that is the only fate I can think of that would be even worse."

I tightened my fingers around his, let myself tip sideways to rest my head on his shoulder. "All right. You're right. That's a very sorry victory."

He turned his head, pressed a kiss on the top of my hair. "If this is losing, I'd rather not win."

I lifted my head off his shoulder and smiled up at him. "I said she won. I never said *we* lost," I murmured, just before he leaned in to kiss me.

His lips were soft against mine and I closed my eyes, pressed into the kiss. His arm wrapped around my waist to pull me closer. I sank readily against him, smiled against his mouth, and then pulled back just far enough to look into his eyes. It was a heartbeat before they opened, and the green, expected though it was, still took my breath away.

I lifted my hand, ran my thumb over his eyebrow, my fingertips through his dark strands of hair. I felt a shiver deep in my stomach—of delight, of wonder. Only a few days ago, it would have seemed impossible to touch him like this. "How did we get here?" I breathed. "Together, like this?"

He smiled, sweetly, unguarded, and my heart leaped. "I wrote you a song," he whispered, and kissed the tip of my nose. "Remember?"

There was more kissing.

But it wasn't *all* kissing. Sometimes it was music, and sometimes it was even planning. That day I had brought a newspaper, but another day it was train tickets. We had three, to leave the Gare du Nord at six in the morning. There was just one piece of the logistics that worried me slightly.

I sat on Erik's couch and twisted my skirt and suggested, "Maybe Mother and I should meet you here."

Erik's brow furrowed. "It'll take far longer to get to the train station if you stop here. It makes much more sense to meet there."

"Yes," I said reluctantly. "But we *could* meet you here…"

His expression cleared and he smiled at me. Then he pulled me closer and kissed my forehead. "I *will* be there," he whispered into my hair. "I promise."

Somehow, at some moments, he had got a little too good at seeing me. Who would have guessed that? I sighed and said, "I know."

I meant it. I believed him. And I worried.

Excerpt from the Private Notebook of Jean Mifroid, Commissaire of Police

7 June, 1882

Still no body. Still no definite answers on the Phantom.

I <u>shot</u> him. He <u>should</u> be dead.

But he should have been dead before. How can I be sure? How can I <u>ever</u> be sure?

Chapter Thirty-Nine

H e stood on the stage of the Opera Garnier, the largest stage in Europe, and looked out over the rows and rows of empty seats. They were barely visible in the shadows, with only a few safety lights burning. It was still dark outside, sun not yet risen, though no light penetrated here anyway, and it was quiet in the Opera. His mind filled in what his eyes couldn't see in the dim light—the glowing red velvet of the seats, the gleaming gold of the decorations, the glittering, newly-hung chandelier above, the sun in the sky of the Opera.

Box Five was just visible, his private sanctuary in the midst of the crowd. So many hours he had spent there, listening to the music fill the air. And later, talking to Meg.

The ghosts of all those symphonies, all those operas, filled the vast cavern of the auditorium. The voices and the melodies, weaving together, and with them, Meg's voice and his own too, as they had slowly found each other through the words.

He had fallen in love in this room, with a woman standing on this stage. He had died in the orchestra pit, only a few days ago.

He had met Meg here, met her properly. When she stood in the center aisle and called him by name, and everything had changed.

He paced to the edge of the stage, leaped down, and walked slowly up the center aisle. He left through the subscribers' door, stepped out between the statues onto the grand marble staircase, the many candelabra along the stairs currently dark. He remembered Mardi Gras, both years he had attended, the crowds of revelers filling this space. How different each year had been.

The front doors of the building were just beyond the foot of the stairs, but he ascended instead, went up one level to walk into the Grand Foyer.   Slightly more light here, the electric lights of the Avenue de l'Opera outside shining through the windows.   He knew where every muse was in the ceiling, knew which bits of the gold decoration were real and which fake.

He halted looking up at the silver face of Charles Garnier.   It felt as though there ought to be something to say.   Some acknowledgment.   But there were no words, and after all—it was only an image.   Only a kind of mask.

He lifted one hand to his hat in salute, then turned away.

He descended the marble stairs and didn't look back as, for the first time in all these years, he stepped out the front doors of the Opera Garnier.   He locked the door behind him, lingered for a moment with his palm against the wood, then continued down the stone steps fronting the building.

He crossed the plaza before he looked back again, at the marble pillars and border of masks, at the looming dome and Apollo, God of Music, surmounting it all.   It had been a good place, for a long time.   His kingdom.   His world.

He reached into the inside pocket of his jacket, drew out a small silver medallion.   He had dropped his trunk at the Girys' house yesterday, to be transported to the train station with their luggage, and Madame Giry had offered him the medallion then.   She had said only that she thought he might value it, and evaded further discussion, or anything approaching gratitude.

He felt the edges of the raised image and engraved words with the pad of his thumb.   A man carrying a child on his back, and the words, "Look at St. Christopher and go on reassured."   The patron saint of travelers, and Erik supposed he could use whatever help he could find.

Slipping the St. Christopher medal back into his pocket again, he turned and walked away through the still Parisian streets.   He had a train to catch.

Mother and I took a carriage to the Gare du Nord, and it was a comfort to remember that we had Erik's trunk among our luggage, with his violin packed away inside. It was still hard to believe he'd leave the Opera, would come to the train station for me. It was, ridiculously perhaps, easier to believe he wouldn't want us to leave town with his violin.

It still gave me a twinge of relief when we alighted from the carriage in front of the station and Erik stepped out of a shadow between two pillars. His cloak seemed natural enough in the cool of early dawn, and his broad-brimmed hat cast enough shadow to nearly hide his white half-mask. I couldn't very well kiss him right there on the street, but we smiled at each other and I took his arm, fingers tight.

Then there was a hubbub of sorting luggage and finding tickets and Mother mostly directing things, as happened every time we traveled anywhere. It felt almost like we could be setting off for Leclair, if not for Erik's mostly silent presence alongside me.

I watched him, trying not to let him see me do it. I noted that his shoulders were tense but at least he smiled at me whenever our gazes met.

Gare du Nord wasn't empty even this early in the morning, but it was sparsely populated, which probably made things easier. There were a few stares, but no one said anything, and Erik didn't run. It all felt distinctly unreal, showing tickets, having the porter take our luggage, stepping onto the train. We made our way through the train and into a private compartment. 20,000 francs a month pays for that sort of thing.

Mother sat down on one bench and I sat next to Erik on the opposite one. I slid my hand down his arm to wrap my fingers around his.

And finally, with a whistle and a roar, the train rolled out of the station, slowly picking up speed, and slowly I could believe it was all really happening. Some final tension in the pit of my stomach, some fear that something was still going to prevent this impossible dream from happening, relaxed as we pulled away from the Gare du Nord.

I looked up at Erik, who was looking out the window, and across at Mother, who had settled behind a newspaper. I was still reading *Frankenstein*, and I could have got it out of my bag. But I had a better idea.

I got up to my feet, automatically balancing against the rocking of the carriage. "I don't want to sit *all* day. Let's go see if we can find the observation car." I extended a hand towards Erik.

I hadn't intended it as a test or a challenge. It was only after he looked up at me, something tight around his eyes, that I realized the obvious, that he likely found the private compartment a relief.

Perhaps I shouldn't have said anything—but before I could properly regret it, he had taken my hand, risen to his feet too and said the perfectly innocuous, "All right."

I glanced at Mother, who was watching us. She discreetly did not offer to join us, but only smiled, a knowing smile, and with a rustle disappeared behind her newspaper. I supposed she didn't think we could get into too much trouble on a moving train.

And as it turned out, the train itself didn't prove too much a trial. It was still very early in the morning, barely light outside the windows, and the aisles were empty. Everyone else in compartments seemed inclined to stay there, and anyone in seats was too sleepy to bother fussing over a man in a mask.

We walked through several carriages and eventually reached a small observation platform at the back of the train. It, too, was empty, and Erik pushed the glass door open so we could step out.

As soon as it closed he pulled me over to one side, out of view of the door, and kissed me. I was more than happy to slide my arms around him and kiss him back.

"I've been wanting to do that all morning," he said at length.

I smiled, bumped my nose against his. "Why do you think I wanted to go find the observation car?"

"Not to see the sun come up?"

"That too," I said, and kissed him again.

We went on kissing as the train traveled east towards the sunrise, towards a sky aflame in reds and golds, fields of clouds forming a magical country in the sky.

We kissed until Erik finally pulled back just far enough to ask, his breath warm on my lips, "What are you thinking about?"

Kissing, mostly, but I'd also been thinking about how we had got here, about the unlikely, improbable threads that wove together to change the shape of a life. "I'm glad I got lost, all those years ago."

I might have had to explain it—but he smiled, and kissed my forehead, and said, "I'm glad I found you."

Also by the Author

The Wanderers
A wandering adventurer, a witch's daughter, and a talking cat – what could go wrong? With damsels to rescue, monsters to fight and Good Fairies to avoid at all costs, you'll recognize elements of a number of fairy tales as Jasper, Julie and Tom set off down the road.

The Storyteller and Her Sisters
A retelling of the Brothers Grimm story, "The Shoes That Were Danced to Pieces," the twelve princesses tell their own story here–about defying their father, who hopes to marry them off to successful champions or behead the ones who fail, in order to rescue twelve cursed princes.

The People the Fairies Forget
Let Tarragon, an unusual fairy, lead you through some familiar fairy tales–and introduce you to some characters you may not have noticed. Like the servants who fall asleep in the castle when Sleeping Beauty pricks her finger, or the young woman who fits into Cinderella's slipper but doesn't want to marry the prince.

The Lioness and the Spellspinners
A brooding heroine with a dark past finds herself trapped on an island where she finds the locals suspiciously friendly–and their talk of magical knitting doesn't reassure her.

Find out more on Cheryl's blog,
Tales of the Marvelous.
http://marveloustales.com/NovelNews

Acknowledgements

My love affair with this story began when I was eighteen years old – thank you, Cate and Panda, for introducing me to the madman in a mask. And thank you, Meaghan, who has been waiting ever since then for this series to finally be published.

Thank you to all the people who let me wax on about the Phantom and this story over the…six? seven? years I've been writing this trilogy—if you remember any conversations like that, I mean you! Thank you to the Stonehenge Writing Group for all the scenes you read and the encouragement you gave that, yes, even for some of you who had never met the Phantom, you liked this story and this character. Erik and I are grateful—Meg too, but she'd be less surprised.

Thank you especially to Karen, Ruth, Kelly, Dennis, and Meaghan, for your beta-reading and invaluable feedback.

I am indebted, of course, to Gaston Leroux, who began it all, and to Andrew Lloyd Webber and Susan Kay, who carried it forward so beautifully. I am grateful to all the men who have portrayed this complicated character in so many ways: first and particularly, Michael Crawford, who will always be the voice of my Phantom; Lon Chaney, Claude Rains, David Staller, Charles Dance, Earl Carpenter, and too many more Webber Phantoms to name. I am grateful too to Terry Pratchett, whose *Maskerade* is the funniest book I have ever read, and whose Christine is surprisingly closer to mine than any other I've seen.

And thank you to Charlies Garnier, for all the inspiration of your gorgeous opera house, and apologies for making you share the credit with a masked Phantom. Erik and I both recognize your genius.

About the Author

Cheryl Mahoney lives in California and dreams of other worlds. She has been blogging since 2010 at Tales of the Marvelous (http://marveloustales.com). Her weekly Writing Wednesday posts provide updates about her current writing, including excerpts and updates on books that are coming soon. She also posts regularly with book and movie reviews, and reflections on reading. She has been a member of Stonehenge Writers since 2012, and has completed NaNoWriMo seven times.

Cheryl has looked for faeries in Kensington Gardens in London and for the Phantom at the Opera Garnier in Paris. She considers Tamora Pierce's Song of the Lioness Quartet to be life-changing and Terry Pratchett books to be the best cure for gloomy days.

A Note on Research

This trilogy has been the undertaking of many years, and has involved extensive research into the Phantom of the Opera, classical music, ballet, the Opera Garnier, and France of the late 1800s, as well as two trips to the Opera Garnier itself. For those wanting to seek out more information for themselves, here are some of the sources that were most useful in this adventure.

Burrows, John, editor. *The Complete Classical Music Guide*

Fenby, Jonathan. *France: A Modern History from the Revolution to the War with Terror*

Gill, Miranda. *Eccentricity and the Cultural Imagination in 19th-Century Paris*

Guest, Ivor Forbes. *The Paris Opera Ballet*

Hall, Ann C. *The Adaptations of Gaston Leroux's* Phantom of the Opera, *1925 to the Present*

Hart, Charles, Richard Stilgoe and Andrew Lloyd Webber. *The Phantom of the Opera.* Really Useful Group, 1986.

Kay, Susan. *Phantom*

Leroux, Gaston. *The Phantom of the Opera.* Leonard Wolf, Editor

Lofts, Norah and Margery Weiner. *Eternal France*

Meyer, Carolyn. *Marie, Dancing*

Meyer, Nicholas. *The Canary Trainer*

Moatti, Jacques. *The Paris Opera, photos*

Perry, George. *The Complete Phantom of the Opera*

The Phantom of the Opera. Directed by Rupert Julian. Performance by Lon Chaney. Universal Studios, 1925.

Phantom of the Opera. Directed by Arthur Lubin. Performance by
Claude Rains. Universal Studios, 1943.

The Phantom of the Opera. Directed by Tony Richardson. Performance
by Charles Dance. Hexatel, 1990.

The Phantom of the Opera. Directed by Darwin Knight. Performance
by David Staller. Hirschfield Films, 1991.

Siciliano, Sam. *The Angel of the Opera*

Schlor, Joachim. *Nights in the Big City: Paris, Berlin, London, 1840-1930*

www.ingramcontent.com/pod-product-compliance
Lightning Source LLC
Chambersburg PA
CBHW060403260626
47160CB00006B/2413